Three rich men and a web of lies…

DIAMONDS
are for Surrender

Three sensational, dramatic novels from
Bronwyn Jameson, Tessa Radley
and Maxine Sullivan

Diamonds are a Girl's Best Friend!

January 2013

February 2013

March 2013

April 2013

May 2013

June 2013

DIAMONDS
are for *Surrender*

Bronwyn
JAMESON

Tessa
RADLEY

Maxine
SULLIVAN

Mills & Boon, an imprint of Harlequin (UK) Limited, Eton House, 18-24 Paradise Road, Richmond, Surrey TW9 1SR

DIAMONDS ARE FOR SURRENDER
© Harlequin Enterprises II B.V./S.à.r.l 2013

Vows & a Vengeful Groom © Bronwyn Turner 2008
Pride & a Pregnancy Secret © Tessa Radley 2008
Mistress & a Million Dollars © Maxine Sullivan 2008

ISBN: 978 0 263 90285 3

025-0213

VOWS & A
VENGEFUL GROOM

BRONWYN JAMESON

Bronwyn Jameson spent much of her childhood with her head buried in a book. As a teenager she discovered romance novels and it was only a matter of time before she turned her love of reading them into a love of writing them. Bronwyn shares an idyllic piece of the Australian farming heartland with her husband and three sons, a thousand sheep, a dozen horses, assorted wildlife and one kelpie dog. She still chooses to spend her limited downtime with a good book. Bronwyn loves to hear from readers. Write to her at bronwyn@bronwynjameson.com.

With heartfelt thanks to Melissa Jeglinski
for her faith in and support of our author-led
series from start to finish.
Thank you, MJ, you are a gem!

One

Kimberley Blackstone's long stride—and the Louis Vuitton suitcase she towed in her wake—gathered momentum as she left customs at Auckland's international airport and headed toward the exit. Despite the handicap of her three-inch heels, she hit the Arrivals hall at a near jog, her focus on grabbing the first taxi in the rank outside, her mind making the transition from laid-back holiday mode to all that awaited her at House of Hammond on her first workday after the Christmas-New Year's break.

She didn't notice the waiting horde of media until it was too late. Flashbulbs exploded around her like a New Year's light show. She skidded to a halt, so abruptly her trailing suitcase rammed into her legs.

Surely, this had to be a case of mistaken identity. Kimberley hadn't been on the paparazzi hit list for close to a decade,

not since she'd estranged herself from her billionaire father
and his headline-hungry diamond business.

But, no, it was *her* name they called. *Her* face the focus of
a swarm of lenses that circled like avid hornets. Her heart
started to pound with fear-fuelled adrenaline.

What did they want?

What the hell was going on?

With a rising sense of bewilderment she scanned the crowd
for a clue and her gaze fastened on a tall, leonine figure
forcing his way to the front. A tall, familiar figure. She stared
in stunned recognition and their gazes collided across the sea
of heads before the cameras erupted with another barrage of
flashes, this time right in her exposed face.

Blinded by the flashbulbs—and by the shock of that momentary eye-meet—Kimberley didn't realise his intent until
he'd forged his way to her side, possibly by the sheer strength
of his personality. She felt his arm wrap around her shoulder,
pulling her into the protective shelter of his body, allowing
her no time to object, no chance to lift her hands to ward him
off.

In the space of a hastily drawn breath, she found herself
plastered knee-to-nose against six feet of hard-bodied male.

Ric Perrini.

Her lover for ten torrid weeks, her husband for ten tumultuous days.

Her ex for ten tranquil years.

After all this time, he should not have felt so familiar but,
oh, dear Lord, he did. She knew the scent of that body and its
lean, muscular strength. She knew its heat and its slick power
and every response it could draw from hers.

She also recognised the ease with which he'd taken control

of the moment and the decisiveness of his deep voice when it rumbled close to her ear. "I have a car waiting. Is this your only luggage?"

Kimberley nodded. A week at a tropical paradise did not require much in the way of clothes. Especially when she was wearing the one office-style dress and the only pair of heels she'd packed. When he released his grip on her shoulder to take charge of her compact suitcase, she longed to dig those heels into the ground, to tell him exactly what he could do with his car, and his presumptuous attitude.

But she wasn't stupid. She'd seen Perrini in action often enough to know that attitude yielded results. The fierce expression and king-of-the-jungle manner he did so well would keep the snapping newshounds at bay.

Not that she was about to be towed along as meekly as her wheeled luggage.

"I assume you will tell me," she said tightly, "what this welcome party is all about."

"Not while the welcome party is within earshot."

Barking a request for the cameramen to stand aside, Perrini took her hand and pulled her into step with his ground-eating stride. Kimberley let him because he was right, damn his arrogant, Italian-suited hide. Despite the speed with which he whisked her across the terminal forecourt, she could almost feel the hot breath of the pursuing media on her back.

This was neither the time nor the place for explanations. Inside his car, however, she would get answers.

The initial shock had been blown away—by the haste of their retreat, by the heat of her gathering indignation, by the rush of adrenaline fired by Perrini's presence and the looming verbal battle. Her brain was starting to tick now. This had to be her father's doing. And if it was a Howard Blackstone publicity ploy, then it had to be about Blackstone Diamonds, the company that ruled his life.

The knowledge made her chest tighten with a familiar ache of disillusionment.

She'd known her father would be flying in from Sydney for today's opening of the newest in his chain of exclusive, high-end jewellery boutiques. The opulent shopfront sat adjacent to the rival business where Kimberley worked. No coincidence, she thought bitterly, just as it was no coincidence that Ric Perrini was here in Auckland ushering her to his car.

Perrini was Howard Blackstone's right-hand man, second in command at Blackstone Diamonds and head of the mining division, that position of power a legacy of his short-lived marriage to the boss's daughter. No doubt her father had sent him to fetch her; the question was why.

On his last visit to Auckland, Howard had attempted yet again to lure her back to Blackstone's, to the job she'd walked away from the day she walked out on her marriage. That meeting had escalated into an ugly word-slinging bout and ended with Howard vowing to write her from his will if she didn't return to Blackstone's immediately.

Two months later Kimberley was still here in Auckland, still working for his sworn enemy at House of Hammond. They hadn't spoken since; she hadn't expected any other outcome. When her father said he was wiping his hands of her, she took him at his word.

Yet here she was, being rushed toward a gleaming black limousine by her father's number-one henchman. She had no clue why he'd changed his mind or what the media presence signified, apart from more Blackstone headlines and the certainty that she was being used. Again. Sending Perrini was the final cruel twist.

By the time they arrived at the waiting car, her blood was simmering with a mixture of remembered hurt and raw resentment. The driver stowed her luggage while Perrini stowed her. She slid across the silver-grey leather seat and the door closed behind her, shutting her off from the cameras that seemed to be multiplying by the minute.

Perrini paused on the pavement beside the hired car, his hands held wide in a gesture of appeal as he spoke. Whatever he was saying only incited more questions, more flashbulbs, and Kimberley steamed with the need to know what was going on. She reached for her door handle, and when it didn't open she caught the driver's eye in the rearview mirror. "Could you please unlock the doors? I need to get out."

He looked away. And he didn't release the central locking device.

Kimberley's blood heated from slow simmer to fast boil. "I am here under duress. Release the lock or I swear I will—"

Before she could complete her threat, the door opened from outside and Perrini climbed in beside her. She'd been closer inside the airport terminal, when he'd shielded her from the cameras with the breadth of his body, but then she'd been too sluggish with disbelief to react. Now she slid as far away as the backseat allowed, and as she fastened her seat belt the car sped away from the kerb.

Primed for battle, she turned to face her adversary. "You had me locked inside this car out of earshot while *you* talked to the media? This had better be good, Perrini."

He looked up from securing his seat belt and their eyes met and held. For the first time there was nothing between them—

no distraction, no interruption—and for a beat of time she forgot herself in those unexpectedly blue eyes, in the unbidden rush of memories that rose in a choking wave.

For a second she thought she saw an echo of the same raw emotion deep in his eyes but then she realised it was only tiredness. And tension.

"I wouldn't be here," he said, low and gruff, "if this wasn't important."

The implication that he would rather be anywhere but here, with her, fisted tightly around Kimberley's heart. But she lifted her chin and stared him down. "Important to whom? My father?"

He didn't have to answer. She saw it in the narrowing of his deep-set eyes, as if her comment had irritated him. Good. She'd meant it to.

"Did he think sending you would change my mind?" she continued coolly, despite the angry heat that churned her stomach. "Because he could have saved himself—"

"He didn't send me, Kim."

There was something in the delivery of that simple statement that brought all her senses to full alert. Finally she allowed herself to take him all in. He was not lounging with his usual arrogant ease but sitting straight and still. Sunlight spilled through the side window onto his face, highlighting the angles and planes, the straight line of his nose and the deep cleft in his chin.

And the muscle that ticked in his jaw.

She could feel the tension now, strong enough to suck up all the air in the luxury car's roomy interior. She could see it, too, in the grim line of his mouth and the intensity of his cobalt-blue eyes.

Despite the muggy summer morning Kimberley felt an icy

shiver of foreboding. Beneath the warmth of her holiday tan her skin goose-bumped. Something was very, very wrong.

"What is it?" Her fingers clutched at the handbag in her lap, gripping the soft leather straps as if that might somehow anchor her against what was to come. "If my father didn't send you, then why are you here?"

"Howard left Sydney last night. Your brother received a phone call in the early hours of this morning when the plane didn't arrive in Auckland."

"Didn't arrive?" She shook her head, unable to accept what he wasn't telling her. "Planes don't just fail to arrive. What happened?"

"We don't know. Twenty minutes out of Sydney it disappeared from radar." His eyes locked on hers, and all she needed to know was etched in their darkened depths, and in the dip of his head and the strained huskiness of his next words. "I'm sorry, Kim."

No. She shook her head again. This couldn't be happening. How could her all-powerful, larger-than-life father be dead? On the eve of his greatest moment, the day when he'd vowed to rub the Hammonds' faces in his accomplishments right here on their home turf.

"He was coming for the opening of the Queen Street store," she said softly.

"Yes. He was due to leave at seven-thirty but there was a delay. Some contracts to be signed."

There always were. Every childhood memory of her father concerned business papers, negotiations, dealing in the fabulous wealth of the diamonds that underpinned it all. She couldn't remember ever seeing him dressed in anything other than a business suit. That was his life.

Diamonds and contracts and making headlines.

"When I saw you at the airport," she said, "with all the cameras and media hubbub, I thought it was to do with the opening. Some strategy he'd come up with to grab attention for the new shop." The awful reality of tomorrow's headlines churned through her, tightening her chest in a painful vise. "They were there because they knew."

While she'd been enjoying her last walk on the beach, her last breakfast of papaya and mango and rambutan, while she'd laughed with the resort staff and flirted with the twenty-year-old charmer seated next to her on the flight home—

"I didn't know," she said on a choked whisper. Despite their bitter estrangement of the past decade, despite everything she held her father accountable for, she'd grown up adoring the man and vying with her brother to win his favour. For thirty-one years he had shaped her decisions, her career, her beliefs. For the last ten of those years she'd done everything she could to distance herself, but he was still her father. "I walked out of the terminal and into those cameras.... How did they know?"

"About your father?" He exhaled, a rough sound that doubled as a curse. "I don't know. They shouldn't have had names this quickly. They sure as hell shouldn't have known you were coming through the airport this morning."

The sick feeling in Kimberley's stomach sharpened. She hadn't worked her way around to that, but now he'd brought it up. Her forehead creased in a frown. "How did *you* know where to find me?"

"When you didn't answer your phone, I called your office."

"Last night?"

"This morning."

Kimberley digested that information. Obviously he didn't

mean in the predawn hours when her brother Ryan first received the news, otherwise he wouldn't have called her office. Wouldn't have found someone—Lionel, the office manager, no doubt—to point him in the direction of the airport. "You didn't call me as soon as you heard?"

"No." His voice dropped to the same harsh intensity that darkened his eyes to near black. "This wasn't something to hear over the phone, Kim."

"You thought it might be better if I heard from a news crew?" she asked.

"That's why I flew over here. To stop that happening."

"Yet it almost did happen."

"Because Hammond's office manager wouldn't give me your flight information over the phone." Ric ground out that information with barely leashed restraint. He didn't need her derisive tone reminding him of his impotent frustration on the drive to and from the city, not knowing if he'd make it back in time to meet her flight. Not knowing if the media would discover her whereabouts when that information had been deliberately withheld from him.

It hadn't been a surprise, just a damn aggravation.

There was no love lost between the employees of House of Hammond and Blackstone Diamonds. The enmity of a thirty-year feud between the heads of the two companies—Howard and his brother-in-law, Oliver Hammond—had spilled over and tainted relationships into the next generation. Kimberley had re-ignited the simmering feud when she took a position assisting Matt Hammond, the current CEO of House of Hammond.

"You can't blame Lionel for exercising caution," Kim said archly, as if she'd read his mind.

There was something in that notion and in her tone that trampled all over Ric's prickly mood. Ten minutes together and despite the gravity of the news he'd brought, they teetered on the razor's edge of an argument. He shook his head wearily and let it roll back against the cool upholstery. Why should he be surprised? From the moment they'd met, their relationship had been defined by fiery clashes and passionate making up.

He'd never had a woman more difficult than Kim...nor one who could give him more pleasure.

When the phone call about Howard came in, he'd made the decision to fly to her without a second's hesitation. As much as he hated what had brought him here, he relished the fact it would bring her home. She belonged at Blackstone's. Ric sucked in a deep breath, and the scent of summer that clung to her skin curled into his gut and took hold.

Just like she belonged in his bed.

"You must have left very early this morning," she said.

"I was on my way back to Sydney from the Janderra mine when Ryan called. An emergency trip, last minute, so I took the company jet. When Howard knew I wouldn't be back, he chartered a replacement for his trip."

"You were already in the air. That's why you were the one to come."

Ric turned his head slowly and found himself looking right into her jade-green eyes. They were her most striking feature, not only because of that dramatic colour offset by the dark frame of her brows, but because of how much they gave away. The trick, he'd learned, was picking the real emotion from the sophisticated front she used to hide her vulnerabilities.

Not that Kim ever admitted to any weakness. She was her father's daughter in that regard. And right now she was working overtime to keep both him and the shock of the news he'd delivered at arm's length.

"It didn't matter where I was," he said, strong and deliberate. "I would have come, make no mistake."

"To tell me my father was d—"

"To take you home."

"To Sydney?" The notion appeared to surprise her, enough that she huffed out an astonished breath. "You're forgetting, my home is here now."

"I haven't forgotten."

After she'd walked out on him, he'd allowed her time to cool down. To think about her hotheaded accusations and to realise they belonged together. Four long dark months of silence passed before he'd come after her…only to find that she hadn't cooled down one degree or come to any realisation other than the certainty their marriage had been a colossal mistake and that her new home was here, in Auckland, New Zealand.

With Matt Hammond as her boss and her protector.

No, he hadn't forgotten anything and the power of those memories fired his temper and sparked between them in the close confines of the slowly moving car. She knew he was remembering that last heated clash in her workroom at Hammonds. The knowledge glittered in her eyes and brought out colour along her high cheekbones as she lifted her chin to speak.

"You said you would never come after me again."

And he hadn't. Pride and the finality of divorce papers hadn't allowed him, but this was different. "This isn't about us," he said tersely. "This is about your father and your family."

Kimberley held the narrowed anger of his gaze for another second before looking away. She closed her mouth on the instant comeback that flew to her tongue, the very inconvenient truth that the Hammonds were her family, too.

Her mother, Ursula, who'd died when Kim was a toddler, was Oliver Hammond's sister. Because of the animosity between the Blackstones and the Hammonds, she'd grown up with a tremendously biased view of her New Zealand uncle and aunt and their adopted sons, Jarrod and Matt. Yet when she'd needed a new job, they'd welcomed her into their business and into their home. Matt had been her friend when she'd badly needed one. His wife, Marise, had never exactly warmed to her, yet Matt had insisted on having her as godmother to their little son, Blake.

For the past ten years these Hammonds had been more her family than anyone on the Blackstone side of the Tasman, but she refrained from saying this out loud. If she'd read the turbulence in Perrini's eyes correctly, then mentioning Matt's name would be like red-flagging a bull. He'd never forgiven Matt for offering her an easy escape from Blackstone's with the plum position at House of Hammond, and the pair had almost come to blows in the Hammond workroom the day Perrini had tried to talk her in to taking him back. Anything she said now would only lead to more hot words and this wasn't the place.

This isn't about us. This is about your father.

How right he was…on more levels than the present.

Their relationship had never been about just them. Therein lay the problem. They'd met at Blackstone Diamonds, they'd bonded while working together to sell the retail jewellery business plan to the board and they'd fallen into bed in a wildly spontaneous celebration of their success.

But Perrini had wanted more. He'd married her to get it,

and his proud new father-in-law had delivered everything an ambitious young marketing executive could want. Power, prestige, a prominent bay in the executive parking lot…and entrée into one of Sydney's richest and most socially prominent families.

In the same sweet deal, he'd won the job of launching the retail business, Blackstone Jewellery, the job Kimberley had been promised and which she'd worked her backside off to earn. The killer blow? When she expressed her disappointment, Perrini sided with her father when he told her she didn't have the necessary skills or experience.

In time she'd come to accept their point, but at twenty-one she'd been wildly, madly in love, and she'd felt only a crippling sense of betrayal over what had led to that point. He'd pursued her; he'd married her; and all to serve his own ambitions.

Today he'd come to take her home to her family in Sydney, but could she trust his motives?

The farther they travelled in silence, climbing familiar streets toward her One Tree Hill town house, the more she realised that his motives didn't matter. The cold, hard reality of his news was finally beginning to pierce her armour of denial.

This isn't about us. This is about your father and your family.

Her father's plane was missing and even without the media's eagerness for photos of his anguished family, she couldn't go to work. Nor could she sit around her house going stir-crazy as she waited for news. With Matt away on a business trip she had no one to call on, no arms to hold her steady, no shoulder to cry on.

From the corner of her eye she could see Perrini's outstretched legs and the memory of his solid support at the airport ambushed her for a moment. A bad, unnecessary moment. She didn't need the comfort of his arms, not anymore, but she did need to go back to Sydney. She needed to be there when news came in of her father's fate.

And she needed to see the rest of her family, to make amends for the years of her absence.

Just the thought of seeing her brother Ryan and her Aunt Sonya, who'd been the closest thing to a mother figure in her upbringing, caused a tight ache in her belly and her chest and the back of her throat. She took a tighter grip on the bag in her lap and on her emotions. Tears would come, she knew, but never in front of Perrini.

"This is your place?"

Perrini's head tilted with what looked like curiosity as he surveyed the neat exterior of her stucco town house from the street where the limo had pulled up. Kimberley nodded abruptly in reply. He'd given the driver this address, so he knew without asking. And now that they'd arrived a new nervous tension gripped her insides with platinum claws.

This was her domain, a haven she'd created for herself away from the craziness of her busy business life. She didn't want Perrini prowling around, casting his long shadow over her privacy, leaving an impression she knew would stick like superglue to her visual memory.

Yet how could she not invite him in, when he'd flown through the early morning hours on top of a return flight to Blackstone's outback mine? Being one of her father's toys, the company jet would be furnished with every amenity and then some, but still...

"Would you like to come in?" she asked quickly, before

caution or nerves could change her mind. "I won't be long. I just need to repack and water my plants and call work to let them know."

One dark eyebrow arched. "You've decided to come?"

"Was there any doubt?"

"With you, Kim…always."

The wry tone of his comment surprised a short laugh from Kimberley and their eyes met with that sound still arcing between them. A hint of the Perrini smile that could render smart women senseless hovered at the corners of his mouth and the blue of his eyes suddenly seemed richer, deeper, sultrier. Everything inside her stilled…everything except the elevated beat of her heart.

Damn him. It wasn't even a proper smile. He wasn't even trying to charm her.

"I'd best get organised," she said briskly, breaking that moment of connection with a rush of smart-woman willpower.

She reached for her door just as his mobile phone buzzed. Leaving him to his call, she let the driver haul her luggage up the steep rise of steps to the closed-in portico that sheltered the front door. She rummaged in her bag for her keys and phone. Walking and talking would save precious minutes and by the time she'd unlocked and waved the driver inside, she'd also apprised Hammond's office manager that she was taking a week of personal leave.

Next, Matt. He needed to know, as her friend and her boss, but she'd barely dialled his number before a hand closed around her wrist, capturing her arm and her attention. Perrini. She recognised the span of his hand, the smattering of dark hair, the scar on his middle knuckle. The black-sapphire cuff links Howard had given him as a Christmas gift.

"Is that your boss you're calling?"

His voice was as tight as his grip and Kimberley blinked her attention away from his hand and on to the terse words he'd spoken. Her jaw tightened with irritation. She was in no mood for another go-round about the nature of her relationship with Matt. "So help me, Perrini, if you still can't accept that I wouldn't sleep with my—"

The rest of her reproach froze on her lips when she looked up into his face. Stark, taut, leached of colour. He exhaled a breath and the harsh sound echoed through the enclosed space. "I wish that were all, Kim."

The phone call.

He had news about the plane, about her father.

Panic beat hard in her veins but she straightened her shoulders in preparation for the blow.

"They've found debris," he said grimly, confirming her worst fear. "Off the Australian coast."

Debris. Kimberley assimilated the innocuous-sounding word. Not wreckage. Not bodies. "Just…debris?"

"No." He shook his head. "They also found one person. Alive. A woman."

A soft sob escaped her lips and she started to tremble somewhere deep inside. Perrini's arm came around her, lending her strength when she might have fallen.

"Who?" she breathed. "Please God, not Sonya, too."

"No, not your aunt." He took the phone from her limp fingers and flipped it shut. "According to Ryan, there's a chance it may be Marise Hammond. Your boss's wife."

TWO

Marise Hammond may have been on Howard Blackstone's charter flight?

It made no sense in Kimberley's shock-muddled brain. Yes, Marise had been in Australia for the past month tying up estate matters following her mother's death. Yes, Marise was capricious and self-absorbed, but not to the extent that she would hitch a ride home with her husband's bitter enemy. She knew how Matt felt about Blackstone Diamonds, and all because of Howard.

Why would she choose to be in his company?

Perrini had no answer and the question had been wiped from Kimberley's mind, temporarily, by the rest of the details he passed on from that phone call. He stressed that the woman hadn't been identified, that Marise hadn't been confirmed as a passenger, that the information was unsubstantiated.

But his contact was a senior officer in the Sydney police force. Surely he wouldn't tell them a woman had been pulled from the water alive without concrete information. Surely he wouldn't provide a name without confidence in her identity.

Surely he wouldn't build up false hope that Howard, too, might have survived the crash.

That notion only struck her while she was packing—if you could call throwing random clothes into a suitcase "packing." There was no rhyme or reason to the process. She didn't want to deliberate over what she might need in the coming week beyond clean underwear, although she made a conscious choice to shed the austere black dress she'd been wearing for work in favour of a pretty white sundress.

She didn't want to contemplate the outcome of this trip.

She didn't want to think about the need to pack sombre black.

Then she caught sight of herself in the mirror and saw that her face contained little more colour than her dress and possibly less than the creamy South Sea pearls in her ears. But it wouldn't have mattered what she wore, her face would be a pale, haunted contrast to the dark hair she'd pulled back in a ruthlessly tight ponytail. Her eyes would still look dazed and lost.

In that instant the last of the indignation that had carried her through the past half hour deflated like a pin-pricked balloon. Weak-kneed, she collapsed to the edge of her mattress amid the bright heap of floral-hued clothes she'd tipped from her holiday suitcase.

From the living room she heard Perrini's deep voice, a low, mellifluous sound that worked its magic on her shattered senses and pulled her back from the abyss. He had to be on the phone— a reminder of the previous phone call he'd taken in the limo— and now that her head was clearer she made the connection.

Marise was alive. Perhaps she wasn't the only survivor.

That faint hope flickered like a slow flame in the centre of her chest. It was okay. She was going home and it would all be okay.

Perrini appeared at her bedroom door, the phone still in his hand. The way he looked at her made her heart skip a beat. "Was that more news?" she asked, eyes wide and fixed on his face.

"No. It was my pilot. The jet is fuelled and ready to go when you are."

Kimberley released the breath she hadn't known she was holding and nodded. "Once I decide what to wear, I'll be ready."

Given the circumstances, it was a ridiculous thing to say. She regretted it even more when Perrini surveyed her, and the haphazard contents of her suitcase, with ruthless focus. Then, with his trademark decisiveness, he crossed the room and pulled her up from the bed and onto her feet. Slowly he surveyed her, from her toes all the way up to her eyes.

"You'll do in what you're wearing," he said, and his eyes smoked with a hint of what she might do *for.* "I always liked you in white."

Kimberley blinked with astonishment. *He was flirting with her? Half an hour after delivering news of her father's possible demise? Unbelievable.*

"I'm not dressing to impress you, Perrini," she said sharply.

He almost smiled and that tightened the screws on her incredulity.

"Give me five minutes—and some privacy—and I'll change."

"No, you won't." He took hold of her hand. "I've put some colour back in your face and some life in your eyes. Now let's go before you start thinking too much and lose it again."

* * *

The trip from Auckland to Sydney passed in a slow-moving daze despite the swift efficiency and supreme comfort of flying in the Blackstone corporate jet. A Gulfstream IV, it was the exact same model of aircraft her father had chartered for his ill-fated flight. She'd asked Perrini about that, after they boarded. After she noted the rich mahogany paneling, the luxurious cream-colored leather seats, the fully stocked galley and ornately appointed bathroom.

Right after he'd pointed out the bed and said, "Feel free to use it. I'm happy to share."

No doubt he was trying to get the spark back in her eyes by employing the same diversionary tactics as back in her bedroom, but that didn't dull the electric awareness that shimmered between them. Was he remembering another private flight they'd taken together?

There'd been no bed on that charter flight from San Francisco to Vegas but it hadn't mattered. They'd improvised. And before she'd come down from that incredible high, Perrini stunned her with a proposal she'd thought as wildly impulsive and wickedly romantic as making love with him a mile up in the sky.

That weekend had been the zenith of ten blissful weeks as Ric Perrini's lover. She'd become his wife in a wedding chapel only Vegas could love, and afterward they'd spent three decadent days in a Bellagio suite ordering room service and indulging themselves in every way possible. She hadn't realised a wedding band would make such a difference, but oh, how it had. It was the difference between good champagne and the vintage French they quaffed that weekend. Another level, impossible to describe or define, that filled her senses and her heart until she wondered if they would explode.

On their return to Australia, they had.

Everything inside Kimberley contracted painfully as she recalled the bliss. She didn't want to remember the freefall plunge that followed their return home…or the shattering pain of hitting rock bottom. So she'd focused on the here and now, and asked Perrini mindless questions about the jet's inclusions and capabilities, and she'd learned that her father had chartered the same model.

Clinging white-knuckled to the armrests during takeoff with the high-pitched wail of the engines in her ears, feeling the forward thrust suck her back into her seat, she could not shut out the image of her father and Marise experiencing the same sensation fourteen hours earlier. Nor could she eradicate the image of all that power and speed crashing from the sky and hitting the sea with devastating impact.

The flicker of hope in her chest wavered and died, and Kimberley's emotions spent the three-hour flight seesawing between numbed disbelief and intense dread of what lay ahead. She took up Perrini's suggestion to lie down because she couldn't bear the thought of looking out the window at the stretch of sea where the plane had gone down. He'd told her that Australian search-and-rescue had mounted an extensive search, but she didn't want to see the evidence.

It wasn't denial, it was self-preservation.

She felt she'd done a decent job of disguising her turmoil. She hadn't succumbed to tears. She'd even managed to feign the easy breathing of sleep when Perrini came to check on her.

It was one of the hardest things she could remember doing, lying there controlling her breathing while he stood in the open doorway staring down at her. Then he'd pulled the light blanket over her prone body. If he'd spoken, if he'd touched her with more than the velvety brush of his knuckles, she might have given in and asked him to stay. To share the bed, to hold her, to distract her in any way he chose.

That's how fragile and alone she'd felt at that moment.

But he'd left as quietly as he'd come and she'd curled up tightly and hugged herself, the same as she'd done so many nights as a child when she would sneak down from her bedroom and hide in a quiet corner of the foyer in their Vaucluse home, waiting for her father to come home from a long working day or a week at the mine or at the end of another overseas business trip.

Now, as they neared that home, the thought that he'd never come home again sunk diamond-sharp talons into her heart. It shouldn't hurt this much, not when she'd come to hate everything about the way he operated, including his screwed-up ethics and his treatment of the Hammonds, who were his wife's family. Not to mention the manipulation of her marriage to suit his own self-centred ends.

Maybe she needed to focus on *that* son of a bitch, instead of a childhood ideal of a father who had never existed except in her imagination.

"Okay?" Perrini asked from behind the wheel of his Maserati. The coupe was all sleek, blue style and eye-catching looks on the outside, with an engine that purred deceptively until provoked. Then it roared to life with impressive power and drive.

This car is your perfect match, she'd told him a couple of miles back. Now, the thick ache in her throat made it impossible to answer his question.

At the next red light he reached across and put his hand over hers, where they lay tightly clenched in her lap. The unexpected gesture was so comforting and so strengthening that she immediately found her voice. "I wish you'd stop being so nice," she snapped. "It makes me nervous."

He cut her an inscrutable look from behind his sunglasses. "A temporary aberration. Don't get too used to it."

"Thanks for the warning," she said dryly. Then she shook her head when she realised that once again he'd shocked her out of her wretchedness. "Thank you," she repeated, this time with sincerity.

"For?" The lights changed and he took his hand back, using it to guide the powerful sports car through the gears as they climbed the curves of New South Head Road.

"For breaking the news to me in person. For rescuing me at the airport and bringing me home. For keeping me together along the way. I do appreciate it, Ric. Thank you."

"You're welcome." They travelled another block before he added, "You called me Ric. I must be making progress."

She'd called him Perrini from their very first meeting, a ruse to remind him of their business relationship because she hadn't trusted his smooth moves or her body's unruly responses to him. They'd had to work together and she'd wanted to keep it professional. She'd fought the good fight for almost two months. And after they'd hooked up she kept on using his surname out of habit—and to tease him when he got all he-man insistent about her calling him Ric.

Now she'd done so to show the sincerity of her thanks. "It was a temporary aberration," she said coolly. "Don't get too used to it."

He laughed, a two-note snort of amusement that pierced Kimberley's numbed senses. It was dangerous, letting him charm her so easily, so quickly, but this was a temporary situation. A week at most, and she would be returning to Auckland. And right now she needed that charm and the sound of laughter because they'd arrived in Vaucluse and were climbing the street lined with multimillion-dollar homes to the most spectacular of all.

Miramare.

For the first twenty years of her life the three-storey white mansion had been Kimberley's home. She'd never been struck by its majesty, its size, its opulence, until now as Perrini downshifted gears to negotiate the thick cluster of news teams waiting outside the security gates, and turned into the driveway. And there it was, rising before them like a Venetian palace. A home fit for the man the media dubbed Australia's King of Diamonds.

A man who'd forbidden her from ever darkening this doorstep again when she defied his will and refused to return to work for Blackstone Diamonds.

A maelstrom of conflicting emotions—resentment, anguish, anticipation, anxiety—stormed through her as Perrini parked beneath the *porte cochere*. Although her gaze was fixed on the steps leading to the grand entrance, she heard the subtle scrunch of leather and sensed him shifting in his seat to face her. Her heart beat like a tom-tom drum high in her chest.

"Good to be home?" he asked.

Now there was a question! Was this home? Would her family welcome her back into their home?

When she'd quit her job at Blackstone's and joined House of Hammond, she'd also deserted her family. That's how it was between the two sides of the family. You chose your team: Blackstone or Hammond. There was no common ground, no fraternity, and it had never been as simple as birth name.

Sonya Hammond was the perfect example. Her mother's much younger sister moved in with the Blackstones as a teenager. Staying after Ursula's death completed her estrangement from her brother Oliver Hammond and his family.

But Kimberley was more worried about Ryan's reception than Sonya's. Her younger brother had endured his ups and downs with Howard but now he headed the Blackstone Jewellery chain, which placed him very firmly in the Blackstone camp. He didn't approve her defection—his word, used when he'd called to try his hand at changing her mind—any more than he'd approved of her affair with, and subsequent marriage to, Perrini.

And Perrini's question still stood unanswered.

Good to be home?

"I'm feeling many things," she said frankly. "Good is not one of them."

"Care to elaborate?"

Slowly she turned to face him. "I wouldn't be here but for one thing."

Their eyes met, the knowledge a shock of understanding that sharpened his expression into tight lines and shadowed planes. If Howard were here, she wouldn't be. It was as simple—and as complicated to her psyche—as that.

Before Perrini could respond, something distracted him and the atypical hesitation caused her to turn back toward the house. Sonya stood on the top step, her willowy figure framed by the open front door. Kimberley's heart beat even harder in her chest.

"She hasn't changed," she murmured.

Still tall, slender, beautiful, her aunt Sonya was dressed elegantly in a skirt and heels, her brown hair pulled back in the same conservative style. A warm smile graced her lips as she lifted her hand in welcome.

She looked so heartwrenchingly familiar, so *Sonya,* that Kimberley struggled to contain the squeal of joy that exploded inside her. Reflexively her hand lifted to the chatelaine necklace she wore around her neck, Sonya's gift on her twenty-first birthday. Each exquisitely crafted antique charm was a symbol. Love. Fertility. Protection. Strength. Eternity.

After the dissolution of her marriage she'd put it away in its box, unworn but not forgotten. Until recently when she'd started wearing it again. She wiped away the tears that blurred her vision, then allowed Perrini to help her from the low-slung car so she could run up the stairs and into her aunt's open arms. Then she knew why she wore the necklace.

It was her connection to home, to Sonya, whose embrace reminded her what it should feel like to come home. Tears she'd refused to cry for her father fell unrestrained as she breathed the familiar scent of her aunt's Chanel No. 5 and felt the comforting pat of her hand on her arm.

I should not have let Perrini and my father keep me away this long. I should not have given them that power.

"I'm sorry," she choked out fiercely through her tears. "I'm so very sorry."

Sonya's hug tightened for a moment as she whispered, "We all are, honey. About everything."

Long before Kimberley was ready her aunt broke the embrace. Taking a half step back Sonya smiled through her own tears as she took Kimberley's hands in hers. "It is so good to have you back home again, Kim, and to see you looking so beautiful…despite the circumstances."

"It is so good to be here, despite everything that has kept me away."

Rough emotion dimmed the light in Sonya's warm hazel eyes. "Let's not talk about that now. Come inside. Your brother is out on the terrace with Garth. I'm sure you can't wait to see them both again. And Danielle arrived a little while ago, too. She flew down from Port Douglas as soon as she heard."

Danielle was Sonya's daughter, and she must have been waiting just inside the door for the perfect moment to make her appearance. She *had* changed. Between seventeen and twenty-seven Danielle Hammond had grown into a copper-haired beauty with her mother's willowy build and a tan befitting her Port Douglas, Queensland home.

Golden eyes welling with tears, she hurried over to embrace Kimberley with the same warmth as her mother and her own special brand of exuberance.

"You brought her," Danielle said fiercely over Kim's shoulder. "I will never doubt your genius again."

"I'm only the chauffeur," Perrini drawled, downplaying his role in the prodigal's homecoming, "and the sometime porter. Where do you want me to take these?"

Kimberley saw that he toted her matched set of luggage, but before she could answer, Sonya stepped into her customary role as hostess. "Take them up to Kim's room, please, Ric. You know where it is."

How? Kimberley wondered, frowning. Afraid of awkward encounters with her father or her brother, she had never brought him home when they'd been lovers. They'd met at his house and they'd kept their relationship quiet at work for as long as they could. Yet out of all the bedrooms and suites spread through the mansion's upper wings, he knew where to find hers?

He disappeared into the house with Sonya, and Danielle's voice cut through her distraction. "How are you coping, Kim…or is that a stupid question?"

"I'm fine."

Danielle's eyes narrowed in a way that demanded the truth, and Kimberley decided that her cousin hadn't changed so much after all. Up close she noticed that beneath the big smile and light sprinkling of freckles, Danielle's complexion was blotchy and her eyes red-rimmed from crying. She had grown up in this house, too, with Howard a larger-than-life presence in her upbringing. She was more a Blackstone than a Hammond, although she'd struck out and started her own jewellery design business as Dani Hammond since moving to the tropical north of Australia.

"I can see that the Port lifestyle agrees with you, but how are you doing beneath the smile and suntan? Is everything working out for you?"

"Don't change the subject," her cousin fired back. "You're the one under inquisition right now."

"I told you, I'm fine," Kimberley assured her, but tears were brewing in her eyes as she reached out to hug Danielle again. A couple of seconds was all she needed to restore her composure and in that time she realised that she'd spoken no less than the truth. Being here, with the people she'd grown up with—the people she loved—she *was* fine. "Has there been any more news?" she asked, straightening and wiping moisture from her eyes. Again.

"No…at least none that your brother is passing on."

Kimberley stilled. "Do you think Ryan heard something he isn't sharing?"

"I had that feeling but when I asked he just about bit my head off. I don't know what's going on with him, Kim. Oh, I know he's shattered about his father, and this waiting around for news is *so* not his style. Mum told me he's been trying to line up extra search aircraft and vessels, despite all that AusSAR is doing. That was *after* he went down to water police headquarters to demand full disclosure. I wouldn't be surprised if he tried to get a spot on one of the search vessels, as well."

Kimberley well knew of her brother's tenacity. "That would have been interesting."

"No kidding."

"Do you think they told him anything new?"

Danielle released her breath on a heavy sigh that blew an errant curl from her face. "Honestly, I don't know. He is just so antsy, I can't help thinking there is more."

"More than his father being missing and him stuck here unable to charge to the rescue?"

"I guess you're right," Danielle mused aloud, although she didn't sound convinced. She tucked her arm through Kim's and tugged her toward the front door. "Let's go in. Knowing Mum, she will be putting together a late lunch for you and Ric as we speak. I bet you haven't had anything to eat all day."

"True, but food is the furthest thing from my mind."

"Do try and have something if only to please Mum. Fussing over us all day is the only thing that's keeping her together. Let her do the same for you."

"I will, but there's something I need to do first."

"Ryan?" her cousin guessed astutely.

Kimberley nodded. *Yes—Ryan.*

Returning from his porter's errand to the second floor, Ric was halfway down the ornate marble staircase that rose from the grand foyer when Danielle and Kimberley came through the front door arm-in-arm. But he only saw one woman.

Dark hair slicked back in an efficient ponytail. Green eyes so recently awash with tears now clear and sparking with renewed resolve.

She'd rebounded from the tearstorm. Good. Bringing her home had not only been necessary but also essential, for her, for Sonya, for all the family. And now that she was here, she was staying. Whatever it took.

"There you are." Danielle released her hold on her cousin's arm as Ric descended the last of the stairs. "I was just taking Kim out to the terrace to find Ryan."

He knew this would be the difficult part of this reunion, hence the warrior-woman look on her face. "I'll take her," he said, smoothly stepping in to claim her hand. "Could you let Sonya know to bring our coffee out there?"

Danielle left them alone, but only after a raised-eyebrow look that took in his proprietary clasp on Kim's hand and a murmured comment he lip-read as "Nice work."

By the darkness that suddenly appeared in Kim's eyes and the jerk of her hand against his, he gathered she didn't miss that knowing look, either. "There's no need to take me any-where," she said frostily. "I know my way to the terrace."

"I didn't imagine you wouldn't."

"Then let go of my hand. You've already given Danielle the wrong impression."

He raised an eyebrow. "That being…?"

"Don't pretend to be dense, Perrini. It's not becoming."

"Are you still hung up on what your brother thinks about us together?"

"Since we're not together anymore, no." She narrowed her eyes at him. "And wasn't it *you* who said this wasn't about us?"

"Throwing my words back at me? That's not like you, Kim."

Her emerald eyes shot fire at him and she tugged harder at her hand. Ric didn't let go. Instead he used the leverage to pull her closer, close enough that the flared skirt of her dress brushed his thighs and her eyes widened with apprehension. In the cool quiet of the atriumlike foyer he imagined he could hear the wild race of her heartbeat…or perhaps it was his own.

He thought about kissing her. When her mouth opened on a silent note of outrage, he ached to bend into that kiss. He imagined he'd get slapped for his efforts, but fear of that didn't stop him. The flicker of vulnerability in her eyes did.

The fierce determination was just a front for facing her brother. Beneath the veneer she was emotionally exhausted by the day's revelations and he knew there would be more to come, if not today then tomorrow or the next day. It was only a matter of time before the wreckage was located and the bodies recovered.

No, he couldn't take advantage of her weakness. Not now. As a compromise he lifted the hand trapped in his toward his lips. He felt her resistance, saw it snap in her eyes even as he turned her arm and delivered a chaste kiss to the inside of her wrist. Briefly it crossed his mind that she might slap him anyway, with words at the very least, but the sound of rapidly approaching footsteps broke the tension and he released her hand as Garth Buick strode into view.

Kim gasped, her surprise this time tainted with delight as

she launched herself at the Blackstone company secretary who was Howard's closest and oldest friend. The fact that they'd remained friends for so long was a testament to Garth's character and loyalty and remarkably even temperament.

He wrapped his arms around Kim with genuine affection, but the eyes that met Ric's over her head were shadowed with gravity. "Ryan's just taken a call from Stavros."

Their contact at police headquarters. Ric's heart stilled. "Bad news?"

"Nothing on Howard," Garth assured them both. "But we finally have confirmation of the passenger list."

"Was it Marise they found?" Kim asked. "Was she on the plane?"

The older man nodded heavily. "Yes. They've just brought her body in to the morgue."

Three

"Her body?" Kim's voice rose on a note of shock. Confusion clouded her expression as she looked from Garth to Ric. "You said she was alive. A survivor. You said they—"

"She passed away on the rescue boat," Garth said gently, "shortly after they took her on board. I'm sorry, Kim. I know you were close."

"No, not really."

A deep sadness imbued her comment and Ric wondered if she was thinking about Marise or her husband Matt, the Hammond Kim *was* close to. Or perhaps the couple's son. His jaw tightened. Dammit, he'd hoped there'd been a mistake. That they'd learn the woman wasn't Marise Hammond, the mother of a small boy, too young and innocent to be the victim of such a tragic loss.

"Are they certain it was Marise Hammond?" he asked.

"Certain enough that Stavros told us before the formal identification process. Unofficially, of course," Garth added.

"When you called me in New Zealand, you mentioned a foul-up with the passenger list."

"Initially there was a Blackstone employee listed," Garth said. "Jessica Cotter. She manages the Martin Place store and was supposed to be going to Auckland for the opening."

The name wasn't familiar to Ric, but he hadn't worked in the jewellery side of the business for almost eight years. "She couldn't be the one they found in the sea?"

"Wrong build, wrong hair colour, wrong clothing. It seems Ms. Cotter had a change of mind and got off the plane at the last minute. Hence the initial confusion over the passenger list."

"So it was Marise Hammond." Sonya's voice cut into the conversation, and Ric swung around to find her standing in the archway leading toward the kitchen. Although her eyes looked shell-shocked, she stood tall and poised and even managed a passable attempt at a smile. "Why don't you go through to the living room? Danielle and Ryan are there and I think we should all be together to talk about this. I've made tea and coffee but if anyone would prefer something stronger, please let me know."

Ryan Blackstone looked like he needed something stronger.
Ric eyed the younger man narrowly, taken aback by the gaunt grey cast to his normally tanned features. It was never a surprise to see Ryan wound tighter than a newly forged spring, especially in Ric's presence, but in all his years at Blackstone's Ric had never seen him unravel once.

Today, as his stark green gaze met his sister's across the wide expanse of the mansion's living room, he looked perilously close to that point.

"Coffee, Ric?"

Sonya distracted him with the proffered cup—black, strong, welcome—for only a second, and he turned back to see Kim bound so tightly in her brother's arms that he thought she might snap. It was a brief, silent embrace with none of the exuberant warmth of her reunion with Sonya or Danielle or Garth, but what it lacked in length and words it more than made up for in intensity.

Feeling like an intruder on this deeply private moment, he looked away and saw that Danielle had done the same. The significance of this particular reunion hit him suddenly and with all the force of a runaway ore truck.

It had nothing to do with their chequered history or Ryan's disapproval of Kim's defection. Nothing to do with any prior competition for their father's approval and affection. Nothing to do with her taking the Hammond side in the long-running family conflict.

Kim and Ryan were all that remained of their family unit. First their elder brother, James, abducted and never seen again. Then their mother's suicide. Now they faced the probable loss of their seemingly indestructible father.

No wonder they clung to each other so tenaciously.

The room where the family gathered opened onto the terrace and front gardens, and rose up through the second storey to a thirty-foot ceiling. Light and air spilled into the vast space via the opened banks of French doors and the stacked windows above, yet the atmosphere strummed with the dark tension of a mausoleum, until it was broken by the faint rattle of cup against saucer.

From the corner of his eye Ric saw Garth quietly take

Sonya's coffee and set it down on a side table. Her quiet "Thank you" broke the silence.

"I'm very sorry to hear about Marise," she continued with a calm composure that belied her distress.

Danielle, sitting beside her, took hold of her hand. "We can't be certain it was her…can we?"

"It was," Ryan said with surprising force. "The passenger list is confirmed. An all-male crew. Howard. His lawyer. Marise Hammond. She was the only female on the plane."

"Well, what was she doing on the plane?" Danielle fired back, undeterred. "I didn't think she would even know Howard, let alone be on speaking terms with him."

Ric put his untouched coffee down. The same question had been circling his head all day, and he didn't like any of the answers he'd come up with. But he could respond to the second part. "She worked at Blackstone's as Marise Davenport before she married Matt Hammond. And unless the tabloids are doctoring pictures now, she was still on speaking terms with Howard in December."

"What are you talking about?"

Danielle asked the question, but Kim studied him with equal bewilderment. Living so far from Sydney, neither woman would have seen the scurrilous piece run by a high-profile society columnist a couple of weeks back. A piece that could easily have been dismissed if not for the accompanying photo.

"*Scene* published a picture of them dining together," Sonya explained, "and hinted that they might be involved… personally."

Danielle's eyes widened with astonishment on her mother's careful choice of description. "Howard and Marise were having an affair? You have got to be kidding!"

"Of course it's not true," Sonya said with some heat. "That magazine is renowned for printing outrageous scuttlebutt and getting away with it by using broad hints rather than actual claims. Marise is married—she has a child. Whatever Howard's involvement with this woman, it was not an affair!"

Sonya's passionate declaration hovered for a long moment unanswered and uncontested, but when Ric caught Garth's eye he knew they were on the same wavelength. Howard's wealth and power and charismatic good looks had always attracted pretty go-getters—reportedly before, during and after his only marriage—and he'd never been averse to casting aside his current mistress in favour of a dazzling new model.

And Marise Davenport Hammond had always been a dazzler. From her time working at Blackstone's, Ric recalled her as a go-getter, as well. She'd put the moves on him and Ryan, too, before striking gold when she met the heir to the Hammond jewellery business at a diamond trade show. But now that she had Hammond's wealth at her disposal, why would she need to turn her eye elsewhere?

"Did your father say anything to you about meeting with Marise?" Ric directed his question at Ryan.

A distracted frown creased Ryan's forehead as he flipped shut the cell phone he'd been checking, but when he looked up his gaze focused razor-sharp on Ric's. "Not a word."

"Garth?"

"I asked him about the photo when it surfaced," the older man replied, "and he told me to mind my own business. In so many words."

Ric could imagine. Howard never minced words and the ones he chose were always colourful. "So you don't think they were discussing business that night?"

Garth shook his head. "I doubt it."

"No way in hell," Ryan added with force.

"Perhaps she was trying to broker harmony," Danielle suggested. "On behalf of Matt and the Hammonds."

Ric's gaze flicked to Kim, who'd sat through the exchange in uncustomary silence. One hand twisted at the charm pendant she wore around her neck and her dark brows were drawn together in a frown. He didn't have to say a word to garner her attention. Slowly her gaze lifted to his. Strikingly green. Pensive. Troubled.

"Marise wasn't involved with business at House of Hammond," she said. "And, no, she wasn't a peacemaker."

"So why was she meeting with Howard and flying on his plane?" Danielle exhaled on a note of frustration. "I guess we might never know."

"Does it matter?" Ryan pocketed his phone, his scowl forbidding. "The gutter press will jump all over this and you can bet they'll rehash that photo and every other sordid detail they can dig up."

Sonya made a soft sound of distress. She knew—hell, they all knew—that the Hammond-Blackstone family tree could provide enough juicy fodder to satisfy the greedy press for weeks. They wouldn't even have to get their hands dirty digging, since most of it had been emblazoned across the front page of every major scandal sheet at one time or another.

"How many cameras were outside the gates when you came in?" Garth asked him.

"Too many."

"Can't they leave us alone, at least for this one day?" Sonya asked.

"No," Ric said wearily, "that's not how they work. We'll

all have to be prepared for the intrusion and speculation and the rehashing of old history. This is going to get a hell of a lot worse before it gets any better."

Kimberley couldn't stomach any more. With an excuse of needing to stretch her legs after her two long flights, she stalked outside to the terrace. Minutes later Ryan came to the open doors and said he had some business to attend to, and unless any news came through in the meantime he would see her in the morning.

She'd noticed his distraction in the living room. Whoever's call or message he'd been checking his phone for every five minutes had not come through. No doubt he would chase that down with his usual ruthless determination.

Restless and wired, she strode over to the arced balustrade that presented Miramare's multimillion-dollar view of Sydney Harbour to perfect advantage. Reflexively, her hands fisted over the sun-warmed wall and she had to force herself to relax her steely grip. She'd escaped the unrelenting tension of the living room and the endless eddying conversation about Marise and Howard.

She didn't want to think about them, to picture them in cahoots, their well-groomed heads together, conspiring Lord knows what.

She didn't want to think about them at all. She just wanted to close her eyes and let the late afternoon sun seep into her body, to relax her whirling mind and melt the icy ache from her belly. If only she could conjure herself onto one of the yachts far below, flying across the sea-blue water with the wind at their backs.

Of course all that was impossible. When she closed her

eyes, she did see Marise and Howard together and she heard Perrini's blunt summation. *This is going to get a hell of a lot worse before it gets any better.* That comment had hustled her from the room before she exploded with a sharp rejoinder.

Worse? How could it get any worse?

A plane had crashed. People had died horribly, innocent people going about their everyday working lives. The pilot and copilot, a cabin attendant, a lawyer travelling with Howard—all real people whose families would be stunned and grieving and asking their own questions about fairness and fate. Perhaps some left loved ones with unanswered questions, but did it matter? Ryan was right about Marise. It didn't matter what she'd been doing that night in the restaurant or why she was on Howard's charter flight. What mattered was how Matt would suffer a brutal hammering from the press as they speculated over every aspect of his family history and his business and his marriage, at a time when he should be mourning the loss of his wife in peace.

What mattered was another child not understanding why his mummy hadn't come home. He would forget her face and her cuddles and her laughter, but later he would grow inquisitive and seek answers. Sadly they would be clouded by every scandalous supposition printed and gossiped about and adopted as truth.

Kimberley knew all about that and the thought of her godson going through the same distress chiselled open a chasm of pain in her heart. She'd been the same age as Blake when her mother hadn't returned from a break at their Byron Bay holiday home. Many years later she'd read all the conjecture over Ursula Blackstone's apparent suicide, her inability to cope with two young children while stricken with grief and remorse over the abduction of her firstborn son. How her depression had deepened over the rift between her brother Oliver and her husband following a loud and belligerent confrontation at her thirtieth birthday party.

At least Blake had a father who loved him unconditionally, who would protect him and explain the truth about his mother. Matt was a good man, a fair man, and a wonderful father. His only mistake was marrying the lethally beautiful Marise.

Familiar footfalls on the sandstone terrace broke into her reverie. *Damn*. After ten years she shouldn't remember such minute and significant detail, but her consciousness refused to forget the cadence of his stride. Or the intense scrutiny of his gaze on her face as he settled by her side.

"You can't enjoy the view with your eyes closed," he said after several seconds.

"I've seen the view a thousand times." Kimberley kept her eyes firmly closed. "I was enjoying the solitude."

"Pity."

Perrini fell silent, but she felt the brush of his sleeve against hers as he leaned forward. She pictured his hands planted wide on the balustrade, his azure gaze narrowed as he surveyed the amazing view. It always blew visitors away, this picture-perfect vista that stretched down the harbour to the famous bridge and beyond.

"I thought you might have been thinking," he said after a moment.

"About?"

"Marise and Howard. You didn't offer an opinion inside." He paused, a deliberate hesitation before delivering the million-dollar question. "Do you think they were having an affair?"

Reluctantly she opened her eyes and felt the impact of his

perceptive gaze—narrowed and as blue as the harbour—
ripple through her senses.

Double damn. She couldn't escape this. She couldn't walk
away.

"Anything is possible," she said, choosing her words
with care.

Perrini's expression tightened. "Stop pussyfooting around,
Kim. You knew Marise better than any of us. What was she
doing in Australia these past weeks?"

"She came over for her mother's funeral. As far as I know
she stayed to tie up some matters with the estate."

"Over Christmas and New Year's?"

"Her mother passed away in December—I doubt she had
much choice. I believe her father isn't well and her sister was
away on a modelling assignment."

"And if there was money involved in her mother's estate,"
he mused, "Marise struck me as a woman who'd be all over it."

Kimberley exhaled through her nose. She would not respond. Speaking ill of Marise now seemed uncharitable and
purposeless. She'd survived a plane crash, spent terrifying
hours in the water, only to pass away among strangers. No
one deserved that, not even a woman who'd deserted her
husband and child for weeks on end with scant excuse for her
absences.

Not even a woman who might have done so as cover for
an affair.

"I don't know Marise as well as you seem to think, so I
don't know what she might or might not have done," she
said. "But I do know what my father is capable of."

"You don't think your stance on Howard is slightly jaun-
diced?"

A humourless laugh escaped Kimberley's lips as she met his gaze. "You know it is. And you know why."

"Ten years is a long time, Kim."

Staring into his shadowed face, she wondered about that. So much hadn't changed, including the way he sparked her temper and her body's dormant hormones with equal ease. Just by standing a little too close. Just by looking into her eyes a little too long. Just by pressing his lips to her wrist and stirring insistent memories of other kisses, against other skin, far more intimate.

"Did he tell you about the last time I saw him?" she asked, regathering her concentration. "When he came to New Zealand to try and snare me back to Blackstone's?"

"I'd like to hear your side."

Oh, he was smooth. He wouldn't give away how much Howard had shared about that horrendous meeting. He'd been the same inside, she realised belatedly. Assuming control of the discussion, asking the leading questions, drawing opinion from everyone else but never offering his own.

She could call him on that—later—but for now she *wanted* to share her side.

She wanted him to know exactly what Howard Blackstone was capable of.

"When I refused his job offer," she said, getting straight to the point, "he sweetened the salary package. More than once. When I told him money wasn't the issue, he asked what it would take. I said an apology."

"I gather you didn't get one?"

"Have you ever heard Howard Blackstone apologise? For anything?"

Something tightened in his expression, but he simply said, "Go on."

"He rejected any notion that *he'd* done anything wrong, but then he accused Matt of stealing me from Blackstone's. He called him a thief like his father, and brought up the whole sorry raft of accusations from Mum's party." Shaking her head, she blew out a heated breath. "That was thirty years ago. I can't believe he still thinks Oliver Hammond stole the Blackstone Rose necklace that night."

"You don't think Oliver took the opportunity to reclaim what he believed should have been Hammond property?"

"No," she replied with absolute conviction. "Oliver wouldn't have taken that necklace if it was handed to him on a silver platter. He despised Howard for cutting up the Heart of the Outback stone and making it into such an ostentatious piece. He hated that he'd put the Blackstone name to the necklace, when it came from a diamond found by a Hammond. And he despised Howard for making such a blatant show of owning it, with all the magazine spreads and having Mum photographed wearing the necklace at every opportunity."

"From what I understand, your grandfather gave the diamond to Ursula. It was her prerogative to do with it as she wished. Eventually it would have passed to her estate," he said with emphasis. "If it hadn't gone missing, the Blackstone Rose would be yours, Kim."

She gave a strangled laugh and shook her head. "No, that was never going to happen. Howard was the sole beneficiary of my mother's estate. And as of last month, I believe I am no longer named in his will."

"He said he was striking you from his will?" Perrini

whistled softly through his teeth. "That must have been some argument."

"You might say that."

His lips quirked at her dry comment but his brows were lowered in serious contemplation as he caught her gaze. "Surely you didn't believe he'd go ahead with it once he cooled down?"

"Maybe not, but what about his other threat? He still doesn't accept that I walked away from Blackstone's—" *and you* "—because of his actions. He blames Matt for actively recruiting me. The last thing he said to me that day was 'Hammond will pay for this.'"

The portentous statement hung for a beat in the still evening air while Perrini made the connection. His blue eyes narrowed. "You think he was sleeping with Marise out of vengeance?"

"I don't know, but I wouldn't be surprised if that's what he wanted Matt to think."

She watched him consider that, his expression guarded. "Did Hammond have any reason to think his wife would cheat on him?"

"Matt didn't discuss his marriage with me."

"But it's possible?"

Kimberley ached to say *no, their marriage was as solid as the Sydney sandstone beneath our feet. Marise valued her husband and her child too dearly to stray.* But she couldn't say it. She looked away, her silence answer enough.

They stood like that for what seemed a long time, side by side at the balustrade, considering the shocking implications. Whether there'd been a clandestine affair going on or not didn't matter. If the tabloids ran with it, if Matt believed it, then Howard's job was done. Whether he was here to enjoy the fruits of his malicious game didn't matter. He'd won.

The thought chilled Kimberley to the bone. This was her father. The man she'd looked up to with adoration throughout her childhood; the person she'd set her sights on emulating when she'd focussed single-mindedly on a career in the precious gems industry.

Unconsciously she rubbed her arms. "How can I mourn such a man?" she asked bitterly. "How can anyone?"

Perrini didn't answer, but she sensed a change in his posture, a stiffening, and felt the warning touch of his hand on her arm. She swung around and saw Sonya standing just outside the French doors.

Had she heard that last comment?

Kimberley felt sick. She would never set out to hurt her aunt, who for some inexplicable reason had always stood by Howard with the same steadfastness as she'd defended him earlier. Over the years there'd been much speculation about their relationship, but Kimberley believed Sonya when she said there'd never been anything sexual between them.

Of course not. He's my brother-in-law, she'd said, sounding offended that Kim had asked.

But she still could have loved the bastard. Kimberley suspected she would mourn him more purely than anyone.

"I know neither of you have eaten all day," Sonya said now, in her customary mothering role, "so I'm going to start dinner early. You will stay, Ric?"

"Thank you," he said easily. "I will."

"Good." Sonya turned as if to leave, then paused. "Your room is made up, as always, so do consider staying over. We'd love the company tonight."

Your room? As always?

Kimberley blinked in confusion at the allusion to regular sleepovers. Her gaze shifted from her aunt to the ex-husband who seemed to have slipped right into her family during her absence. No wonder he'd known where to locate her bedroom when he'd taken her luggage upstairs.

"I'm not going anywhere," he assured Sonya with a smile, but when he turned his gaze on Kimberley the warmth of that smile didn't reach his eyes. They darkened with a message that felt like a vow.

I'm not going anywhere.

Four

True to his word, Perrini stayed that night and through Friday, as well. He left only once, following a call from his office Friday morning, and even then he waited until after Ryan had arrived before leaving.

"Does he think we womenfolk will fall apart without a big, strong man standing guard?" Kimberley asked Danielle across the remains of their breakfast.

"I would hardly call Ryan's presence *standing* guard. He hasn't stopped pacing since he arrived!"

Kimberley watched Ryan's impatient stride back and forth from shadows to sunlight at the far end of the terrace, the ever-present phone at his ear and a forbidding frown on his face. "He should go in to work," she said. "At least then he might feel like he's doing something useful."

"He *is* doing something useful."

Sonya's soft words came from beside Kimberley's chair, and she turned back around to find her aunt had brought fresh coffee. She set it down before continuing, her tone as close to a reprimand as she ever managed.

"Ryan is handling all the calls that are coming in, the same as Ric did during the night and early this morning, and which I know I can't deal with at the moment. He will ensure we hear any news as soon as it comes in. And if the police need to find us—" her eyes met Kimberley's briefly, her meaning clear in their tear-shrouded anxiety "—then this is where they will come."

With quiet dignity, she gathered up some of the breakfast dishes and walked away. Last night they'd learned that Sonya had given all the household staff leave. On Perrini's recommendation, of course.

So, okay, she understood the need for caution with the estate under siege from the media. Especially as Perrini already suspected someone in the know of leaking her flight arrival details to the Auckland press. She understood, but she reserved the right to feel snippy about his air of authority regarding all things Blackstone.

Ten years ago she'd stood toe-to-toe with Perrini and accused him of marrying her to become a Blackstone. She'd asked if he'd considered changing his name, since it was so obvious that Howard was treating him like a surrogate golden son. And she had felt like a meaningless pawn, her only value the Blackstone name and birthright.

To establish herself and to prove her worth she'd had to leave. And in her time away it seemed that Perrini had performed exactly as accused. He'd not only scaled the corporate ladder at Blackstone Diamonds, he'd become a part of the Blackstone family with a room at his disposal and the kind of easy rapport with Sonya and Danielle that only comes from constant contact.

She could only presume his relationship with her father had progressed to the same degree, and in her mind's eye she saw the self-satisfied look on Howard's face when they'd returned from that momentous vacation in San Francisco. When they'd decided, on a whim, to fly to Vegas for a weekend and he'd surprised her with the "impromptu" proposal.

She swallowed tightly, her throat constricted with raw, bitter emotion as she recalled Howard's words when they'd walked hand-in-hand onto this very terrace and told him their news.

"Welcome to the family," he'd said, jumping to his feet to shake Perrini's hand and clap him on the back. "You never fail to disappoint me, Ric."

Kimberley had felt the snub like a body blow then, and now it seemed as though her ostracism was complete. She was the outsider in her own family, and she'd made little effort to bridge that gap. Gathering up the rest of the breakfast plates, she pushed to her feet. "I'm going to help Sonya with the dishes."

Over her coffee cup, Danielle arched her brows. "You know how to do dishes? You have changed, cuz. Colour me impressed."

"Danielle has just suggested that I've changed." Straightening from packing the dishwasher, Kimberley met Sonya's constrained gaze across the impressive width of the Miramare kitchen. "But it seems you can still rely on me to say what I'm thinking, without thinking. I'm sorry, Sonya. I was feeling tetchy earlier when I made that crack about Ryan, but I wouldn't have said what I did if I thought you might overhear."

"The same as last night?"

How can I mourn such a man? How can anyone?

Kimberley blanched as she recalled what Sonya had over-heard on the terrace the previous evening, but she refused to be a hypocrite even to spare her beloved aunt's feelings. "I'm sorry you heard that, although I'm not sorry I said it."

Sonya shook her head sadly. "He's not all bad."

"Why do you always defend him," Kimberley shot back, "when he's been such an utter bastard to so many people?"

"He's been good to me, always. He provided me with a home and paid for my education after my father passed on. And he's done the same for Danielle. I could not have wished more for my daughter than what's been provided in your father's home."

Kimberley thought about her cousin, with whom she'd chatted long into the night about her designs and the materials she worked with and her fledgling business in Port Douglas. They had so much in common. And how could she dispute Sonya's claim? "I want to disagree on principle," she said after a moment, "but Danielle is so warm and lovely and talented and smart. She is a credit to her upbringing. You must be very proud."

"I am, but it's not only my doing, Kim. Did she tell you that Howard helped her with the capital to set up her business?"

"Yes, she did." But Kimberley couldn't help thinking there must have been something in it for Howard.

"He would have done the same for you," her aunt said gently, "if you'd stayed."

"I never wanted my own business."

"Then he would have advanced you at Blackstone's, the same as he's done with Ryan and Ric. He loved you, Kim. Whatever else he may have done, whatever you hold against him, never forget that."

There was so much heart in Sonya's delivery, so much conviction, that Kimberley longed to believe her. Who didn't yearn for their parents' love? But Howard had too many strikes against him and the acrimony of their last encounter still burned in her stomach. He'd done nothing honourable, nothing to earn back the love he'd crushed like a worthless bug ten years before. And nothing in his attempted reconciliation suggested it meant anything to him beyond vengeance against the Hammonds.

Some of that resentment must have shown in her face because Sonya continued with the same earnest intensity. "I remember when you were born and Ursula told me how overjoyed he was to have a daughter. He chose your name, you know."

"After the location of his mining leases?" she asked.

"Honey, you know that's not the reason. When you came kicking and screaming into the world a week early—January twenty-sixth, Australia Day—he wanted a significant name, something fitting to mark our national holiday. He chose Kimberley because it's his favourite part of Australia, because of the region's natural beauty, and also because it is home to so many treasures. That's you, Kim. You were always his treasure. Don't ever forget that."

Early Saturday morning, the pilot's body was pulled from the water and AusSAR started making noises about calling off the search for survivors. Prepared for this eventuality, they had a team on standby to continue the search for the wreckage on the seabed. But Ric hadn't expected it this soon. Until now he'd managed to harness his impatience and frustration, but all morning he'd been on the phone to every official contact he could find or make, only to be quoted policies and procedures until he ached to shove them back down officialdom's collective throats.

He tossed the phone onto the armoire and dragged a weary hand over his face. He needed a shave. He needed sleep, too, not the restless minutes of shut-eye that were interrupted too soon by another phone call, another worried executive needing reassurance, another headline about the company's future to repudiate.

The spread of papers across the table he'd commandeered as a desk in the top-floor living room of the Vaucluse mansion told the tale. It *had* gotten worse, even more swiftly and viciously than he'd predicted two days earlier, and it wasn't all about scandal. Today's business pages speculated over who would lead the billion-dollar business and hinted at the possibility of a power struggle.

The buzzards hadn't even waited for a body to be found before starting their nasty work, damn them.

He needed a break from those screaming headlines, and when he paced onto the patio, he found the perfect distraction.

Kimberley lounging on the pool deck.

That she wasn't wearing a bikini was only a minor blip of disappointment because the sleek, black one-piece clung to her killer curves and exposed the tanned length of her legs as she settled on one of the loungers. Even more spectacular than the harbour view, he mused, leaning his hands against the railing and drinking in the sight.

She'd changed some over the years, growing into the sophisticated sexiness she'd only promised at twenty-one. Yet she'd lost none of the strong will. None of the firebrand that had snared his attention from the second they locked eyes across the Miramare dinner table ten years ago.

Watching her now whipped a new frustration through his veins—a resentment of every one of their years apart, of every barb aimed in vengeful anger, of the pride that prevented him from chasing her down and dragging her home where she belonged.

He didn't allow the feeling to take hold. She *was* here now, and getting her to stay was a mission he could sink his teeth into, one that wouldn't leave him floundering like this morning's exercise in futility. Right on cue his phone buzzed again, but he gave it only a cursory glance as he strode through to the bedroom he'd barely used the past two nights.

He was taking a break. Alone with Kimberley. She'd been avoiding his company, or distancing him with a cool politeness he figured was for Sonya's benefit. Ric preferred her sharp-tongued frankness, and alone on the pool deck he might just get a healthy dose.

If not, at least he'd get some exercise.

Swimming laps of the serene Miramare pool was a poor substitute for pounding through the Bondi surf. That was Ric's exercise of preference. Pitting himself against the unpredictability of the ocean's surge and pull every morning set him up for the volatility he faced at the rockface of business. He relished that challenge, in the water and in the workplace. Pity it had taken him this long, through too many dead-end disappointments, to realise he needed it in his woman, as well.

He turned up the tempo, churning the pool's surface with the power of a sprinter's strokes. Another lap, forging through his own wake, still wasn't the challenge of open water, but it dispelled the last of the morning's frustration and breathed life into his dulled senses.

He climbed from the water, those senses already honed on

the only occupied piece of poolside furniture. She was reclining, but not relaxed. Even from a distance he could see the tension in her posture, in the slender fingers curled around the edges of her lounger.

He knew she'd see his presence as an intrusion. A small grin tugged at his mouth as he recalled the evening she'd arrived, when he'd intruded on her solitude up on the terrace. His grin stretched when he imagined her outrage when he—

Still dripping from the pool, he stopped beside her and shook his head like a wet dog.

Kim didn't disappoint. With a gasp of shock she bolted upright and whipped off her water-dotted sunglasses. Her eyes fired with green sparks. "What the hell do you think you're doing, Perrini?"

He finished pulling a lounger right alongside hers and stretched out. "Drying off."

Damn, it felt good to see that blaze in her eyes. And to smile, genuinely, for the first time in days. Being around her always made him feel alive...in all kinds of ways, he added, as she began drying her dark lenses on the nearest soft cloth.

Which happened to be the softest part of her swimsuit.

Ric took full, unapologetic advantage of the show, even after she noticed the downward drift of his gaze and stopped polishing. "Nice suit," he said, meeting her eyes again. "I'm glad you packed it."

"I borrowed it from Sonya." She shoved the glasses back over her eyes, hiding the irritation in her expression although she didn't bother keeping it from her voice. "She told me you were working."

"I was."

"I assumed she meant at your office."

"I have a makeshift office upstairs," he said casually, closing his eyes and feigning his own relaxation. "In the living room next to my bedroom."

"Don't you have a home to go to?"

"I do. At Bondi."

She didn't answer right away, but he sensed a change in her mood and felt her alert gaze on his face for several seconds before she asked, "The same one?"

"Yes. Why do you ask?"

"I thought you might have cashed it in," she retorted. "Although if property values in the eastern suburbs are still on the rise, then I suppose it's a smart investment."

"That's not why I kept it."

"Why did you?"

Surprised she would ask such a leading question, he opened his eyes and turned to look at her. She'd pushed her glasses on top of her head, and her candid green gaze and the intimacy of lying side-by-side—as close as if they shared pillow talk—kicked him low and hard.

"Because I like living there."

Something flitted across her expression and was gone before he could catch it. And when she replaced her sunglasses and rolled onto her back to stare up into the blue summer sky, he knew that moment of connection was gone. Even before she sniped, "If you like your home so much, why do you spend so much time here?"

"Ahh."

Kimberley turned to glare at him through her designer lenses. "What is *ahh* supposed to mean?"

"Sonya mentioned you had problems with the 'standing guard.'"

That comment she'd made at yesterday's breakfast. She should have known he would hear about it. Not that she wouldn't have said the same to his face, but she hated the thought of her words being repeated behind her back. "Do you and Sonya discuss me often?"

"Would it be much of a disappointment if I said no?"

Damn him and the dark silkiness of his voice. Damn him for coming down here parading his assets in those Daniel Craig swimmers. Damn her foolishness for watching those powerful assets rise from the water, for wanting to know about his house, for longing to say yes, *I loved living there, too, even for such a short time.* For that split second of yearning for a place they'd once been, a time they could never wish back. Too much had been said, too much unsaid, too many years had passed.

"No," she said finally in answer to his question. "Not if it's the truth."

An uncomfortable silence stretched, broken only by the murmur of traffic from the streets far below and the mournful hoot of a distant ferry in the harbour. Kimberley closed her eyes but she couldn't shut him out. She felt his narrowed gaze on her face. Dissecting her expression, divining for emotion.

Damn him.

She shoved her feet to the ground, but he stopped any further retreat with one mildly delivered comment. "Walking away again?"

"That's a cheap shot," she snapped over her shoulder.

"A fair observation, I'd say." With a seriously distracting play of muscles across his abdomen, he pushed upright. "Care to tell me what's really bugging you?"

Kimberley's gaze snapped back to his knowing blue eyes.

Oh, yes, he'd noticed her distraction. "Do you mean what's bugging me right now?"

"About me being here."

He didn't mean here, now, on the pool deck. She knew that. And she was glad, because admitting she was bugged by his state of undress would seem petty in the least. Revealing at the most. She didn't mind telling him what bothered her about his continual presence at Miramare, however.

"It's not just you, it's the endless waiting." She lifted her hands and let them drop in a gesture of undistilled frustration. "You and Ryan and Garth—at least you're kept busy with taking calls and keeping up with what's going on with the search. I didn't realise how hard this would be, just sitting around and waiting and feeling…excluded."

"We've kept you updated."

"Exactly. *You've* had control, *you've* done the updating, which shuts me out no matter how much information you pass on. I can answer a phone. I can speak for the Blackstones. I wouldn't find it any hardship to say 'no comment' or 'no further news.'"

"And if the person on the phone is Tracy Mattera or Max Carlton or Jamie O'Hare. Would you have no-commented them?"

"How can I say? I don't recognise the names."

"Mining production manager, human resources manager, Howard's driver," Ric supplied matter-of-factly. All three had called him that morning. He hadn't plucked the names out of thin air, although the doubt on Kim's face suggested he had done exactly that. "All real people, all employees of Blackstone's."

"Which I am not," she said tightly. "I get the message."

Ric watched her turn away and get to her feet, her shoulders as tight as her voice, her backbone rigid. He could let her walk away again. This wasn't the time or place for this discussion, but she had provided the perfect opening. She wanted a purpose. She needed something to occupy her mind.

Perhaps this was the right time....

"It doesn't have to be that way, Kim."

She swung back around, her hands stilled in the process of tying a lime-green sarong around her hips. "Are you suggesting I return to Blackstone's? When I have a job I love and a home in New Zealand? Why would I even consider doing that?"

"Because you're a Blackstone."

"That hasn't changed."

"Other things have," he said with quiet resolve, coming to his feet and meeting her gaze across the width of the loungers. "The board of directors is seven strong. Currently that's Ryan, Garth, your uncle Vincent, David Lord, Allen Fitzpatrick."

"You—" she tapped finger against thumb, counting off number six "—and my father."

Ric inclined his head in confirmation. "Chairman, managing director...and, with Ryan and Vincent, one of three Blackstones required on any sitting board, according to the articles of constitution."

"And you're thinking about a replacement?" With her quick brain, she'd caught on immediately. But the dark flash of her eyes and the tone of her voice indicated that she didn't like the taste of that catch one little bit. "Isn't that a little premature?"

"The board is due to meet Thursday this week. I imagine we will have news by then, and the directors will look at appointing a replacement. That may sound callously quick, but as directors we have a duty to our shareholders and our staff—

at the moment that duty is projecting stability in the face of press that's suggesting otherwise."

"The power struggle between you and Ryan?"

Obviously she'd read today's business pages. Ric's jaw tightened. "Don't believe everything you read in the papers, Kim. The board will decide Howard's successor as head of the company, when and if it has to. There won't be any fight."

She had a comeback—something acerbic, by the flare of her eyes—but the melodic chime of a ringing phone distracted her. With a quick, "Excuse me, I'm waiting on a call," she ducked down to retrieve the flip phone from beside her lounger. The distraction in her eyes turned to something like relief when she read the caller ID.

"I have to take this," she said shortly, already turning away.

Hammond, Ric surmised, cursing the timing. *The last person he wanted in on this decision.*

Phone at her ear, she'd already started to walk away, but in several long strides Ric caught up and put a hand on her shoulder.

Kimberley whirled around as if she'd been scalded. "One minute," she said into the phone. Then to Ric, "Excuse me?"

He didn't allow her rapid turnaround to dislodge his hand. Instead he fastened his hold on her smooth, warm skin until her eyes widened slightly and he knew he had her full attention. Then he said, "When the board meets, your name will come up. Think about it. This is your chance to be on the inside, to shape something positive from this disaster."

Her deep green eyes snapped. "How?"

"As part of the force that determines how Blackstone's goes forward into the future."

* * *

Kimberley had so many questions, so many rejoinders, but Perrini silenced them all with the latent power of that last statement. She watched him stride back toward the house, her heart beating too fast and too hard as the implications raced through her brain.

She could make a difference. She could solder broken links. She could make up for her father's mistakes.

Then his long, decisive strides carried him inside and out of her sight, and she felt as though she'd walked into the shadows. Reflexively she rolled her shoulder, which still bore the imprint of his touch, and remembered the phone call. Matt. Damn. For the past three days they'd been playing phone tag, and now, finally, they'd managed to connect and she had left him on hold.

Just because Perrini had unsettled her again, first with the heat and the texture of his hand on her bare skin, then with the juicy enticement of righting the Blackstone wrongs toward her uncle and her cousin.

"Matt?" She swung around, phone to her ear. "Are you still there?"

"I'm here."

She released a soft gust of relief. "Thank you for holding. I was just in the middle of something."

"I can call back."

"No, no. It's okay. He's gone. I'm done. I'm just so glad I've finally found you with feet on the ground…your feet are on the ground?"

"I'm in Sydney," he said in short, succinct contrast to Kimberley's delivery. She was pacing, too, unable to stand still. "Landed this morning."

"Where are you staying? The Carlisle Grande? Why don't I come in. We could have coffee or even dinner, if you're free. Is Blake with you?"

"This isn't a trip I'd bring my son on."

His cold, clipped tone brought Kimberley's pacing to a brickwall halt. She palmed her forehead in her hand. How stupid and thoughtless. He'd come to identify Marise's body, lying cold and lifeless in a city mortuary. How could she have asked about bringing Blake?

"I'm so sorry, Matt." She didn't know what else to say, so she said it again. "So very sorry for your loss. Especially this way."

"Is there an easy way to lose your wife?"

"Good God, no, of course not! I meant the headlines and the tabloid frenzy. I can only imagine that's as bad for you as for us."

"No," he said after a heavy beat of pause. "I don't think you can imagine."

He was right, and she felt too choked up with emotion— and with the foot she couldn't seem to keep out of her mouth—to answer for several taut seconds. In person this would be easier, the same as it had been with coming home and seeing Sonya and Ryan. "Can we meet for coffee?" she asked again.

"I won't be here any longer than it takes to arrange a funeral."

The shock of that last word turned to ice in Kimberley's veins. She rubbed her free hand up and down her arm. How could her skin be so warm when she felt cold to the core? "When you've made the arrangements," she said stiffly, "please let me know when and where. I would like to be there."

"It will be a private burial. No cameras. No headlines. No Blackstones."

Kimberley understood his point. She knew pain had honed his voice to that diamond-hard edge but she still felt the rejection like a slap. It brought her head up and put a sting into her response. "I'm sorry I won't be there, for you, for Blake, for Marise. But with Howard gone, surely it's time to put this Hammond-Blackstone animosity to rest so we don't have to choose sides. I hate that—I'm sure Sonya does, as well. I've been approached about a possible position on the board of Blackstone Diamonds, and perhaps that is a good place to start mending the broken links."

"A conflict of interest with your position at Hammonds, wouldn't you think?"

"No, I don't think that has to be the case. The business rivalry has only come about through the old feud and personal bitterness, some of which was between Howard and me. With that over now—"

"No." Matt's objection was low, but delivered with such chilling finality that it sliced right through Kimberley's argument. "It's not over. After what Blackstone has done to my family, it can never be over. Not until everything the bastard took from us is restored to Hammond hands. Since one of those things is the wife I'm burying next week, I don't give that outcome a chance in hell of succeeding. Do you?"

Five

"That's all for now. Thank you, Holly."

Ric closed his office door behind the PR assistant who'd delivered the press clippings from Tuesday morning's papers. It didn't matter that there'd been no new developments in the search for the jet's wreckage or that no further bodies had been found, the headlines kept on coming. This week the focus had shifted from the present to the tragedies in Howard Blackstone's past, everything from the kidnapping of two-year-old James Hammond Blackstone thirty-one years ago to Ursula Blackstone's suicide and the disappearance of the Blackstone Rose necklace.

"This isn't news," Ryan said as he tossed a national broadsheet onto Ric's desk with barely concealed fury. "I expected better from them."

Ric didn't expect anything from the media except more

sensational headlines. They'd stalked Howard Blackstone throughout his life and now they haunted him in death, with the biggest scandal—the possibility of an illicit affair with Marise—still hovering over them like a fat black thundercloud. So far they'd reported nothing beyond her positive identification, running poignant photos of Matt Hammond's grief-ravaged face as he arrived in Sydney to claim her body, but following tomorrow's supposedly private burial the storm of speculation would build. As sure as thunder followed lightning.

They had to do more than wait it out. Ric owed that to Howard, to his staff, to the shareholders.

He didn't return to his desk but chose a central position where he could face the other two men, the seated Garth and the prowling Ryan, to explain why he'd called them to his office at the company's Sydney headquarters after days of monitoring the search from the Blackstone home. "We've waited as long as we can but in the absence of new developments, it's time to move on. We—"

"Move on?" The words exploded from Ryan's mouth. "No. We're not giving up yet, Perrini. Who are you to say we abandon my father?"

Ric met the sharp spear of the younger man's gaze without flinching. He'd been prepared for the hostility. Ryan wouldn't like him taking the initiative in calling this meeting any more than he'd like what Ric had to say. "I'm not suggesting we give up anything. Not the search and not this company your father built up from nothing but an exploration lease and his belief that diamonds were there to be found. Howard wouldn't appreciate us sitting on our hands, waiting for an outcome of a search that could go on for weeks."

Garth made a sound of agreement. He folded the paper he'd been scanning and placed it neatly on top of the others. "I can hear him now, growling in horror at the share devaluation."

"The price is still sliding today?" Ric asked.

"Down another five since opening. At this rate every second analyst will be tipping us as a prime takeover target by the end of the next week."

"It's not the raiders I'm concerned about."

Ryan turned in front of the window, hands on hips, framed by the city skyscape at his back. "Who are you concerned about?"

"Matt Hammond."

"Still holding him accountable?"

Ric's jaw tightened although the blow had been aimed much lower. He didn't give Ryan the satisfaction of responding. Instead he zeroed in on the reason he'd called them together. The threat of a takeover, not by an anonymous corporate raider or venture capital consortium, but at the hands of a man motivated by vengeance. "Howard holds fifty-one percent of the Blackstone Diamonds stock." He turned toward Garth, the company secretary, who was also the executor of Howard's will. "Can you confirm how that will be distributed?"

"Equally between you, Ryan and Kimberley."

"No chance he wrote Kim out of the will as he threatened?" Ric asked.

Garth shook his head. "He was set on that course when he returned from his November trip to New Zealand, but maybe he thought twice after he cooled down. Maybe I managed to talk him out of it. God knows, I talked long and hard enough. And maybe he took his lawyer along on this trip with a new threat of disinheritance. Whatever the reason, his will remains unchanged. That three-way split of his company stock still holds." The older man's eyes narrowed astutely. "I take it you're concerned about Hammond pursuing Kim's share, the way he went after William's ten percent?"

Two months ago Howard's older twin brothers, William and Vincent, each had owned a stake in Blackstone Diamonds. Then Hammond took advantage of rumours of a falling-out between the brothers. Needing cash in a hurry William had seized the chance to unload his stock at a premium price, and he'd been dirty enough on Howard to relish selling to his adversary.

"He wouldn't have to be that aggressive in chasing Kim's stock," Ric said. "She wouldn't be looking for instant profit. He would only need to spin a good story, convince her she was doing the right thing, and with those two bundles and whatever else he can pick up on this depressed market, it's conceivable he could acquire a majority share."

"We know he's not a player. He's only doing this for one reason." Ryan's expression was as hard and dark as black diamond. "The son of a bitch would gut the company."

Garth grunted in agreement. "We need Kim on our side. Any chance she would reconsider returning to Blackstone's?"

"I'm working on that," Ric said. His gaze shifted to Ryan. "As long as there are no objections."

"She's a Blackstone. She should never have left." There was a world of condemnation in the words and in the other man's expression as he faced Ric down. "Makes me wonder what you intend offering to bring her back from Hammonds."

"A fair question."

"Do you have an answer?"

"I'll offer whatever it takes," Ric said with steely resolve. "Leave it in my hands. I will bring her back."

"You're not wearing the new dress?"

Kimberley hesitated on the staircase, her gaze dropping from Sonya's arched eyebrows to the plain oatmeal linen sheath she'd changed into at the last minute. Okay, so she'd changed several times. Possibly half a dozen. And during that process the dress Sonya talked her into buying had been relegated to the very back of the queue. Not that she didn't like the soft, inviting fabric or the leopard-spot print—even the sexy touch of lace was growing on her— but it was just too unbusinesslike for a dinner that was all about business.

"This is more suitable," she said, lifting her head and continuing resolutely down to the foyer.

Sonya had paused, a stem of roses in each hand, in the middle of arranging a massive vase of freshly cut blooms from the Miramare gardens. She raised her elegantly shaped brows even higher. "I thought the purpose of today's shopping expedition was to choose a dress for tonight."

"That was our *excuse* to go shopping," Kimberley said with a wink. Then, over her shoulder, as she proceeded through to the living room, she said, "I would never have got you to agree to come along otherwise."

And they'd both needed to get out of the house. Kimberley hadn't thought she would miss the presence of Perrini and Ryan and Garth, after they'd taken their mobile phones and their constant grim-faced pacing and returned to the city megalith that housed the headquarters of Blackstone Diamonds.

Danielle had left, too, to apply the final touches to her collection for the annual Blackstone Jewellery show. Each year the event launched the latest in-house collections, as well as showcasing an emerging young designer. This year was Dani Hammond's big break.

This is what you've worked so hard for, Sonya had said, encouraging her reluctant daughter to return to her Port Douglas studio. *I have Kim here now, so I won't be alone. You still have work to do, so go, be inspired, be brilliant. Make me proud, make Howard proud...and make those critics who pooh-poohed his choice eat their words!*

Without them all, the house echoed its vast emptiness. Kimberley had felt the impact most acutely when she'd woken that morning. Wednesday. Marise's funeral day. Beautiful, headstrong, self-assured Marise was dead and for the first time Kimberley forced herself to face the reality that her father, too, was gone. This house, which had always been a reflection of the man and his taste for the grand, the opulent and the glamorous, would forever feel empty without him and the ever-present party of business and society acquaintances he brought home.

Sonya felt the emptiness, too. Kimberley had taken one look at her aunt's haunted eyes and restless hands as she fussed around preparing a breakfast neither of them would eat, and she'd decided they both needed a distraction.

Perrini provided it with a phone call and what had sounded like an off-the-cuff invitation.

"Dinner?" she'd asked. Her heart kicked up a beat and her free hand curled around her pendant charms. "I don't think that—"

"You need to eat? To get away from that house for a few hours? To discuss details of my proposal about the Blackstone's board vacancy...."

Oh, yes, he'd been clever. He'd known over the weekend that the waiting and inactivity were making her stir-crazy, and he'd picked the perfect time to lure her with the board position and the prospect of changing old animosities from the inside. Then he'd left her a day too long to think it over. Now she was hungry for more information, to find out exactly what was going on at Blackstone Diamonds…and why she'd been targeted for the Blackstone-only board position.

That's the only reason she'd accepted his invitation. That's why she'd gone with the plain business-meeting dress, despite playing along with Sonya's fancy to choose something fun, flirty, and way different from her usual classic style. The shopping trip to her favourite Double Bay boutique had been a game, a ploy, a distraction to take both their minds off the funeral in progress just a couple of suburbs away.

It had nothing to do with tonight's "date."

Now, as she wandered the living room unable to sit or stand or settle, Kimberley wished she'd insisted on meeting Perrini at the restaurant instead of letting him railroad her into the "more convenient" pickup. Being all dressed up and waiting for a man to arrive on her doorstep only played into the nerve-jangling notion of a real date.

She should have asked him to call when he left the office. Then she could have timed this better. Perhaps she still had time to go upstairs and change her earrings. Or to pin her ponytail into a chignon. At least that would fill some—

The chime of the doorbell echoed through the cavernous interior and startled Kimberley's jumpy heart. He was here. About bloody time.

"I'll get it," Sonya called.

Seconds later Kimberley heard the murmur of voices followed by the deep rumble of Perrini's laughter. She'd already taken several strides toward the foyer but the punch of that sound brought her up short. Laughter, so unexpected, so familiar to her female heart.

A hot charge of anticipation rocketed through her veins, tightening low in her stomach and tingling through her skin. She so wasn't ready for this. She needed a minute or two to compose herself, to restore her cool poise…time she didn't have as footsteps and the melodious notes of Sonya's voice heralded their approach.

At the last second, she scurried for the nearest chair and picked up a glossy from the side table. When Sonya said, "Kim, Ric's here," she managed to lower the magazine with surprisingly steady hands. Her smile was cordial, calm, controlled. Then she looked up into the deep sapphire of his eyes and her heart lurched like a poleaxed drunk.

"You're here," she said nonsensically.

Not the opening line she'd rehearsed—that was supposed to be a cool *you're late,* as she swept past him and strode out to the car—but better than thanking him for being here and bringing laughter into the emptiness.

"Ready to go?" he asked.

She put down the magazine. "For the past twenty minutes."

One of his brows rose marginally. "Nice to know you've acquired punctuality."

The subtle jibe at the past, referencing one of the flaws she'd fixed in the new grown-up version of Kimberley Blackstone, cooled the remaining impact of his arrival from her blood. Ignoring his proffered hand she rose to her feet and, after kissing Sonya on the cheek, swept past Perrini and out to his car. Marcie, the housekeeper, opened the front door and allowed her to proceed unimpeded. If only they had valet parking she could have swept all the way to his car and into the passenger seat.

Instead she was left beside the locked Maserati cooling her three-inch heels. She'd chosen them to help level out the height difference and therefore the power dynamic, although she still needed an extra couple of inches to bring her eye-to-eye with Perrini's six-one.

Why in heaven's name had he felt the need to lock his precious car?

Arms folded, she tapped her toe and frowned back toward the still-open front door. Several minutes later he appeared, and paused to speak to Marcie. Okay, she was honest enough to admit that he looked bloody good. Even though he'd likely come straight from the office after a twelve-hour day, his charcoal suit was immaculate, his white shirt crisp, his sapphire tie perfectly knotted.

But it wasn't only the expensive hand-tailoring, it was the way he wore the clothes. Whether he was striding into a meeting wearing one of his suits or sauntering by the pool in nothing but a brief pair of swimmers, he had a unique combination of cool authority and kick-ass confidence that drew attention to the man rather than the external trappings.

The effects of that long, open inspection were still rippling through Kimberley's body when he bent and kissed a blushing Marcie on the cheek, and peeled away to jog down the steps. The remnants of a smile softened his mouth and she had to work hard to maintain her irritation.

"Don't you trust our staff?" she asked, inclining her head toward the locked car.

"Force of habit." The doors popped with a scarcely audible snick. He opened her door, then waited until she'd slid inside before he leaned down to meet her eyes. His were no longer smiling. "For what it's worth, I wasn't expecting to see any staff."

Kimberley recognised the pointed dig. "I couldn't see the sense in keeping loyal, long-serving staff laid off for fear they may leak private information, when it is obvious the press is getting whatever details they want from their own sources."

"Are you referring to Marise's supposedly private funeral?"

"That's one instance." It had been mentioned in more than one of today's newspapers, which made her mad enough to spit. "They seem remarkably well-informed about everything."

"It's their job to be." Perrini's expression tightened with his own irritation. "Seat belt."

"I'm not a child. I know—"

She sucked in a breath as he short-circuited her indignant protest by leaning across to retrieve the belt. In the process his arm brushed the side of her breast and she felt the fleeting contact reverberate low in her belly and pull tight in her nipples.

Damn.

He stilled a moment—or perhaps that was just her, her heart, her senses—before clicking the belt into place. Then the dark heat of his eyes locked on hers and he spoke in a low and rough-edged voice. "I know you're not a child, Kim, despite indications to the contrary."

Indications to the contrary? What the hell did he mean by that?

The door thudded shut, leaving her quivering with suppressed wrath for the six seconds he took to round the car and slip into the driver's seat. Kimberley counted to six again, while he started the engine and she controlled her urge to shriek those questions.

"Indications to the contrary?" She managed to sound cool and composed. And adult.

"This decision to reappoint the household staff without consulting me—did you have a reason other than to thumb your nose at me?"

"Without consulting you? I'm sorry, but I didn't realise you were now the head of my household."

As he powered through the security gates and into the street, he cut her a narrow look. "I didn't realise you consi-dered yourself a part of this household."

Touché.

Kimberley inhaled long and deep. Provoked by his remark about her childishness, that head-of-my-household comment had just slipped out. "You're right," she admitted in a more reasonable tone. "I'm only a visitor, but I did consult with Sonya before calling any staff back on duty. I didn't think she needed the extra work."

"Perhaps she does."

That perceptive comment deflated the last of Kimberley's resentment. How could she remain piqued when they were on the same wavelength regarding Sonya? "Yes, she does…to an extent, which is why I asked the cook to take an extra week of holiday leave. Sonya enjoys the kitchen and that's enough for the moment. Plus with Marcie in the house she has both help and company."

Another sidelong glance. "You aren't enough help?"

"In the kitchen?" Kimberley laughed dryly and shook her head. "You know what happens when I'm allowed access to a cooktop!"

For a heartbeat their gazes caught and a decade-old memory arced between them. Burning bacon, a shrieking smoke alarm and Kimberley hopping from one foot to the other, yelling for help.

Her husband of six days had picked her up fireman style and bundled her back to the bedroom. *In here,* he'd said, *you can burn and scream all you want.*

"Things change in ten years," he said now.

"Some things. Others stay the same."

Stationary at a traffic light, Ric leaned his forearm on the wheel and turned to study her profile more closely. She'd tied her hair back, worn minimal makeup and jewellery and one of those blend-into-the-background dresses whose only plus was the fact it ended short of her knees. Rather than diminishing her beauty, the austere look drew all attention to her face. With that amazing, contrary combination of fire and ice, of strength and vulnerability, of have-me mouth and hands-off eyes, Kim Blackstone would never blend into any background.

"What hasn't changed?" he asked softly.

For a moment he thought she would ignore his question, but then she rolled her head against the seat and the answer was there in her eyes, in that moment, in the crackle of sexual awareness.

This hasn't changed.

From the moment she'd strutted into his life, fresh from a two-year apprenticeship with a diamond master in Antwerp and bursting with a passionate impatience to overhaul the marketing of Janderra's rare coloured diamonds, she'd lit his senses with white-hot desire. For seven and a half weeks she'd kept him at bay with her sharp tongue and cutting lines. *That* hadn't changed, either. The same distrust, the same defence mechanisms, the same defiance that put her in the beige background dress instead of the stunner Sonya had described her buying today.

The light changed to green and Ric urged the Maserati forward. The engine's smooth growl reverberated low in his belly. If Kim didn't feel threatened by this undiminished sexual spark between them, then she wouldn't feel a need to employ those obvious defences. She was working to keep *him* at arm's length, he realised with a delayed jolt of perception. She tried to keep her own desires in check.

First time around he'd allowed her time and space while he enjoyed the challenge, the pursuit, the anticipation. This time the stakes were higher. He wasn't playing games; he was playing for keeps.

From the corner of his eye he caught the almost imperceptible lift of her chin. Defence mechanism number one. A precursor to speech, used when preparing for verbal battle.

Deep inside Ric smiled in anticipation. *Bring it on, babe. I'm ready.*

"I may not have learned how to cook," she said, circling back to her earlier comment about kitchen helpfulness. "But I have changed in other ways."

"How?"

"I'm more cautious now. I don't make snap decisions. I weigh my options so I can make an informed choice."

With the position on the Blackstone's board, for example. That's where she wanted to lead the conversation; that's why she'd taken her time in choosing her words so cleverly. A pity and a waste, since he wasn't ready to go there. They were within five minutes of their destination and an inevitable disruption.

Their long, involved and probably heated discussion was

for later, without interruption, so he let her leading comment take this conversation in another direction. "Such as deciding to wear that dress—" his gaze swept over her before returning to the road "—instead of the new one?"

"I beg your pardon?"

"The new dress you picked out in Double Bay this afternoon."

"Sonya," she said on an accusatory note. "I can't believe she told you about that!"

"Not nearly enough, as it happens. Why don't you fill in the gaps."

"You want to hear about our shopping expedition?"

The incredulous look on her face was priceless. Ric stifled a grin. "I want to hear about the dress and why you decided not to wear it." He let his eyes drift over her in lazy speculation. "Was it too short? Too low-cut? Too revealing?"

"All of those things," she replied without missing a beat.

"Then I can't wait to see you in it," he murmured.

"I doubt that will happen."

"Spoilsport."

The start of a smile lurked around the corners of her mouth but she looked away quickly, peering out the side window in sudden rapt interest. He noticed the exact second her pseudo-interest turned real. Her shoulders stiffened, her head snapped around. "Where are you taking me?"

"My place. Is that a problem?"

"You said dinner. I assumed you meant at a restaurant."

"I could get a table at Icebergs if you'd prefer," he said mildly. "Although I can't promise we'll have privacy to talk or that our tête-à-tête won't appear in a society column tomorrow."

Indecision ghosted across her expression.

"Which wouldn't be all bad," he mused. "It'd give them

something to talk about other than Howard and Marise."
Flicking on an indicator, he pulled over to the side of the road
and reached for his mobile phone. "I can call ahead and secure
a table if you don't mind being noticed dining with me. Or
we can eat at my place, as planned, with the privacy to talk
business and no risk of interruption.

"Your decision, Kim. What's it to be?"

Six

Perrini was too damn clever by half! Kimberley quietly simmered while she chose privacy, just as he'd set her up to do. They had business to discuss and if he tried baiting her again as he'd done over the dress and just now over the restaurant, then she might feel inclined to throw something at him. She would prefer if *that* didn't appear in any society columns, thank you very much.

Which didn't mean she felt comfortable returning to the house where they'd spent so many nights and weekends of their affair, plus their short, drama-filled ten days of marriage. During the days they'd worked side by side with cool, professional restraint, and in the evenings they'd driven into this street, this driveway, this garage, and torn into each other with a fevered passion that could not wait a second longer.

"You're not nervous about coming here?"

Kimberley blinked herself out of the minefield of memories. Carefully she relaxed her fisted fingers and moistened her lips. "Should I be?"

"I don't see why."

But there was a dangerous glint of heat in his eyes as they rested briefly on her mouth, and she wondered if he, too, was recalling the times they hadn't made it upstairs with all their clothes on. When they'd slaked their hunger for each other here in his car, or in the foyer leading off the garage, or in the slick elevator that glided between the three floors of this uniquely designed contemporary town house.

"Do you live here alone?" she asked.

The question had been brewing, unacknowledged and unspoken, ever since the day by the pool when he'd told her he still lived here. Now seemed the time to ask. Before he took her inside.

"At the moment," he said after a beat of pause, "yes."

Now, what was that supposed to mean? Had there been a live-in lover, one who'd recently packed her bags and departed? Or did he have someone waiting in the wings, all primed and ready to park her stilettos under his bed?

The thought crept up like a thief and ambushed her with unbidden images. Perrini with a faceless, nameless woman. Her hands sliding inside his shirt. Her mouth opening to his kiss. Her arms pulling him down to the bed.

No. Kimberley shut down the visuals with a vicious shake of her head. And while he opened the passenger door and ushered her from the car to the foyer and into the elevator, she struggled to tamp down the impact of her irrational possessiveness. She had no right to it. She had no claim on him.

Business, she reminded herself. *It's not about us.*

But in the confines of the closet-size lift, she became hyper-aware of the whipcord tension in his body and the heat emanating from his skin despite the layers of fine Italian tailoring separating their shoulders, their arms, their hips. Those ten-year-old memories of greedy mouths and impatient hands and swiftly shed clothes worked back into her consciousness, blurring the imagery until the nameless woman's face became hers.

Her hands, *her* mouth, *her* arms drawing him onto the bed and into her body.

"Hungry?"

The velvet murmur of his voice spent a moment meandering through her fantasy before Kimberley snapped her errant mind back into focus. "Yes, I am." Cool. Somehow she managed to sound very cool. "What are we eating?"

"Seafood. For expedience I ordered ahead. I hope you don't mind."

"That would depend on what you ordered."

"Blue swimmer crab. Roasted scallops. Ocean trout. Catch of the day with aioli and Murray River salt."

Although her taste buds had started to shimmy in anticipation, Kimberley merely nodded. The real test was in the final course. "And for dessert?"

"Ah, so you still start your order from the bottom of the menu? That hasn't changed?"

She tilted her head, enough that she could favour him with a silly-question look.

Amusement kicked up the corner of his mouth. "Zabaglione and Roberto's signature gelato."

"Which is?"

"Good. Very good."

Her taste buds broke into a dance just as the elevator doors slid open at the top level. And she realised with a jolt of shock how little notice she'd taken of her surroundings downstairs. Here the changes hit her full in the face.

Ten years ago the house had been newly built and decorated in stark white to play up the clean lines and irregular angles. But with the open plan and abundant windows, light had bounced off every wall with blinding impact. Many times she'd teased him about the need to don sunglasses before entering his house.

Not anymore.

Evening sunlight still beamed through the glass doors that opened onto a large curved balcony, but the effect had been softened with earthy tones of cream and pale salmon and rich moss green. Kimberley paused in the centre of the living room to take in all the changes. In the dining room one feature wall was painted with a mottled sponging of peachy cream. The artwork, the plants, the polished timber floors and terracotta sofas packed with plumped cushions, even the gilded shades on the unusual light fittings, all complemented the warm palette.

She finished her slow 360-degree inspection to find Perrini watching her from behind the kitchen bar. A bottle of wine and two glasses sat before him on the waist-high counter.

"What do you think?" he asked. "Did I get it right?"

There was something in his stillness, in the deliberate casualness of his question, that caused her heart to thump hard against her ribs.

He'd listened. The night she lay on one of the matched pair of snow-white couches with her head in his lap and described how *she* would decorate this area. He'd remembered.

She completed another turn as if she was still making up her mind, and then she lifted her arms and let them fall with the same fake casualness. "It works for me. Do you like it?"

"Overall, yes." The hawklike intensity of his expression softened as he switched his attention to opening the wine. "I could have done without the peachy colours but Madeleine insisted."

Kimberley's heart stopped for a beat. Of course he hadn't done it himself. How stupid to imagine him matching colours and cushions with her long-ago Sunday musings.

She wandered over to inspect a large abstract canvas, then on to the glass doors where she stared blindly out at the view. "Madeleine?" she asked.

"The decorator. She had her own interpretations on the brief I gave her."

Not the live-in lover stewing in her imagination, but a professional. It was nothing personal, nothing to do with Kimberley at all, which was a very good thing. It was bad enough that she still felt an intense sexual pull every time he got too near, she didn't need the emotional resonance of discovering he'd decorated to her specifications, to please her, to welcome her home. It was much better to acknowledge that he'd taken her overall idea and used it to inspire the overhaul. She couldn't be disappointed. She would not allow herself that weakness.

When Perrini arrived at her side and handed her a glass of white wine, she thanked him with a smile. "Even if you painted the walls lime-green, it wouldn't matter. This—" she raised her glass to indicate the view "—would always be the focus."

He opened the doors and Kimberley wandered out to stand at the wrought-iron railing. Low down to her left Sydney's most famous beach was littered with people despite the late hour. Some swam, some strolled, others sat on the golden slice of sand and scanned the horizon, as Kimberley did now, for a sailboat or a cruiser or a cargo ship chugging out to sea.

It wasn't quiet, thanks to the traffic on Campbell Parade and the summer tourists cruising the beach promenade—but Kimberley welcomed the sounds and sensations that regaled her body, even the sensual buzz when Perrini came to stand close by her side. The past week sequestered at Miramare and focussed so completely on the plane crash and its deadly consequences had numbed her to the wider world. She'd needed to get out, somewhere like this, a place that breathed life into her senses.

"I love this aspect," she said with soft reverence. "Not to mention the view."

"Is that why you bought your town house in One Tree Hill?" he asked after a moment.

Unable to make the connection, Kimberley shook her head. "What do you mean?"

"Its similarity to this place. The high aspect, the view, the architecture."

"I don't think they're even close to alike. My total floor space would fit on one of your levels with room to spare. And as for the view—" she expelled a breath that was part wry laughter, part disbelief "—how can you compare? You have a version of this postcard panorama from every window. I have to stand on tiptoes in my highest heels to get the tiniest glimpse of Manukau Harbour, and that's only from my deck."

Perrini didn't respond although she felt the long, warm drift of his gaze all the way down her body until it reached her leopard-print heels. And for that length of time she wished she had worn the new dress with its matching print and silk-cloud fabric. She wished the evening could continue in this easy harmony, that she could kick off these heels and indulge her sensual self with the wine and the food and the company and yes, even the dangerous tug to desire.

She wished she could forget her past hurts and everything that had happened this week and just live in the moment.

"I don't come out here enough." Perrini's voice, low and reflective, interrupted her reverie. "The view is a waste when I don't take time to enjoy it."

"Do you still work those punishing hours then?"

"When I have to."

"No one ever *has to,*" she countered with subtle emphasis. "They choose that course, for whatever motivation drives them. Ambition, money, ego, security, insecurity."

With Perrini she wasn't certain which applied. For all his charm and extravagant good looks, he possessed an inner toughness and a determination to succeed. She knew he'd been raised by a single mother, that he'd worked his way through school and a business degree, but he'd never really opened up about his childhood. That was just one more regret she'd taken away from their relationship. He'd only ever shared what he'd chosen to, withholding so much of the important stuff.

"Which is it with you, Kim? What motivates you?"

"The work," she said simply.

"Still?"

"Yes, still."

He studied her a moment, his blue gaze shadowed in the gathering dusk. "What about that ambition you used to talk about, that craving for a top-floor office at Blackstone Diamonds? You used to see yourself as your father's successor. What happened to that dream?"

"A dream is all that was ever going to be, Perrini. You know that."

"No," he contradicted, "I don't know that and neither do you. Everything is about to change at Blackstone's. If you haven't revisited that dream lately, then it's about time you did."

Kimberley's heart was beating hard. She hadn't revisited those old dreams, old ambitions, the stuff of her childhood, in more than a decade. Since her return she hadn't looked beyond the directorship proposition and the chance to end the old feud that had rent the two branches of her family apart.

Did she want to be part of the family company?

Did she harbour that leadership ambition anymore?

The chime of the doorbell broke the intense moment. Perrini straightened, lifting his head. "That will be dinner. Roberto's food is too good to keep waiting. Let's continue this discussion after we eat."

Ric kicked himself savagely for bringing up business prematurely and destroying the relaxed ambience established on the balcony. Dinner provided a temporary distraction. While they enjoyed the simply prepared but stunningly flavoured food, they talked about Roberto's restaurant, her recent holiday, the frustrating lack of progress with the search, Danielle's departure—everything but the unfinished business that hovered between them.

Now he watched her put down her spoon and push away the glass dessert bowl. "That's the best you can do?" he asked, eyebrows raised at her unfinished gelato.

"As hard as it is to believe, yes. Everything was divine but those scallops were my undoing."

"Would you like coffee?"

She shook her head.

"A liqueur? I have cognac or tokay—"

"Nothing, thank you. Let's just get on with why I'm here."

Ric inclined his head at her blunt request. It was time to get down to business, but not here at the dinner table. "Let's go through to the lounge. You can put your feet up and relax while we talk."

"Oh, I very much doubt that," she said softly, bringing a smile to his lips. But she set her serviette aside and pushed back her chair. "Still, let's do this away from the crockery. Just in case the discussion gets heated."

With that in mind, Ric suggested she sit at the far end of the sofa. "That lamp is damn ugly but it cost a fortune. Best keep it out of your reach."

Amusement softened the curve of her mouth as she took the proffered seat. "Wise decision. The base looks solid enough to make quite a dint."

"This doesn't have to be a confrontation," Ric said evenly.

"No, although our history suggests there is that possibility. Especially when the subject of Blackstone Diamonds enters the discussion."

Ric couldn't argue with that claim; he couldn't even say it was all bad. When they'd worked together on the business plan for Blackstone Jewellery, their heated debates had been more than intellectual foreplay, they'd sparked new angles and creative solutions. They'd complemented each other in the office, as well as the bedroom, and that's what he wanted again. That heat, that spark, that connection.

That's what he wanted and that's what he would have, but that didn't stop him wanting to prolong their current harmony.

He didn't want to wipe that glint of humour from her expressive eyes. But he did, as soon as he settled opposite her on the second of the suede sofas. The smile faded from her face even before he spoke. "Let me at least get my proposal on the table before you arm yourself," he suggested.

"Would that proposal be the board position or the dream job you dangled in front of me earlier?"

"Let's start with the directorship."

She nodded briefly. "I have given that some thought."

"And?"

"Matt suggests it would be a conflict of interest with my present position at House of Hammond."

No surprise that she'd discussed his preliminary approach with her boss. Ric had expected as much, but that didn't stop his jaw tightening in annoyance. "Your boss is right," he said shortly. "You couldn't continue to work for him if you took on this directorship."

"Why would I choose a board position over the job I have—a good job that I love?"

"Because that's all Hammond will ever offer you. A job. Second in charge," he stressed, when he saw an objection fire green sparks in her eyes. "But where is the future beyond that? Matt Hammond will never cede power to anyone but another Hammond."

"Not everyone craves power, Perrini."

He met the condemnation in her eyes head-on. "You used to. You came back from Europe, your head crammed with ideas and your heart fired with passion. You couldn't wait to make changes, to put it all into practice, and you couldn't do that from the sidelines. I recall you saying as much the day you stormed out of your father's office."

"I left Blackstone's for many reasons," she said tightly. "That was only one of them."

"You made those reasons crystal clear when you left, but things have changed. You have a personal stake in the company now."

Her forehead creased with a frown. "What do you mean?"

"When your father's will is read, you'll become one of three major stakeholders in Blackstone Diamonds."

"No." She shook her head adamantly. "Howard wrote me out of his will. He said—"

"Whatever your father intended when you had that row, a new will was never filed. I checked with Garth, who is executor of his estate. You *will* inherit a third share of Howard's stake in the company, and that is significant equity. With it comes the power to implement change. From the forty-third floor you can see dreams through to reality. You can heal rifts. You can right wrongs."

Ric watched the storm of possibilities flare in her eyes for several long, weighty seconds.

"That's powerful rhetoric," she said.

"It's not just rhetoric," he responded without hesitation. "This next few months will be a tough time for the company. The share price is already taking a beating on the back of this week's negative publicity. We can't sit tight and ride this out. We need to play the game smarter. We want you working with us to generate positive press, Kim. We want you back at Blackstone's."

"We?"

"Senior management. Ryan, Garth, myself."

"'Generating positive publicity' sounds more like a PR

specialist's dream job than mine," she countered after a moment's consideration. "Why don't you hire a consultant?"

"We don't want a slick consultant. We want you and your sharp brain and your industry knowledge and credentials." He leaned forward, hands linked loosely between his knees, but there was nothing casual about the insistent strength of his gaze. "We want to present a united front, Kim, to show we're not dwelling on the past but moving forward with the next generation. And we want your name quoted in the papers, your face in front of the cameras."

Her brows arched with a hint of derision. "I thought you were using Marise's supermodel sister as the 'Face of Blackstone's'."

"Briana Davenport is the 'face.' We're proposing you as the 'mouth', a role for which you're eminently qualified."

Unexpected amusement sparkled at the back of her eyes. "Aren't you concerned that my mouth will create more trouble?"

"Only for me," he acknowledged dryly, "and I'm big enough to take it."

It was an innocent remark, designed to show he appreciated that her mouthiest moments had always been reserved for him. But when she didn't fire back an instant retort, and when the glow in her eyes warmed with a different fire, the harmless jest grew teeth that gnawed through the thickened silence. There were all manner of things he ached to tell her about her mouth, how he'd missed the bite in these exchanges, how he lived for the moment it opened beneath his, how he dreamed of its sweet-spice taste.

This wasn't the moment. The only task that mattered right now was luring her back to Blackstone's, and he couldn't risk ruining his chances.

He shoved to his feet and strolled toward the open doors

to breathe the familiar, salty air, to clear the buzz of another seduction from his brain.

"If I took this position—" her gaze, direct and unwavering, met Ric's as he swung around "—who would I be working under?"

"That would depend on the project," he replied carefully, ignoring his libido's grunt of response to her wording.

"The projects being...?"

"The big one is the launch of the latest jewellery collections. I'm guessing Danielle would have told you about the gala show?"

"A little." She tried for cool, but failed to hide the sparkle of interest that lit her expression. "It's next month, right?"

"February twenty-ninth. Even without recent events, this year's show has special significance."

"The ten-year anniversary of Blackstone Jewellery," she guessed without hesitation. "So, the usual birthday celebrations, continuing promotions, ad campaigns?"

"All that."

"I'm guessing this would be well covered by the marketing department. What, exactly, would I be doing?"

Looking into her eyes, Ric felt an adrenaline punch of response. *This* is what he'd missed—her quick pickups, her sharp comebacks, the verbal duels that were never predictable but always stirred something vital inside him. "If I knew, then I wouldn't need you."

"I?" she countered. "Not the royal *we?*"

"Interchangeable." He figured she knew that anyway. It's why she'd asked who she'd be working under. "In this case, you'll be working with Ryan and his staff, supplementing the marketing plan to generate positive press for the Blackstone brand in general and the launch show in particular. As for how you do that—" he spread his hands expansively "—that's your job. To explore the possibilities."

"And answerable to Ryan?" she murmured after a moment's consideration. "He would be my boss?"

"On this project."

"And overall?"

"The new CEO, as appointed by the board."

"Meaning there's a fair chance it will be you."

"An even chance. Ryan is a Blackstone, a significant point in his favour. But if I am appointed—" Ric narrowed his gaze on hers as he closed the space between them "—is the prospect of working beneath me a deal breaker?"

She came to her feet and faced him with cool pride in her stance and etched in her expression. "I wouldn't return to work for my father, why on earth would I consider working for you?"

"Because we need you, Kim. Blackstone's, your brother, the company, each and every member of our workforce—we need you working with us. I sincerely hope you understand what I'm offering is on behalf of the management team, and that you won't let our past stand in the way of the Blackstone future."

Seven

Kimberley's heart drummed like a jackhammer against her rib cage. Poor, foolish, easily swayed thing wanted to believe in his sincerity even while her brain chirped a warning to beware his motives.

"I'm not a naive twenty-one-year-old now," she began, her voice surprisingly even given the rough cadence of her pulse. "I won't be taken in by your sweet rhetoric and I won't be used just because I'm Kimberley Blackstone."

"Used?" Perrini's eyes narrowed dangerously. "I've never used you, Kim. Not in any sense."

"You still don't see that pursuing and marrying your boss's daughter in order to secure a plum promotion—"

"Let's get one thing straight. I always wanted you, the woman, enough that it didn't matter that you were Kimberley Blackstone. From where I stood that was a big, fat strike against you, not just because you were the boss's daughter but because you inherited so many of Howard's pain-in-the-ass qualities."

She must have looked as outraged as she felt, because he expelled a harsh-sounding laugh and shook his head.

"You said you didn't want any of my rhetoric, so let's try some home truths. You're stubborn, cynical, opinionated, but on the flip side there's your quick brain and your passion for this business, your honesty and humour and the way you lift your chin whenever you take a stance on something you believe in. Yeah, just like that," he said in a low, rough-edged voice that resonated through her blood. "Whether it's right or wrong, it doesn't matter. You stand by your word and that's one of the many reasons I pursued you. Not with any ambition other than to have you. In any and every way that I could."

The silence following his speech crackled with the undistilled passion of his delivery. This wasn't the smooth charmer, the slick orator, the silver-tongued lover. This was a side Perrini showed so rarely that it stunned Kimberley into silence.

"That day in the Hammond workroom," he continued, "you said you should never have married me."

"And you agreed." Finally she found her voice, although it rasped with raw emotion. "You said our marriage was a mistake."

That coldly conveyed summation had pierced her heart like a spear of ice, before shattering into a hundred frosty shards. The final, chilling end of that argument and of their union.

"It was a mistake," he said bluntly, stunning her all over again. "I married you for the wrong reason. I thought I was calling your father's bluff."

"What do you mean?"

"That Christmas, before we left for our holiday in San Francisco, he had a word with me over a quiet whisky. He knew we were lovers—maybe he had all along—and he played the outraged father. Said he didn't appreciate us creeping around behind his back and suggested, forcefully, that if I wanted to bed you, I could damn well marry you."

That was so like Howard, Kimberley couldn't summon a quarter-carat of shock. She'd known her father had orchestrated their marriage; she just hadn't known the details. At the time she'd been too outraged, too shattered, too betrayed to believe any explanations.

And now…at least now she knew what had prompted Perrini's out-of-the-blue proposal. "So you thought, why the hell not?"

"I wanted you here, in my home, every night, every day. So, yeah, I thought why not marry you? I sure as hell didn't expect we'd be welcomed home with open arms. I'd married his only daughter—the Blackstone heiress—in a Vegas chapel. I expected your father would be livid."

Instead Perrini had been rewarded hugely for taking the initiative. He'd passed the Howard Blackstone test. He'd proven he had balls.

And Kimberley, if she'd played along, would have been relegated to the subordinate role of wife and mother, a part she could never even pretend to play. Infuriated, she'd lashed out at them both. When Perrini sided with her father, she'd walked.

"It didn't quite work out how any of us expected," she said. "Even for Howard."

"Especially for Howard. He wanted you back at Blackstone's, Kim. He was just too proud and stubborn to admit it."

Perhaps, but now she would never know. Regret and sadness thickened in her throat. "It's history now. All of this. We can't go back and change anything we did or said."

"No, but you're letting that history influence your decision."

"And I shouldn't?"

"That's up to you. But just so everything is clear and aboveboard, let me say this." His eyes narrowed with a dangerous glint of purpose and challenge. "I want you back at Blackstone's and I want you back in my life. Whether you accept the business proposal will have no bearing on the personal. They are two separate entities."

"And if I say no. If I return to New Zealand?"

"Not far enough to keep me away."

Kimberley's mouth turned dry. Her heart was beating hard and fast, but she lifted her chin and met those determined blue eyes without a backward step. "I shall take that into consideration when making my decision."

Perrini inclined his head in acknowledgment. "Do that," he said shortly. "We'd appreciate an answer before next week's board meeting."

When will you be back to work? I need to know tomorrow, if not sooner. If you can't reach me, talk to Lionel.

Matt's message greeted Kimberley when she checked her phone that night, a cool, clipped reminder that Perrini wasn't the only man waiting on her decision. She couldn't sleep and pacing through the vast emptiness of the Vaucluse mansion, she had never felt more alone.

She longed for the familiar comfort of her Auckland town house...and then she didn't.

There, too, she would be alone and pacing with no one to

talk to. For the past decade Matt had been her sounding board, but she sensed their friendship would never be the same again, even if she chose to return to House of Hammond.

Paused outside the door to Sonya's suite, she raised her hand to knock but then let it fall away. Sonya would listen and might even dispense advice on her dilemma, but that guidance would not be impartial. There were two sides, the Black-stones and the Hammonds, with a yawning abyss of mis-understanding between.

The prospect of breaching that gap appealed more than ever after Perrini's potent speech. Kimberley's pulse kicked up a beat. For all his talk of dream jobs and the tempting notion of working on the Blackstone Jewellery show, healing the family rift spoke most directly to her heart.

But did she want to return to Blackstone's, to work for a business founded on her father's shady acquisition of the Hammond mining leases? To this day the Hammonds claimed Howard Blackstone wooed Ursula Hammond and befriended her father only to get close to the mines. The fact that Jebediah Hammond signed over the lease to Howard on his death bed only bolstered those claims.

Could she work for Blackstone's now that she knew the full story?

Could she separate the business and the personal and work with Perrini, knowing he aimed to pursue her with the same ruthless purpose he'd employed ten years before? Could she resist the powerful pull of their attraction...and did she even want to?

It was the hardest decision of her life and in the end the choice was hers to make alone. She would not be rushed into it; she would make an informed decision. To do so she needed to see the Blackstone Diamonds of today, to assess the current business structure, to determine whether she even fit anymore.

Did she want to work for Blackstone Diamonds?

Kimberley strode into the ground-floor foyer of the Blackstone Diamonds building the next morning and came to an abrupt halt. Her gaze skimmed from the manned security desk to the high-tech scanners to the ID tag displayed by an employee as he hurried through to the bank of elevators. The nervous anticipation that had swirled in her belly during the taxi ride to the city settled to a leaden weight.

What had she been thinking? That she could simply waltz in the door and wander around at her leisure? Stupidly, she hadn't thought ahead. She'd wanted to come here, to see what had changed, to test her instinctual response to the workplace she'd left ten years before.

Not that the new security checks were an insurmountable problem. At nine-thirty on a Thursday morning, Perrini, Ryan and Garth would all be entrenched at their desks. A quick phone call to any one of their offices and she would be whisked up to the rarefied atmosphere of the upper levels.

That wasn't what she wanted.

Belatedly, she recognised the implausibility of her goal. Blackstone Diamonds had grown into a gargantuan corporation, its multiple departments spread over scores of floors in the soaring tower. This was not an atmosphere that invited idle wandering. Imposing, isolating, impersonal, it was a world apart from the House of Hammond.

Kimberley rubbed the goose-bumped skin of her bare arms. In a moment of defiantly dark humour, she'd decided to wear the new dress. It wasn't nearly as daring as she'd allowed Perrini to believe, but in the air-conditioned confines of the building she wished she had at least grabbed a jacket. Not that she was staying. In fact—

"Can I help you?"

She turned, expecting to see one of the covertly uniformed security guys. Instead she found herself eye-to-eye with the most prettily handsome man she had seen outside the pages of the fashion magazines. Golden hair. Smooth tanned features. Vivid blue eyes rimmed by outrageously long lashes. And a dazzling toothpaste-commercial smile that widened as recognition sparked in his eyes.

"Miss Blackstone," he murmured. "I couldn't help noticing that you looked a little lost. Can I help you find your way? If it's clearance that you need—"

"No." Then, to soften the nerve-honed sharpness of her answer, she smiled. "Thank you, but I'm not going inside after all. I've changed my mind."

"Your prerogative." Amazing, but his eyes really did twinkle. Like a perfectly matched pair of brilliant-cut blue diamonds. "I hope we'll see you back here soon, and if you ever need clearance, call me. Max Carlton. Human resources manager."

He lifted his hand in farewell, and as Kimberley watched him pause to swap a short greeting and bring a smile to the stern face of the security-desk custodian, she couldn't help smiling herself. Perhaps she should have taken him up on his offer, but did she want the slick showman's tour? Not really. Although an hour or two of his pretty face and disarming smile would be no hardship.

Feeling infinitely better for the short interlude and inspired by Max Carlton's eyes, she walked outside and turned right into the morning sunshine. She hadn't given up on her day's task. She was just starting where she should have started all along.

Blackstone Jewellery's Sydney store was a short walk up-town from the office tower and occupied a prime corner site in a historic sandstone building that also housed the five-star Da Vinci Hotel. Kimberley had shied away from even a passing glance at this and all the Blackstone stores during her business travels. After watching the evolution of the latest over-the-top opulence across the street in Auckland, she'd expected similar here.

How wrong could she have been?

The building was grand, yes, but in a classic, traditional sense. The signage was discreet and window displays spare, spotlighting individual pieces against monochrome back-grounds. She paused, captured by the unique design of a gold-pearl-and-diamond necklace. Around the corner a larger display set a collection of retro-style diamond brooches and earrings against deep ruby velvet.

When she finally swung through the revolving door into the air-conditioned interior, her heart was beating thickly with a strange combination of pride and anxiety. *This* was how she'd visualised Blackstone Jewellery when she'd brought the plans to her father the very first time. She felt almost at home as she slowly circumnavigated the open downstairs gallery. The air of exclusive, expensive class reminded her of House of Hammond, although she doubted anyone at Blackstone's would appreciate the comparison.

The click of high heels brought her head up suddenly and snapped her mind out of introspection. A slightly built woman was descending the staircase from the first floor with hurried steps. When she caught sight of Kimberley, her eyes widened slightly in recognition and her worried frown turned tail into a welcoming smile. The smile transformed her face, although her silver-blond hair combined with an austere black dress to highlight her pale air of fragility.

"I'm Jessica Cotter, the store manager," the younger woman said, as she reached the ground floor. "Welcome to Blackstone Jewellery."

"I'm Kimberley Blackstone…although I sense that's superfluous information."

Jessica nodded. "You won't remember, but we were at school together," she continued, a hint of nerves clouding her pretty brown eyes. "You were a senior when I started P.L.C., which is why I recognised you and now I'm making a very unprofessional first impression."

"I caught you on the hop. I should have let you know I was coming in," Kimberley said with an apologetic smile. "I was just passing, and curiosity got the better of me." Which was only a small diversion from the truth. "Would you believe I've never been in a Blackstone store?"

"Then you have come to the right one. This is our flagship store, the first location we opened almost ten years ago. Let me show you around."

"Thank you." Kimberley smiled. "As long as I'm not keeping you from your work."

"Not at all. Is there anything in particular you would like to see?"

"The pearl-and-diamond pendant in the window. Is that by one of your in-house designers?"

"Xander Safin," Jessica said with a nod. "His last collection is one of my favourites. Earth Meets Sea. His aim was to offset the brilliance of diamonds from our Janderra mine with the lustre of coloured pearls."

"If the necklace in the window is any indication, I would say he succeeded."

Jessica's pretty brown eyes lit with warmth. "Come upstairs and I will show you some of Xander's other pieces."

They spent more than an hour poring over the various designs and designers, comparing their preferences for various cuts and settings. Although her name was familiar, Kimberley didn't really remember Jessica from school. After doing the math she'd calculated her age as midtwenties, which was young to manage such an important store. She wondered about the other woman's history, although she didn't doubt her knowledge of jewellery or her passion for the job.

A like soul, Kimberley thought. A woman she could work with if she returned to Blackstone's.

"Are you involved with the February show?" Kimberley asked.

A shadow crossed the other woman's face momentarily but then she looked up, her smile bright and fixed. "Yes. I have been working with Ryan...with Mr. Blackstone. We have some fabulous collections this year. Will you be coming to the show?"

Good question. Would she still be here? Or would she be back in enemy camp and struck from the invitation list? "Well, I hope I'm invited," she said lightly.

Jessica's eyes widened in horror. "Blackstone Jewellery was your idea, your vision. Of course you will be invited to the anniversary celebration."

"I will hold you to that, because I'm really looking forward to seeing the Dani Hammond collection."

"You are in for a treat," Jessica said, the glow of a secret smiling in her eyes. "Dani has such a talent for making her designs come to life."

"I don't suppose you have anything of hers in store?"

"No, unfortunately. The samples we have for the show are under lock and key and Ryan would have my hide if I showed them to anyone." Then, as if suddenly realizing what she'd said, her eyes rounded in horror. "I'm sorry, I didn't mean—"

"I know my brother well. You have cause to look out for your hide." Jessica looked even more dismayed by that reassurance, and Kimberley scrambled to ease her discomfiture by turning her attention back to the jewellery. "Could I possibly have a closer look at the necklace I pointed out downstairs? The Xander Safin?"

"Of course," Jessica said with obvious relief. "I will just go and get it for you."

She returned a minute later with the necklace, which was made up of three broad strands of pavé-set diamonds finished with golden drops of South Sea pearls. "This," she said, holding it up to Kimberley's throat, "would look fabulous with your dramatic colouring. With your hair up, a plain strapless gown. White or silver, I think. See?"

Kimberley saw. It was an exquisitely designed and crafted piece. And beneath the bright showroom lights and the gleam of enthusiasm on Jessica's face, she also saw the shadows beneath her eyes. Jessica Cotter. Suddenly she recalled why the name was familiar—not from school, but from the original passenger list for her father's fatal flight. This was the employee who had cheated death with a last-minute change of plans.

No wonder she looked fragile.

Something of her thoughts must have shown in Kimberley's

expression, because the other woman's smile dimmed. A hint of consternation crossed her face as she locked the necklace back in a display case. "I'm sorry. I get a little carried away when I find someone who shares my enthusiasm."

"Don't apologise. I was thinking of something else," Kimberley assured her. "My mind was miles away."

Jessica looked up, her eyes large and dark and troubled as she discerned where Kimberley's mind might have been. "Kimberley...please accept my condolences for your loss. I know with the lack of news and everything that's been written in the papers, this is a difficult time for you and...for all your family."

"Thank you." There was little else she could say, and when an awkwardness descended she grimaced at her watch. "I have monopolised you long enough for one morning. Thank you for your time and for showing me through the store. I enjoyed it very much."

"It was my pleasure."

"I will call in again." Kimberley smiled and tucked her bag beneath her arm. "Perhaps next time you can talk me into buying that necklace."

Jessica returned her smile but it didn't quite reach her eyes. Secrets, Kimberley thought, as she made her way downstairs.

The girl has something going on in her personal life, which is why she missed that plane and why she is still alive and why she has that haunted look in her eyes.

Immersed in her thoughts, she almost ploughed into Ryan coming out the revolving door and moving with his usual bulldog-after-a-bone tenacity. Steadying her with a hand on each arm, he scowled over her shoulder and up at the floor above before focussing narrowly on her face. "What are you doing here?"

"And hello to you, too, little brother."

The frown suddenly changed tenor, as if he'd shifted gears to finally take in the significance of her presence here at Blackstone Jewellery. "This the last place I'd expect to find you. What's going on, Kim?"

Eight

After Kimberley admitted that her visit to the Martin Place store was part of an inspection tour of the Blackstones' business, Ryan walked her back downtown for a tour of the office complex. Ryan, being Ryan, made it the potted version but that was all right with Kimberley. She preferred to make up her own mind, without the rah-rah rhetoric she might have expected from someone like Max Carlton. Or Perrini.

In the high-speed elevator they zoomed their way to the executive floors, and the sudden pitch of her stomach had less to do with that speed than the prospect of seeing Perrini. How adolescent. Kimberley gave herself a stern mental slap but her nervous anticipation only escalated with each passing floor. So much for keeping business and personal compartmental-ised. Perrini had always been so much better than her at that distinction.

The lift slowed and stopped several floors short of their destination. Patrice Moore, an accounting whiz she remembered for her expert input on the jewellery store business plan, stepped on board. Her smile was instant, warm, genuine. "I heard you were in the building. Nice to see you back, Kimberley, despite the circumstances."

"Thank you. I'm glad you're still here."

"Why wouldn't I be?" the other woman said. "They look after me well."

The lift pinged open at the top floor, and Patrice offered a few sincere words of sympathy before striding off down the corridor. Ryan steered Kimberley in the opposite direction, away from the offices of the senior executives and toward the boardroom. As they walked she felt his inquisitive scrutiny of her face.

"I didn't expect to see so many familiar faces," she admitted.

"You thought we'd have driven them all away with our evil business practices?"

Kimberley laughed and shook her head. "Not exactly. I guess I just...I don't know what I expected."

"Our staff is a large and recognised part of our success. We're proud of our retention records and of our recruitment program."

They turned into the spacious vestibule outside the boardroom and Kimberley cast a quick eye over the comfortable seating, the low tables and the artwork, before returning to the issue of staff. "I have to tell you I was most impressed with your manager at Martin Place. Is she one of your recruits? She's quite young to be managing a store."

Ryan paused with his hand on the door to the boardroom. Kimberley couldn't see his face but she could see the stiffness in his shoulders for the brief moment before he turned around. "Jessica has been with the company since she left school," he said. "She knows our product inside out. She's earned every one of her promotions."

From his sharp tone, Kimberley wondered who might have suggested otherwise, but she didn't get a chance to ask. Ryan was already moving on, opening the door, and gesturing for her to precede him inside. For now she let it go, her mind and her heart and the nerves in her stomach distracted by the long, gleaming cherrywood table lined by tall-backed chairs.

"The many seats of power," she murmured, trailing her fingertips from chair to chair as she strolled the length of the room. She could imagine her father seated at the head of this table, completely in his element, the master of all he surveyed.

She snuck a glance at her brother, found his eyes on that same chairman's place, his expression fixed and forbiddingly stern. The rigid set of his shoulders as he'd paused at the door now made a different kind of sense. He'd been bracing himself for this. For seeing that chair and what its emptiness represented.

Quickly she closed the space between them and placed a hand on her brother's shoulder. Even if she had the words, she doubted her ability to push them past the lump in her throat, especially after she glanced up and saw Ryan's jaw struggling to contain his emotions. Lord, she thought she'd moved past this. That she'd accepted, with the news of Marise, that Howard was gone.

A mobile ringtone shattered the intense moment, and with a last comforting squeeze she stepped back to allow Ryan access to his phone.

"Yours," he said curtly, his gaze skating off Kimberley's as if uncomfortable that she'd witnessed his momentary turmoil. "I'll leave you to take it in private."

"Thank you." If this was Matt returning the call she'd

placed earlier, then she would need that privacy. "This may take a while," she told Ryan. "I've seen all I need for now so I will see myself out. We'll talk later, okay?"

"A word of warning. Don't let Ric Perrini under your—"

"I'm a big girl now," she cut in. "Rest assured, Perrini won't be getting under anything of mine."

Ryan nodded briefly and was gone in a dozen swift strides. When he closed the door behind him, Kimberley retrieved her phone and sucked in a breath. It was Matt. The moment of truth. Her stomach clenched as she put the handset to her ear.

"Matt. Thank you for calling back." Through the phone, she heard the high-pitched prattle of a child's voice and Matt's deeper response. "Is Blake with you?" she asked.

"Rachel—the nanny—brought him in on the ferry."

"He loves that ferry ride." Kimberley's voice thickened, remembering her godson's barely contained excitement as he recounted imaginative "sightings" of dolphins and whales and submarines. "Can I say hello?"

"He's on his way out."

Kimberley's heart dipped at Matt's cool reply. Her hand gripped more tightly around the phone. How could she leave and risk cutting herself off from her godson? Or was the damage already done?

"When are you coming back?" Matt asked. Then, when she didn't answer right away, his voice dropped another chilling degree. "*Are* you coming back?"

"I've been offered a job at Blackstone's."

"You have a job, at Hammonds. Surely you're not considering this offer."

"Considering, yes," Kimberley admitted. "But there is an

awful lot to think about and I hate the thought of leaving you short staffed at such a difficult time."

"Lionel is managing the shortfall."

She pressed her lips together for a moment, fighting the awful sense of being torn in two. The redoubtable Lionel always managed, and so did Matt.... "But that isn't the point. I don't—"

"No," Matt said, cutting her off cold. "The point is, you're contemplating this move after everything Howard Blackstone has done. Your decision should be simple—either you can work for that bastard's company or you can't."

"He's my father, Matt, and he's gone. Please respect that this is a difficult time for me, as well."

"If you're suggesting that you're mourning a man you spent the past ten years despising, then you're not the person I thought you were."

Stung by the frosty slap of those words, Kimberley lifted her chin. "If you can't understand my position, then you're not the man I thought you were, either."

"I understand," Matt said curtly. "You're a Blackstone. That's all that needs to be said. I shall take this as your resignation from Hammonds, as of last week."

Patrice Moore alerted Ric to Kim's presence in the building. "Any truth in the rumour she's coming back?" the accountant asked in her usual forthright manner.

"News travels fast," Ric said noncommittally.

"You're not kidding. It'll be in the gossip columns tomorrow."

Ric didn't doubt it. At least that would be a positive piece of press, unlike the rest of the current rumour-mongering about Blackstone's. For a good ten minutes after Patrice left his office, he fought the urge to hunt Kimberley down to find out if the rumour bore any truth, or if her tour of the offices meant she was closing in on a decision.

During the drive back to Vaucluse last night she'd asked for time and space to reach that decision, and he had no idea what she'd been thinking or if he'd miscalculated and gone too far in revealing his intentions toward her, the woman.

He'd wanted her to know where he stood, and where she stood, so there would be no misunderstandings when he made his move. When he brought her back from Auckland, he'd thought he could be patient. That he could wait until after her father had been laid to rest and the ensuing commotion had settled down.

That was before he'd taken her to his house…and let her leave without touching her.

He'd spent a restless night rueing the outcome of his self-control, and the restless heat in his blood had not been cooled any by his predawn plunge in the ocean. That heat surged again now, knowing she was here, on this floor, and not knocking on his office door.

With a low growl of impatience he shoved to his feet.

Ten minutes he'd given her, and that was all the patience he had.

He found her in the boardroom, and the first sight of her stopped Ric dead in his tracks. Dead but for the rush of arousal that quickened his pulse.

Beyond the long stretch of the table, she stood at the bank of windows looking out at the city. Sunlight slanted through the glass and burned ruby sparks in the loose fall of her hair. The same God-given rays sliced through her dress, silhouetting every curve of her body in mouthwatering detail.

That image, and his body's response, riveted him for several long greedy seconds before he took in the bigger picture. The tense set of her shoulders. Her absolute stillness. The fact that she was so lost in thought that she hadn't noticed his arrival.

It struck him then how small and isolated she looked against the expansive view of Sydney city that stretched beyond the boardroom windows, and his initial surge of lust thickened to a deeper, richer need. Gently he closed the door, but the quiet sound was enough to bring her swirling around, both hair and dress alive with that momentum. Their eyes met down the polished length of cherrywood, and he caught a glimpse of that same vulnerability he'd detected in her stance.

Then she lifted her chin. "Did Ryan tell you I was here?"

"I heard via the office grapevine."

"Word travels fast."

"All the way to the top floor." He paused halfway down the room, pacing his approach, checking the urge to charge forward and claim the softened curve of her mouth. "Is this the dress you didn't wear last night?"

"Yes," she said, sounding surprised. "How did you know?"

"You gave away the vital clue last night." He debated whether to continue, but what the hell. He felt prickly enough to tease her. Hang the consequences. "You said it was revealing."

She blinked once, slowly, realisation dawning in her eyes as she quickly looked down and then around at the light at her back. A hint of colour traced her cheekbones but she didn't rush away. She just raised her eyebrows a little and said, "In future I will be more careful about what I wear into this room."

"You see yourself in this room in the future?"

Her shoulders straightened with what looked like resolve and she nodded once, the gesture as tense as her posture. "Yes. I've decided."

"Good," he said simply. *Get the business done. Then celebrate.* "The job and the position on the board?"

"Both…if the other directors agree."

"They will." He halted his progress through the long room beside one of the credenzas parked along the wall. Close enough, for now. "What made up your mind?"

"A combination of factors," she said carefully. "I do regret cutting myself off from my family, and you were right about my dreams and my future and the difference I can make. I want to be part of shaping the future of Blackstone's."

"Your tour through the building helped?"

"Yes, and visiting the Blackstone Jewellery store. I felt at home there, seeing the heart of the business."

Ric shook his head. "Those polished gems aren't the heart, Kim—they're just the pretty face. The heart and soul of Blackstone Diamonds is way up north, in the red Kimberley earth."

"The Janderra mine," she conceded softly. "Of course." Then she blew out a rueful breath. "Would you believe after all these years in the diamond business, I've never visited a mine?"

"Easily fixed."

She straightened slightly. "Oh, I wasn't fishing for an invitation."

"I didn't think you were. But as a director you need to visit Janderra to get the full scope of this business, to meet the key personnel, to be able to do your job."

"Then, thank you. I would like to do that."

"I'll make the arrangements."

"For when?"

"I was planning to fly out there early next week, to address concerns about new workplace agreements and about the future management. That'll be the ideal opportunity for you to look around." Ric's gaze fastened on hers, straightforward and challenging. "If you don't mind an overnight stay."

Something flared in her eyes, a sign that she felt the low simmer of awareness between them. But she didn't acknowledge it. She moistened her lips and fixed her gaze resolutely on his. "Why would I mind?"

"With the ongoing wait for news on your father, I thought you might prefer to stay close to Sydney."

"If we're using the company jet, we can turn around and come back if necessary. We'll only be three hours away at most."

"Four."

She nodded. "So, what's next? What do I need to do to get started?"

"I'll organise an office for you."

"Which department?"

"You'll be working from this floor."

"No," she said, shoulders straightening. "This is the territory of senior executives. Hardly appropriate for the position you offered me."

"Suit yourself." Ric spread his hands expansively. "But you'll be in close consultation with those executives. Having you nearby would be convenient."

"Perhaps, but I'll also be working closely with the other departments—PR, marketing, the jewellery division. To be honest, I would rather if my office weren't up here on this floor."

Ric considered her answer. Cool, logical, matter-of-fact. But there was something else, something that tinged her high cheekbones with warm colour and deepened the green of her eyes. "Too close to me?" he asked.

"That shouldn't be a factor."

"But it is, isn't it?"

She pressed her lips together, a hint of annoyance flitting across her expression before she replied. "You're right. That shouldn't be a factor. I will consider whichever location you deem appropriate, as long as it suits my workspace requirements."

Her tone was formal and stuffy and so unlike Kim, Ric had to suppress a smile. The prospect of an office too close to his unsettled her. Good. "When do you want to start?"

"Yesterday."

Ric unleashed a smile as he straightened and pushed away from the credenza. "Monday might be more convenient, but we can get started on the formalities now." In half a dozen businesslike strides, he closed the space between them. "Welcome back to Blackstone, Kim."

He took her hand in what started as a formal handshake, but when he felt the faint tremor in her fingers and saw the stirring of emotion in her eyes, his grip on her hand tightened. "You've made the right choice," he said softly. "You belong here. You—"

"Don't." She shook her head abruptly. "Please, don't go all understanding on me now. That is not what I need."

"Perhaps you do."

"Oh, no. I definitely don't." She expelled a little burst of air.

"It's been quite a day. Seeing Blackstone Jewellery for the first time and talking to Ryan. Then making my decision. I spoke to Matt just before you came in, and Blake was there—"

Her voice cracked on the boy's name and so did her composure. He saw something like desperation in her eyes as she tugged her hand free and swung away. Nothing could have hit Ric as hard as that wounded fracture in her voice or the sign of tears looming in her eyes.

He put his hand on her shoulder. A gesture of comfort, he told himself, but it wasn't enough. He shifted closer, his simple touch expanding until his palm cupped her shoulder and his fingers encountered the smooth warmth of her skin. Dipping his head, he pressed his lips to her sunwarmed hair. Perhaps that would have been enough if she hadn't made a choked sound of distress.

It sounded like, "Don't," but he paid no heed. With a hand on each shoulder, he turned her into his chest and tucked her close. The tickle of her hair against his chin, the scent of orchids and spice in each breath, twined around his senses and thumped in his pulse.

This was where she belonged. Right here. In his arms.

He would hold her, just hold her, while his hands soothed the bare skin of her arms and the delicate fabric that cloaked her shoulders and her back. Leopard print. With lace peeping from the shoulder straps and the hemline. Underwear aside, it was one the sexiest things he had ever seen her wearing and with each stroke of his hand his control slipped another tenuous notch.

"This dress," he muttered thickly, his fingers giving up the fight and tracing the delicate line of lace down one shoulder blade, "is not coming on the Janderra trip."

He felt the flutter of her breath against his throat, the tension in her shoulders, the live-wire jolt of his fingertips on her skin.

"Of course not." Her voice sounded low, breathy. Turned on. Or at least that's how Ric's body interpreted the husky edge. "It's completely not appropriate for work."

"Then it's lucky you're not yet on the payroll."

She went perfectly still, and he knew exactly what was ticking through her agile brain. *Inappropriate. Work. My boss's hands on my skin.*

Beneath those hands he felt her gathering control. Every cell in his body growled a fierce objection. No way in this life or the next was he letting her go.

When she started to pull away, his hands slid to her upper arms and held her in place; his eyes on her face did the same.

"And since you're not," he said, low and dangerous, "I'm not bound to let you go."

Her nostrils flared as she drew a quick breath, and a new awareness shivered in the air between them. "Even if I ask?"

"Are you asking?"

A beat of pause, the green-diamond flash in her eyes, the quick lick of her tongue to moisten her lips, was all the time Ric allowed for her answer. Then he lifted a hand and touched his thumb to her mouth. He felt the warmth, the moisture, the shudder of her exhalation, and was lost.

He lowered his head and took her mouth with the hunger of years of wanting and the ache of the past week's emotion. It was no gentle exploration, no tender assault, not once she responded with her own longing, with her hands at last on his arms, his shoulders, twining around his neck to draw him more fiercely into the kiss.

With a low growl, he changed the angle of contact so he

could have more of her, more of the sweet heat he craved. When she welcomed him into her mouth, he tasted the impact all the way to his groin. It was sharp, intense, an exquisite surge of lust that he wanted to assuage, here and now.

Hands on her back, he pulled her closer until their bodies were flush and the kiss exploded with a silken savagery. Thigh to thigh, hip to pelvis, breasts to chest, she was everything he remembered of raw heat and unrestrained passion...and still it was not enough. He cupped her buttocks and lifted her against him, all the while turning and backing her toward the credenza.

Breaking the kiss, he lifted her onto the sleek cherrywood surface and her hands slid forward to cradle his face. Her thumbs stroked the corners of his mouth, the effect a gentle contrast to the rough rasp of their breaths. Their gazes locked for a long moment as he palmed the smooth warmth of her thighs, his thumbs circling inward with the same erotic motion as hers.

At first he thought the vibrating hum was her response to his touch. Then she touched a finger to his lips in a shushing gesture, her mouth turning down in a frown. "That's your phone. Don't you think you should answer it?"

"No," he growled against her throat. "I don't."

But she slipped her hand into his jacket pocket and retrieved the phone. "Ryan," she mouthed, hitting the answer button and holding the receiver to her ear.

Ric's growl turned into an internal groan...until she sat up straight, her eyes big and stark in her suddenly pale face.

"What is it?" he asked.

With a trembling hand she passed over the phone. "He's just taken a call from the search area. They've located the wreckage."

Nine

Closure, finally, Kimberley rationalised once the initial spear of shock had dulled. The interminable waiting was over. They could mourn Howard's passing, make arrangements for his funeral service and burial, satisfy the press with final statements, move on at a personal and business level.

Unfortunately it wasn't that simple.

An initial inspection located only three bodies in the wreckage, meaning one of the men—and the marine police couldn't even speculate on whether this was passenger or crew member—remained missing. Due to the depth of the water and adverse weather conditions brewing off the coast, the recovery operation could take several days. The process of formal identification would require the use of dental records and DNA matching, which, their police contact warned them, could take weeks rather than days.

Looming over it all was the real and sobering possibility that the lost body might never be found...and that it could be Howard.

The waiting continued. Kimberley appreciated being included in the inner information circle this time, and for that she thanked Perrini. Or she would once they got through the weekend and the incessant phone calls. As the Blackstone PR mouthpiece she'd decided to be more open with the press, in the hope that regular statements and updates would result in more factual stories and less speculation.

So far it seemed to be working. Several business and social commentators had already reported on the prodigal daughter's return to Blackstone Diamonds, and she'd taken a deep breath and agreed to an interview for a magazine piece at a date to be fixed. Positive press, she reminded herself, when her heart palpitated at the thought of such public exposure of her private self.

"Good start," Perrini said, in one of their few moments alone. It was late Saturday afternoon and the official gatherings and press updates had given way to the personal. Garth, her uncle Vincent and two of Howard's yacht club cronies had called at various intervals during the afternoon to offer sympathy and support. None had left. Sonya's tea had given way to Howard's best whisky, and Kimberley had retreated to the terrace for a brush with solitude.

That's where Perrini found her and those small words of praise resulted in an inordinate rush of satisfaction. Perhaps because his expression conveyed more than words, perhaps because she was enjoying their stolen seconds of privacy a little too much. Perhaps because, for a whisper of time, their incendiary boardroom kiss sizzled the air between them.

She liked that it wiped her mind of the deathly images imprinted in the past forty-eight hours, that it melted the icy weight of angst in her stomach, that it focussed everything on this moment, this connection, this enlivening flame in her senses.

"I hope it's the right start," she said in response to his comment…and because she couldn't resist the thinly veiled allusion to what lay unfinished between them.

"It is." Arrogant, supremely certain, his gaze lingered on her mouth for a telling second before drifting back to her eyes. "I like that you seized the opportunity and ran with it."

"I gather you're talking about the magazine article?"

"Of course…unless you prefer to talk about us."

Did she? Her heart skipped an erratic beat as she met the still intensity of his gaze. Asking too much, too fast, too soon, that look sizzled through her, charging her senses with renewed memories of their white-hot kiss and the press of his body hard against hers. A loud burst of laughter from inside the house broke the connection, reminding her they weren't alone. Reminding her that she'd given no thought to discretion in those crazy lost-to-the-world moments when he'd lifted her onto a cherrywood sideboard.

And that she'd given no thought to what was next.

"No." She lifted her chin and shook her head resolutely. "Not yet."

"When you are ready—" for a scant second his fingertips skimmed the back of her hand, a touch as dark and hot and double-edged as his words "—you know where to find me."

He left soon after, but those final words and his dark, velvet touch kept Kimberley intimate company throughout a night of little sleep. She woke early, out of sorts with herself for chickening out of that talk, not just the previous evening but ever since she learned of his intentions. He wanted her. Five minutes of hot magic in the boardroom had demonstrated that desire. But on what terms?

And what of tomorrow?

Did she even want to know, when the answer might reveal future needs she could not deliver?

Her heart constricted with an aching trepidation that sent her rocketing out of bed, too antsy to lie still any longer. She pulled on three-quarter yoga pants and a sports singlet, comfort clothes that made her feel no less comfortable in her own antsy skin. She needed to get out, to escape the claustrophobic press of this house and her restless mind.

What she needed was a long, energetic walk. Her mind conjured her favourite jaunt of old, the path that dipped and rose from beach to clifftop between Bondi and Bronte. Open air, the sea breeze on her skin, the challenge of attacking steep rock stairs and on a leisurely return trip, sinking her toes into the silky Glamarama sand...

Yes. That's exactly what she needed.

It was early, so early that she beat the notoriously early-rising Sonya downstairs. If she left now she might also beat the Sunday crowds who flocked to the popular coastal walk. Although she'd been given carte blanche access to the extensive Miramare garage, she dithered several minutes before jotting a note and grabbing the keys to Sonya's compact Mercedes.

Fifteen minutes later she parked at the northern end of Bondi Beach and attacked the mile-long stretch of sand at a testing pace. Despite the early hour she wasn't lonely, passing steady walkers and being overtaken by the serious exercise nuts. At the top of the first steep rise she paused to catch her breath and to absorb the stunning moment of daybreak over the Pacific horizon. Far below, waves crashed and foamed against the dark shelves of rock; far above, real estate battled for a share of the compelling view.

One of those houses was Perrini's.

Would he be up, enjoying his first coffee on the deck outside his bedroom? Or was he still asleep, long limbs spread-eagled across the king-size bed, covers kicked free by a restless, over-heated body?

The image took root in her brain, and she couldn't pry it loose. Nor could she prevent herself turning back and then taking the detour up the steep hill to the headland. When she turned into his street her heart was pounding, not from exertion but with nervous tension.

She didn't know what she was doing here. From the street-side, a privacy wall and the steep drop of the site protected most of his house from view. She had no clue if he was home or not. The sensible course of action would be to turn around and hotfoot it back to the car. The nonsensible, risky, spur-of-the-moment thing involved her mobile phone and a speed-dialled number.

A light came on in a second-floor window. His bedroom. Her stomach tightened with a new and different tension.

"Kim." The deep morning huskiness of his voice curled through her, tightening to a stark ache low in her belly. It was desire. It was loneliness. It was the lure of a light in his bed-room window and the sound of her name on his tongue. "It's hellish early. Is everything all right?"

"Yes." No. *Not exactly. Why hadn't she composed some-thing to say before hitting that button?* "I was just wonder-ing if you were home," she finally managed to say. "I'm in the neighbourhood and I just—" She closed her eyes, her fingers tightening in a deathgrip around her palm-size phone. "I seized the opportunity and ran with it."

He opened the door before she rang the bell, and for several electric seconds they stood in silence, their eyes locked. Kimberley did notice that he wore trousers and nothing else—nothing except a narrow-eyed look of intense, primal concentration that would have knocked her off her feet if he hadn't snaked out a hand and pulled her inside.

Vaguely she registered him reaching out to push the door shut behind her. Mostly she registered the scent that clung to his skin, the unique combination of expensive soap and male heat she'd labelled Ricaroma way back then. It still had the power to make her hormones sit up and pant.

For a long, thick beat he studied her face, her heightened colour, the jut of her tightened breasts in a top not designed for aroused nipples. "Do you want to talk?" he asked, and those female hormones rolled over and begged.

"No." She met his hungry look, direct, honest. "Not talk."

One of the things she'd always appreciated in Perrini was his ability to judge the moment. He could match words with the smoothest orators on the planet, but he knew when talk wasn't necessary, when action spoke with the greatest eloquence.

Without a word he led her by the captured hand to the elevator. From ground floor to second, he kissed her with the exact intensity she needed to eat away the last flutter of nerves. As he backed her toward the master bedroom, those first greedy seconds eased into a sultry meeting of lips, tongues, mouths.

Oh, yes, the man knew when and how to use his mouth to devastating effect.

In the doorway he paused, to tug the elastic from her pony-tail, to drag her singlet over her head, to hold her arms trapped while he took her in with a low, thorough look that screamed through her senses. This was her chance to slow things down and rethink, to step away from temptation and think this through.

From the moment she'd turned on the clifftop path and caught a glimpse of the ivory stucco walls, the jutting balconies, the glint of daybreak on bedroom glass, she'd been steel to a magnet, powerless to resist the pull. She didn't want to think. She wanted to feel, to drive the past days from mind and body with the purest, most absolute, life-giving pleasure. The kind she had only experienced in this man's expert hands.

Stretching up, she kissed the raspy line of his jaw, the indent in his chin, the velvety fullness of his mouth, and they sunk into another long, deep soul kiss that waltzed them in perfect, thigh-brushing synch toward the bed. She lapped up the dark flavour of his mouth, savoured the heat and texture of his hands as they palmed her shoulders, her upper arms, the blades of her shoulders.

Eventually he eased the connection with a delicate trail of nips from her bottom lip to her jaw and earlobe. "Shave," he muttered, demonstrating the need with a momentary brush of his whiskery cheek against hers.

"Shower," she murmured, thinking about her earlier exertion and then his beautiful, big, shower-with-friends-size room.

Thinking about him, naked and wet, his hands sliding over her skin, filled her veins with a heavy, languid beat. Their gazes connected and the same primal drumming burned in his eyes and tightened his expression. He lifted a hand, knuckles skimming over her hair before he twisted a hank around his fingers and urged her closer. When her taut nipples came into scorching contact with the hard wall of his chest, all the air left her lungs in a fractured gasp.

Eyes locked on his, she shifted her hands from his waist to the front fastening of his trousers but he stilled her fingers beneath the flat of one hand. "It's been too long," he told her bluntly, "to stand much play."

"Too long…without?"

"Without you." The honesty of that statement and its inherent message—this is you, this is different—resonated through her blood and into her heart. When he released her hair and his fingertips teased across the rise of her breasts, she swallowed a lump of hot, desperate desire.

"Same," she said, stepping out of her shoes, her hands already peeling down her pants until she stood naked before him. "I'll turn on the shower."

He didn't let her shave him but he joined her beneath the double showerheads. He stepped straight into her arms and into a kiss that was strong and bold and without pretence. They explored each other's bodies with the same intense, unhurried thoroughness, until his hands moulded her bottom and drew her up against his thick arousal. Their mouths came apart but their gazes held the connection as he rocked her slowly, deliberately, stoking the restless fire and testing the tenuous limit of their control.

For a second Kimberley could do nothing but ride the wave of erotic pleasure that flooded her, then he lifted her and she wrapped her arms around his neck and her legs around his sleek, wet flanks. She felt him, hard and hot between her legs, and need—unbearably intense—swelled in her breasts and in her female core and in her heart.

Eyes linked with his, she saw the momentary hesitation and felt the slight withdrawal, and guessed its cause.

"No," she whispered, not wanting to break the moment, only wanting him inside her like this, with nothing between them. "There's no need."

"You're protected?"

"I'm…yes. There's no risk of pregnancy."

Something fierce flared in his eyes, a blaze of possessiveness that caused her heart to contract and ache with the truth of the statement. *No risk of conception, unless by some miracle.* Then he carried her from the shower to the dressing room. He set her down on the vanity, the cool marble surface a shockingly erotic contrast to her overstimulated skin and to the heat of his hands. They spanned her waist, drawing her forward while he fed on her mouth, her throat, her breasts.

When he fingered her slick heat, she moaned into his mouth and then his hands on her thighs opened her and anchored her when the first measured thrust of his body filled her with unbelievable heat and sensation and with a vicious jab of regret for their years spent apart.

In the supercharged intensity of that intimate coupling, Kimberley saw the same complex mix of sensual awe and conflicted emotion in his eyes. She lifted her fingers to his mouth and felt the warm slough of his breath when he spoke low and ardent. "Welcome home, babe, where you belong."

She wrapped her legs higher, drawing him deeper and pulling him into a kiss that strengthened their intimate connection. Beneath her hands the harshly etched muscles of his back reflected his restraint as he started to move with a slow, controlled cadence. The pleasure was exquisite, immense, impossible.

Her hands slid lower, relearning the shape of him as her

body relearned the power of his restrained strength with each deep thrust. She traced the long planes of muscle, the dimples at the base of his spine, the taut muscles of his behind.

And when she reached lower still, a deep shudder racked his body. His head lifted, eyes fiercely hooded as he dragged her bottom lip between his teeth and changed the angle to rock deeply against her pelvis. He didn't need to touch her anywhere else, didn't need to do anything except look at her. He drove her to a climax that shattered into a spray of vivid brilliance in her blood and in her flesh and in her heart.

Ric leaned his unashamedly bare hip against the doorframe and watched her come awake with the quickness he remembered from the past. No slow stretches and yawns for Kim, her eyes opened clear and focussed, her brain already geared for action. Despite the second thoughts he imagined ticking through her agile brain right now, he smiled with satisfaction, not only because he'd taken her to bed and made love to her another time with complete, inventive thoroughness, not only because she was still here and he was thinking about a third time, but because she looked so right in his bed.

"I wondered if you'd ever wake."

"Worn out," she murmured. The contented light in her eyes as she found him watching her was a kiss to the heart. "What time is it?"

"Quarter after midday."

"You're kidding." A frown formed between her brows. "I didn't expect to be away so long."

"That's a problem?"

"Only that I took Sonya's car. She might wonder...."

When she swung her legs out of bed, Ric abandoned his

nonchalant stance and moved swiftly to prevent her exodus. He sat on the edge of the mattress, trapping the sheet beneath him. Unless she wanted to slide butt-naked from under that sheet gripped across her breasts, he had a captive audience. He intended having that talk now, and finding out what prompted her surprise visit.

"How long did you expect to be gone?" he asked.

"When I left home, it was to do the Bronte walk. That's all."

"And this—" he gestured between them with his fingers "—was a spur of the moment impulse? Alternate exercise? What, exactly?"

"An impulse," she admitted, hunching her shoulders into a tight shrug. "After this weekend, everything about the crash seemed a little too real and…graphic. I wanted to take an hour to forget about searches and victims and means of identification. I wanted those images out of my mind."

"Did it work?"

"Yes." Her gaze lifted, stark and luminous with the same emotion that coloured her voice. "Thank you…not only for this morning, but for everything this weekend. I appreciated being included in the meetings, even though Ryan disapproved. And thank you for allowing me to make the media statements."

"That's your job."

"I'm not officially on the payroll until tomorrow," she pointed out. Then said, "Thank you for calling Danielle and getting her back so swiftly. Sonya needed her family around her this weekend."

"No need to thank me," Ric said quietly. "She's the closest I have to family."

"I noticed."

"And you don't approve?"

"I don't *understand*," she clarified. Then she shook her head and blew out a breath. "No, that's not quite right. I think I understand all too well."

Alerted by the edge to her voice, Ric's gaze narrowed on her face. "What is it you think you're seeing here, Kim?"

"My father welcomed you with open arms when you married me, and it wasn't only as an approved son-in-law. He'd always looked on you as a surrogate son, a replacement for the one he'd lost."

This revelation wasn't news to Ric, he'd always suspected that part of Ryan's antagonism toward him was based on a similar belief. But that didn't make it any easier to swallow. Not when coming from Kim. Not when it was just plain ludicrous. "Howard never saw me as a substitute for James. Why would he, when he believed James was still alive?"

Eyes wide and appalled, she sat up straight and stared at him. "Are you crazy? My brother was taken thirty-two years ago. Despite all the investigations and all the reward money my father offered, there were no leads that didn't peter out a mile down the road. How could you suggest that he's alive?"

"I don't believe it any more than you do, but Howard refused to give up hope. That was his one weakness. His inability to let that go."

"His inability to let go," she said fiercely, "was always his weakness."

She had a point. And if his reason for being on that plane was tied up in his vengeance against the Hammonds, then it had turned into a fatal weakness.

"What about you?" Ric lifted a hand and threaded a loose

tress of hair behind her ear, leaning in to follow with his lips. "Are you able to let go of the past? To start again here and now? Will you stay?"

Ten

Ric couldn't talk her into staying Sunday night, but before he finished kissing her goodbye he had convinced her to fly to Janderra with him on Monday afternoon. With the crucial board meeting on Thursday and concerns about the still-depressed share price spreading edgy malcontent through some factions of the company, this wasn't the best time to be out of the office. But he didn't want Kimberley there, or at the Vaucluse house, when the police brought in the bodies. For once Ryan agreed with him.

They took off late afternoon in the company's Gulfstream, and this time she sat beside him and accepted the comforting grip of his hand at takeoff. Although she didn't miss the chance to point out, "I'm not a nervous flyer, you know that. It's just that last flight from New Zealand, I couldn't get out of my mind that we were flying over the same stretch of water where the jet went down. That I could look out the window and see—" She blew out a rough laugh. "Silly, because given the expanse of the Tasman the odds would be miniscule."

"Not silly." Ric lifted their linked hands and pressed a kiss to the delicate skin on the inside of her wrist. "FYI, I'm using this excuse to hold your hand. Humour me."

"FYI, humouring you is not part of my job description."

"Can be added. It's fluid."

She gave him a look.

"So, how did you spend your first day?"

"Meeting staff, reading annual reports, getting the lay of the land. There's been a lot of change, a lot to catch up on."

A helluvalot. And businesswise he would allow her to catch up. As for everything else, he stood by what he'd told her in his bedroom. There and then they'd let the past go. They were starting over. "Did Max get the formalities sorted out?"

"Ah, Max, a bright spot in the middle of all those balance sheets," she said with a grin. "The man should come with a warning."

Ric's gaze narrowed. He knew Carlton's reputation as a charmer. Everyone east of the Great Divide knew, but hell—

Laughing at his grim expression, Kim shook her head. "Relax, Perrini. He didn't offer to hold my hand or anything. We just met over coffee and talked for a while. He was very helpful, clueing me in on staff politics. Oh, and he recommended Holly McLeod as my assistant."

"Good choice."

"I met her and I agree, except I don't need a permanent PA."

"You are entitled," he said, "as an executive and a director."

"Which doesn't mean I need to take up the perk," she retorted. "I will utilise Holly when necessary. She impressed me already, putting together a dossier on the jewellery show at short notice."

"Have you had a chance to look at it?"

"Briefly."

Something in her expression focussed Ric's attention on her face instead of his contemplation of how much she'd changed. Ten years ago she'd taken every perk as her due as a Blackstone. He approved this change. Very much. "Problem?" he asked.

"Briana Davenport," she said, a frown between her brows and in her voice. "The model used in all the promotional materials for the show. I haven't worked out if she's a problem or an opportunity yet." After a moment's hesitation she asked, "How well do you know her?"

"I've met her at a number of functions and from everything I've seen and heard, we couldn't have chosen a harder-working or more amenable model as 'the face of Blackstone's.' Are you concerned because she's Marise's sister?"

"Precisely. I'm worried about what spin the media might put on that, now that they've started chewing over the juicy prospect of a Howard-Marise affair."

Ric swore silently and succinctly. "You saw that column, then?"

"It's my job to see columns like this morning's," she said matter-of-factly, shaking her head at his question. But he saw the anger darken her eyes. "It's also my job to think about future ramifications. What if Briana sells family secrets to one of these gossip magazines?"

"She wouldn't do that. She isn't the type who chases attention."

"She's a model…she's a Davenport. Are you sure about that?"

"Briana may be Marise's sister," Ric said with conviction, "but that is where the resemblance ends."

Kimberley made a mental note to call Briana Davenport on their return from the outback, to arrange an informal meeting where she could form her own opinion. Then she turned her focus to the trip and to renewing her opinion of the man at her side. Until now she'd acted impulsively, in succumbing to his kiss, in going to his home, in falling into his bed, but from here on she needed to be honest with herself about where this was leading and what she expected from their relationship. And the first step to honesty was acknowledging that Perrini could never be a casual lover. He was her ex, her boss, the only man who had ever owned her heart…but was he the same man ten years later?

Today he was more relaxed than she'd seen him since her return from New Zealand, and she liked to think that present company had something to do with his upbeat mood. They'd always connected in conversation, in ideas and interests, which stimulated their exchanges—both verbal and physical—with an extra element of excitement. That hadn't changed.

But the following day at the mine, as she watched him roll up his sleeves and don hard hat and boots to go onsite at the gaping open pit, she realised that his laid-back demeanour might have as much to do with Janderra itself. This was a Perrini she'd never seen before, equally at home addressing the site managers or leaders of the indigenous community or climbing into one of the huge ore trucks to chew over the concerns of the mine staff. Recalling the day in the boardroom when he'd told her that this was the heart and soul of Blackstone's, she wondered about *his* heart and soul.

When Kimberley first met Ric Perrini, she'd judged him as the perfect Blackstone representative, as eye-catching and expensive and charismatic as the stones at the company's foundation. Now she was intrigued by his hidden facets—and by the original, rough diamond from which he'd been hewn. What drove his ambition, his love of the beautiful and the exclusive, his loyalty to a man who'd manipulated him into an ill-fated marriage? By the end of their first day at Janderra, Kimberley's curiosity had not only been reignited. It flamed blue-hot with her need to know.

Tracy Mattera, one of the mine executives, had invited them to a barbecue dinner at her home in the Janderra township. Having met the all-business, khakis-and-boots-wearing Tracy at the mine site, Kim hadn't pictured her as a mother. So it came as something of a surprise when they were greeted at the door of an unprepossessing, ranch-style home by another version of the thirty-something woman.

This Tracy looked younger, softer, prettier in shorts and bare feet and freshly washed blond curls, with a baby perched on one hip. She greeted Kimberley with cool politeness and Perrini with a big welcoming smile, and Kimberley gained the distinct impression the other woman had pulled back from greeting him with even more enthusiasm.

That initial prickle of knowledge was barreled over by another stronger rush of female response when Perrini scooped the toddler from Tracy's arms and swung her high in the air. The sound of the little girl's giggles, the sight of Perrini's wide grin, the fierce tug of longing as their eyes met over a mop of baby-soft blond curls, arrowed straight to her heart and to an emptiness deep at her woman's core. And it only intensified when a little boy of six or seven shuffled into the room, skinny legs weighed down by full-size cricket pads, bat and ball in his hands. Tracy's expression clouded. "Oh, Cam, no backyard cricket tonight. Ric has brought a…friend."

"Kim won't mind," Perrini said easily, and still tense from that awkward introduction she didn't realise his intent until her arms were filled with wriggling baby girl. She didn't mind—the proposed game of cricket, the baby, anything—but she had been caught off guard and that unpreparedness must have shown on her face. Uttering a hasty apology Tracy reclaimed her child.

"Please, I don't mind," Kimberley reassured her, but it was too late. With a cool smile Tracy hurried off to fix them drinks and Kimberley was left feeling oddly bereft after one token moment of sweet-scented baby in her arms. Hugging her arms lightly she looked up and her gaze collided with steady blue perception.

He'd paused at the ranch slider, one hand tossing and catching the well-used red cricket ball, the other resting lightly on Cam's shoulder but his attention was fixed entirely on her, catching her unguarded, her emotions stripped bare. For a moment she thought he would say something, but Cam tugged at his shirt, recapturing his attention, and they continued on to the backyard, a picture of man and child that reached into her emotional heart and squeezed it like a vise.

"You were quiet tonight," he said later, driving back to their accommodation. For a second she felt the sidelong touch of his gaze, felt its perceptive impact shiver through her. "Should I have warned you about the kids?"

"I'm that transparent?"

"Usually, no."

But at that one moment, yes. Since then she'd had plenty of time to collect herself and to prepare an answer that, while not the complete truth, wasn't a lie. "I am going to miss Blake. Tonight I realised just how much."

"I wondered if I'd done the wrong thing thrusting Ivy on you."

"Only from Tracy's viewpoint." Then, when Perrini looked puzzled, she shook her head. *Men. Perceptive one second, clueless the next.* "She didn't exactly approve of me, did she?"

"She didn't approve of you breaking my heart," he said lightly. "Give her time. She'll get over it."

He was kidding; she knew it in her mind and yet that didn't stop her heartbeat thickening with a longing. *Follow his lead,* she cautioned herself. *Keep it light.* "I gather you've been friends a while?"

"Twenty years, give or take. We started at the mine together, the same day, same shift. I've known her kids since birth."

Another part of his life she'd known nothing about. The knowledge irked. "It might have helped if I'd known some of this history beforehand."

"Helped, how?"

"I don't know. Maybe if I'd known you were close friends I wouldn't have been taken aback when she all but kissed you at the door and when you grabbed hold of Ivy. Instead I was left wondering about your relationship—"

"You thought I might be their father?" he interrupted, his voice a rough rasp of astonishment.

"No. *No,* that didn't even cross my mind. I meant your relationship with Tracy. I thought you might have been lovers."

"You were jealous?"

"Yes," she admitted after a moment. "If she knows you better than I do, then I'm jealous of that."

"You know me."

"No," Kimberley countered, shaking her head. "Whenever I've asked about your background, you provide the minimum of facts with a what-does-it-matter shrug. What do I know about you? You were born in Italy, and came to Australia with your mother when you were a baby. You grew up in West Australia. After your mum died, you worked to pay your way through university. One of those jobs was here at the Janderra mine. And after finishing your business degree you got an entry-level job in the marketing department at Blackstone's."

"That's my background, not me." His words might have been deliberately dismissive, but the determined set of his features and the long sidelong glance he cast over her face were anything but casual. "If you want to know me, move back to Bondi. Live with me. Work with me. It's as easy as that."

"No, that's easy for *you*. Tell me just one thing," she continued quickly when his blue gaze snapped in protest. "Why did your mother come to Australia? Why did she stay, when she had no family here? That must have been difficult for her, especially as a single mum."

"Just *one* thing?"

His tone was dry, one eyebrow lifted in sardonic query, but Kimberley wouldn't be put off by semantics. "One thing in several parts," she justified. "Why Australia?"

"My father was Australian. Mum came out here to find him."

"And did she?"

"Apparently." He hitched a shoulder, the what-does-it-matter gesture exactly as she'd described. "I was too young to remember. That didn't work out but Mum decided to stay. She had no reason to go back to Italy."

"She didn't have any family?"

His mouth thinned with impatience or irritation. "There is Perrini family, but they didn't approve of the pregnancy or her decision to keep me. They wouldn't have welcomed her back."

Perrini family. That she'd never known about, that he'd never mentioned. Family that had cut him out. Her heart beat hard with renewed curiosity and with silent empathy. "Have you met any of your family?" she persisted.

"No. Nor do I ever want to."

Kimberley turned in her seat, better to study the hard set of his profile. "You aren't curious about your grandparents and…are there uncles, aunts, cousins?"

"I called once, when Mum was dying. Her father didn't want to know her, he didn't want to know me. That's not family."

"Your grandfather," she murmured on an appalled breath. "Is he still alive?"

"I don't know. I don't care. The only relevance is how that little episode taught me to appreciate family that does care."

"Like the Blackstones?"

"Like Sonya. Like Tanya and her kids." His eyes were Antarctic cold, but beneath the frosty expression was more, the kind of emotion that told her this mattered. Very much. "Just so you're clear—I've never aspired to be a Blackstone. If I wanted that kind of a family, one that picked and discarded its members like Howard has done with his family, then I have Pappà Perrini in Turin."

The previous night she'd insisted on sleeping alone in her room, citing Perrini's words—which annoyed him to no end—about keeping their business and personal relationships as two separate entities. Tonight he showed her to her door and after a kiss that claimed complete possession of her mouth and her heart, she took his hand to lead him inside. Something snapped tight and intense in his expression.

"No," he said, low and rough-edged. "Not tonight. I am not a man to be pitied."

It's for the best, she told herself as his retreating footsteps echoed through the hollow corridor of the executive accommodation complex and found a matching resonance in her heart. If she called him back, if she made love to him now with her emotions so exposed, he would question her motives and any words of love that crept from her tongue.

Instead she stripped and showered and fought the impact of his rejection by chewing over all she'd learned, her heart analyzing the impact of his family's callous abandonment. He'd only been fifteen, damn it, and watching his mother—his only parent, the only family he knew—dying of cancer. No wonder he'd never mentioned his family. No wonder he'd reacted so heatedly when, in the dustup of their marriage, she'd accused him of wanting to become a Blackstone. No wonder he'd bonded with Sonya and retained a strong friendship with Tracy, both single mothers doing a wonderful job with family, just as his own mum had done.

She couldn't help wondering if his ambition—his near ferocious drive to succeed—stemmed from a need to prove himself to an old man in Turin who'd not thought his grandson worth knowing. And when she left her bed and wavered by the door, wanting to go to him, to hold him, to make love with the whole man she now recognised for all he'd overcome and all he could be, she heard his closing words and her hand dropped away from the doorknob.

Pity was not something Perrini's pride would ever accept,

and the next morning she sensed a barrier—a subtle coolness in his eyes, a focus on last-minute business he conducted alone—that prevented her broaching the subject until they were airborne on their return to Sydney late in the morning. And then she had to lean across the table between them and place her hand on the papers he was reading and weather the irritated slice of his frown.

"This won't take a minute," she assured him, lifting her chin and meeting the blue reserve in his eyes. "Thank you for bringing me out here. You were right—Janderra is the heart and soul of the business."

He inclined his head in acknowledgement. "Is that all?"

"I wanted to thank you, also, for sharing what you did of your past...although you were wrong to claim it irrelevant. It all matters. It all made you the man you are and you were right—that is not a man to be pitied." In his eyes she saw the look of rejection, and quickly she leaned forward to trap his hand beneath hers on the tabletop. "Tell me one thing before you pull away. This last week—when you kissed me in the boardroom, when you pulled me into your foyer last Saturday morning—was your desire driven by compassion or pity over Howard? Is that why you wanted me?"

"You know it wasn't."

"Then can you accept that I wanted you last night? That I want you now?"

Something shifted in his expression, his eyes flared with heat, and Kimberley's heart breathed a heavy sigh of relief.

"Now?" he asked softly, turning his hand beneath hers to capture her fingers and draw them to his lips. "On a business trip?"

"Now," she said, "on our lunch break."

* * *

By the time they arrived back in Sydney Kimberley knew she was ninety-nine percent back in love with him. She fell the final one percent during the board meeting held on the following day. It wasn't only how he introduced her, not as Howard's daughter but by acknowledging her standing in the industry and her creative vision, which had spawned Blackstone Jewellery ten years earlier. It wasn't just the standing ovation he led when the board formally accepted her as the new interim director. It wasn't even his decisive leadership of the meeting, or the overwhelming vote of confidence that led to his appointment as interim Chairman and CEO of the company.

No, the moment when she allowed herself to fall that final percent came in a singular second after the announcement of Howard's successor was made, when he sought her eyes as if her approval was all that mattered. And in that instant of connection and clarity, she saw the man he'd become and it didn't matter where he'd come from or what had brought him to this point.

In all his facets he was the perfect cut for her, and the knowledge thrilled her and soothed her and scared her in equal measures.

As Ric anticipated, the remains of the crash victims were recovered from the wreckage while he and Kim were returning from Janderra. The exhaustive identification process had commenced and despite the dark pall cast over proceedings by Howard's as-yet-unresolved fate, the meeting ended on an optimistic note. Rick had wanted to take Kim out for a celebratory dinner... after she'd packed her things and moved into his house.

To his chagrin she'd agreed to neither.

"Let's not rush into anything this time," she'd said. "And wearing my PR hat, I would suggest that any celebration of your appointment is done in private."

"That's not what I want to celebrate," he'd pointed out. "But since I can't toast your move into my home, how about we enjoy a quiet dinner from Roberto's?"

She'd agreed. They'd eaten. And since she now sat on his sofa, her feet curled up beneath her and a second glass of Dom Pérignon in her hand, Ric couldn't complain about the outcome.

"Do you think Ryan will stay on?" she asked.

Halfway to sitting down beside her, Ric paused. "Has he mentioned leaving?"

"No, nothing like that. But he can't be happy with your appointment."

"Which is interim," he reminded her. "If he doesn't think I'm the right choice, then he can lobby for change."

"Do you think? The other directors made it clear that they believe Howard handpicked you as his successor. It must have been tough for Ryan to hear that his own father preferred another man for the job he coveted."

"That's not why Howard or the directors chose me. Your brother's still young. I have a solid eighteen-year history with Blackstone's. I started in the mines—I've worked across the divisions, from marketing to retail to export. Today's vote was an issue of experience and seniority, not preference."

"But is that the way Ryan will see it?" she asked, her voice soft with empathy. "I know how he feels. I've been in that position."

"Howard chose me back then for the same reason, Kim."

"Seniority and experience. I know." Her shrug was casual, belying the whirl of emotion in her eyes. "But that didn't help soften the blow." With a shuddery sigh, she leaned her head against the back of the sofa to stare up at the ceiling. "I wonder what *he* thought of today's events. If he's sitting there with a smug look on his face because you're in charge and I'm back here as he always intended."

The pensive edge to her voice as she conjured up that spirit of their past loosened a great knot of emotion in Ric's gut. He watched her sitting there beside him, with the mahogany gleam of her hair and the smooth tan of her bare arms and the sweet curve of her hip... Hell, she was so damn beautiful it hurt.

"I'm pretty sure he would approve of us."

Slowly she turned her gaze on him. "Ironic, isn't it? In life he tore us apart, but his death has brought us back together."

"He won't come between us again," Ric promised. "Not Howard or Blackstone's."

For a long moment his resolute words hung in the night between them, a solid vow, a promise he would keep. Kim moistened her lips, her gaze shadowed as she dipped her head to take a sip of her champagne. "Is that all that was wrong between us back then?"

"We were young. What we had—" he didn't know how to describe it, what words would encapsulate that potent passion "—hit us quick, before we'd worked out what we wanted."

"*I* was young," she corrected in a rueful tone. "You always gave the impression that you knew exactly what you wanted."

"I knew I wanted you. The first time I saw you. I knew."

"Despite the hard time I gave you?"

"Despite Ryan's disapproval and the threat of career suicide." He waited a beat, expression serious before continuing. "You accused me of getting everything I wanted when I married you."

"And did you?"

"Yes." The shock of that admission registered in her eyes and when she would have looked away Ric leaned forward and captured her chin in his hand. "I got the advancement, the prestige, the chance to prove myself. And while I wasn't ever a substitute for your brother, I did get to feel like I was part of a family. Sonya has that knack."

A hint of disquiet shimmered in the depths of her eyes. "That mattered?"

"Family is everything. Yes, it mattered. It all mattered, until you were gone."

For a long moment she sat in silence, a faint tremor of emotion in her eyes and in the skin beneath his fingers. Then she murmured, "And now I'm back."

"Then let me know you are. Move in with me. Come out to dinner, have your photo taken on my arm. Let me know I'm not just an impulse or a distraction. Let me know, and let the world know that you're back and you're mine."

Let's not rush, Kimberley said in careful answer to that heart-stoppingly ardent declaration, but four hours, three glasses of Dom and two orgasms later she had agreed to move into Perrini's house. And to accompany him to a formal Sydney Festival event the following Tuesday night, not only as a representative of Blackstone's, but as a date.

And to start calling him by his given name.

Ric. Ric. Ric. She practiced in time with the tap of her heels as she hurried through the Pitt Street Mall en route from the designer floor of David Jones' city store to Martin Place. *Ric. Ric. Ric.*

The repetitive cadence triggered memories of the night

before, when he'd held her on the edge of release, their fingers joined high above her head while he stared into her eyes and insisted she call him Ric.

"Only when I come?" she'd asked.

"That'll do nicely for a start."

The mere memory coloured her skin as she shouldered through the revolving door of the Blackstone's store, her hands filled with shopping bags and the hangered gown she'd chosen for the reception. Only five minutes late. Which, given the way she'd been chasing her tail all morning, was something of a miracle.

She'd called Jessica Cotter yesterday to make the appointment, right after Perrini—*Ric*—had reassured her that attending the reception was a good idea.

"A Blackstone presence won't be expected," she'd argued. "We're in mourning."

"Not expected," he'd countered, "which makes it a sound promotional ploy. The rags are buzzing with Marise and your father. Let's give them something else to talk about."

Resigned to becoming society-column fodder, Kimberley decided to make the best of it. She would wear Blackstone jewellery and a designer gown to set it off. Hence her shopping expedition and her appointment with Jessica, who met her at the top of the stairs. Her curious eyes took in Kimberley's plastic-protected burden. "You brought the gown with you? Perfect."

"I've come straight from DJ's," Kim admitted. "Where I came perilously close to calling you and begging for your help in deciding."

"You should have," Jessica said with a warm smile. "I would have been happy to help."

"Oh, you did. When I was here last week, you described a gown—strapless, white or silver." While she spoke, Kimberley unzipped the bag to reveal her choice. "And here it is."

"The dress looks divine," Jessica said softly. "This reception you're going to…is it the one at Warralong House?"

"I'm not sure. It's for one of the highlight acts at the Sydney Festival—the dance company performing at the Opera House."

"That's the one."

There was something in the younger woman's voice—a note that sounded almost wistful to Kimberley's ears. "If you would like to go," she said with a smile, "you can have my ticket. I'm really not a fan of these affairs."

"I don't think my presence would be appreciated, even if this gorgeous dress fit me. Now, let's see what we can find for you. Are you looking for something subtle? Classic? Sophisticated?"

"Something that photographs well," Kim said, putting aside her curiosity about Jessica for a moment. "That is the main thing. And since I'm representing Blackstone's, it definitely has to be diamonds."

Eleven

Even though coloured stones—especially the rare Janderra pinks—were the Blackstone trademark, Jessica put her in white diamonds.

"Better for my colouring," she told Ric as he took his sweet time about fastening the fabulous multistrand necklace. "What do you think? Enough bling for a Blackstone?"

His fingers lingered on her throat, a deliciously warm contrast to the cool weight of the stones against her skin, but he didn't answer right away. Seated at the dresser applying a final brush of bronze to her cheekbones, Kimberley looked up and caught his gaze in the dresser mirror. Then he let his eyes do the talking with a long, lazy sweep over her near-backless gown, her bare arms and shoulders, the hint of cleavage above the silvery sheen of her fitted bodice.

"You don't need the bling, Kim." Leaning forward, he

covered the necklace with his hands. His thumbs blocked out the fat diamonds in her ears. "See?" he whispered at her ear. "You dazzle without them."

Wow. The impact of his inspection, his words, his breath against her skin, pooled low and hot in Kimberley's belly. She drew in a breath that wasn't quite steady, closed her compact and set it down on the top of the dresser. "Do you want to go to this party?"

"Not particularly."

His voice was as casual and deliberate as the drift of his fingertips to the sensitive skin beneath her earlobe.

Kimberley shivered deep inside. "We could stay home." She leaned back against his black dinner suit and felt the erotic imprint of his arousal in every female cell. "I've never made love in a quarter million dollars' worth of diamonds."

"We will rectify that," he promised, and his mouth replaced his hands, trailing a string of delicate kisses to her hairline. "After we've let the world know you're going home with me."

She pointed out the flaw in his logic while they drove to the glamorous Point Piper venue. It helped distract her from what she saw as an ordeal ahead. She'd never liked society soirees, and she had a feeling she would hate being studied and whispered about when she appeared on her ex-husband's arm.

But after the first half hour and the obligatory pose for a society snapper, she found herself enjoying the evening much more than anticipated. Part of that pleasure was due to the outdoor setting, in the terraced gardens of a historic harbourside mansion. Part was knowing she had the party's hottest date at her side, feeling his hand at her back, catching his rescue-me glance when he'd been shanghaied by yet another predatory female. She might have felt sorry for him if he wasn't inviting the interest, with his killer smile and smooth conversational skills.

But her biggest delight came from the knowledge she would be going home with him, and the expectancy that built with every touch and every captured glance. The pleasure bubbled away inside her, a secret smile couched in optimistic hope that this time around things might just work out.

They'd already started to wind their way back up the garden toward the house and the exits, taking their time, heightening the anticipation, when she saw her brother's familiar tall frame. She did a double take. "I didn't expect to see Ryan here. I wouldn't have thought this would be his thing," she murmured, although how would she know what Ryan's thing was? She knew nothing about his private life. She studied the statuesque blonde at his side. "Is that his date?"

"No, that's the wife of the one of the festival directors. I met her earlier."

"Is he dating anyone?" she asked after a moment.

"I have no idea. That's not information your brother would share with me," Ric replied dryly.

But Kimberley was recalling Jessica's odd reaction to tonight's party and the vibes Ryan had given off when she mentioned Jessica's name the day he showed her around the office complex. "You don't think he might have something going on with Jessica Cotter?"

"An employee? Hell, no. You know his opinion on that issue."

Ten years ago she'd known his disapproval of her and Ric's relationship, a distaste born from Howard's affairs with several secretaries. But that didn't stop her wondering and besides that curiosity, she'd wanted to catch up with him ever since last week's board meeting. To say what, she didn't quite know, but she didn't want that old enmity resurfacing. Her return was supposed to heal rifts, not drive a wedge in them.

"I'm going to say hello."

"Uh-uh." He hooked his arm around her back and pulled her snug against his side. The promise in his eyes and the heated spread of his fingers against her bare back smoked through Kimberley's senses but she made a valiant attempt to rally.

"I won't be a minute."

"You can say hello to your brother tomorrow. It's time to go home," he said, dipping in to melt her objections with a short but devastating kiss. "I have a hankering for diamonds."

It was just a line. As he loosened his bow tie and flipped the studs from his dinner shirt, he met Kimberley's eyes in the mirror of her dresser and told her he only hankered for her, unadorned. Drawing her to her feet with the sensual power of his words and his voice and his cobalt gaze, he carefully, deliberately, went about unadorning her.

First, he unzipped the platinum gown and let it fall in a pool at her feet. Next, the lacy slithers of underwear, the sky-high heels, every diamond pin in her hair, and last he removed each glittering piece of jewellery until she stood naked before the full-length mirror. Then he stripped her completely bare by looking into her eyes and telling her that this was how he wanted her—just her, Kim, without a glimmer of Blackstone's between them.

When he vowed to kiss every inch of bared skin, she felt a momentary ripple of disquiet but he chased that away with the moist touch of his lips at the base of her spine. When he turned her in his hands, one kiss following the next over her flanks and hips and belly, he noticed the scar in her belly button for the first time. Although she tensed momentarily, the velvety brush of his thumb and then the moist heat of his kiss against the tiny mark released the last vestige of self-preservation.

"Keyhole surgery," she explained on a whisper of breath because his mouth shifted lower. "Women's stuff…it's okay."

His hand stilled on her belly, enveloping her emptiness with heat and a reverent pressure, and in that moment it was okay for the first time in a very long while.

"You've stopped." She stretched, a sinuous movement designed to distract and provoke. "If you do manage to kiss every inch, then I promise to reciprocate."

Distracted and provoked, he fulfilled his promise and so did she, and the memory of that amazing connection—when he was inside her, reminding her of what mattered and what didn't—still steamed through her senses three days later.

"You left suddenly the other night."

Ryan's voice cut into her sensual memory and Kimberley turned, letting the elevator she'd been about to board go without her. The smile that was never far from her lips these past days bloomed to full effect as she greeted her brother. Not smiling, but that was Ryan, and despite his unwelcoming expression she was glad they'd finally caught up. "We were on our way home when we saw you. Did you enjoy the reception?"

"No. Going up?" He indicated the vacant lift with a nod, then followed her inside. "I didn't expect to see you there."

"Part of the strategy," she said, "to demonstrate that Blackstone's is hail and hearty and moving forward. We want to show we're not stalled by grief or backpedaling due to the negative press."

"And moving in with Perrini…is that a strategy for the good of the company?"

Quiet words, but their implication froze Kimberley's smile. "No. That would be a strategy for the good of me."

"I hope so, Kim."

"Look," she said tightly, reading a wealth of meaning behind those words. "I understand your grievance with Ric and I know you're feeling raw at the moment. Perhaps this isn't the best time for this conversation."

"The best time would have been before you got involved with him again. I shouldn't have let him assume control of this deal."

The lift glided to a smooth halt at her floor, but Kimberley's stomach kept on moving. She hit the button to hold the doors shut and looked into her brother's eyes. Not hard, cold, hostile, as she'd expected, but churning with something that looked like self-recrimination. "What do you mean?"

"We all wanted you back here, Kim—none of us liked you working for Hammond—but Perrini always held him accountable for busting up your marriage. That gave him extra motivation." He expelled a harsh breath, and the sound shivered like a chill of precognition all the way to the marrow of Kimberley's bones. "That, and his need to have a Blackstone at his side at that board meeting."

No. *No.* She shook her head, rejecting the awful clawing sense of déjà vu. "He didn't have me at his side. My return to Blackstone's has nothing to do with my personal relationship with Ric." But the words sounded hollow, booming with the memory of that day when he'd introduced her, when he'd sung her praises, when he'd sought her gaze across the boardroom table.

Had everyone noticed that connection? Was she such a blind fool?

"Your return was the talk of the office," Ryan confirmed. "Especially after you took off to the outback."

Just the two of them. In the company jet. Of course there would have been talk, talk that was only confirmed by the society columns' pictures of them together—a reunited couple—in this week's papers.

But that didn't mean Ryan was right, or that Perrini had used her to further his own ambitions. "He would have won that vote," she told Ryan, "with or without my support."

"You're wrong. He needed you as leverage in that board-room. He said he'd do whatever it took to get you back, and it seems that you let him."

Her brother's words struck like a slap, bringing her head up and washing the blood from her heart. "Then perhaps you should have warned me of this earlier."

"I did."

That day in the boardroom, when she'd said she was a big girl, that she wouldn't make the same mistake again.

She sucked in a breath, struggling to hold herself together and managing to do so by repeating those same words in her mind. She would not make the same mistake again. She would not assume too much. She would find out the whole story, from Perrini, before making any rash judgements.

Ric wasn't in his office and his PA knew nothing of his whereabouts other than he was not due back until midday. Kimberley knew he had a lunch meeting with several depart-ment heads, he'd told her that morning, after he'd returned from an early swim and they'd talked about their plans for the day over breakfast on the deck.

At the time she'd been smiling, thinking *I could get used to this start to every day, this routine, this simple bond of sharing. This man who filled my heart.*

Right now that same heart was knotted and tense over Ryan's disclosure. Quite likely she was overreacting or Ryan had misinterpreted. He saw Ric as his adversary and had always been a little too keen to point out the negative aspects of his ambition. That reasoning didn't ease her anxiety.

Too restless to settle, too tied in knots to concentrate, she paced to her window. The lunch meeting would keep him tied up for most of the afternoon and if she left this discussion until after work she feared it would grow and fester and explode in a heated volley of accusations. She didn't want that. She wanted a calm, controlled conversation.

Tomorrow was her birthday. Ric was taking her to a private retreat in the mountains, where the staff and he would pander to her every need. If she didn't get this sorted now, she feared the fallout might cast a shadow over their plans.

She tapped her phone against the palm of her hand for a moment before turning it over, decision made. With a finger that quavered only slightly, she dialled the number of his mobile phone.

Ric's phone buzzed as he was leaving the car dealership in the newly purchased Porsche. He could have taken the call handsfree but when he saw Kim's name on the caller ID he chose to pick up. Her voice he preferred in his ear, private and intimate, a gift to his hormones.

He grinned as he steered the sports car over to the kerb with a gentle caress of the wheel. She handled superbly—smooth, responsive, amenable, with a fiery strength beneath the sleek, sophisticated exterior. Pretty much like the woman he'd bought it for, as part of the birthday package. He aimed to make her very, very happy and very, very appreciative.

He flipped open the phone. "Any chance you can take a quick break?"

"I…yes." She sounded slightly taken back, the frown obvious in her voice. "I need to talk to you. That's why I called."

"Sounds ominous," he said lightly. The beat of silence afterward sounded even more so. His grin faded. His hormones subsided. He switched gears instantly, to the implications of her need to talk. "Meet me out the front in fifteen minutes. Look for the silver Porsche."

She hesitated beside the kerb, a frown drawing her brows tight. *Jump in,* he'd said, but by her expression he might as well have said *jump into the shark tank.*

She drew a breath, snapped her gaze to his. "Can we go somewhere private, somewhere we can just…talk?"

Everything about her, from her choice of words to her troubled eyes to her fingers tapping the frame of the opened door—to the fact that she hadn't seemed to notice he was driving a strange car—stirred a warning in Ric's gut. This wasn't business. This was about them. "If you get in before I score a ticket for loitering in a no-stopping zone, then I'll find somewhere private. We'll talk."

That got her moving. Although once she'd slid into the low seat and buckled up, she sat tense and motionless while he negotiated the midmorning traffic.

"You want to give me a hint?" he asked, stopped at a red.

For a second he wondered if she would answer. If she'd even heard. But slowly she turned her head to look at him. "I ran into Ryan this morning."

The alarm in his gut shrilled. He should have guessed this would be a Blackstone doing, that Ryan wouldn't take his defeat last week lying down. The light changed and he scooted ahead of the traffic, picking a route to a quiet residential area close to the city centre.

"And he's told you something to sour your perception of me?" he guessed. His voice sounded mild, matter-of-fact, his question measured—a surprise when his blood rankled with a mix of anger and disappointment. Forget mild. He cut her a sharp look. "Why the hell would you even listen to him?"

"I'm not taking his word, Ric. I want to hear your side of the story."

She used the word *story*. A piece of fiction. Good choice of word, he thought. He turned down a dead-end street and found a park outside a neat row of terraces. He switched off the engine and turned in his seat. "Then you'd better spell out the charge I'm answering to."

She nodded, her gaze not quite steady on his. He could tell she was collecting herself, choosing her words carefully, and the idea of that self-censorship fired his irritation like an accelerant.

"No pussyfooting," he said shortly. "Just say what you have to say, Kim."

Her chin came up. "Did you say you would do 'whatever it takes' to get me back to Blackstone's?"

"Yes," he said without hesitation. "That's exactly what I said."

She blinked, the shock of disillusionment bright in her eyes. Before she could respond Ric leaned closer and captured those wounded eyes with the resolute strength of his.

"I said it and I meant it, Kim. When I went to New Zealand, I had a simple agenda. Getting to you before the media, doing whatever I could to soften the blow of the news about your father and bringing you home to your family. But as soon as I climbed in that car with you and you turned those eyes and that tongue of yours on me, I knew I wanted more.

"Make no mistake, Kim," he said, low and serious, "I was always going to do whatever I could to get you back."

"Even offer me a directorship in the company?"

"That had nothing to do with my personal agenda. I told you the night you came to dinner. Business and personal, two separate entities."

Nearby a small dog started to yap, distracting her attention. He could tell she remained ambivalent, chewing over his words and searching out the argument points.

"I thought we covered all of this that night," he continued brusquely "If there's anything else I didn't make crystal clear, or if your brother passed on any other information for the purpose of creating trouble, he—"

"That wasn't his purpose. His concern over your motives is genuine. And so is mine."

"You choose to believe him over me?"

"I want to understand, that's all. Everything that led to your offer and why you targeted me. No one has convinced me why I was so indispensable. Why me and not Uncle William? He has the necessary Blackstone name, plus he's spent a lifetime in the mining industry. He invested start-up capital in the company and yet his name didn't come up once at the meeting last week as a prospective director. Why not? Did he turn the offer down? Or was it Howard's daughter you needed on your side at last week's meeting?"

Ric heard the last sentence loudest. It hung between them, heavily shaded with the true nature of her distrust. "William had a falling-out with Howard last year over selling his stake in the company. He would have been our last choice."

"Because he sold his shares?"

"Because he sold to Matt Hammond."

That bald pronouncement shocked a disbelieving laugh from her mouth. She started to say something, then shut her mouth and shook her head before trying again a second later. "Matt isn't a market player. And he despises Blackstone's. William owned a substantial holding. Why would Matt outlay such a significant sum on opposition stock?"

"For the joy of sending Howard apoplectic."

This time she didn't laugh in either shock or incredulity. She looked away, staring blindly out the side window. When she finally turned her eyes back on him they shimmered with more than disbelief. Wounded disillusionment dimmed their dark beauty, but not the spark of her voice or the pride that held her chin high. "So this all comes back to vengeance. Matt acquired Blackstone shares and you couldn't risk me siding with him, not if I'm to inherit a sizeable parcel of shares."

"That's only the business equation."

"Wasn't there an element of payback in the personal, too?" she asked, bitterness sharpening her tone. "Because Matt took your new plaything?"

"No. I always wanted you. For me. For what we are together. Hasn't this last week meant anything to you? Hasn't it shown you what I want with you? I don't know what else I can say to convince you."

"Perhaps you can't. Perhaps the mistrust and the doubts have been eating away at me too long. Perhaps the scars are too deep. Perhaps what you told me last week in Janderra explained too well why you have to keep climbing that ladder, doing whatever it takes, to prove yourself better than the Blackstones or the Perrinis back in Italy. To show your mother did the right thing and that you're the equal of everyone in this world. Perhaps I'll never be able to trust that you want me—just *me*—not the Blackstone name and all the power and privilege that comes with it."

The resonance of her passionate declaration engulfed them in the long, weighty aftermath. It was reminiscent of another time, another place, another fight, one Ric had made a prideful mess of, but this time he wasn't letting go as easily. He was all out of words but he had one remaining weapon, and he aimed to wield its power ruthlessly.

With a decisive efficiency of movement, he turned, buckled and started the engine. "Buckle up," he said shortly. "We're going for a drive."

"Take me back to the office," she said. And when he ignored her, joining the link road to the Harbour Bridge, she sat up straighter. Indignation coloured her cheeks and desperation edged her words. "You can't make me go with you. Let me out."

"You're coming with me. You're listening to me. Then you can make up your mind."

"And if I won't listen?"

He cut her a sideways look of lethal intent. "If you can look me in the eye and say you don't love me and that I don't have a chance to prove myself worthy of you and your Blackstone name, I will let you out right now, here or wherever you demand."

Eyes blazing, she stared him down, but when she opened her mouth to speak, the words didn't come. The truth glimmered in her eyes, rare and precious as green diamond, for one unguarded second before she looked away. And Ric's heart started beating again.

After he forced that silent admission, Kimberley was too wrapped up in miserable anguish to care where he was taking her. It didn't matter. He could talk about wanting her until he was blue in the face and she would listen and it would make no difference. Wanting her had never been in dispute. Respecting her, trusting her, seeing her as more than a Blackstone and a boardroom asset to be won back from the enemy—those were the things she needed and which she feared she could never earn from Ric Perrini. He'd played her again, using her to get the result he needed for his future at Blackstone's, and her misery was compounded knowing how swiftly and easily she'd fallen into his plans.

And now he knew that she loved him.

Could this hurt any more? Was there anything left to bring her right to her knees?

Dimly she heard the rumble of his voice as he spoke on the phone, and with a sharp mental slap, she forced her mind back into focus. She was pitiful, wallowing in the pit of despair she'd dug for herself while he'd moved on, calling his PA and cancelling the lunch meeting.

"Do you need to clear your schedule at the office?" he asked.

Ah, yes, her handcrafted position at Blackstone's. A paste

job. And not even a good one, she realised, now that she saw it with the clarity of hindsight. Yet she'd been seduced by the dazzle of Perrini's description, by the picture he'd painted... the one she'd wanted to see. It was her own contemptible fault, because she'd wanted it to be the real deal. She'd wanted that youthful dream, engraved into her heart the first time her father took her into the Blackstone's workrooms to see the magical transformation of rough diamond to polished gemstone.

"If you do, Vina can make the calls," Perrini continued.

Kimberley shook her head. She didn't need his PA. There wasn't much to cancel. "I'll call Holly. I have an appointment late this afternoon. Do I need to cancel or will we be back by then?"

"Cancel it."

She did, not because of that terse demand but because the appointment was to meet Briana Davenport for the first time at the Da Vinci's elegant Louvre Bar. Whatever the outcome of this mysterious drive, Kimberley knew she would be in no mood for polite small talk over drinks with Marise Hammond's supermodel sister.

"What is this about?" she asked after flipping her phone closed. While she'd been wallowing they'd crossed the bridge and turned east through the affluent middle harbour suburbs, heading toward the northern beaches.

"I'll tell you when we get there."

Twelve

When was fifteen minutes later.

Where was a cul-de-sac high on a bluff overlooking the Manly peninsula.

He killed the sports car's engine, and before Kimberley had a chance to take in more than a first impression of peace and space and elevation he'd strode around and opened her door.

"Come on," he said, leaning down to unbuckle her seat belt. "I have something to show you."

For a split second his eyes met hers, and if she didn't know better she would have read the shadows in their depths as nervousness. Then he straightened with his usual smooth efficiency and she huffed out a breath. Not nerves, just determination to turn her around with whatever smoke-and-mirrors show he had planned.

Gathering her cynicism around her like a cloak, she stepped

from the car's cool interior into the late morning heat. His hand at her elbow steered her from the paved footpath toward a thickly grassed block that rose from street level to meet the brilliant blue of a cloudless sky. Kimberley's heart fluttered into an edgy beat that rippled like goose bumps over her skin despite the summer sun. Either nerves or the steep slope they climbed turned her knees wonky, but he steadied her with a grip on her arm.

"You should have told me we were hiking. I would have chosen more appropriate foot—" Her breath caught on a gasp as they crested the rise and she caught sight of the view. Not just harbour, not just beaches, but bushland and treetops. "Who owns this land?" She turned on him, regathering her resolve to deflect whatever he threw at her. "Why have you brought me here?"

"It's mine." A muscle jumped in his cheek. "I bought it nine years ago, after my wife left me."

After she'd left…Kimberley shook her head, not comprehending. "Why?"

"When I first joined Blackstone's and when you met me, my ambition was all about proving myself, just as you said."

"Proving yourself to whom?"

"The boss at BJ Resources who tossed my application aside because I didn't attend a GPS school. Every pizza shop and liquor store I ran deliveries for. The family who excommunicated my mother when she disgraced the Perrini name with her pregnancy." He turned away suddenly. Hands on hips, he stood surveying the view for a long, breathless moment. Then he exhaled and turned back to face her. "The Blackstone directors. Howard. You."

Every one of those telling revelations punched a huge chip

out of Kimberley's resolve. *This* was the Perrini he'd never exposed, the real man beneath the polished facade. Although a part of her ached to pick apart each of those clues, another recognised that the details didn't matter. Concisely and eloquently he had told the complete story.

"And this?" she asked, gesturing at the land around them. "What is this to prove?"

"When I came to New Zealand to bring you home, I had the deeds to this block of land in my pocket. Proof that I wanted a future together, that I was looking forward to the time when we'd build a home here. I chose this land with that future—*our* future—in mind. I could see us bringing up our children here. There's a school right down there." He pointed off to their right, and Kimberley closed her eyes, her heart pounding so painfully hard she felt it in every cell of her body. "And over there is the beach where I'll teach them to swim and surf.

"I bought this block as a proof of my commitment to our future and the only thing that's changed is that the future is now. I want everything I see here—the home, the kids, the family—and I want them with you."

She squeezed her eyes shut in a vain attempt to block out the picture he painted, but she couldn't block out his low, gruff-voiced intensity. She couldn't block out the realisation that *this* was his dream—not success in the business world or chairmanship of the board or her return to his life and his bed, but this family that he'd never had. It seemed so simple, so attainable, and yet it was the very thing she could not give him. That knowledge drove a shard of pain right through her heart, as she lifted her chin to face him.

To tell him.

"I'm not the woman in that picture, Ric."

His head came up, jaw rigid with determination. "Why not? Is it this place?"

"No. This block is— God, you know what it is!" He might as well have reached right into her heart and plucked it out. "I can't give you everything you see here. I am not your future, Ric. I *can't* be. I can't have those children."

Kimberley thought she'd reached rock bottom when forced to acknowledge her love, but that was before Perrini revealed the future she would share with him in a heartbeat if she thought that future could be happy. That was before she told him that any conception would be a miracle pregnancy and he couldn't disguise the shock of raw regret that crossed his features.

Then she struck rock bottom.

Recovering rapidly he demanded details of her surgeries, first for endometriosis and then to remove the resultant adhesions, and she recited facts and statistics. True to form he steamrolled over medical opinion, stating they would see fertility experts, investigate IVF, whatever it took.

Kimberley was starting to despise that phrase. "And if I don't want to have babies?" she asked, her heart breaking with the lie. "Have you considered that I might not share your vision of happy families? That my dream may be something else entirely?"

His head came up, and his gaze narrowed. "Because of your mother's postnatal depression? Are you afraid of history repeating itself?"

"No," she said softly, unable to latch on to that ready-made excuse. "My mother lost a baby. She must have suffered incredible guilt."

"Then what?" When she would have turned away, he

closed in on her, taking her stiff shoulders in his hands, forcing her to face him. "The truth, Kim."

"I can't give you what you want, Perrini. Can't you accept that?"

His grip and his features tightened with a combination of frustration and determination. "Our future isn't dependent on you having my babies," he asserted. "You can't chase me away that easily."

Chin high, she gathered together the tattered shreds of her resolve and faced him down. "I have fulfilled my end of the deal. I came here. I listened. And I've made up my mind. Now, please take me home…to Miramare."

Ric took her to the Vaucluse mansion, as she demanded. When he parked the car and handed her the keys, she gave him a bewildered look. After the tense silence on the drive back from Manly when she'd shut down his every attempt to discuss her stance, he figured any look she gave him, other than total acquiescence, would have set his teeth on edge.

Unfortunately doe-eyed bewilderment didn't.

"The car's yours," he said roughly, folding her stiff fingers around the keys. "Happy birthday."

She puffed out a breath. "I…I don't know what to say. I can't—"

"'Thank you, Ric,' would do for a start," he said over the top of her protest.

There was only so much rejection a man could hear in one day and Ric had reached his limit. If he hadn't just handed her the keys to the only ready transportation, he would have turned and walked away. Not for good—he was far from done with Kimberley Blackstone—but for now.

Turning on his heel he took the steps to the mansion two at a time, ignoring the protests that followed in his wake, and greeted Marcie with a strained smile as she opened the door. "Is Sonya in?"

"She's out the front, in the garden." The housekeeper shot a worried look out the front door. "Is Miss Kimberley all right?"

"She'll be in shortly. She's just deciding what to do with her new car."

As he strode inside he took his phone from his pocket and switched it on, frowning at the list of missed calls. Ryan, more than once. He checked the text messages and stopped in his tracks.

Halfway back across the foyer he met Kim coming in. Her phone was in her hand and her eyes sought his, wide with the unasked question. He nodded. *Yes, he'd got the same message.* Although he saw the shield come up in her eyes, he kept on walking and took her resistant body into his arms.

They'd identified Howard's remains. The waiting was over.

He helped her through the formalities with the coroner's counsellor, stayed for the family meeting to discuss funeral arrangements, and for the dinner Sonya insisted they eat. Afterward Kim suggested he looked tired. He ignored the thinly veiled hint. He wasn't going anywhere.

"Kim's right," Sonya said, reaching across to place her hand over his. "You do look worn-out. Why don't you go home? It was lovely having your company for dinner, but you don't have to stay and babysit me. In fact, I'll be going upstairs myself soon. So, please, both of you, go home."

"I'm staying here tonight," Kim said after a beat of awkward silence. Then, for the first time since they'd received the news six hours earlier, she met his eyes. "You can take the Porsche. Please."

"The Porsche?" Sonya asked, looking between them with curiosity. "Do you have a new car?"

"An early birthday present." His eyes locked on Kim's, daring her to disagree. "Thank you for the offer of its use, but I don't need a car. If you're staying, then so am I."

Her eyes flared, her lips thinned, but in front of Sonya she said nothing. Several minutes later, while he answered Sonya's question about why he'd chosen that particular car, she quietly excused herself. Suspecting she would lock her bedroom door, he didn't allow her too much start and caught up on the first-floor landing.

"I will see you in the morning," she said stiffly, turning to her door as if she expected him to continue upstairs to the room he normally used.

"No." He closed the space in six easy strides. "You'll see me now."

"Don't do this," she whispered. "I can't handle this fight, not tonight."

The fragile edge to her request cut him to the quick. He lifted a hand and touched his knuckles to her cheek, to the dark fall of her hair, and then he bent and kissed her forehead. "I'm not here to fight, baby, I promise you that."

Too drained by the day's emotional seesaw to resist, Kimberley let him into her bedroom. The idea that he might use sex as a weapon to wear down her defences should have stirred her to anger, instead it only deepened the ache in the middle of her chest.

She showered quickly and when she unlocked the bath-room door to an empty room, she breathed a sigh of relief. He stood outside the French doors on her small balcony, out of reach of the one bedside lamp, and when she slipped into bed she turned that off, too.

Four nights she'd spent at his Bondi home, and already she felt the strangeness of lying alone in bed. In the dark her heart-beat sounded too thick, too fast, too needy. She heard him come inside, heard the rustle of clothes as he undressed, and she held her breath. But he didn't come straight to bed. He showered, too, with the door open and the light slicing across the bedroom while the air filled with the sound of running water and her body softened with images of his naked body and her heart ached with the pictures he'd painted on an impossible future.

Then the water shut down, the bathroom light went out. Tension held her limbs rigid, her fingers curled into her pil-low, while she waited for the dip in the mattress, the flutter of the sheet, the heat of his body behind hers, his arm closing over her and drawing her back into the spoon of his body.

"Relax," he murmured near her ear and she shivered at the touch of his hair still wet from the shower. "I'm just going to hold you."

She closed her eyes, willed her body to relax. He didn't just hold her. He held her and he talked to her, random memories of her father that were in turn funny and infuriating, irreverent and respectful. When the tears finally came he held her more tightly and soothed the tremors with long, calming strokes of his hands.

Afterward she tried to turn away, but he wouldn't let her. Patiently he broke down her defences and made love to her with heartwrenching tenderness, filling the hollowness with his healing heat, and opening her heart to a deeper, stronger ache. This was the man she wanted, the only man she had ever loved, and she could not give him what he most wanted.

Much later, when his body felt slumberously heavy against hers, she hugged his arms tight to her chest and whispered into the dark, "I can't give you what you want."

And she felt the press of his lips to her neck, the stir of his breath as he spoke. "Let me be the judge of that."

The following days swept by in a blur of activity, with ongoing funeral arrangements and the preparation of press statements and the continual stream of condolence calls. Kimberley smiled graciously through each and every one until her cheeks ached with the effort. Through it all Ric remained at her side, a source of solid support and extra despair.

"What am I going to do with you?" she whispered on Monday night, after he'd stormed her defences again with his body and his sweetly destructive tongue.

"You could give up this intransigence," he replied sleepily. "You will in the end. You know it, I know it. I'm not going away."

Perhaps he was right. Perhaps she was being falsely stubborn, obstructing what was meant to be. But there was something holding her back, a complex combination of the babymaking issue and her lingering mistrust of his motives in wanting her back.

"I need a sign," she muttered as she traipsed along Pitt Street on Tuesday morning. She'd been on her way to the jewellery store when Garth called and asked if she could meet him at his office. Another detail to sort out for the funeral, no doubt. She'd turned back and had almost reached the Blackstone building when she caught sight of Ric crossing the street, his stride long and purposeful, his expression creased in concentration. Her heart did a little bump, just from the unexpected sighting. Ridiculous really, when she'd seen the man step naked from her bed that morning.

Perhaps this was the sign she'd asked for. As infinitely simple as that *I-see-you* bump of her heart. Her heartbeat accelerated with the thought, wanting with a painful kick of intensity to believe that it could be this simple.

As straightforward as him crossing the street on this block at this precise moment.

She stopped, a smile starting to curve her lips as she prepared for the moment when he stepped onto the sidewalk and saw her. Perhaps she should walk right up and kiss him—not a quick hello peck but a passionate embrace right here in the middle of Tuesday morning. Her smile kicked up, contemplating his surprise, but then a woman pushing a stroller brushed past her, blocking Ric from view momentarily.

When she saw him again he was picking up something from the footpath—a tiny, pink shoe—and handing it to the young mother. The woman's harried expression turned to a smile when he hunkered down to put it back on the toddler's foot. Then he straightened and the expression on his face— a concentrated dose of purest longing—trampled Kimberley's heart to the street.

The sign she'd asked for was simple after all. As simple as a baby's dropped shoe.

Ric saw her ahead of him hurrying into the Blackstone's lobby, but when he called her name she kept on moving. He increased the length of his stride, concentrating his effort on intercepting her at the elevators. He didn't know how much detail Garth had given her, if any, and before she stepped into that office she deserved some warning.

As he passed through the security scanner he called her name again, but her sage-green dress and the swing of her dark ponytail disappeared into a lift. With a last Herculean dash he managed to get his hand in the gap between the rapidly closing doors, reversing their direction at the last second. As he stepped into the car, she sucked in a breath that flared her nostrils and widened her big green eyes.

He swore softly. "Garth's told you already."

"I'm on my way up to this office now, so, no. What is this about, Ric?"

"Your father's will," he said shortly. "There's been a new development."

"New development?" she echoed.

"A lawyer from Ian Van Dyke's firm called Garth this morning."

"The lawyer who was on the plane."

Ric nodded. "That's right. An estate lawyer who's been doing work for your father for some time now. Apparently a new will was drafted and signed that day, before they got on the plane."

"And they've just found it?" She choked out a laugh. "Did it fall behind a filing cabinet?"

"I don't know what happened. I imagine this meeting will shed some light on why this document took so long to come to light, and its contents."

"I don't think the second part is too much of a mystery, do you? He told me he was writing me out."

"Don't jump to conclusions, Kim. This could be anything from a complete shake-up to a few cosmetic changes. I think the second is more likely, given the thing was signed and witnessed in an airport lounge."

"The documents that delayed the flight," she said softly.

The lift stopped at the top floor. The doors glided open, but he could see by the pallor of Kim's face and her white-knuckled grip on the charm pendant around her neck that she wasn't ready for this meeting. "Ryan's not here yet," he said, turning her toward the boardroom. "Come and sit down for a minute."

A minute probably wasn't going to do it, Kimberley thought, as she sank into a chair in the director's lounge. Ric had gone to let Garth know she'd arrived and where to find them when Ryan showed up. Whether it was a minute or ten, she appreciated the chance to collect herself.

She knew in her heart what this lawyer would tell them, but it wasn't the threat of imminent disinheritance that had knocked the wind from her lungs. It was the sum of all that had happened this month, and the realisation of all she'd changed and all she stood to lose. She'd left the job she loved at House of Hammond, thinking she had a personal stake in the future of Blackstone's. In the process she'd lost the respect and friendship of her cousin Matt. She might never see her godson grow up.

And she'd learned what had forged Perrini into the man he was today, a man with a mark to make on the world and a need for family, a man she loved for all he'd become and all he could be. A man she didn't believe she could ever make truly happy.

The door opened and he came back into the room, his eyes instantly finding hers. Whatever he saw in her face meshed his brows into a tight frown. He pulled a chair over in front of hers and sat, close enough that their knees bumped when he leaned forward to take her hands in his. He held them tightly for a moment until the trembling stopped.

"If I'm not a stakeholder in Blackstone's," she said finally, picking the one thing she could focus on without falling apart, "this whole month has been for nothing."

He studied her silently for a second. "Let's assume that this new will is what you suspect. That doesn't have to change your position or your directorship at Blackstone's."

She huffed out a breath. "How can I stay on knowing my father didn't want me to have any part of the company?"

"Do you want to stay?"

"It isn't that simple."

"It can be," he said, gripping her hands more firmly and shaking them with a quiet insistence. "If you would just accept that things don't always have to be difficult."

"Things, such as?"

"Let's start with this will. *If* your father has disinherited you, it's because you had a blow-up row. He hated that you wouldn't play by his rules in his sandbox. He hated who you chose to play with instead. That doesn't mean he didn't love you or that he wouldn't be damned pleased to see you back here."

"It would seem I have a problem recognising love."

"It would seem," he said dryly, but his expression tightened with his trademark strength of purpose. "I gave everything I thought I could offer the other day, but maybe I should have stuck to the simple, and the simple truth is this—I don't care if it's Manly or Bondi or Janderra or the moon, I just want to make a home with you, a life with you."

"And if I don't believe it's that simple? If I believe it's a family you yearn for?" Her voice grew thick, choked with emotion that swelled in her chest and squeezed her heart. "I saw your shock when I told you I couldn't have babies."

"Hell, yes, I was shocked. You were telling me about surgery, about your inability to conceive, about big things in your life and your body that you'd never mentioned before. Of course I was shocked and concerned—for *you,* not for me."

She shook her head slowly, not wanting to reject the sincerity of that message, but not ready to accept. "I *saw* you out in the street before, when you picked up the little girl's shoe. I saw your face when you held little Ivy, when you bowled a cricket ball to Cam. You say you just want a home and a life, but I *saw* the look on your face. I can't give you that, Ric, and that's about me, not you. I want to be able to give you happiness. Maybe that's what love is. It tears me in two because I can't give you what you want."

"Kids? A family? Yes, I want, I'm not going to lie about that, but there are other means, other methods, and if that doesn't work out we foster or we adopt from overseas or we do whatever it takes, because you're the only woman I've ever wanted as my wife and the mother of my children. No one else can give me what you do."

"Difficulties?" she asked on a hoarse exhalation, not quite a laugh, not quite a cry. "All those pain-in-the-backside qualities you mentioned I'd inherited? I guess no estate lawyer can take those from me!"

A spark that looked something like triumph and something like love kindled the sapphire depths of his eyes. "Wouldn't want to try," he murmured, and his clasp on her hands changed tenor, softening, deepening, along with his voice and the thickening thud of her heartbeat. She so wanted to believe him, to take that final leap of trust. "I went ten years without you making my life more difficult and more of a delight. I don't want that again. Ever."

"How do you do that? How can you make this sound so easy?"

"It's as simple as trusting our love and deciding you want to marry me again, for the right reasons this time."

"The right reasons?"

Lifting their joined hands, he tapped her knuckles to his heart. "I love you, Kim. It doesn't matter what Howard's will does or doesn't say, whether you choose to stay at Blackstone's or not. Nothing will change the simple truth of my love. Your choice—do you want to marry me, love me, give me everything I could ever want?"

The lingering spectre of doubt shadowed her face and her eyes as she started to shake her head. He stopped her with the most effective move of all, leaning in to take her lips in a kiss more eloquent than any words.

"You, babe," he said against her mouth. "You're all I want, all I need, all I cherish."

His next kiss started gentle, and was everything his words promised. Honest, direct and everything she could ever want in a kiss and in her man. Dizzy with the heady promise of a simple future, she leaned nearer and closed her eyes and he took the invitation to deepen the contact, to taste her capitulation on her lips and her tongue.

She could have gone on kissing him forever but a knock at the door interrupted and brought them crashing back to the present. Kimberley didn't mind. She smiled into his eyes and said, "Yes, I will marry you, for the right reason. The simplest reason. I love you, Ric Perrini."

He kissed her again to celebrate that moment and that admission, then he pulled her to her feet. "Are you ready for this?"

Kimberley nodded, the smile in her heart spreading to her lips. "Let's go and see if you've made a very poor choice of bride."

"I haven't," he said with absolute conviction. His hand tightened on hers, linking their fingers, sealing their bond of love. "That's the simplest truth of all."

* * * * *

PRIDE & A
PREGNANCY SECRET

TESSA RADLEY

Tessa Radley loves traveling, reading and watching the world around her. As a teen Tessa wanted to be an intrepid foreign correspondent. But after completing a bachelor of arts and marrying her sweetheart, she became fascinated with law and ended up studying further and becoming an attorney in a city practice. A six-month break traveling through Australia with her family re-awoke the yen to write. And life as a writer suits her perfectly; traveling and reading count as research and as for analyzing the world... well, she can think 'what if' all day long. When she's not reading, traveling or thinking about writing, she's spending time with her husband, her two sons—or her zany and wonderful friends. You can contact Tessa through her website, www. tessaradley.com.

With heartfelt thanks to Melissa Jeglinski
for her enthusiastic support for the
DIAMONDS DOWN UNDER continuity.
Thanks also to the five authors who created this
series with me—and a special thanks to
Bronwyn Jameson for generously sharing her
knowledge and experience.

One

"It's time to wake, sleeping beauty." The voice was deep, dark and achingly familiar.

Jessica Cotter's eyelashes fluttered in response. A masculine hand cupped her shoulder and stroked her skin. Her lover's touch. Warm and secure under the down duvet, Jessica gave a small moan of contentment and snuggled deeper under the bedclothes.

"Wake up, Jess."

Even through the mist of sleep she sensed him coming closer, bending over her. Instead of kissing her, he pulled the covers back. Screwing her eyes tightly shut to resist the onset of the day, Jessica curled into a ball and murmured a protest.

Then she caught his scent. One hundred percent pure male. Turn-on sexy. A hint of the heat they'd shared in the dark of the night still clung to the air. The protest became a soft moan. She shifted against the sleek satin sheet, stretched a little. Her body arching toward him, her eyes still closed, she waited for his touch.

His fingers tightened on her flesh. This time he gave her shoulder a little shake.

"Get up, Jessica!"

She opened her eyes. It took a moment to get her bearings.

Ryan Blackstone's penthouse.

The morning of his father's funeral.

Howard Blackstone's funeral. Little wonder Ryan wasn't in the mood for—

"Wipe that. You don't need to get up yet." He interrupted her thoughts. "I'll shower first. I need to get moving. Take your time."

Jessica sat up, wide awake now, and reached for the covers intent on hiding her suddenly inappropriate nakedness. She need not have worried. Ryan was already turning away.

She collapsed back against the pile of pillows and felt a hollow heaviness filling the pit of her stomach. The sound of the shower hissed in the bathroom. A sideways glance at the clock on the bedside table revealed that it was much later than it should be.... Damn, she'd overslept.

They both had.

The running water stopped. Jessica didn't move. She waited. The bathroom door opened and Ryan emerged, towelling his dark hair, surrounded by steam billowing out of the bathroom behind him.

He was utterly, unashamedly naked. His wide chest bare, his narrow hips lean. The most gorgeous male she'd ever known. Jessica watched furtively from under her lashes as he glanced at the Seamaster on his wrist, made an impatient sound and headed for the walk-in closet.

She closed her eyes.

God, this was going to be difficult.

"Are you asleep again?" Even with the hint of impatience, his voice was deep, a sexy rasp that never failed to ignite her senses.

Her eyelids flicked open. Immaculately dressed in a dark suit that contrasted with the crisp white cotton shirts he preferred in Sydney's February heat, he was picking his way through the clothing they'd torn off last night and dropped on the floor. Jessica felt herself flush at the memory. He must've read something in her face because his eyes darkened with secret knowledge and he came toward her. He reached the bed and bent over her, planting a muscled arm on either side of her, and his eyes softened.

"You are the most tempting woman in the world," he murmured.

He smelled clean and fresh—of soap and man. "And you're easily tempted?"

"I could stay here the whole day."

His words cast a shadow over her thoughts. So much would happen today. Howard Blackstone's funeral…the will reading…the discussion she needed to have with Ryan. Yet, despite everything hanging over her, he was irresistible.

One last kiss. That's all, she promised herself. Jessica threaded her arms around his neck and tugged.

"Hey." He landed on the bed beside her, his face so close to hers she could see the jade hue of his irises, the verdant richness that never failed to set her heart pounding. His jaw was tanned and smoothly shaven, his features strong and bold.

His hand stroked a tendril of hair out of her eyes. "You look tired. Pale. There are shadows under your eyes this morning. I shouldn't have kept you up so late."

"No problem." She forced a smile to conceal her worry about him. Their predawn lovemaking had held a certain desperation. The disappearance of his father's jet and the subsequent recovery of Howard Blackstone's body had blighted Ryan. On her part, the desperation came from other causes…a sense of time running out.

Irrevocably.

She changed the subject. "You're meeting Ric before the funeral, aren't you?"

At the mention of Ric Perrini, interim chairman of Blackstone Diamonds and his sister's husband, Ryan's mouth tightened into a hard line. "No. I'll have plenty of time to talk to him afterwards."

Jessica hesitated, then said softly, "Today is going to be hard on Kimberley as well." Ryan's sister had returned to Australia after her father's death having spent the previous ten years working for Matt Hammond, the son of Howard Blackstone's most bitter enemy—his brother-in-law, Oliver.

"I know."

Jessica almost said, "Go easy on her," but bit the words back at the last minute.

Ryan wouldn't want her counsel. She was only his lover, after all, not his wife.

Heck, she was less than his lover—she was the secret mistress that no one was supposed to know about. With a touch of dark humour Jessica wondered what people would say if they knew that the cool blonde who ran Blackstone Jewellery's Sydney store in the day came apart in the boss's arms under the dark cloak of night.

Shock. Horror. A Blackstone sleeping with a lowly member of staff? A mechanic's daughter living with a groomed-for-greatness millionaire?

A hand stroked her hair. "You know what I want more than anything in the world?"

Ryan's voice was soft, mesmerizing. For a moment Jessica

wished that the world outside these walls—the Blackstone family, Blackstone Diamonds and public expectations—could melt away. That there was only them: Jessica and Ryan. That she could curl up in his arms and never leave.

If only...

"What do you want?"

"To climb into that big bed beside you, kiss you here—" he pushed aside the cover a fraction of an inch and touched the soft skin at the base of her throat "—and celebrate life, rather than death."

He matched his actions to his words. The kiss landed on target. Jessica swallowed, her throat moving convulsively under his mouth. Then his lips moved up along her neck and landed on her mouth.

Jessica moaned.

"Open your mouth, honey, I need you."

There was a desperation she'd never heard from Ryan before. Obediently her lips parted. His mouth plundered the softness, his tongue exploring the inside of her sensitive bottom lip. Jessica moved restlessly, her arms tightening around his neck to a stranglehold. She did not want to let him go. Ryan was breathing hard when he lifted his head, and his eyes were wild.

"God, I could stay here all day. What an easy way out." His head dipped again.

The kiss was frantic and Jessica ached for him. His desire to take the easy way out, to escape, hammered home how much he dreaded the coming day. The funeral was the final proof that his father was gone. Forever. She rubbed her hands along his shoulders, wishing she could take the hurt, the pain, away from him.

He pulled back. "See how responsive your body is?" Ryan slipped a hand under the cover. "Your breasts have swollen already. I noticed last night how taut they are."

Jessica went cold.

She grabbed his wrist to stop his hand moving toward the curve of her belly. She hadn't seen any change in her body yet. Only felt the warning signs. "We haven't got time for this." Rolling away from his touch, she said, "You better get going or you'll be late."

"And you better get up, too."

"I will." She gave him a weak smile. "As soon as you're gone."

He blew out hard and raked the fingers of both hands through his hair. "I suppose it's better that way. Once you get up and start dressing I'll never get out of here. But first…"

He bent forward and placed his lips against hers for a long, lingering moment. It was a gentle kiss. Tender. A sharp contrast to the desperate passion that had gone before. "Thank you for last night."

Jessica's heart tore in half.

Ryan didn't know it yet but last night had been goodbye… although she was already wavering. Maybe another week…

He rose to his feet. A dark sombreness shadowed his eyes. "Don't be late for the funeral. And don't—"

"Don't do anything that would give us away." That hurt. Especially today. "I know."

Astonishment turned his eyes the colour of sunlight on jade. "I was about to say don't do anything that might distract me."

Her throat went dry. "Go, Ryan."

Jessica watched him stride out of the bedroom, heard his footsteps on the highly polished nyatoh wood flooring in the airy lobby. Only when she heard the elevator doors slide shut did she get out of bed.

Her stomach rolled. Bile hit the back of her throat. Jessica ran. She barely made it to the bathroom before she started retching.

Afterwards she washed her face with cold water, her hands trembling. Then she finally looked up into the mirror above the basin into her pale face with its wide-set brown eyes, the smattering of caramel freckles standing out in sharp relief. She looked absolutely ghastly. But she held her own gaze. No more pity. No more guilt. *Today*, she told herself. *You break it off today.* As soon as the funeral is over.

Before the evidence was there for everyone to see.

Ryan stood on the roughly hewn stone steps of the historic church where his father's soul was about to be rendered to immortality…or consigned to hell, depending on your view of Howard Blackstone.

There was no room for grey emotion when it came to his father, Ryan mused. You loved him…or you hated him. He had loved his father. But their relationship had not been an easy one. The midday Sydney sun beat against his back, causing sweat to bead uncomfortably inside his collar. He loosened the top button of his shirt and inhaled a deep breath.

He caught a whiff of the scent of churchyard roses. It reminded him of Jessica. The image of her spread across his bed this morning flashed through his mind. He recalled the temptation she'd offered…the desire to succumb to the passion that flared so wildly between them, and the craven impulse to push the hard reality of the day aside. He felt again his all-consuming hunger for her, for the relentless passion they shared each night that left them spent afterwards. A passion that kept him bewitched, despite that brief flare of mistrust after his father's plane went missing. A dark moment of suspicion that he'd abandoned as quickly as it had come.

From inside the church came the strains of organ music. *Abide with me*. His chest tightened.

Turning his head, Ryan glanced at the group of sombrely dressed men gathered around the hearse containing Howard Blackstone's coffin. Except for Ric, all of them would have attended his mother's funeral twenty-eight years ago. From where he stood he could see inside the hearse, could see the mahogany coffin studded with brass detail. Inside that fancy wooden box lay his father. An emotion too powerful to name choked him. His father…

"It's almost time to go in." Ric's husky voice was like a splinter of glass under his skin. Ryan spun to confront the interloper that his father had always put ahead of him, treating *him* like the eldest son.

"Give me a minute to say goodbye to my father," he snarled.

Something flashed in Ric's eyes. Ryan glared at him. The last thing in the world he wanted was Ric Perrini's sympathy. Instantly the emotion vanished and Ric's eyes returned to their usual unreadable expression.

Ryan swung away. The organ music grew louder, spilling out the open church doors. Ryan inclined his head and murmured a silent prayer. With his *Amen* ringing in his head, he brushed past Ric and headed for the rear of the hearse.

Ric's hand came down on his shoulder. "I need a quick word with you."

Ryan stiffened and he hesitated for a moment before giving a curt nod. "Sure."

They walked a short distance away and stopped beside a tall yew hedge. The sun fell across Ric's face, highlighting the shadows beneath the very direct blue eyes. "First off, you need to know that no one here today is sorrier about the loss you've suffered than I."

Ryan wondered whether the bulk of Ric's sorrow came from the rumour that his father had changed his will shortly before his death. Under the original will Ric—rather than Howard's own children—stood to inherit the majority of Howard's shareholding. Was Ric fazed by the possibility of coming into less shares now? By the possibility of Kimberley failing to inherit any shares at all?

Ryan narrowed his gaze and tried to read Ric's expression as he said, "Garth told Kim that Howard changed his will." Garth Buick, one of Howard's oldest friends and the company secretary of Blackstone Diamonds was a trustworthy source.

Ric's eyes grew shadowed. "He's warned Kim not to expect too much. Not after her defection to the House of Hammond."

From personal experience Ryan had a pretty good idea of how badly their father would've reacted. Ten years ago Ric had been appointed head of the new Blackstone retail division, making Ric second in power only to his father. Ryan had resigned from Blackstone's to go work for De Beers in South Africa. He'd needed the time away from Ric, from Howard and from Blackstone's. Howard had been madder than a riled copperhead snake at what he'd termed "Ryan's desertion."

When Ryan had eventually returned, older and wiser, his father had welcomed him back with a coolness that warned him that his desertion had not been forgotten—or forgiven— even though he'd been appointed head of Blackstone Jewellery, the retail arm of Blackstone's. The past had always lain between them, a chasm too vast to bridge. Until Ryan had taken steps to close it and told his father two weeks before Christmas that he wanted a bigger say in the company. Howard had seemed satisfied.

If Howard had changed his will back in December, it was very likely that his own share had increased—at Ric's expense.

It would not make the already strained relationship between himself and Ric any better. But inheriting the additional shares would certainly send out a message about his father's confidence in him, and put him in a much stronger position to be voted chairman of the board at the Blackstone Diamonds board meeting next Monday morning.

Pushing his thoughts aside, he came back to the puzzle posed by the new will. "But surely Kimberley will still get Mother's jewellery and a sizeable number of shares? Dad would never strip her of those." Those shares had given Ryan a few sleepless nights. Together Kimberley and Ric would hold a formidable block of stock...and votes. Who became chairman of Blackstones, he or Ryan, might depend on whether Kim inherited any shares—and on how she voted them.

"We'll know soon enough." Ric was frowning. He glanced in the direction of the church doors, then back at Ryan. "Kim thinks Matt Hammond will be in there. You and I have had our differences, but it's important we present a united front today."

Ryan stared at Ric. Since his sister had come back to Australia, she'd taken charge of public relations at the company. She'd had her work cut out controlling the fallout that had followed the downing of the chartered jet with their father— and Marise Davenport, the woman reputed to be his latest mistress—on board. With her bereaved husband, Matt Hammond, buying Blackstone Diamonds stock and triggering dangerous rumours of a takeover, the newspapers would soon be sniffing around for any signs of cracks within the company management.

Slowly Ryan nodded. "Yes, Matt Hammond will be in there, gloating in the front row. He's been telling every reporter who cares to listen that he'd be here today 'to make sure the bastard's buried'." Ryan knew his father had many enemies. But it rankled that Matt, the son of his mother's only brother, shared the view. And publicly, as front page news, at that.

Matt Hammond was a traitorous bastard—no different from his father, Oliver. And now he'd all but declared war on the Blackstones. If war was what Matt wanted, that's what he'd get.

Turning away, Ryan headed for the hearse, and rapped out, "Okay, time to go."

The coffin rolled out of the back of the hearse. The funeral director, ridiculously attired in cutaway black tails and a top hat, placed atop the coffin the floral arrangement that Kimberley had ordered. Pure white lilies and snowy freesias. His mother's favourites, his Aunt Sonya had said, because Howard had always sent them to her to celebrate special occasions. As the coffin slid past him, Ryan caught a hint of the fragrance and for a sharp instant a memory of sunshine and laughter sliced through his mind...of a time long ago, when there had still been happiness in the Blackstone home.

And then the image was gone and reality bit in. What was left of his father lay under that pile of blooms, pulled out of the plane wreckage that had been recovered a few weeks ago. It was hard to believe he'd never hear that gruff voice again. Never have the chance to prove to his father that he could run Blackstone's with the same expertise and energy that Howard Blackstone had.

The six pallbearers took up their positions. Ryan was up front, Ric on the opposite side. Garth Buick fell in behind Ric, while Kane, a Blackstone cousin, stood behind Ryan. Bringing up the rear were Howard's two older brothers— Kane's father, Vincent and William Blackstone.

Ryan's mouth tightened at the sight of William Blackstone. Two months ago his uncle had sold his ten-per-cent holding in Blackstone Diamonds to Matt Hammond—and set a chain of events in motion that were currently causing havoc at head office.

Ryan bent to pick up the handle nearest him. "Right, let's go."

They hoisted the coffin up. He met Ric's level gaze over the top of the mahogany and fought not to let his turmoil show. More than anything in the world he wanted to prove that he could do the job he'd been denied during his father's lifetime—that of chairman of Blackstone Diamonds.

The music rose to a crescendo as they entered the church and the coffin handle rested heavily in Ryan's hand. A quick glance in the direction of the front pew failed to reveal Matt Hammond. Surreptitiously, Ryan scanned the mourners for Jessica's pale hair, but failed to find it. She'd be here some-where. For a brief moment he thought about the passion they'd shared last night, the kiss this morning, and he felt himself relax. Jessica's generosity as a lover, the comfort she'd so wordlessly given him, had made the day bearable.

They set the coffin down beneath the pulpit, where the priest waited to start to the service. Kimberley beckoned from the front row, and Ric and Ryan filed into the pew.

Once seated beside Kimberley, with Ric on her other side, Ryan took another look around. No sign of Matt Hammond. Nor Jessica.

"She's right at the back," Kim whispered.

Ryan frowned at his sister. "Who is?"

"Jessica." Kim raised an eyebrow. "That's who you're looking for, right?"

Ryan didn't answer.

Nor did he glance back to confirm his canny sister's sus-picions. Instead he fixed his gaze on the lonely coffin in the front of the church and almost sighed with relief when the priest started to speak, sparing him the need to answer.

As he listened to the priest, Ryan couldn't help wondering how Kimberley had known. She'd had always been good at reading people, but Ryan had thought he'd done a great job of hiding his affair with Jessica. So how the hell had Kim gotten wind of it?

No one knew.

He'd made sure of that.

The heat in the packed church pressed in on Jessica and the priest's voice started to fade. She squeezed her eyes shut against the wave of nausea that swept through her and by sheer willpower kept down the meagre slice of toast she'd eaten earlier.

"Honey, are you all right?" Her mother's whisper pierced her misery.

"Yes." Another wave of nausea hit. "Maybe not," she muttered through gritted teeth. Her mother didn't know about the baby…and Howard Blackstone's funeral was the last place she'd pick to make that announcement.

Morning sickness. What a misnomer. It was already noon. All-day sickness would be more accurate.

"Come, let me help you out."

"Out?" Her eyes flew open and she stared at her mother in disbelief. "You mean *leave* Howard Blackstone's funeral?" That thought was enough to make her feel ill all over again. She'd sat with her parents in the farthest back corner to avoid attracting attention. That was hard enough given her father's wheelchair. Leaving now would undo all that.

Her mother nodded. "You need to get some air. You're as white as a sheet, Jessica."

A woman with a black hat that resembled an upside-down flowerpot turned and glared at them. Jessica gave her a weak smile. Placing her hand on her mother's, she mouthed, "I'll be fine." Right.

Sally Cotter didn't look convinced. "If you say so."

The black flowerpot turned and glared again.

Jessica closed her eyes and admitted to herself that she felt dreadful. Relief swirled through her when the congregation rose and started to sing the final hymn.

"I'll see you outside." She slipped past her father's wheelchair, making for the door. Outside she gasped in a lungful of fresh air. Moments later she stood in the restroom. After splashing water over her face, she felt cooler and a little better.

Her doctor had given her a prescription for morning sickness, but she'd been reluctant to take the pills. Instead she'd nearly been physically ill in the midst of Howard Blackstone's funeral. Jessica shuddered. What would Ryan have said? What rumours would have flown around? It didn't bear thinking about. Quickly she opened her bag, found the box and broke the seal, then swallowed down a tablet.

Closing the door behind her, Jessica came around the corner and saw that service was over. The mourners were spilling out the church, down the stone stairs. The sun was bright and in the hedges she could see blackbirds hopping about. The drained, ill feeling receded. She looked around for her parents but couldn't locate them. They must still be inside. She started up the stairs.

Before she could sidle through the press of people, Ryan reached her. "Jessica, I didn't see you in there. Surely you didn't stay outside?"

"I sneaked out just as the service ended, I needed the bathroom."

"Thank you for being there." There was an unaccustomed fervour in the eyes that scanned her features.

"How could I not? He was your father."

"And your boss."

"No, you're my boss," she said lightly, peering up at him through her lashes.

"Don't look at me like that!" Tension invaded his features and his eyes turned molten. "It's hard to believe, but I want you. Right now."

"Ryan!" Excitement stirred inside her, a world apart from the awful nausea that had hit her less than ten minutes ago. "What would people say?"

"Right now I don't particularly care." He caught her arm. "Jess—"

"Careful." She pulled free of his grasp. "People will talk. Believe me, later you *will* care."

Before he could reply she took off up the stairs and disappeared into the crowd, her heart beating at Ryan's unexpected intensity.

Ryan nosed the sleek black BMW M6 through the Victoria Street gate into Rookwood Cemetery and followed the hearse as it crawled along a winding lane past lines of graves. Turning into the older burial section Ryan drove slowly beside the Serpentine Canal edged with lush plantings of agapanthus, before pulling the BMW in behind where the dark hearse had stopped.

Swiftly alighting, Ryan made his way to the raw gash in the ground where a fresh grave yawned near a Norfolk pine. He set his expression, determined not to show what this day was costing him.

Ryan's stride hesitated as he glimpsed his grandfather Jeb's grave, just beyond his mother's. Beside him, his aunt Sonya paused at Ursula Blackstone's—her sister's—grave. Ryan put his arm under his aunt's elbow. She gave a start, and he patted her arm, at a total loss for words.

"I sometimes come to tend the rosebushes that Ursula planted for James. She used to visit every Sunday afternoon to tend them. I'm lucky to get here once every couple of months." Sonya's voice was thin. "Now Howard has joined them, too."

The plaque beside his mother's grave, flanked by Remember Me rosebushes, read *In memory of our missing son, James, we will see you one day.* Howard Blackstone hadn't even allowed his wife to reserve a piece of cemetery for James—the plaque was all Ursula Blackstone had to remember her son by. A tragic reminder that his parents had never seen their first-born son after the day he'd been kidnapped.

"Perhaps now the three of them are reunited." Sonya followed his gaze.

"Maybe." Ryan thought about his father's stubborn refusal to accept that James was dead. Howard had retained investigators for decades to chase a stone-cold trail. Maybe Sonya was right. In death they might all find peace.

But one thing was for certain, Ryan wouldn't need to plant rosebushes to remember his father. Howard Blackstone's strength and drive and determination were branded into him. His unspoken legacy.

They strode to the edge of the open grave prepared for his father, and Sonya started to cry in earnest. Awkwardly Ryan put his arm around his aunt and looked wildly around for his sister. Instead of seeing Kimberley, he found himself staring into the angry eyes of Matt Hammond.

From across the open grave Matt's lips moved. "I'll show you you can't mess with my family and get away with it." The words carried on the wind to where Ryan stood.

Ryan speared the other man with a furious gaze, tension coiling through him until he felt he might snap. Somewhere in the thicket of trees a kookaburra cackled. Damn bird!

Beside him, Sonya shifted restlessly. Ryan tightened his hold on her arm and she stilled.

The priest started to speak. Ryan closed his eyes for the reading and tried to absorb the solemn rhythm of the words. Then, without knowing how it happened, he was holding a fistful of earth. Stepping forward, he parted his fingers letting the red earth slip through his fingers onto the coffin.

Dust to dust.

The surge of emotion took him by surprise. His throat tightened, hot. Someone grabbed his hand. *Kimberley.* He jerked and swung away from the grave.

"Are you okay?"

He nodded, breaking free and blindly pushing through the press of the crowd, intent on getting to the back where no one would be watching. Where he could grieve in peace.

Jessica.

Had she come? He scanned the mourners. His gaze came to rest on her slim figure, her pale hair drawn off her delicate features. She wasn't standing alone as he'd half expected, a fish out of water at Howard Blackstone's funeral. Nor was she grouped with the Blackstone employees. Instead she stood a distance away with an older couple. A man in a wheelchair and a woman who on second glance looked vaguely familiar.

His attention returned to Jessica, devouring her, wishing they were a lifetime away from the cemetery and the sad memories it held. She lifted her hand in a little wave.

Ryan gave a brief nod in response and, feeling oddly comforted, turned his attention back to the grave for the final prayer. When he opened his eyes, it was to see Jessica pushing the wheelchair toward a row of parked cars.

She was leaving.

Ryan strode after her. "Jessica," he called once he was clear of the crowd. But she didn't hear and helped the man into an unfamiliar car. Ryan started to sprint. He reached her as she was about to climb into the driver's seat. It certainly wasn't Jessica's Toyota. She didn't respond to his questioning glance at the car, so he simply said, "You'll come to back to the house?"

Her brown eyes were evasive. "I've never been. So I don't think so." She glanced at the couple in the car. "I need to get my parents home."

Her parents? "Introduce us," Ryan demanded, ducking his head down to stare into the car.

"Mum, Dad, this is Ryan Blackstone," she said with a reluctance that unaccountably annoyed Ryan. With the amount of press coverage he and Kimberley had gotten in the past month, her parents would've known at a glance who he was. He supposed he should be grateful that she hadn't introduced him as her lover.

"My parents, Sally and Peter."

Her mother gave him a sweet smile. But her father's eyes were more critical. He wondered what had happened to put her father in a wheelchair. And then he wondered whether her parents knew he was their daughter's lover. Hell, he'd never thought of what she might've told them about her private life. Never considered that she might have to lie to the people she loved.

Her parents. Her friends.

A rush of shame surged through him. With his insistence on secrecy, he'd made things very awkward for Jessica. And why? Because he didn't want it to be public knowledge that he was sleeping with a member of his staff. Had be been grossly unfair to Jessica?

Stepping away from the car, he drew Jessica with him. In the distance the kookaburra laughed again. "Please come to the house, to Miramare, Jess."

"I don't think—".

For a brief moment he felt a strange sense of being abandoned. "I want you to come."

Her head jerked up at the suppressed urgency in his voice, her eyes widening. He read confusion, turmoil...and something else in the caramel depths.

"You've never invited me there before. So why now? I doubt the rest of the staff will be there."

He had no answer for that. At least not one that he understood himself. All he knew was that he wanted to be able to look across the room, and see her slim figure, hear her calming voice.

She was still waiting for an answer. Dropping his voice, he said, "I haven't mentioned it before, but there's talk that my father's changed his will...."

She must have seen something of his turmoil and anger in his eyes because after a brief pause, she nodded.

"I must see my parents home first."

"Jessica," her mother interceded, poking her head out the window. "Let's go past the Blackstone mansion. I can drive home from there."

"I don't want you driving, Mum. Not today." Jessica exchanged a long look with her mother that had Ryan feeling like he'd missed something vital. "I can call a cab to take me after I've dropped you and Dad off. And I'll catch another cab home later."

"All the way to that lonely apartment of yours in Chippendale?"

"I'll take you...home...later," Ryan added quickly. If her parents thought she was still living in the apartment she'd rented in Chippendale after moving to Sydney, that must mean that after almost a year her parents still didn't know she'd moved in to his penthouse. What had it taken for her to maintain that deception? Both of them only used cell phones, and there was no landline in the penthouse. Yet he knew Jessica visited her parents at their home on the outskirts of Sydney every weekend—without him. But he'd never thought how hard it must be to keep her mother from visiting her in return.

"That's sorted. I'll see you later." Ryan stepped away from the car with a feeling that he'd just averted a major crisis that he hadn't seen coming.

Two

Ryan barged out his father's study, past Garth Buick's out-stretched hand, and strode blindly down the corridor, feeling like the bottom had just dropped out of his world. Ahead of him he could see Matt Hammond walking with long angry strides toward the front door—showing no intention of staying for refreshments.

"Ryan." At the sound of his sister's voice the sinking feeling in his stomach intensified.

Kim was whiter than the lilies that had rested on his father's coffin, her eyes glassy with shock. For the first time in years he reached for her, his own hands shaking. She was as stiff as a board in his arms. Ryan drew her into the music room next door, out of sight of curious eyes, and kicked the door shut.

"The old bastard," Ryan said bitterly.

"How could he do it? How could he disinherit me?"

Kim's voice was muffled against his suit lapel. "I'm his daughter, damn him."

"He left your shareholding in the company to someone who doesn't even exist. James is dead." Above her dark head, Ryan shook his head at the craziness of it all. Except Howard Blackstone had never been the tiniest bit insane.

A coldhearted bastard, sure.

Manipulative, yes.

But not crazy.

Except in one respect—his dogged belief that his first-born son was still alive. Somewhere.

"There's no way James is going to magically come back to life in the next six months to claim the shares—or Miramare." Ryan tried to comfort Kimberley and thought he might be making headway when she relaxed a little in his arms. James's ghost had haunted the mansion since his disappearance as a toddler. Perhaps it was fitting that his father had left Miramare to his dead brother.

"Even if he doesn't, the shares left to him will be divided between you and Ric." Kimberley sounded bereft. "I get nothing—except that cold, clear clause that he intentionally disinherited me."

Which meant he and Ric would still have an equal shareholding. Right until the end, his father was pitting them against each other.

"Dad had no right to leave Mother's jewellery to Marise Davenport." A picture of the vampish Marise flashed through Ryan's head. A flamboyant redhead, Marise had worked for Blackstones in the marketing department. He'd never paid her much attention, even though she'd tried to snare his interest often enough. It clearly hadn't stopped her. She'd snared a bigger fish. His father. In addition to his mother's jewellery she'd gotten a seven-figure cash bequest as well. Not that it did her much good now that she was dead.

And his sister had inherited nothing.

"I'm going to challenge the will." Kimberley's voice was harder than the scintillating diamond she wore on her ring finger. Ryan had never heard her use that tone before. "All my life I've been trying to get him to recognize my worth. I'm not letting him get away with it."

"It won't be easy." Neither of them had heard the door open. Ric filled the doorway. "His will states clearly that he intended to disinherit you—that was his dying wish."

Kim tugged free of Ryan's arms and rushed to her husband, "Oh, Ric, he couldn't have chosen a better way to hurt me."

"Shh, love. He's gone. Your father can only hurt you if you allow him to. You make your own happiness." Ric bent his head and placed a loving kiss on Kimberley's lips.

And suddenly Ryan felt like an intruder, an outsider to the tightly bound unit of two that his sister and Ric created. Feeling utterly alone he stepped past them into the corridor outside.

Men in suits stood in huddled clusters in the entrance hall at the foot of the double stairway, with its ornate filigree balustrade, discussing the shocking contents of the will. They grew quiet as he approached, their eyes curious. Ryan shook hands with a couple who offered condolences on the loss of his father as he passed.

The only good thing to come out the will reading was the evidence that his father had viewed him equal to Ric. But Ryan had never been able to fill the void that James's loss had created.

The emptiness within him expanded. He changed direction and headed for the grand salon, where the majority of the mourners had congregated. As he entered, the rich fragrance of fine coffee hung in the air. The sound of chatter was almost overwhelming. Had Jessica arrived yet? He searched the throng, until his gaze rested on a familiar fair head. As if drawn by his gaze, Jessica turned, her caramel-brown eyes filled with concern as they met his.

And for the first time since the funeral, the hollow feeling in his chest started to recede.

Jessica's heart softened as she took in Ryan's tight, strained expression. This last month had been hard on him. At least with the funeral and the will reading behind him, his life should regain some balance. Then she remembered his comment about a new will.

Perhaps not.

Certainly the Ryan crossing toward her was far from settled. His eyes were stormy, his jaw hard and set. Apprehension sank like a stone in her stomach. When he reached her side, she turned to him and murmured, "So the rumour was correct, Howard changed his will?"

"Yes." His voice was harsh. He pushed his hands through his groomed black hair. "Kim's been disinherited."

"Oh, no." Jessica put her hand over her mouth to stifle her gasp of horror. She'd heard there'd been some friction between Kim and her father. But her concern about Ryan subsided a little. "But you're okay?"

The look he gave her held rage and pain. "My father has left thirty per cent of his shareholding to my brother."

"Your brother?" Jessica blinked, trying to work that out. "But your brother—"

"Is dead!" Ryan cut across her. "Only my father never accepted that. He never gave up the hope of one day finding James."

Jessica's breath caught in her throat. *"He found him?"*

"No." Ryan's face darkened. "But according to Garth, Dad

was jubilant before his death. He thought he had a lead."
Ryan shook his head. "James disappeared thirty-two years
ago. I find it hard to swallow that my hard-headed father was
being led on a wild-goose chase by some two-bit charlatan."

Jessica's heart ached for Ryan. She moved a little closer
and wished they were alone, so that she could put her arms
around him and give him the hug he needed right now, even
though she suspected he'd push her away if she tried to hold
him close. He'd shut himself off. And she took care not to
touch him, not to do anything that might compromise the
understanding they'd always shared.

No one must know that they were lovers.

Not even today.

Yet she couldn't help feeling an unexpected surge of sympathy for Howard Blackstone, a man she'd always silently
despised. How terrible to have lost a child…to never be able
to bury his remains and say goodbye.

The thought of losing her unborn baby already filled her
with anguish. *How had Howard and Ursula coped?* "So what
happens now? If there's no brother to actually inherit, who
will inherit your dead brother's share?"

Ryan gave a laugh that held no humour. "In six months' time
it will revert to me and Ric in equal shares. That's in addition
to the thirty per cent we each inherited under the new will."

"Then that will be the end of it, won't it?" Jessica stared up
into the handsome features she'd come to love so much. The
jade eyes, the strong nose and beautifully moulded mouth…

A mouth that tightened into a hard line, lending a toughness to Ryan's almost-perfect face. "I don't think it will ever
end. When James died my family fell apart. He was the first-
born son. The heir."

Understanding dawned. "So you tried to take his place? To
be the son your father wanted?"

He gave her a slanted look. "I'll never be that. And I wasn't alone in trying to please my father. Kim worked hard, too. Both of us excelled at school. I made the cricket and rugby teams and I competed in triathlons. I did everything I could to—" He broke off and looked away. He gave a sigh. "What does it matter? My father is dead."

And Ryan felt as if he'd never lived up to his father's expectations, Jessica concluded. It gave her insight into the man whose secret mistress she'd been for the past two years, showed her a glimpse of his character that he'd always kept firmly hidden. A part that she probably would never have discovered if it hadn't been for the new will.

Was this the real reason he held her at an emotional distance? Did he feel he was incapable of being loved?

"But at least my father didn't leave the lion's share to Ric," he said with a hint of satisfaction.

Jessica drew away. The intense rivalry between the two men—and the manner in which it consumed Ryan—had always concerned her. "Now that your father's gone, you and Kim and Ric will have the task of steering Blackstone's—"

"Ric's not a Blackstone. I'm the only surviving son. Under my leadership the profits on the retail side of the business have grown enormously. I've proved myself. Control of the board should be mine."

Jessica started to speak, chilled by the inflexibility Ryan had revealed, then bit the words back. What would be the point? Ryan had never listened to her. And from his set expression he wasn't about to start now.

Jessica took a tentative bite of a shortbread biscuit she'd taken off a passing waiter's tray. Nothing untoward occurred. Her stomach didn't heave. So she took another cautious bite.

Ryan had left a couple of minutes ago with Garth Buick

and now stood across the room with a group of dark-suited men, all wearing sombre expressions. No doubt he didn't want to be seen overlong in her company—in case it drew unwelcome speculation and more gossip.

But the attempt to wind herself up about his secrecy fell flat. The conviction that she needed to end her relationship with Ryan tonight was starting to waver. It had been such a terrible day for him, especially with what he'd told her about his brother's death.

Perhaps she should delay for another week. After all, she'd originally intended to break it off with him after the New Year, when she'd first discovered that she was pregnant. She'd already delayed once, because his father's jet had gone down—why not again? What would it really matter? Ryan spent so much time at work, so little time home, that he was unlikely to notice the changes to her routines and her body.

She turned away, determined not to give anyone a reason to suspect her connection with Ryan. A little distance away, Jessica saw Dani Hammond, Ryan's cousin and an up-and-coming jewellery designer. Her work would be featured in the launch of the new season's Something Old, Something New jewellery collection amidst much fanfare at the end of the month. The funeral of the young woman's uncle was hardly the time to go and introduce herself as a business associate, Jessica decided.

She started at the touch on her arm.

"Jess?"

Jessica turned to find Briana Davenport, one of Australia's most popular supermodels and the "face" of Blackstone Diamonds beside her. Briana's sister Marise had died in the plane crash with Howard Blackstone, along with the pilot, copilot, cabin attendant and Howard's lawyer, Ian Van Dyke. A terrible tragedy. And today Briana looked nothing like the smiling, glamorous figure who adorned billboards and double-page spreads in *Vogue Australia*. Although she wore a beautifully cut black dress that screamed couture, she looked pale and tired, her eyes red from crying, and her glorious golden-brown hair pulled back from her face into a tight knot.

"Sweetie, how are you holding up?" Jessica asked. Briana was as good a friend as any that Jessica had made since moving to Sydney. They'd met through work and the friendship had grown. Because of Briana's hectic modelling schedule they didn't see each other often—which, given her peculiar arrangement with Ryan, suited Jessica to perfection.

Briana gave a wan smile. "Two funerals in less than a month is tough to deal with. Even though Marise and I weren't close, I find myself crying at the oddest times."

"That's understandable. Don't be too hard on yourself." Jessica touched the other woman's arm. Fortunately Briana didn't know—few did—that *she* was supposed to have been on that plane with Howard. *She* should have died, too. *She* should've been buried, instead of standing here patting Briana's arm like a fraud. Jessica shivered.

She had been lucky....

If it hadn't been for Howard's obnoxiousness, she would've been dead. She'd never thought that she'd be grateful for that.

"You know what the worst of it is?"

Briana's words brought her back to the present. "What?"

"People are saying that Marise was Howard's mistress. I mean that's disgusting...he's more than thirty years older than her." Briana sniffed and fresh tears glimmered in her eyes.

"Ignore it." Jessica advised, deciding not to upset Briana further by commenting on Howard Blackstone's well-known appreciation for younger women in recent years. "It will pass. The media will soon find a new scandal—and then they'll leave the Blackstones alone. There are no hard facts to sustain that scurrilous rumour."

Briana gave her a strange look. "Haven't you heard?"

"Heard what?"

"At the will reading—"

"What about the will reading?"

"Marise inherited an astronomical sum of money under the will."

Ryan hadn't mentioned that. Jessica thought about how she'd had to drag every morsel of information out of him. Wasn't she important enough for him to share the crises that were happening in his life?

It underlined that breaking off with him was the right decision. Their relationship had no future. She had to end it, quickly.

"Marise also got Ursula's jewellery collection. Of course it means nothing now that she's dead." Briana's eyes grew dark with pain.

Poor Kimberley! Her mother's jewels had gone to a stranger. "No, I hadn't heard about that."

"And Marise's son, Blake, inherited a trust fund. People are already speculating that my nephew is Howard Blackstone's illegitimate son."

"Oh, my goodness! If that's true, Matt Hammond is really going to hate the Blackstones now. That would make the boy Ryan's—"

"Baby brother." Briana nodded. "It's terrible. The papers are going to have a field day with it once they find out."

"Oh, no." Jessica knew Briana was right. This would not give the Blackstones the privacy they badly needed in their time of grief. "Poor Kimberley. Poor Ryan. And poor Matt

Hammond." Jessica's soft heart melted for Matt. If Marise had cheated on him with Howard, and he saw Kimberley's return to Blackstone's as Howard's daughter abandoning her job with the House of Hammond, was it any wonder that the man was bitter? She could certainly understand Matt's statements to the papers that he wanted to be here today to see Howard buried. In his position, she'd have wanted to see Howard buried alive!

Briana wiped her eyes. "Shh, Ryan's coming over to say hello." She forced a small smile and held her face up for a brief, social kiss. "I'm so sorry about your father."

"Thank you." Ryan didn't glance at Jessica. "Can I get either of you ladies a drink? Coffee? There's even champagne—some people are celebrating my father's passing," he said darkly.

"I need something strong," Briana muttered. "Help me drown my sorrows." Then an expression of horror crossed her face. "Ryan, that was awful. I didn't mean it the way it came out."

"I know you didn't." He patted her shoulder. "Everyone is walking on eggshells around me right now, it's a relief to hear something that comes out wrong. Why don't you join me with a small sherry?"

"Thanks." Briana gave a sigh of relief. "I think I will."

"Jessica?" At last he looked at her and smiled politely. "What would you like?"

"I'll have a cup of tea, thanks." Her smile was equally polite, but inside she was smouldering at his cool distance, the civil facade that gave away nothing about the passion they shared every night after work.

"Tea? In this heat? Are you certain?"

She nodded. "Perfectly." She bit back her comment that he knew exactly how she liked it. "White with no sugar."

Both women watched him weave his way through the crowd

in search of a waiter. "He's such a handsome man," Briana said. "I can't believe he isn't married or at least attached."

Jessica couldn't help wishing that Briana knew about her and Ryan. But Ryan had been adamant that their affair should remain secret. Which meant that from time to time this happened: the idle speculation about Ryan's good looks, his girlfriends, his prowess in bed. It never failed to sear her with jealousy. It was when she most wanted to wring Ryan's wretched neck for putting her in this predicament. But she'd been so blinded by the stars in her eyes that she'd agreed to the arrangement. So she did what she always did at such times, she tried distraction. "Does Blake resemble Howard in any way?"

Briana's eyes widened in dismay. "Jess, don't tell me you think—"

"I don't know what I think." Jessica decided honesty was the best tactic. "But a lot of people are going to be searching for a resemblance. So you might as well think about whether there are any for them to spot."

A frown creased Briana's forehead. "I'm not sure. Blake does have dark hair…and the cutest smile. I'll have to take a look at the photos at home. I don't see him very often, with him living in Auckland and all the time I spend overseas on assignment. Poor mite. He won't have a mother. But maybe I can still play some role in his life. I'll have to speak to Matt about visiting more often."

"I'm sure Matt would appreciate your help." But Jessica couldn't help thinking of Ryan. If the rumour proved true, how would the existence of yet another brother affect him? Blake was a child. But he was a child under the guardianship of Matt Hammond. A man who had made it clear that he was out to destroy the Blackstones.

A waiter arrived and Briana helped herself to the dainty glass of sherry, then he handed Jessica a cup of tea.

"Look." Briana tilted her head in the direction of a trio of women who kept snatching avid glances in their direction and then leaning forward to whisper to each other. "They're talking about me. About Marise. I hate this."

Jessica threw the women a hard look. They had the grace to look discomfited and turn away. "Maybe they're just admiring you, sweetie."

"No, I heard them say Marise's name." Briana sounded quite upset. She set the sherry down on a table behind them. Jessica followed suit and the teacup clattered against the saucer.

"Gossips!" Jessica glared after them. "Don't they realize she's your sister?"

"We were never as close as I would've liked," Briana confided.

Jessica didn't know Marise. She'd been working in Melbourne and later Adelaide, while Marise had worked in the Pitt Street head office in Sydney. But the office chatter had been that Marise was a man-eater. Not long afterwards she'd married Matt Hammond and then Blake had been born. The gossips had speculated that she'd trapped Matt into marriage by getting pregnant.

Jessica shuddered at the thought and touched her stomach. What kind of marriage would that create? Perhaps Marise had outsmarted Matt. Perhaps she'd already been carrying Howard's child. What kind of woman would do that?

Only a very conniving kind of woman.

The kind of woman that a sweetie like Briana would've found it difficult to relate to. "Maybe Marise wasn't a woman's woman."

"She wasn't a sister's sister, either. I never really understood her." Briana looked around and lowered her voice. "A while back, when she was here for Mum's funeral, she asked to leave something in the safe in my apartment. I said yes. I looked inside the other day, and I discovered she'd left some stones."

"What kind of stones?"

"I don't know. Pink stones. I told Matt I'd found some of Marise's jewellery. He said I should keep it. But how can I do that, Jess?" Briana looked troubled. "I mean, if Matt doesn't want them, they really should go to Blake. They might even be valuable. What if they're diamonds?"

Jessica frowned. "Why don't you get someone to appraise them? There are a couple of people I use." The group in front of them shifted and through the gap Jessica could see Ryan talking to his sister, their dark heads close together. "Quinn Everard is very knowledgeable and has a great reputation, but he's a busy man. Stan Brownlee over in Manly is very good, too."

"I'll call you at the store later this week for their contact numbers," Briana murmured.

"Sure." Jessica was still watching Ryan. Even from here she could see his concern and affection for his sister in every line of his body. How she craved the same for herself. Although he cosseted her, and spoiled her with gifts and jewellery, Jessica had never felt as though Ryan *needed* her. She'd always been highly conscious that he was a Blackstone…and she was nothing more than his mistress.

"You could do a lot worse than Jessica. She's very nice."

Ryan froze. He'd ignored his sister's earlier comment in the church, hoping it was nothing more than a wild guess. But she'd never been the type to let up. And if she found out about his affair with Jessica, that would make his opposition to her relationship with Ric years ago on the basis that they worked together seem very odd.

But how was he supposed to explain that what he had

with Jessica had just…combusted? He'd never meant for it to happen. Hell, he still wasn't sure how he'd landed in bed with her after one of his monthly business trips to Adelaide to check on the store. All he could remember was being drawn relentlessly to Jessica in one the most intense connections of personal chemistry he'd ever experienced. Sexual attraction had blown away his intentions of keeping the stunning store manager at a healthy distance. After a year of illicit monthly bouts of passion, the role of manager of the Sydney store had become vacant and he'd persuaded Jessica, despite her reluctance, to take the transfer to the flagship store.

"What do you mean?"

"Oh, come on." Kim rolled her eyes. "This is me, Kimberley, your sister you're talking to. That distant facade doesn't cut it with me. And you're old enough to be starting to think about needing a wife…a family."

Ryan felt his lips twitch at his sister's irreverence. Then he said, "What makes you so certain that I'd want a wife like Jessica?"

"I know there's something between you two. Don't worry, I'm not going to pry. But she's bright and pretty—and she's doing a great job with the Sydney store. Look after her so that she doesn't decide to give up on you."

At his ferocious frown Kimberley pulled a face. "I just want you happy."

"I'm not into commitment, nor do I want a family."

"Oh." Kim's exclamation held a wealth of understanding. "Does Jessica know that?"

"Yes," he bit out.

"So there is something going on between you!"

His glare at Kimberley intensified. "You think you're so smart! Getting back together with Ric has given you the wedding bug. Why don't you find—" he looked around a trifle desperately "—Briana or Danielle or even Aunt Sonya a spouse?"

"Okay, I can take the hint. I'll mind my own business and leave you alone."

But after Kimberley had moved away with her nose stuck pointedly in the air Ryan found himself pondering what she'd said. *Look after her so that she doesn't decide to give up on you.*

Was Jessica dissatisfied? There'd been that argument they'd had about his spending Christmas at the Byron Bay beach house without her. She'd wanted to spend Christmas with him, but he'd been determined to spend the time with Howard to follow up on the discussions on how his own role within the company could be enlarged. Romance had been the last thing on his mind over the festive season. Jessica had sulked and spent time away with her parents instead. Then, in January, there'd been those horrific hours after his father's death when he'd been unable to locate her. And tangled in that had been the terrible suspicion that he'd never dared think about. Even now he thrust it from his mind.

If he thought back over the past month he'd have to say that she'd been quieter, more reflective, but he'd been so tied up in the catastrophe of his father's death—and the struggle to hold Blackstone's together in the face of all the public scandal—that he'd barely noticed. Perhaps he *was* too distant with Jessica.

But she'd always been so understanding.

And they were both so involved in their careers. That was one of the things that had drawn him to her. She didn't cling. Or demand. She was happy with what they had…or at least that was what he'd always believed.

Until Kim had started confusing him.

Did Jessica want more from him? And could he offer more? He shook his head. *No.* He'd never wanted a family.

But if Jessica was unhappy…

That was the last thing he'd wanted. He liked her…a lot. Perhaps he had been unfair to demand she keep their relationship a secret. Would she be happier if it were public knowledge? That certainly didn't mean he'd be marrying her. But if she were unhappy, that might go some of the way to stemming her dissatisfaction.

If Jessica didn't work for him it would be much easier. He'd been concerned about that from the outset, mostly because he hadn't wanted the kind of rumours that had surrounded his father. The endless, lewd speculation about his "secretaries." But Jessica was a hardly a secretary, she was a very capable store manager. If she didn't work for Blackstone's it would all be a lot simpler.

Across the room he could see a waiter offering her a glass of champagne, and Jessica's smiled refusal. He couldn't ask her to give up her career at Blackstone's, to go work somewhere else, simply because he didn't want to be seen sleeping with his store manager. Just the thought of letting her go disturbed him far more than he cared to admit.

Yet if his sister had worked out there was something between them, it wouldn't be long before others did, too. Jessica had moved in with him and had sublet her apartment—after much persuading from him. Sooner or later somcone was going to discover that.

Ryan rubbed his jaw. There would be gossip. Endless media speculation. But did it really matter that much what people thought of him sleeping with his staff?

He started to cross the room to where Jessica still stood talking to Briana, the beautiful brunette whom half the men in the room would give their eye-teeth to meet. Yet it was Jessica's delicate features that held him captive. He'd almost reached them when an immaculately manicured hand settled on his arm.

"Ryan, so sorry about your father." Kitty Lang skipped to keep up with him, her long gold earrings swinging wildly beneath the bleached-blonde curls. "I heard that he left a fortune to that Marise Davenport." She tapped his arm and gave him an arch look. "Howard was always a bit of a ladies' man." Her giggle grated. "She worked for him a couple of years ago, didn't she?"

Ryan stopped and examined Kitty warily. "Marise worked for Blackstone's—in the marketing department. Not for Howard personally," he bit out, hating the way she made the word *work* sound. No doubt there was a good dose of the green-eyed monster at work. Kitty was rumoured to have been one of his father's mistresses. Not that Ryan paid much attention to the speculation. He'd learned long ago to try and ignore it.

"He always did have an eye for a pretty girl. And so much easier when they worked for Blackstone's. Keep it on the payroll."

His stomach turned. With distaste, he started to extricate himself from Kitty's clutches. This kind of talk was exactly why he hadn't gone public with his relationship with Jessica. The boss-sleeping-with-employee thing was so sordid. He'd been saying for years that Blackstone's should have a no-love-at-work contract.

Yet he'd have broken it.

"It wouldn't surprise me if Marise was already on her way out and that pretty little blonde was warming Howard's bed. He always liked blondes." Kitty ruffled a hand through her platinum curls. "And she works for Blackstone's, doesn't she?"

Something tightened in Ryan's gut. He went on red alert, every nerve end quivering. "Who are you talking about?"

"That girl."

"Which one?"

He followed where Kitty was pointing.

Jessica. "Jessica has never worked for my father." She worked for him! Let Kitty dare try intimate Jessica was one of his father's "secretaries."

"I saw them." Kitty wore an expression of catlike satisfaction.

"Where?" he challenged, praying that she'd spout some nonsense.

"I was flying a client on a charter to Fiji to look at a property." Kitty was a top-class realtor. "It was at the airport. They were arguing."

"That's it?" He stared at her. "That was enough for you to decide they were having an affair?"

"You had to see them together. It was their body language. The way she was talking to him. Lots of emotion. She was angry. But it was the kind of anger you only show someone you know very well."

Like a lover.

That's what Kitty meant.

But Jessica hardly knew his father. Ryan cast his mind back to the occasions he'd seen Jessica and his father in the same room during the eight years she'd worked for Blackstone's. Jessica went very quiet when his father was around. They never talked. No doubt Jessica had been a little in awe of his overpowering father.

Although he had to admit that after he'd discovered that Jessica was booked on the flight that went down he'd wondered why she'd been on the passenger list. Briefly. And he hated himself for the flare of suspicion. He'd suppressed it brutally for a whole month, refusing to even descend into the realm of those dark thoughts. Now Kitty was bringing it all back. He wasn't going there. Ryan sucked in a deep breath. "That means noth—"

"It was on the evening that Howard disappeared. He took her by the elbow, she struggled, then she went with him to board the jet."

"But she wasn't on the jet when it crashed." He tried to argue against what Kitty was saying. But it was getting harder. Jessica had been on the original passenger list. He'd nearly died when he'd seen that. And when he hadn't been able to reach her on her cell phone he'd assumed the worst....

And then he'd come home after the worst day of his life to find her watching television.

Giving himself a shake, Ryan turned away from Kitty, from the poison she was mouthing. Kitty must've made a mistake. Her convincing tale rang through his head. Perhaps she was lying...but why? She didn't know about him and Jessica.

He would ask Jessica about Kitty's allegations, and there would be a reasonable explanation. There had to be. He couldn't bear the alternative.

Jessica was pouring herself a cup of tea when he came up beside her.

"Would you like a cup?" she asked him.

Ryan noticed that she didn't look at him. No secret little smile. Nothing. She kept her attention firmly on the cup she was filling. How had this gap between him and Jessica developed? In future he was going to work on making her feel more valued. "I'll help myself to some coffee from the pot." He moved to the next table where one of the catering staff was filling cups with steaming coffee from a pot.

"Don't say that!" The irritated note in Jessica's voice behind him caught his attention. Jessica raising her voice? Ryan did a double take and turned his head. Jessica was standing with her hands on her hips, looking unmistakably annoyed.

"That's nothing more than vicious gossip. You should be careful what you say."

The target of her outburst had turned scarlet with mortification. What was Jessica so upset about? Ryan scanned the gathering. Briana had disappeared. Kitty was watching Jessica from a distance away, her mouth open in surprise. She caught Ryan's eye and mouthed *See?*

The tightness in his gut was back. Ryan rubbed his eyes. Had Kitty stumbled on the truth? Was his lover also his dead father's mistress?

Seated in the plush leather passenger seat of the BMW, Jessica tilted her head against the headrest and glanced across at Ryan. His hands were clenched on the steering wheel, leashing the torque of the powerful car, his knuckles white as he concentrated on the road ahead and his profile etched against the afternoon light, his nose long and straight, his hair springing back from the distinctive widow's peak.

The funeral was done.

She sighed.

"Tired?" he asked.

"A little." More than a little. Weariness seeped through her. Her feet were sore from standing around in high heels and her back ached. The nausea had returned, a reminder that it was time to start eating better for herself and the baby. She'd use her tiredness as an excuse tonight to sleep in the guest bedroom—as Ryan sometimes did when he came home late, so as not to wake her.

She had to find the strength to end it. She couldn't bear him to touch her tonight. Last night she'd said her goodbyes with every soft kiss, with every gentle stroke of her fingers. They would never make love again.

Never.

"What were you arguing with my father about on the day he died?"

His words slammed into her tired brain with all the force of a sledgehammer.

"Pardon?" Jessica hedged, and her heart lurched in her chest before starting to pound unsteadily. She'd hoped that Ryan would never learn about that awful confrontation.

"You were arguing with my father at the airport. I want to know what it was about."

You.

But she wouldn't tell Ryan that. He probably wouldn't believe her anyway. As much as she detested the man, Ryan idolized Howard Blackstone and strove to follow in his father's footsteps, even though she suspected that hidden behind Ryan's ruthless veneer had been a need for his father's respect.

"It wasn't exactly an argument." She crossed her fingers. "We were just talking."

"The person who saw you said it looked very personal—very emotive. Like you knew each other very well."

Oh, God.

This discussion she didn't need. Not now, not after the funeral. Ryan deserved good memories of his father—not her tainted, far-from-impartial opinion of Howard Blackstone.

She stalled. "Who told you we were arguing?"

"It doesn't matter." He shot her a frowning glance before directing his attention back to the road.

It doesn't matter. Jessica looked away, staring out the side window. For the past two years she'd lived in a fool's paradise. While she'd never expected a proposal of marriage when she'd moved into Ryan's penthouse a year ago, she'd certainly fantasized that Ryan would come to love her. The attraction between them had been so strong, so fierce and overwhelming from the first, that she'd been so sure love would follow.

Heck, she loved him. That's why she'd given in to Ryan's

urging and applied for the store manager's position of the Sydney store when it had come available. Even though she'd worried a little that she'd only gotten the job because she was sleeping with the boss. And even though Sydney was the last city in the world where she wanted to live.

She'd made the move so that she could spend more time with him. But she'd never expected his insistence that their affair remain a secret. And after a year she was still no more than a millionaire's hole-in-the-corner mistress.

Since her return, he never invited anyone over—not even his sister, certainly not his father. When she'd asked why no one visited, he'd told her that he valued his privacy and that he saw enough of his family at work. He had his own social life, his own set of friends he met for dinner in exclusive restaurants, a life he lived without her.

No more! She touched her belly. It wasn't about *her* anymore. Now she had a baby to think about. A child who deserved more than life on the outer edges of Ryan Blackstone's existence.

"You were having an affair with him." Ryan interrupted her thoughts.

Frowning, she tried to make sense of what he was saying. "Who's having an affair?"

"You!" he said, his voice harsh with impatience and anger. "*You* were having an affair with my father."

Three

"What?"

Jessica stared at Ryan in shock. The ugly accusation hung between them. Jessica had a feeling of being a distance away and seeing Ryan as if for the first time. Of looking at a total stranger.

"You honestly believe I was sleeping with your father?" She almost laughed in disbelief. It was so utterly off base. "You're joking, right?"

"No, I'm deadly serious." He slowed to a stop at the traffic light and pulled up the handbrake with unnecessary force. He flashed her a dark, smouldering glare, full of hard suspicion and anger. The tight set of his mouth and the tic in his jaw revealed his perturbation.

Jessica's heart sank. He did believe it. This wasn't some sick joke.

How the heck was she supposed to react to this bombshell?

She wanted to rage at him, scream, get out the car and storm off into the baking afternoon heat. But she suppressed the melodramatics that weren't her style. Struggling with her own anger, she aimed for a composure she was far from feeling. "You have some basis for this?"

"That's all you can say? Ask me if I have evidence?"

Jessica remained mute, refusing to be drawn further, refusing to defend herself against such a ghastly accusation. The silence turned icy.

The light changed to green and the car moved slowly forward. With a curse, Ryan pulled off the road and raked his fingers through his hair. Then he turned sideways in his seat to face her. "I'm trying to give you the benefit of the doubt."

"That's big of you." Jessica couldn't stop the sarcasm slipping out. It was clear that beneath the benefit of the doubt he'd given her, suspicion still lurked. Insulting, unspeakable suspicions that make her feel soiled and sick to the stomach.

"I even dismissed Kitty's comments as troublemaking—"

"Kitty!" Jessica felt no surprise. Kitty Lang was every bit as catty as her name suggested.

"So was it a lover's quarrel that Kitty witnessed? Was my father breaking it off with you, to take up with Marise? Or was he having an affair with Marise all along and you found out about it and confronted him?"

"I'm not answering that." Jessica had no intention of telling him what the fight with Howard had been about.

"Have you got nothing more to say?"

She shrugged. "You've made up your mind that Kitty's told you the truth, so what do you want me to say?"

"Tell me it's not true." But his eyes were watchful, weighing her every movement, and Jessica knew that he would pick apart any avowal of innocence. An ugly, cold, hollowness seeped through her.

She shook her head. "What's the point? You clearly don't trust me and haven't for some time, if you've had suspicions about this." Pain sliced into her soul. That he even had to ask her whether it was true shattered her, enraged her. She wouldn't stoop to offering an explanation.

"At least tell me that it wasn't you talking to my father at the airport that night."

Blood started to pound through her head at his insistence. She couldn't give him the reassurance he sought.

After a moment he sighed. "You were supposed to fly to Auckland the afternoon before the crash on a commercial carrier, for the opening of the new store the next day. You didn't go. All you ever told me was that you'd changed your mind. I shoved aside the fact that that your name was on the passenger list for my father's flight. I dismissed it as a clerical error, a glitch in the bookings with several employees going to Auckland. With my father dead, I was too damned relieved that you hadn't flown that night. But I think you did change your flight. You decided to fly with my father...and then for some reason you never went."

She stared at him, her heart thudding in her chest, and said nothing. She'd missed the commercial flight, and the rest of the flights had been booked solid. She'd waitlisted herself for several of them, waiting at the airport on standby, watching each darn plane take off into the night sky. Spending several hours in Howard Blackstone's revolting company on the flight to Auckland had been a last resort...until she'd seen Howard while they were boarding, heard what he'd had to say. No way in hell had she been prepared to spend time in Howard's company after that altercation.

But Ryan didn't deserve an explanation. Her hands knotted in her lap; her nails dug into her palms. Ryan could believe what he damn well wanted. She no longer cared.

"That's it? That's what caused your suspicions? A change of flight?" She tried to laugh it away.

He hesitated, then his gaze hardened. "More the fact that you never bothered to let me know about your change in plans."

Jessica turned her head and stared blindly out the side window. She and Ryan had argued. She'd wanted to spend Christmas with him, but it hadn't suited him. They hadn't spoken while they'd been apart—she'd been upset. Then, while staying with her parents, she'd found out she was pregnant. And suddenly she had to decide how she was going to deal with it all.

No cats. No kids. No press. No diamond ring.

Those were his terms for their affair. By the end of the holiday she'd known she had only one choice: to break it off with him. She'd intended to take a couple of days off after the opening of the Auckland store to give her time to shore up the courage, and end their affair on her return to Sydney.

Except she'd never made it to Auckland.

And then his father's plane had gone missing.

Afterwards everything had come apart. It had taken ages for the search-and-rescue team to find his father's body. Ryan had been so distraught that Jessica couldn't bring herself to desert him in case he needed her. And knowing how he felt about commitment, there was no way in the world that she could tell him about the baby.

But now the end had come. Because Ryan Blackstone needed no one—least of all her.

"Hey," Ryan caught Jessica's arm as they exited the elevator into his two-storied penthouse apartment and pulled her around to face him. "Don't retreat into silence. We need to talk this out."

Deep down he clung to the growing hope, fuelled by her

angry reaction, that she hadn't betrayed him, hadn't been his father's mistress.

Jessica was his.

Surely she knew that.

His body certainly recognised her as his woman. His fingers had unconsciously started to move, to knead the soft, silken skin below her elbow. Standing this close, he was surrounded by the scent of roses from her perfume, heady and intensely feminine. Already his body was hardening, in tune with every breath she took, aware of every move she made. As soon as she'd explained everything to his satisfaction, they would kiss and make up.

He could barely wait.

His blood was already pumping a little faster through his veins as the primal lust she aroused so effortlessly took hold. He wondered if they'd have time to make it to the bedroom or whether he'd take her here on the carpeted stairs.

But first she owed him an explanation.

A little shard of unease pierced him.

What if Jessica *had* been his father's lover? Would he be able to forgive her? He comforted himself that the fantastic sex they shared would have to be enough. He'd just watch her very carefully in the future, keep her satiated so that she had no need to stray ever again. He told himself that the bitter emotion the thought of Jessica with his father aroused was nothing more than rage at her betrayal. He could get over that. He would forgive her. As long as she understood it must never happen again.

"I want the truth, Jessica. Then afterwards…" His voice trailed away, but he could feel the betraying heat glaze his eyes, the voracious hunger tighten his muscles until he felt he might snap.

"Afterwards?" Her face was cold. Frozen. "What do you

mean *afterwards*? After accusing me of having an affair with your father, you think I want to screw—"

"Hey, calm down." He leashed the annoyance that flashed through him. Surely Jessica knew that what they shared was more than that. But he'd never seen her like this. So passionless. Hard. He loosened his grip on her arm and stroked his fingers over her skin. He glimpsed the sheen of tears. Then she blinked and the veil of moisture was gone.

Jessica slapped his arm away. "Don't touch me!" Her voice cracked and she swung around and headed for the stairs.

"Where are you going?"

"To pack."

"Pack?" Disbelief rolled through him. "What do you mean pack?"

She turned, a hand on the banister, and looked down at him. "It's over, Ryan. It's been over for a long time. But I was too stupid to notice."

Two steps took him to the bottom step. "What do you mean it's over? You can't leave—"

"Watch me. I'm going to walk out the penthouse, out your life and—"

"Out my life?" Alarm bells rang loudly in his head. What the hell had gotten into Jessica? "What about Blackstone's? What about your job?" And what about making love with him?

She stopped at the top of the stairs. "It's always about Blackstone's, isn't it? You don't have a heart, Ryan, you have a glittering lump of carbon inside you. Don't worry, I'll stay. I'll help Kimberley arrange the launch of the Something Old, Something New collection at the end of the month. I won't leave you in the lurch. But in a couple of months I'll be moving on. So start looking for someone to replace me."

Replace her? He stared up at her, aghast. How could he ever replace her?

"Wait." She couldn't simply walk out. He needed her. "You can't do this."

"Watch me." She raised her chin.

Jessica had a soft heart. She was a pushover. "My father was buried today. Doesn't that mean anything to you?"

"Because I'm supposed to be his mistress?"

"No—" He searched for the right words. Had his father dumped her? If so, his instincts to keep his relationship with her secret had been good. What a ghastly scandal there would've been if it had come out that both he and his father had been sleeping with the same woman. A woman who worked for Blackstone's. God! What a mess.

"I'm very sorry for your loss, Ryan." Her face was set and pale. "Hard as you may find it to believe, I never saw much to admire in your father. He was arrogant and conceited, and he had an appalling view of women."

"You sound as if you hated him," Ryan said slowly, trying to read her expression beneath the stony anger.

Jessica blinked. "Not hate."

"Then what?"

Jessica hesitated. "Despise. I despised him. I became your mistress despite your father. Why do you think I never argued when you never offered to take me to your family gatherings?" She gave him a twisted smile.

Ryan eyed that smile. There was a lot more to her relationship with his father than met the eye. Maybe his suspicions had been misguided...but then why hadn't Jessica set him straight?

"I didn't want to spend my precious free time with a bastard like Howard Blackstone," she continued, her usually tender eyes flashing. "Do you know what's really funny?"

"What?" Ryan asked warily, certain he wasn't going to find the answer at all amusing.

"I became your lover despite your father's terrible reputation for bedding his secretaries. I told myself you were different, that you were nothing like your father—"

"He struggled to come to terms with my mother's death, he loved her. My father was a great man."

"Was he?" She lifted an eyebrow.

"Howard Blackstone built a successful empire. He was a well-known humanitarian."

"He was a terrible father. He made more enemies than friends." Jessica ticked Howard's shortcomings off on her fingers. "Believe me there is no woman less likely than I to be your mistress. For more than a year I've lived with you here, been your kept woman, but it's over. I'll never be any man's mistress again."

Ryan stared at her. Had Jessica expected him to *marry* her? Hell! He'd liked her, enjoyed her company and absolutely lived to make love to her, but he had no intention of marrying anyone. She knew that. She'd accepted that. "If this is about getting a marriage proposal out of me, then it *is* over." Ryan flung the words at her. "Because I don't want—or need—a wife. I told you that at the outset."

Jessica gave a snort from the top of the stairs. She disappeared into the room they'd shared and Ryan decided to wait downstairs. He picked up a newspaper and settled down in his favourite chair. She'd calm down, he told himself as he heard the muffled sounds of movement upstairs. It would all blow over.

Ten minutes later she reappeared, carrying a suitcase. "I'll send someone over for the rest of my things," she said over her shoulder as she strode past.

Dropping the paper, he rose to his feet. "Jessica, you need to think this through."

She hit the button for the elevator. "I've thought of nothing else for months."

Months? He did a double take. "If you walk into that elevator it's over. I won't come running after you."

"I don't expect you to." The doors slid silently open. Without a backward glance, she walked into the waiting cage.

The organ that Jessica had referred to as a glittering lump of carbon felt a pang of something...something Ryan could identify only as regret.

The board meeting Ryan had been waiting for with such eager anticipation was over.

Without looking at the other board members, Ryan made his escape, desperate for space and a reprieve from the arctic air-conditioning. Shoving his hands in his pockets he walked out of the impressive building that housed Blackstone Diamonds' head office and jostled with lunchtime shoppers on Pitt Street who had taken advantage of the Monday lull to visit a host of boutiques in the nearby malls.

When he'd come back from golf on Saturday and sailing on Sunday, Jessica had not been waiting at the penthouse with her ready smile and soft voice. A sense of emptiness had nagged at him all weekend. The penthouse had seemed sterile and the music he'd played on his state-of-the-art sound system had echoed hollowly around the immaculate interior. There'd been no relaxing out on the balcony overlooking the harbour as the sun sank, while the wind tugged at Jessica's tousled hair.

But Ryan refused to be emotionally blackmailed. She would come around.

As for this morning's meeting, it had been disastrous. Ryan's blood still boiled at the memory. He'd argued that public confidence demanded that a Blackstone be chairman of the board—particularly with the company under threat of a takeover from Matt Hammond, Kimberley's former boss.

His uncle Vincent had agreed.

But the rest of the board had not felt the same way. Ric Perrini had gotten the chairmanship he had coveted.

"Ric may not be a Blackstone, but his loyalty is not in question. He has far and away the most experience, and he's married to a Blackstone." The words of one of the directors still rang in Ryan's ears.

And his sister had hovered, halfway down the table, clearly torn between wanting to stand by her husband and to maintain the truce with him.

The old seething resentment against his brother-in-law was back in full force. But at the forefront of Ryan's mind as he stalked down the street was the determination that tonight he would not return to an empty penthouse.

He rounded the corner into Martin Place, and continued until he reached the discreetly elegant Blackstone's signage outside the imposing facade of the heritage building that housed the largest and most profitable of all the jewellery stores he controlled.

At least the stores were a success no one could take from him. His vision and planning had led to increased profits, expansion and new stores and designs for jewellery that the market loved.

With a nod he strode past Nathaniel, the liveried doorman who had worked here for the past ten years, through the revolving doors and into the airy gallery-style ground floor, empty of everything except a towering modern black marble sculpture in the centre and glass display cabinets built into the walls.

An incisive glance revealed that a batch of pale pink diamonds recently cut in New York had already been set in modern settings of white gold and placed in the wall-mounted display boxes. Ryan paused. The pieces looked stunning. Yes, they would whet the appetite of the discerning shopper.

The best and biggest stones mined at the Blackstone-owned Janderra mine were still sent to Antwerp for cutting and were available for inspection only by appointment.

The surge of pride for all he'd achieved took him by surprise. He was responsible for the glittering success of the stores. Even his father had known that....

After the humiliating defeat he'd just suffered in the boardroom, he would make the launch of the stunning collections timed for the Northern Hemisphere summer so magnificent that the cognoscenti would be talking about it for months.

Buoyed with new-found enthusiasm, he made for the impressive stairway that led to the next floor—where the majority of walk-in business was conducted.

At the top of the stairwell lay the salon-style showroom, with its thick marbled columns and glittering crystal chandeliers, redolent with the rich patina of wealth.

Ryan's gaze landed on Jessica and he froze. She was facing away from him, talking to Holly McLeod, a PR assistant involved in helping with the organisation of the Something Old, Something New showing that would take place in the spacious downstairs lobby later in the month.

Jessica hadn't contacted him over the weekend to collect her possessions. By now, with time to cool down, she'd surely have realized the tactical mistake she'd made. By tonight he was determined to have her back in his bed—where she belonged.

At the thought, his hormones went wild, and he gave her a very subtle, intensely sexual once-over. She was wearing a silky blouse in an oyster shade and a pair of smartly tailored pale grey linen trousers cool enough for the Sydney heat. A strand of lustrous pearls at her neck and a pair of snakeskin heels high enough to be sexy completed the outfit that managed to strike a balance between stylish and sensual.

She reminded him of the pale pink diamonds he'd been

admiring downstairs, so cool and impervious on the outside but inside the fire sparkled with a brilliance that was breathtaking.

Ryan reined back the raw need that the sight of her unleashed. He would handle her with care, with a fine meal and plenty of flattery. He couldn't afford for her to walk out of her job—not with the show so close. Jessica was too sensible to walk away from Blackstone's. She'd never allow her personal life to jeopardise her future. Her career would always come first.

They were similar in that outlook.

But he didn't need to stand here and stare at her all day. Jessica was his lover. He knew every inch of her covered flesh intimately.

Ryan strolled forward. "Jessica, a moment, please."

She turned her head. Ryan found himself staring into blank, polite brown eyes. "Good morning, Ryan."

The chilly formality took him aback. "I need to talk to you." He glanced at Holly. "Privately."

But Holly was already moving away, the picture of efficiency in a tailored white shirt and black trousers, her long dark hair caught up in a sleek ponytail, a leather folder clasped to her chest.

"Look, about Friday night—"

"If this is not work-related then I'd rather not discuss it right now. I have details I need to finalise with Holly."

She started after Holly. Ryan reached out and grabbed her. It didn't take a rocket scientist to know that Jessica was signalling that this conversation was at an end.

"I have work to do!"

As she spun to face him, Ryan stared at her, flummoxed. Jessica had never spoken to him in that sharp voice. Even during working hours when they'd kept each other at a professional distance—at his insistence—she hadn't been this distant. He let her arm go.

Alarm fluttered through him. For the first time he considered the possibility that he might've lost her—that she really wouldn't be coming back.

He regrouped rapidly. "Let's have lunch—"

"I'm really busy, Ryan."

"Dinner then."

"I'm going to my parents for dinner tonight."

He'd imagined she'd be staying with her parents. If not, where the hell was she staying? He'd find out tonight. "What time will you be finished? I'll pick you up, and we can go for a drink first—" He broke off as she shook her head.

"I'm bringing Picasso back with me. I can't leave him alone on his first night at my apartment."

Picasso? His frown deepened. Who the hell was Picasso? Oh, yes, her rag-bag cat.

No pets. No kids. No press. No diamond rings. Those had been the ground rules of their affair. He wasn't sure which item on the list he detested most. They all reeked of the insidious ways that women curtailed a man's freedom. If he'd allowed the cat, the designer elegance of the penthouse would've been transformed into off-the-rack homeliness before he'd had time to take a breath. The excuse that he hadn't wanted the animal in his penthouse in case it wrecked the expensive furnishings had worked. Now she was taking it back to her apartment….

Her apartment?

He stiffened. "I thought you'd sublet your apartment?"

"No." She met his gaze levelly. "You ordered me to sublet it and assumed I had. I wanted to keep it available. I wasn't sure when I'd need it."

Her words rocked him. She'd been expecting this. Months,

she'd said on Friday night. *I've thought of nothing else for months.*

Why? Why had she planned to break it off? If it hadn't been because of his father, then who? He cast his mind back, trying to remember any man she'd mentioned, talked about. No one attracted a red flag. But then she had her own social life, as he had his. "Is there someone else?"

"Of course not!" Her eyes were flashing.

He pushed away the festering thought of Jessica with his father. "You're telling me no other party is involved in our breakup?"

Her gaze slid away from his. "Why the postmortem, Ryan?" Then her breath caught and the eyes that snapped back to his were filled with remorse. "Sorry, that was tactless."

She was hiding something. There was someone. He reached for her hand. "Jessica—"

"Not at work, Ryan." She yanked her fingers free. "Someone might see."

The tingle from the brush of her fingers against his lingered. He shoved his hand into his pocket and stared at her through narrowed eyes. After a moment he dismissed the half-formed suspicion that she was mocking him and swivelled to scan the room. "No one is looking."

It occurred to him that he had no clue what was going on inside her beautiful blonde head. Suddenly he wished he hadn't insisted on their maintaining separate sets of friends, separate social lives. But then he'd never expected *her* to be the one to break it off.

God, how had this happened? Of all the countless beautiful women he'd dated, how had this one managed to get under his guard?

"Meet me for dinner tomorrow then, after work."

"To discuss work?"

"No, to talk about us."

"There is no 'us.' It's over, Ryan." She gave an impatient sigh and brushed the blonde tendrils off her face. Then she hurried away, calling Holly's name, and he stared after her.

An icy determination filled his gut. Ryan tilted his head to one side and narrowed his gaze as he considered his options. He couldn't do anything about losing the chairmanship of the board…yet. But he was damned if he would lose Jessica.

That afternoon Jessica couldn't get Ryan's bleak expression out of her mind as she flipped through a brochure featuring carefully selected pieces of the Something Old, Something New collections being launched at the end of the month.

It certainly wasn't because she'd left him.

More likely it was the realisation that his father was gone forever that had turned his handsome features into a haggard mask. She couldn't help feeling guilty about breaking it off with him.

But she'd had no choice.

It was best for herself…and her baby. After all, what did she want with a man who made it clear that he wanted nothing more than a secret mistress—one whom he believed could leap into bed with his father?

But it was the best solution for Ryan, too. With all the problems facing Blackstone's, the last thing Ryan needed right now was the additional scandal of a pregnant secret mistress erupting in the public eye.

Nor was she ready to tell him about the baby yet. She couldn't bear for him to accuse her of deliberately getting pregnant. Or ask her to abort the child he would never want. It was her problem, not his. And she wanted this baby, *his* baby, with a desperation that astonished her.

She turned the page, and stopped at the glossy photo of a stunning Xander Safin piece. Quickly she made a call to Xander and arranged a time to meet him in two days to show him how magnificently the brochures had come out.

When Holly returned later with the next pile of brochures to show her Jessica was unprepared for Holly's question. "Did you read the memo from head office?"

She searched Holly's blue-green eyes for a clue. "What memo?"

"The e-mail memo announcing that the chairmanship has been decided."

Tiredly Jessica brushed her hair off her face and dropped her gaze to stare blindly at the brochure. *The chairmanship of the board.* The position that Ryan had wanted most in the world.

"I've been so busy I haven't had a chance to go through my e-mails yet. What was the outcome?" She waited, tensing. He'd lost so much with his father's death, she couldn't bear it if he lost this, too.

"Ric Perrini was voted in."

Jessica squeezed her eyes shut. Then a horrible thought struck her. Her eyes snapped open. "When?" Then more urgently she asked, "When did this happen?"

"This morning. Just before lunch."

Jessica swore softly.

Holly looked at her with a slightly startled expression.

Ryan must have come straight from the board meeting to the store. He'd asked her to lunch. And she'd sent him away. Had he come to share what must've been a devastating blow with her? Then the next realisation hit her. *That* must be the reason he'd looked so terrible. Nothing to do with their breakup. Nothing to do with her at all. It was all about Blackstone's.

Holly was playing with a small solitaire pendant that hung

from a gold chain around her neck. "He'll be okay. Ryan is such an iceman, nothing gets to him."

Jessica blinked. Was that how people saw Ryan? As an iceman? Was she the only one who saw beneath the diamond-hard exterior to the volcanic emotions below? The anger. The passion. The mix of turbulent emotions that made up the complex man she loved but did not always understand.

Holly looked concerned. "I really thought you knew."

"Don't worry about it. I'll read the e-mail later. I'm glad you told me. I'm sure Ryan will be disappointed. But Ric will make a fine chairman."

By the following day, everyone knew that Ric Perrini was now chairman of the board, and Jessica's heart ached for Ryan. But she wouldn't allow herself to weaken and call him to offer sympathy. She had to think of herself first now, and their baby.

She didn't see him that day—too much must be happening up at the corporate office in Pitt Street. But when she got home after swimming at the local pool in the hope that exercise might help her sleep better tonight in her lonely double bed, it was to Picasso's frantic complaints—and her newly activated answerphone blinking.

Ryan.

Jessica's first thought was of him.

Then she remembered that Ryan didn't even have this number. The message was from her mother, to whom she'd given her number earlier in the day. When Jessica pulled her cell phone out of her Fendi bag, she saw she'd missed four calls from him during the afternoon. She sank into a chair and put her head in her hands. Who was she kidding? Finally, she picked up the handset and punched in the cell phone number she knew by heart.

"I heard about the chairmanship, I'm sorry. Is that why you came down to the store? To tell me?"

"That's why you called me?" he asked. "To commiserate?"

After that crack, she wasn't telling him that she'd been worried sick about him. "Why else?"

"I see." He sounded strange.

"Ryan…?" He didn't respond. "Do you want me to come over?"

"Come over or come back?"

"I'm not coming back." A deafening silence met her stark statement. Jessica bit her lip. Should she have softened her refusal? No. There was no going back. Not to what they'd had. And Ryan wasn't capable of offering her more.

Then he sighed softly. "Don't worry about coming over. I don't need pity right now."

Pity? Jessica nearly told him exactly what had almost been on offer. Her body…her heart…her soul. Their baby.

Fool. Ryan Blackstone certainly didn't need a ready-made family—or her love!

Four

The following evening Ryan came to an abrupt stop on the threshold of the Louvre Bar, where he'd invited Ric and his sister for a truce-sealing after-work drink to celebrate Ric's appointment as chairman of the board. After a day spent soul-searching, he decided it was time to put his disappointment behind him, and throw his support behind Ric.

He'd arrived early. And the sight of two pale heads close together caused his teeth to clench until his jaw hurt.

Jessica and Xander Safin?

Was Xander the reason why Jessica had ditched him? For the first time Ryan considered Xander as a man rather than Blackstone's hotshot jewellery designer. Tall and lean. Indisputably good-looking with high Slavic cheekbones that gave his features an exotic mysticism that few women would be able to resist.

Too engrossed in each other, neither of them had seen Ryan. Right now Xander sat far too close to Jessica for Ryan's liking, his pale grey eyes sparkling and his hands moving expressively in the air as he spoke, while Jessica listened, nodding and interjecting the occasional comment.

Jessica's ability to listen was the quality that singled her out from every woman Ryan had ever known. And he missed the companionable silences. Jessica made it easy to relax, to be himself.

Hell, it had been less than a week and already he missed all that.

Ryan found an empty booth and dropped down onto the leather bench seat. From this angle he could still see them. He hadn't even known she saw Xander outside work. But when Jessica said something that caused Xander to fling his head back and laugh out loud, it became evident that they were very much at ease in each other's company.

His own fault!

He'd been the one to insist that they maintain separate social lives. Even though he'd been totally faithful to Jessica during their time together, he hadn't wanted a clinging vine when he finally ended their relationship. And now his separate-space philosophy had come back to bite him in the ass.

Jessica was an attractive, intelligent woman. No doubt there was a queue of men waiting to take his place. Starting with Xander-bloody-Safin.

Ryan found he didn't care for that idea at all.

"What's Jessica doing with him?"

He glanced up to find Ric sliding into the booth opposite him holding two beers, one of which he slid across the table. Ryan took it with a nod of thanks and looked around for his sister.

Before he could reprimand Kim, she'd rushed into speech. "I didn't tell him. Promise. He worked it out."

Ryan swallowed his annoyance. "I suppose it makes my reaction to you two—" his glance took in Kim and Ric "—all those years ago seem completely hypocritical?"

"Is that why you took such pains to hide your affair with Jessica?" Ric's gaze was fearsomely direct. "You didn't want it known that you were sleeping with the staff, when you've always been so vocally against it?"

"Relationships in companies always cause tension." Damn, but he sounded pious.

"Not always." Kim smiled slowly at Ric.

Ryan envied the easy confidence between them, the love that his sister deserved. "Just look at Dad."

"He'd fire his secretaries when they took his attentions too seriously." Kim shook her head. "Those poor women."

"Exactly. And his office would be in chaos for weeks."

"So why did you start something with Jessica if you knew that you'd probably end up firing her…if she's fool enough to fall in love with you?"

His sister's words hit him in the gut. Jessica, in love with him? No chance of that. Especially not after he'd accused her of sleeping with his father. And if his accusation had been wrong, then she'd have every right to be hurt and disappointed in his lack of trust. If he'd screwed that up, would she ever let him close again?

For a moment Ryan contemplated ignoring his sister's question. Then he shrugged. "I thought this time would be different. That I could control it." Hell, he'd gotten that wrong.

"Like you control everything else?"

Ryan glared at her, and she held her hands up. "Okay, I take that back."

"It was never intended to be anything more than a temporary affair. Jessica knew that. I knew Dad wouldn't approve of the relationship, either. He's always made it clear that I needed to think with my head when it came to women. Connections are—were—important to Dad."

"Because her family's not wealthy?" Kim asked. "That's

ridiculous. She runs the Sydney store with formidable acumen, she has an eye for design, she knows what the consumer wants and she has flair. Fashion nous."

"I never realised you were such a fan."

His sister drew an audible breath, then said quietly, "We've spent a lot of time together in the last month. I'd like to think that I can count her as a friend."

"I'm sure Dad wouldn't have minded Jessica being my 'friend'—he had enough of those himself." Ryan's mouth curled. "But I don't think he would've been too happy to find out she was living in my penthouse."

"She's living with you?" Kim's eyes were wide. "Why the secrecy?"

"Then what's she doing here with Xander Safin?" Ric interjected.

Trust Ric to cut to the heart of it. "We broke up," Ryan confessed reluctantly.

"Oh, Ryan." Kimberley shook her head in aggravation and her dark hair swirled across her shoulders. "Sometimes you puzzle me. She's the best thing that could've happened to you…and you worry about what Dad would think?"

Maybe his sister was right. He'd behaved like a jerk. But he couldn't help saying defensively, "You know what it was like, Kim. Always having to do the right thing. You know the price of disappointing Howard Blackstone." For far too long he'd tried to be the son his father wanted. To win his father's approval. The time had come to live his life on his terms— and to stop being a Howard Blackstone clone.

Kim met his gaze. "Dad is dead. And we're not children anymore. I've told you before, you could do a lot worse than Jessica Cotter, little brother."

"That's probably academic. Because it doesn't look like

Ryan will get the chance." Ric tilted his head in the direction of the other couple.

Ryan's gaze cut across the bar in time to see Jessica reach up and place a kiss on Xander Safin's mouth.

Jealousy slashed through him. Damn them! Jessica had no right to be kissing other men. She belonged in his bed, not in Xander Safin's arms. Jessica was his woman—and his alone.

The anger at her desertion came back in full force. He tore his gaze away from the couple and looked into his brother-in-law's all-seeing eyes.

"Let's get the hell out of here, before I take him apart with my bare hands," he muttered, his throat raw. He'd known that *something* had happened to force her to end their relationship. Xander-bloody-Safin had happened.

He shook his head to clear it of the rage. How could she have turned to another man to match the passion that they'd shared? Or had she'd felt neglected. Had she believed that he was ashamed of her?

"No, need," Ric replied. "They're leaving. If you want her back you're going to have to move swiftly. She's clearly not going to sit around moping over you."

Dammit, Ric was right. He'd been hoping that she'd realise her mistake, that she'd cool down and come back. But seeing her so cosy with Xander caused Ryan to reassess. If he didn't move fast, he might lose her for good.

Jessica belonged to him. What he needed was a way to force her to spend time with him. And this time he'd do things differently. This time he'd make sure she was so enthralled that she wouldn't look at another man.

But right now Ryan could do little except watch as the woman he wanted more than all the pink diamonds in Janderra walked out the bar beside the tall blond jewellery designer, turning heads as they went.

* * *

Jessica found that the days had been spinning past, faster and faster. She was busy and the store buzzed with customers. On top of all that, helping with the organisation for the approaching jewellery show meant even more unrelenting pressure. Each night she returned to her apartment utterly exhausted. She put the extreme fatigue down to her pregnancy. But she knew it would all be worth it once the baby was born. She couldn't wait to hold the life that grew within her.

When she walked into the store on Friday morning, bracing herself for another long day before the weekend, the last thing she expected was to find Ryan waiting in her office, a cup of coffee cradled between his hands. He looked relaxed and perfectly at home in her domain. By contrast, she felt harassed, a little ill as the scent of the coffee reached her…and a lot late.

He unfolded his legs and rose to his feet as she entered.

"Don't worry about getting up." As always his perfect manners triggered a softness deep inside her.

Jessica subsided into her chair behind the desk. She'd just come from an appointment with her doctor. She'd mentioned her tiredness, the drained feeling and he'd upped her iron intake. When Dr. Waite told her that the nausea should start receding now that she was in the second trimester, she'd wanted to kiss the man in gratitude.

Then he'd told her that she could look forward to being a little absentminded in this trimester. Jessica had groaned aloud, thinking of all that needed to be done for the launch. She couldn't afford to be scatter-brained. Not now of all times.

As Ryan sat down again, Jessica turned on her computer and reached for her PalmPilot. "I don't remember that we had an appointment," she said pointedly.

"We don't." Ryan took a sip, his green eyes examining her over the top of his mug. "But I wanted to let you know before the others that I'll be moving down here for the next few weeks in preparation for the launch."

"Here? You'll be working here?" Jessica's heart sank.

He nodded. "Think about it. It makes perfect sense."

"But Kimberley's also involved and she's working out of head office." So why the heck was he moving down here? His constant presence was going to mess with her head.

"Kimberley is only involved with the publicity. Holly McLeod and a couple of others working with her are all based at Pitt Street, so it wouldn't be a good idea to move my sister down here." He rocked back in the chair and took another sip of coffee. "I want to be where the heartbeat is. The place where the show will take place. The place where our jewellery is displayed, where the customers visit."

"But where will you sit?" She tried to remain calm and rational and not reveal her utter horror at what he was saying to her. "You'll want somewhere quiet, where you can work. Most of the space here is taken up by the salon, a couple of appointment rooms, which are heavily used, the vaults and storage space. You certainly can't use the staff canteen." She didn't care if she sounded unwelcoming. She didn't want Ryan around all day long, a daily reminder of all that she had lost.

It would be too painful.

And it increased one hundredfold the chances of him discovering that she was pregnant.

He shrugged. "I'll find somewhere. There's a small boardroom next door that I can use."

"But the plugs are too far from the table to be any use for your laptop." She knew that Ryan never remembered to charge the batteries, and he hadn't gotten around to upgrading to wireless like the rest of the senior management team. "And there's no phone extension."

"I can use my cell phone." He peered sideways. "You have enough plugs here to run a power station. I can always share your office if I need to use my laptop."

Oh, no!

She'd moved out his penthouse, now he planned to move into her office. If it wasn't so upsetting, it might be farcical.

"I'll be out of town for some of the time. And you're on the floor a lot," he added. "There should be plenty of space for both of us."

She stared at him, aghast. She'd been spending her lunchtimes in her office with the door closed and her feet up to stop her ankles swelling in the heat. And she'd been taking short breaks through the day when the tiredness plagued her. With Ryan under her feet, it wouldn't take him long to start asking questions. Just the thought was enough to make her shudder with dread.

"Suit yourself. You're the boss." She looked away and tried to look unconcerned as she logged her password into the computer.

"I'm going to need your help, Jess."

Her heart ached at the tender, familiar way he spoke the shortened version of her name that only he used. "With what?"

"With the jewellery show." He hesitated, then said solemnly, "Some people are muttering that we should've cancelled the showing, given my father's tragic death. I think that those rumours were started by our competitors and the press have been eager to run with them. I want the show to be a tribute to my father, to be the best that's ever been done."

Put like that, how could she refuse? "Of course, I'll help you." Then she thought of something she'd been meaning to ring him about. "I'd like to collect my things over the weekend. Will tomorrow be convenient?" Since she still held a key to the penthouse, she could slip in sometime during the morning, while Ryan played his regular Saturday round of golf with a group of businessmen who held powerful jobs.

The silence stretched.

She glared at the computer screen. "Or perhaps next week some time?"

"Not next week, I'll be going to Janderra for part of the week so I won't be able to help you pack."

That caught her attention. "But what about the races?" The annual St. Valentine's Diamond Stakes, sponsored by Blackstone Diamonds, would be held next week in Melbourne. Jessica had been considering giving the event a wide berth this year. Prickles of tension spread across her skin. Last year she'd spent the day pretending to barely know Ryan and the night going wild in his arms....

"It would be a pity to miss that." She glanced at him, hoping that none of her memories showed in her eyes.

A frown pleated his brow. "I'm too busy to go to Melbourne. You can collect your possessions tomorrow, if you want."

He stood. Seconds later he was gone, taking his empty mug with him, and all of a sudden Jessica felt bereft. She placed her hand on her stomach. Earlier, she'd heard the baby's heartbeat. It had been noisy, although the doctor had said that part of the noise had been her own heartbeat in the background. But it had made everything so real, so thrilling.

And even though Ryan had always made it clear he had no intention of being a family man, what had been missing when she'd heard the baby's heartbeat had been Ryan at her side to share the wonder.

Jessica swiped the access card that controlled the elevator that went up to Ryan's Pyrmont penthouse apartment in the luxurious complex overlooking the harbour. It felt odd to be entering the elevator, riding up to the empty penthouse, the place where she'd lived in a temporary waiting-for-the-shoe-to-drop manner for the past year. Today would be the last time she'd come here.

The doors hissed open. She stepped out…and stopped dead.

Instead of the vacant apartment she'd expected, Ryan sat in the living room, the weekend papers scattered over the leather couch beside him. Dressed casually in a pair of black jeans and a white polo shirt, he looked unfairly breathtaking.

"You're supposed to be at golf," she accused, struggling to recover from the shock. *Why was he here?* His Saturday morning round of golf was sacred, he never missed it. Everywhere she turned lately, Ryan was there, larger than life, dominating *her* life.

"I thought you might come this morning." Was that a hint of satisfaction in those rich green eyes? "I skipped golf so that I could be here to help you."

"But—" Jessica broke off. She didn't need his help. She must look like a fish, with her mouth opening and closing as she tried to think of something to say. "You didn't need to do that," she said lamely.

"Oh, but I did." He swept the newspapers aside and rose to his feet. "You've lived here for a year. How could I let you leave like a thief in the night?" Despite the polite words, his eyes were full of turbulence.

Jessica gnawed at her lip. He was going to make this difficult. "I'll be fine, honestly." She glanced helplessly at her watch. "If you go now—"

"It's too late for me to play today."

"But you could still make the second nine—"

With the wave of his arm he dismissed the golf game, and

his mates. "I organised them a fourth already. They don't need me."

"Neither do I," she murmured rebelliously.

He stilled. "No, I don't suppose you do."

The edge of cynicism in his voice caused her to say, "What's that supposed to mean?"

"You have Xander Safin now to satisfy your…needs."

"That's a disgusting thing to say. Xander's a colleague. We have a working relationship."

"And you kiss all your colleagues?" His voice was soft, lethal.

Jessica blinked. Then she thought frantically what he could be talking about.

A kiss?

Of course! She'd kissed Xander goodbye the other night. "You should have come over and said hello rather than watching from wherever you were hiding. That was a good-night kiss to the friend that Xander has become."

He tipped his head to one side, examining her. "You want me to believe you didn't leave with him?"

He already believed she'd been his father's mistress. His bad opinion of her couldn't get any worse. "I don't care what you believe. But I'm telling you I went home alone." She brushed past him. "Goodness, you have a low opinion of me. First you accuse me of being your father's mistress, now I'm Xander's lover. Make up your mind!"

From behind her, he murmured, "Put like that it does sound a little excessive. I believe you that Xander is nothing more than a colleague."

"Gee, thanks."

"You don't have to leave, Jess. You can come back."

She swung around to face him, unable to believe what she was hearing. Before she could reply he'd pulled her into his arms. The dark turmoil had vanished from his expression, replaced by a primal intensity she recognised. Her heart quickened as he said, "Hush, don't say anything. Just think about this."

This turned out to be a kiss so hot, so passionate, that Jessica gasped as his lips slanted across hers. Instantly he pressed the advantage. His tongue swept into her mouth, tasting her like she was the sweetest thing in the world. He groaned and his arms tightened around her. Jessica was conscious of his height, of the hard wall of his chest, of his strength and her own femininity.

Then she became aware of the length of his erection pressing against her.

"No!" That was exactly what had landed her in the bind she was in. And she wasn't about to compound her mistake by landing back in Ryan Blackstone's bed.

He raised his head. "No?"

"I don't want this. I want to go home."

"*This* is your home, Jessica."

She wrenched herself out his arms. "This place? My home? Never!" His startled expression was almost comical. "Do you think that a million-dollar love-nest with great artwork—" she gestured to the abstract Fred Williams landscape on the wall "—and a professionally designed interior with fancy wooden floors and leather couches is what I would call home?" This was no space for a kid to grow up. "It's such a showplace, you didn't even want my cat here."

"Bring the damn cat then. If that's what it will take to make you happy."

"It's not about Picasso."

He frowned. "Then what *is* it about? You say that Xander's not the reason you left. Nor is your cat. So why did you go?"

Jessica drew a deep shuddering breath. "How can you ask

me that when you believe I could be your father's mistress while living with you?"

He held up a hand. "Wait, I've been thinking about that." For an instant a hint of vulnerability flashed in his eyes. "I got it wrong. I apologise."

"Thanks! And that's supposed to make me happy?" She glared at him, the hurt back in full force. How dare he have doubted her even for a minute? She sighed in frustration. "You turned my life upside down. An apology is not going to fix it. This is not like putting Humpty Dumpty back together again. You and me…it's not going to work, Ryan."

"Hang on." He looked so bewildered that she wanted to pummel him. "We were happy together."

He'd been happy. She'd have done anything to keep him happy. She shrugged. "It was all on your terms."

"I told you I didn't want marriage—"

"I'm not asking you to marry me," she interrupted before he could say anything more hurtful. "I don't even think marriage would make it right anymore." By his darkening eyes she knew that shocked him. "Since coming to Sydney I can't help noticing how much like your father you've become."

He narrowed his eyes. "You knew I wanted to be chairman of Blackstone's, that I wanted more, a bigger role in the company."

"How much more do you need? Surely you have enough wealth and power to keep you happy for your lifetime." She glanced at his set expression. "It doesn't matter, Ryan. This— us—was never going to last. It's better for it to end now." She sighed. "Are you going to help me pack or not?"

His lips drew into a flat, straight line. "You're making a mistake."

It would be a bigger mistake to stay. Ryan didn't want a baby, a family. And even if he asked her to stay after she told him that she was pregnant, how could she tie him down to a situation he'd been honest enough to tell her he never wanted? He'd come to resent her and the baby, and she wouldn't be able to bear that. She had no choice but to get out of his life. And later, when things had settled down a little, when she'd started to show and could no longer hide her pregnancy, then she'd tell him about the baby he didn't want.

It would be too late for him to demand that she abort their child.

There was an awkward moment when Ryan entered the showroom on Monday morning carrying a bulky black briefcase. His eyes met Jessica's across the vast space, and one look at his face told her that Ryan hadn't forgiven her for not crawling back into his bed when he crooked his little finger.

Jessica tensed, dreading the next round of recriminations, then spotted the woman dressed in a flowing, turquoise dress behind him, bracelets jangling on her slim arms. Iridescent opals arranged in flowers bloomed on a circlet of silver that nestled against her throat. She looked like Persephone, the goddess of spring.

Jessica gave her a smile, grateful for the reprieve from meeting Ryan alone after their last searing encounter.

"Jessica, you know my cousin Danielle, don't you?" Ryan asked, halting beside the row of chest-level display cases that served as a counter, and setting the briefcase down.

"We didn't meet at the funeral. But we've spoken on the phone." Jessica moved from behind the counter where she'd been giving Candy, one of the sales team, a set of instructions, and shook hands with his cousin. "I'm sorry for the loss your family suffered."

Sadness clouded Dani's eyes. "Mum and I miss him terribly."

Jessica resisted the unkind temptation to retort that many

didn't miss Howard Blackstone for a moment. Including herself. No, that would be unnecessarily cruel. And she wasn't sinking to Howard's level.

"Excuse me, I need to make a couple of calls," Ryan cut in. "I'll use your office, Jessica."

"Of course." *Their* office now, according to what he'd told her on Friday. It was going to be impossible to share that small space with such a big man. Jessica refused to run hungry eyes over Ryan's tall, broad frame. Reminding herself that she was mad at him, she kept her attention on Dani. "I've always called you Dani because that's the name you run your business under. Do you prefer Danielle?"

Dani grimaced. "To my family I'll always be Danielle. But in Port Douglas everyone knows me as Dani. They also know me dressed like this." She gestured ruefully to her colourful dress. "I'm flying back to Port Douglas straight after this, so don't tell my mother that I didn't wear a business suit to the store. She'd be embarrassed. And you can call me anything you want."

Jessica laughed, warming to Dani's refreshing candour. "My Mum has things she'd like me to do, too. Like find a nice man and get married."

"Mine, too." Dani grinned conspiratorially. Then she spotted the pile of brochures for the launch on the glass-topped counter. "Ooh, are any of my designs in here?"

"Take a look," Jessica invited. "The images of the designs you sent came out beautifully."

Dani Hammond was a breath of fresh summer air. Jessica couldn't help smiling at Dani's enthusiasm as she leafed through the pages, her eyes glowing with delight.

"Gosh, this stone is stunning. Imagine cutting that." Her tone held awe. "I'd be petrified at the thought of making the first cut."

Jessica peered over her shoulder. "Amazing, isn't it?

That's the Desert Star, the first of the big stones that came out the Janderra mine after it was first opened. It will be on display as part of the history of Blackstone's, but it's not for sale."

"My uncle showed it to me once when I was a little girl. He told me that it was flawless. Colourless. I remember the fire that flashed inside the heart of the stone and I told him that it couldn't possibly be called colourless. Not with all those sparkles."

"It's in the vault. Would you like to see it again?"

"Please!" Dani dropped the brochure and leapt forward, hoisting up the briefcase that Ryan had carried in. "I've brought some of my pieces for the show with me. They'll need to be put in the vault, too."

They made their way to the vault set behind the showroom. It had no windows, no natural lighting and the bright electric light shone starkly over the banks of metal-fronted drawers. Jessica unlocked a drawer, lifted out a box and flipped it open to reveal a solitary polished gem twinkling against black velvet.

"Let me see." Dani's voice held wonder. And for a moment Jessica could imagine the little girl she must once have been.

Jessica passed the box over. "It may not be a fancy coloured diamond like the most valuable stones mined at Janderra, but the colour and clarity are superb. Just over eleven carats, a D-colour, internally flawless cushion-shaped diamond. Hard to believe that much beauty is nothing more than atoms of carbon bonded together."

"Ooh, an old mine cut." Dani's eyes stretched wide. Her fingers touched the stone with reverence. "Howard was right. This stone is truly colourless. And the fire. The brilliance. Look at the symmetry, and how the light dances from facet to facet. It's a wonderful job. Aaron Lazar was a master cutter. I'm so envious of his talent." Dani looked up at Jessica.

"Lazar also cut the Heart of the Outback—the stone that my grandfather gave to Auntie Ursula and Uncle Howard just after James was born. He and Howard were business partners—that's how my Auntie Ursula met and married Howard."

"Ryan doesn't talk about his mother." Jessica couldn't resist probing for information. "I heard she committed suicide when he was little."

"He was only three when she died." Some of the radiance and sparkle drained from Dani's golden eyes.

Jessica half wished she'd never mentioned it.

"Mum says as a toddler Ryan used to stand by the gate, clutching the bars, waiting for his mother to one day come home. Once he understood that she'd died and gone to heaven, he used to ask the postman if there were any letters for him. He told Mum that even in heaven he was sure Ursula would remember to send him a postcard."

Jessica's heart cracked wide open for the lonely little boy he'd once been.

Then Dani seemed to give herself a mental shake. She looked round theatrically and whispered, "It's all part of the family scandal. The stuff we never talk about."

Did that mean Dani wasn't going to be any help in filling her in on the dark spaces in Ryan's life? Jessica took the hint and went back to the subject of diamonds. "I've heard about the Heart of the Outback. Over a hundred carats in the rough before Howard had Lazar cut it into five stones and assembled into a necklace called—"

"—the Blackstone Rose. Those five cut stones must have been stunning. Four of them were seven carats and the fifth, a pear-shaped stone, weighed almost ten carats." Dani shook her head. "No wonder my Uncle Oliver—that's my mum's brother—was mad as anything about it."

Jessica stilled, reluctant to interrupt lest Dani remember that she was talking to an outsider. And she was very much an outsider—despite her relationship to Ryan. Howard Blackstone had made that clear enough the last time she'd seen him. She would never be accepted into the Blackstone fold. She didn't have the right connections, the right pedigree that Howard wanted for the woman who married his son.

Dani perched herself on a waist-high steel safe that held a fortune in jewels. "That fancy pink diamond brought nothing but bad luck to our family. The necklace was stolen on the night of Ryan's mum's thirtieth birthday party." Dani gave a theatrical shudder. "And the fights and accusations haven't stopped since."

Jessica had read the speculation in the press about the events of that scandalous long-ago night. Knowing Howard, Jessica privately agreed with the notion that Howard had stolen the necklace himself to rip off the insurance company. Not that she'd ever admit that to anyone—especially not to Ryan. And the insurance company must've leaned that way, too, because they'd never paid out on the theft, much to Howard's reported rage. "The press had all sort of theories about who stole it."

Dani sighed. "It did horrible things to our family. You know, after that my Uncle Oliver never wanted to see my Mum or my Auntie Ursula again. He'd only come to the party because his wife begged him to come and put an end to the feud between himself and Howard. But instead of making things better, they only got worse after the necklace went missing. Not that Uncle Howard ever took it out on Mum or me. He was like a fairy godfather to me."

Howard Blackstone? A fairy godfather? Jessica gave Dani a sideways look of disbelief.

Dani intercepted it and tossed her head, and her coppery curls bobbed around her freckled face. "Is it that hard to believe Howard had a softer side?"

"Frankly, yes." Jessica thought of the overbearing, domineering man she'd grown to know.

"He was hard on Ryan and Kim. Perhaps it was different for me because he didn't have the same expectations for me. Or maybe he'd mellowed a little by the time I grew older. He did so much for me. He even loaned me money—interest free—to set up my business. Without Howard I'd still be backpacking around Asia, and I'd never have gotten the chance to pursue my dream of creating my own designs."

"Designs that will be a runaway success at the show at the end of the month." Jessica decided to change the subject. She'd never be able to be cool and rational about Howard.

Dani looked unaccustomedly nervous. "I hope you're right, Jessica."

"I am. Believe me on this. Dani Hammond is going to be the hottest name in town."

Dani gave a lopsided smile. "There's some kind of irony in that. A Blackstone event making a Hammond famous." Then all humour left her eyes. "I hate this stupid feud. At the funeral I wanted to go say hello to Matt Hammond. He's my cousin, after all. But he looked so hard and angry that it felt disloyal to Howard's memory, and I couldn't bring myself to do it."

Sadness seeped through Jessica. "I hate it, too. So many tensions." Between Ryan and Ric. Between Ryan and Matt Hammond. "Why can't it just end?"

"My mother says that Uncle Oliver fought with his father because he thought that the Heart of the Outback should have been his. Granddad gave it to Uncle Howard and my aunt Ursula when James was born. To celebrate. After James's kidnapping, Uncle Oliver said that it served Howard and Ursula right that their son had been taken. They'd stolen what was rightfully his, so the diamond put a curse on them."

How could anyone have been so cruel? Jessica knew she

would die if her child was taken from her. But perhaps it hadn't been so simple....

"I heard that Howard accused Oliver of kidnapping James," Jessica said.

"But it wasn't true—"

"Oliver Hammond stole the Blackstone Rose off his sister's—my mother's—neck." Ryan's harsh interruption made Jessica jump.

But he hadn't finished. "Like father, like son—now Matt Hammond is trying to steal Blackstone shares. What else could one expect from a Hammond?"

Her mortification at being caught gossiping was overtaken when Jessica caught the flash of hurt in Dani's eyes. *Damn.* Didn't Ryan realize that he'd hurt Dani with his bullheaded reaction against the Hammond name? "I thought you had some calls to make?" Jessica tried to stop him saying anything that might make matters worse.

Ryan's face was set, and his green eyes were colder than a frozen lake in winter.

"I own this store, remember?"

Jessica flushed at the pointed rebuke. She'd just been reminded of her place. He gave the orders. Not her. He was the boss. ·

Dani slid off the steel safe where she'd been perched. "I should go. I've got a plane to catch."

"Don't leave on my account, cousin."

Dani raised an eyebrow, flags of colour high on her cheeks. "I'm not sticking around if you're in a bad mood," she said with the candid familiarity of someone who had grown up in the family.

Ryan's face cracked into a smile. "Sorry! I always think of you as one of us. I forget that you have the misfortune of bearing the Hammond name."

"And Hammond blood beats in your heart, too," Dani retorted.

"Still as forthright as ever. I pity the man who tries to tame you, pumpkin."

Jessica envied the easy familiarity between the two of them. But his statement describing Dani as *one of us* only emphasised how much of an outsider she was. And how right she'd been to end the sorry excuse for a relationship that they had.

After Dani had gone, her hurt spilling over, Jessica turned on Ryan. "That was rude."

He looked startled. "What? Calling Dani 'pumpkin'?"

"Accusing the Hammonds of being nothing more than a pack of thieves."

"I was referring to Oliver Hammond and his son. Dani knows I don't mean her."

"Does she?" Jessica narrowed her gaze. "Or does she think you despise her, too?"

"She's my cousin, for Pete's sake." His tone grew heated. "As she pointed out, my mother was a Hammond so I'm half Hammond, too. But that doesn't change the fact that Oliver is nothing more than a liar, a cheat and a thief."

"He's your uncle *and* Dani's uncle. But Dani's still not a Blackstone, even though she grew up amongst you. In her position I'd feel torn in two."

"You would?"

"Yes! She's caught in the crossfire. Do you know she wanted to greet Matt at the funeral, but she was worried about being disloyal to Howard's memory?"

"That's commendable. Dani's always been a loyal little thing."

"But Howard is dead!" Jessica wanted to shake him. God, but he could be intransigent. "She and Matt are alive. He's her cousin. And yours, too. Don't you think it's time to bury the hatchet?"

"In Matt Hammond's head?"

Jessica threw her arms into the air. "I give up! I can't talk to you. You're the most stubborn—" She broke off. Why was she allowing herself to get all worked up? Jessica drew a deep breath. Turning away, she placed the sparkling Desert Star into its box with careful hands and put it back in the drawer. "Thankfully this has nothing to do with me. I only work here."

But even that was not permanent. Once the baby was born...

"Matt is out to destroy Blackstone's." Ryan had moved up right behind her. Jessica stopped breathing. "Everything my father and I—and even Ric," he added grudgingly, "have worked so hard to build is in jeopardy."

Something is his voice caught her attention and she swung around to face him. "Do you really believe Matt can damage Blackstone's?"

Ryan nodded, and his eyes glittered in the artificial light. "Yes, he can. Matt is out for revenge. At any cost."

"Do you think it's because—" She broke off.

"Because my father stole his wife?" Ryan shrugged. "I don't know. And I don't particularly care who my father's mistress was."

For a moment something flashed in the depths of his eyes as he looked at her. A hint of pain...or something else? Ryan must be hurting that his idol, his father, was proving to have feet of clay. But who knew what really went on behind that handsome face? It was entirely possible that he thought the speculation about Howard stealing Marise from Matt was a bunch of rot— because he'd already decided *she* was his father's mistress.

Then he growled, "But I'm not going to let Matt destroy Blackstone's."

Five

The emerald turf of Flemington racecourse provided a dramatic backdrop for the jewel-bright silks worn by the jockeys. In the parade ring, the best of this year's fillies circled. Some walked on a loose rein, while others snatched at the bit and kept breaking into a trot, showing high spirits.

"Beautiful, aren't they?"

At the sound of Ryan's rough voice, Jessica lowered the binoculars.

He was dressed entirely in black. A black suit, black shirt and highly polished black Italian shoes. He looked debonair, dangerous…and every inch a Blackstone. "I wasn't sure that you were coming."

She met his gaze squarely. "I certainly didn't expect to see you here. You said—"

"That I was going to Janderra?" The satisfaction in his voice alerted her.

He'd deliberately misled her!

Why? To ensure that she came to the races? Had he thought—correctly—she might back out if she'd known he would be in the Blackstone box today? Yes, that was it.

Seething, she lifted the binoculars.

"Which filly do you fancy?" he asked at her shoulder.

"I don't bet." It sounded so prim that Jessica almost groaned out aloud.

"I know that. But last year you picked the winner before the race had even started."

"I'm surprised you even noticed." In the past two years they'd barely looked at each other at the racetrack. Absolute discretion. No one could've guessed they were lovers.

"I notice everything about you," Ryan murmured softly. "I even remember that full skirted black dress you wore last year…and how I unlaced the tight corset top afterwards."

Jessica stifled a soft groan. She didn't want to remember how after the St. Valentine's Ball—after pretending to be nothing more than boss and employee—she and Ryan had gone back to the apartment the Blackstones maintained on the spacious top floor of a sought-after building. Or how they'd shared a bottle of Taittinger in the hot tub.

Those memories were far too seductive.

And nothing like that would happen tonight. Because tonight she would be staying in the five-star Ascot Gold Hotel. Alone.

A chestnut filly pranced past in front of them, sunlight burnishing the bunched muscle of her hindquarters. The jockey wore black silks with a large pink diamond emblazoned on the front and back. A Blackstone horse.

"What's that filly's name?"

"Diamond Lady." Ryan barely looked at the horse. "Do you remember how we spent the next day in bed? Only getting up for a meal in the evening?"

She'd been totally in his thrall.

"Jessica…Ryan!"

Jessica gave a start of surprise. She could've kissed Briana for the timely interruption. Wearing a stunning silk yellow dress that only a very confident woman could pull off, her golden-brown hair artfully curled around her face, Briana walked beside a tall, dark-haired stranger.

"Jake Vance," Briana announced. "Jake, meet Ryan Blackstone…and my friend, Jessica, who manages the big Sydney Blackstone's store."

Jake's smile was wide and white. She'd heard the name before but Jessica couldn't remember where. Had Briana found comfort in her time of loss? Jessica sincerely hoped so.

"Are you ready to go up to the seating enclosure?" Briana asked.

"Yes," Jessica responded hastily. The company would dilute Ryan's attention.

"So, Jess, who do you favour to win the Blackstone stakes?" Jake Vance asked.

"Diamond Lady." Jessica didn't miss a beat.

Both Briana and Jake laughed.

"I should've expected that," Jake said wryly.

"I'm going to place a bet on that filly." Ryan started to move away.

"Not on my opinion, I hope," Jessica said in alarm. She'd simply repeated the name she'd heard seconds before. "There's no scientific basis to my choice."

"Maybe it's a woman's intuition," Briana mused. "I think I'll put a bet on Diamond Lady."

"Then I'd better, too," Jake added.

Jessica dropped her head into her hands. "Don't blame me when you all lose your hard-earned cash," she called after them and made her way to the Blackstone seating enclosure.

Five minutes later the other three arrived. "Jess, my bet didn't even break the bank." Briana dropped into the seat beside her.

Jessica met her friend's smiling eyes. "It's good to see you here, sweetie," she said softly. "And I'm so glad to see you with someone other than Patrick."

Briana waved a dismissive hand. "Jake and I aren't serious. I needed to get out and Jake invited me. That's all."

"Maybe it will develop into something special."

"Oh, you…romantic!" Briana laughed. "We need to find you a guy. You haven't dated in the all the time I've known you."

"I'm trying to talk Jess into going to dinner with me tonight." Ryan approached holding two tall tulip glasses filled with champagne.

"Thank you," Briana took one. Then she turned to Jessica. "Oh, Jess, you can't refuse an invitation like that!"

Jessica shot Ryan a killing look. *Wanna bet?* "You can't take me to dinner. You need to make an appearance at the St. Valentine's Ball after the races—and I don't have a ticket," she said with quiet triumph. She'd refused the offer of a ticket to the ball back in Sydney, intending to have an early night.

"You can be my partner." Ryan grinned at her.

What was he doing?

Before Jessica could object, Briana smiled and said, "That's settled! Why don't the four of us sit together tonight?"

Great. Now Briana thought she'd matched the couple of the century. Jessica wanted to brain Ryan. Instead she made do with looking away and ignoring him. After years of secrecy, now that their affair was over he wanted everyone to know they were a couple? It didn't make sense.

But she didn't have to go. "It's black tie—and I haven't brought a suitable dress along." All she had was the white linen suit she was wearing. Dressed up with a stylish black hat and a silver camisole and her familiar pearls, it was smart enough for the races but nowhere near formal enough for the ball. Last year she'd worn a floor-length lace dress in the palest shade of aqua.

"That's easy to fix," Briana declared. "I have a deal with a couple of designers to show off their clothes. They'd have no problem with dressing you." Briana already had her cell phone in her hand. A moment later she was speaking to someone with the unlikely name of ZinZin.

Jessica glared at Ryan. He lifted his glass in a silent toast. What had he gotten her into? And why now, of all times? The very last thing she wanted was to be seen out in public with him and have people adding two and two and coming up with pregnant when she started to show in a few weeks' time.

"That's settled. Cinderella can go to the ball," Briana said with some satisfaction as she ended the call.

Jessica bit back an acid comment. She would go to the ball as Ryan's partner. It would be worth it to keep that smile back on Briana's beautiful face.

"Oh, the horses are off!" Briana got to her feet.

A thrill surged through Jessica and her irritation with Ryan was forgotten.

"Sorry." Briana sat down, laughing, too. "But it's always so exciting when the horses leap out onto the track."

"Even a hardened businessman like me finds it exciting." Jake winked at Briana.

Was it serious? Despite Briana's denials Jessica hoped so. Briana deserved some happiness after her abortive previous relationship. Jessica had never cared much for Patrick—too smooth. Too charming. Jake, on the other hand, looked tough and ruthless. Jessica frowned as she tried to remember where she'd heard his name. Briana didn't need more hurt after the rough time she'd had recently.

"Here they come!" Ryan's exclamation had her leaning forward to squint at the horses in the lead bunch. "And Diamond Lady is right up there."

The fillies thundered past the stands, the jockeys bent over their necks, their bodies in rhythm with the horseflesh beneath them. The roar of the crowd was deafening.

"She might make it!"

The excitement in Ryan's voice was contagious. Jessica grabbed his hand, squeezing it tightly as the horses flashed past the finish line. The sight of the chestnut filly and the jockey's pink and black colours magnified on the huge television screen on the opposite side of the track led to loud whoops.

Briana swung to her, a delighted smile on face. "See? I didn't lose a cent."

"Yes!" Ryan punched the air.

"Diamond Lady won!" Jessica couldn't believe it. Without realising it, she found herself on her feet, jumping up and down in delight.

Ryan pulled her into his arms, hugging her, his face blazing with triumph. And then he kissed her.

It was a quick kiss, full of elation and joy. But their eyes caught and held.

Hurriedly, Jessica said, "Shouldn't you be down in the winner's enclosure to present the trophy?"

Ryan dropped his arms and stepped back. "Kim's doing the family honours this year. I've done it all the years she's been away in New Zealand. Ric's down there with her."

A pang of disappointment pierced her as he moved away. It seemed like aeons since she'd last touched him.

"Besides," Ryan continued, "it's much nicer up here in the box, sipping French champagne and sitting with you. Can I top up your glass?"

Jessica set her glass down. "I've had enough. I still have to drive back to my hotel and get ready for the ball."

Then Briana was saying, "Where are you staying, Jess? I'll have ZinZin send over a selection of dresses for you to try on."

"The Ascot Gold Hotel." For a mad moment Jessica wished she knew what Ryan had been thinking when he looked at her with that strange intensity.

"I'll meet you in the lobby at seven." Something glinted in the depths of Ryan's green eyes.

The dress that Jessica had chosen from the selection ZinZin sent over was soft and feminine. The wraparound style made her confident that the thickening waist only she knew about didn't show.

A soft mix of palest apricot and rich creams, the gown hung to the floor in fine pleats and emphasized the lustrous glow of her skin. She'd put her hair up. A pair of flawless diamond studs that Ryan had given her last Christmas twinkled in her ears. She knew she looked good. Picking up a small sequined bag and the pashmina wrap that ZinZin had matched with the dress, Jessica made for the door.

Downstairs, Ryan was waiting for her, wearing a white dinner jacket and a black bow tie.

For an instant his sheer male beauty took Jessica's breath away and she stilled, then she moved forward. "I hope I didn't keep you waiting."

"No. I'm staying in the hotel as well."

"Here? At the Ascot?"

Ryan nodded. "Kim and Ric are staying at the apartment. There's really not enough space for me there, too."

Jessica could imagine that Kim and Ric's renewed closeness might cause Ryan to feel like a spare part. While the apartment was undeniably luxurious, it was a lover's retreat.

Jessica had wondered in the past if Howard Blackstone had bought it as a lover's nest to share with his latest "secretary."

"You're staying here because of the ball?" It was highly unlikely that Ryan had chosen to stay here because of her, Jessica told herself. Ryan couldn't have known—or cared—where she was staying.

His gaze shifted away. He held out an arm. "Come, we don't want to be the last to arrive."

And thereby attracting even more speculation than their arrival together already would.

The St. Valentine's Diamond Ball was held in the ballroom of the Ascot, a vast room lit with dozens of brilliant chandeliers. Silver cutlery glittered on the round tables, which were covered with snowy white tablecloths and adorned with sprays of ivy and tall elegant white candles.

They made their way to the main Blackstone table where Kim and Ric, Briana and Jake and a host of familiar faces from the Melbourne Blackstone's Jewellery store were already seated.

After greeting them, Briana said, "That dress looks stunning, Jess. I knew ZinZin would find something perfect for you."

"It was perfect advice."

"You look almost—" Briana paused "—voluptuous tonight."

Jessica gave a self-conscious little laugh. But apprehension stirred. She couldn't afford for Briana to guess....

"I guess I've picked up a little bit of weight lately."

"It suits you." Briana's eyes scanned her face. "You're glowing."

"I noticed that, too." Ryan leant forward. "You're growing more beautiful every day, Jess."

Even Briana looked startled by this observation.

"Flatterer," Jessica exclaimed quickly, and resisted the urge to place her hands over the barely noticeable curve of her stomach hidden by the artful pleats of the soft fabric.

"You're not talking about Ryan, are you?" Kim entered the conversation. "My brother never wastes time on flattery. What did he say?"

"Never mind." Jessica could feel herself flushing.

Kim's gaze grew knowing. Jessica grew even hotter. "Can we change the subject please?" she begged.

Kim came to her rescue. "I hear you predicted Diamond Lady's win today. I hope you had good odds on her."

"Um...I didn't bet." Jessica latched gratefully onto the change of subject.

"But everyone else did," Ryan added, and gave her a slow smile that caused tingles to run up and down Jessica's spine. She looked away hastily.

Briana instantly piped up about her winnings and Jake added that he'd been lucky enough to predict the trifecta. Then Briana passed a comment about financial sharks that suddenly set a lightbulb off in Jessica's head.

Jake Vance...financial shark. Corporate raider. Of course! How could she have forgotten a name that so often appeared in the financial pages.

During dinner the lively debate about horses and predicting winners continued. Jessica didn't contribute much—she was too aware of the man seated at her side.

When Ryan's chair scraped back, she gave an inward sigh of relief. No doubt he intended to circulate. She would have a reprieve from his overwhelming presence for a little while.

"Dance?"

Ryan stood beside her chair, his hand outstretched. Did she really have a choice? Reluctantly Jessica rose to her feet.

On the dance floor he gathered her close. She intercepted some speculative glances from several of the surrounding couples.

"We shouldn't be doing this."

Ryan's brows drew together. "Why not?"

"Everyone will think we're a couple."

Ryan's response was to draw her closer still. "Maybe we should be."

"No!" That couldn't happen. "It's too late for that. I don't want people to think—"

"I don't particularly care what they think."

That was Ryan. Arrogant. Outspoken. And then he blew her preconceptions away by saying, "I want you to be happy. So if it makes you unhappy to be this close to me, just say the word and I'll let you go."

"Let me go?" She looked up into his face. "You mean you'd stop dancing and return me to the others?"

"If that's what you want."

He would, too. She heard the resolve in his voice. And he'd probably never ask her to dance again. Then she'd never be held this close to him again. Jessica didn't know if she could bear that.

So instead of pulling away, she stayed in his arms, so close that she could feel the steady beat of his heart against her cheek. The moment to back away was gone.

"You smell so good," he murmured, nuzzling her hair. His fingers trailed across her back. "You feel so good."

Little shivers shook her. Had he missed her? It would be too much to hope for.

Even if he had, what would change? Ryan had no desire for a wife or a family. The high-flying corporate executive life he led was a world away from what Jessica had realised over the past six weeks she wanted. A family home, a man with time to spend with her—to watch their child grow up. She didn't want a man who was driven by power and profit. If the truth be told, deep in her secret heart, she wanted a man who loved her more than anything in the world.

And that man could never be Ryan.

Yet she fit against the hard angles of his body as though she'd been made for him. And as he shifted to the music her body swayed with him. That tantalising hand slid down her back, to rest on her hips and waves of dizzying longing swept her.

She'd missed this closeness.

She missed lying curled against him in the dead of the night. She missed hearing his husky voice saying her name. She missed seeing him seated across the breakfast table from her. She missed *him*.

Without thinking about it, she snuggled closer. Ryan's arms tightened and his cheek moved against her hair. The warmth of his body and a subtle hint of the expensive aftershave he wore surrounded her.

When the song came to an end, he held her for a heartbeat past the end. Then he let her go.

A wild emptiness filled her. She stood an arm's length away from him and it felt as if he were a world away.

Jessica shivered again as loneliness sliced through her.

"Come." His arm came around her shoulders and he guided her back to the table where Ric and Kim sat, their faces close together, totally absorbed in each other.

Ryan picked up her evening bag and her pashmina. "I'm taking Jessica home," he declared. "Say our farewells to Briana and Jake."

Kim looked startled, then she smiled.

Jessica thought about objecting to Ryan's high-handedness. But one look into his smouldering eyes and the flash of rebellion subsided.

Once they left the ballroom, the music dimmed and Jessica became aware of the simmering silence between them. It deepened as they entered the elevator. Ryan's index finger hovered over the control panel. "Which floor are you on?" His voice was rough.

She told him.

The silence returned. A living, breathing force that pushed them apart. Jessica stared at the red digital numbers flashing as they passed by each floor. When the elevator stopped and the doors opened, she bolted out.

"I'll see you to your room."

"It's not necessary," she said in a strangled voice, not daring to look at him. But he paid no heed and strode beside her down the carpeted corridor.

Jessica was aware of every muffled step it took them to reach her room. She could feel herself becoming more breathless with each passing second.

She halted and fumbled in her bag for the access card, conscious of her chest rising and falling.

"Invite me in, Jess."

She looked at him then. In the muted light of the corridor she glimpsed heat in his eyes…and the same tension that filled her lonely heart.

She knew what she wanted.

"Yes," she whispered and his eyes flared until they became as dark and unfathomable as midnight.

"Good," he purred, then took the card from her nerveless fingers and swiped it. The door clicked open, the sound overloud in the night.

He pushed the door open and Jessica stepped through into the bedroom beyond.

Six

"Come to me, Jess."

Ryan stood beside the bed, his features stark with want.

"I can't." Paralysed with fear that if she let him touch her, she might never again find the strength to leave, Jessica folded her arms tightly across her chest and watched as Ryan approached. The glaring overhead light fell across his face, highlighting the taut cheekbones and turning his eyes to blazing emerald.

"Meet me halfway, then. For tonight."

One night…

"Only for tonight?"

He hesitated, then nodded, a swift jerky movement.

She could do one night, couldn't she? Jessica took a step forward. Then another. Before she knew it she was in his arms.

His hands pressed her against him, uncompromising. The pashmina slipped to the floor, and his hands confidently stroked the naked skin that the low-cut back left exposed. But instead of resisting, instead of resenting his demonstration of dominance, desire exploded through her. She made a little keening noise in the back of her throat.

His lips came down on the side of her throat, under her jaw, and she tipped her head back and muttered incoherent sounds of desire. The mouth that closed over hers was hard and hungry and she responded with an alien, unladylike wildness she'd never shown before.

He groaned and his fingers dug into her upper arms. "God, this is happening much faster than I expected."

His hips surged forward and Jessica was conscious of his hardness pressing into her, conscious of the life that lay in her womb where he'd already impregnated her. The knowledge was strangely erotic.

But it reminded her that she wasn't as reed slim as the last time she'd been in his bed.

"The lights," she whimpered. "Turn the lights off."

"I want to see you. I want to feast my eyes on every naked morsel of your flesh."

She shuddered. "No."

He pulled away, staring down into her eyes. Into her soul. "Why the sudden shyness, Jess?"

"I'm not shy." She buried her face in his shoulder, the fabric of his jacket hiding her expression. "But I don't want you to see me."

"But I've seen every inch of you before." The tension threaded through his voice subsided a little, replaced by gentle amusement.

Her heart contracted. "But tonight is…different."

"How?"

"Because…" *What to say?* She certainly couldn't tell him about the fuller curves that she didn't want him to see.

"Because we're not really together anymore." She writhed at the deception. But if she told him...

That would be the end.

No cats. No kids. No press. No diamond rings.

He would walk out the door. She'd hear from his lawyers. It would soon be too late for the suggestion of a face-saving abortion—her greatest fear, given the wealth and power of the Blackstones. Yet she was confident that Ryan wouldn't walk away from his financial responsibility. He'd send her a maintenance cheque for the child every month. But he would never touch her again.

And she'd missed his touch.

He might not love her but he still wanted her with the same hunger that had always raged between them. For tonight—for only one night—she would be his. And he would be hers. It would have to be enough.

He released her. She felt cold. Then the room plunged into darkness.

"Okay, if I'm not allowed to see you, I'll touch you. I'll remember every bit of your skin with my fingertips."

The husky, evocative words caused her breath to quicken. His fingers touched her cheek in the darkness, warming her, driving out the chill. One finger traced her cheekbone, before they all speared into her hair, pushing out the pins. She felt the soft locks fall around her face.

Shivers of desire shook her, growing with every passing second. The sensation swept through her, heating her blood, heightening her anticipation.

His other hand cupped her jaw, tilting her face up. Then his lips touched hers in the darkness, ever so gently, with light, unsatisfying kisses that teased as much as they provoked. Her lips parted, inviting him in. Wanting more... wanting him.

But instead of deepening the kiss, he let his tongue trace her lips, driving her wild.

She wanted more.

More pressure.

More passion.

And a thousand times more pleasure than the tender butterfly touches gave her.

"Kiss me," she whispered impatiently against his mouth.

He lifted his head. "I am."

"Kiss me properly."

He stilled. "Why don't you show me how you want to be kissed?"

Jessica hesitated. If she kissed him, he'd know exactly how much she still wanted him. So what? Desiring him wouldn't mean revealing her other secrets. Like how much she loved him. And how much she missed him. Nor would he find out about the baby.

So long as the lights stayed off.

So why the hell not? She'd show him how she wanted to be kissed. Properly. Or maybe not so properly. Maybe tonight was the time for a little improper behaviour. Tonight she'd be the woman she never would have dared to be in the past.

She had nothing to lose.

"Okay." Her voice sounded husky, unfamiliar. "But first this needs to go." She slipped her hands inside his white dinner jacket and pushed it from his shoulders.

"Whatever you want." It was a rough whisper.

The fabric rustled. Jessica's arms circled his waist and deftly caught the jacket as it slid off his shoulders. She tossed it in the direction of the armchair she'd seen earlier and heard it land with a soft plop. She ran her hands up and down his back, loving the feel of the hard ridges of muscle either side of his spine under the sleek silk of his shirt.

His body vibrated with tension. "Now are you going to kiss me?"

"Wait."

He gave a theatrically loud sigh.

She brought her hands back to the front, so that she was no longer touching him. "Do you want me to stop?"

He groaned. "Jess, don't tease!"

"Tease?" She smiled into the darkness. "*This* is teasing?"

Feeling ahead of her, she stopped when the fabric of his shirt touched her fingertips. Careful not to brush his skin with her fingers, she lifted his silk dress shirt away from his body and tugged the snaps undone.

This time his groan was louder. "You're killing me."

Quickly Jessica yanked the shirt out of his pants and attacked the bottom snaps.

"Kiss me. Touch me, dammit."

"Your wish is thy mistress's command, oh Master." With great deliberation, she snaked her fingers up his bare chest, ignoring his harsh intake of breath, until she reached the last of the remaining snaps. She hunted for his bow tie and tugged it loose. An instant later she dealt with the final snaps.

The shirt fell to the ground with a faint whisper of sound.

Next her fingers tangled with the buttons of his fly. She released him and peeled his briefs off. He was trembling, shaking under the brush of her fingers, his body wired with tension.

"Come here." His voice was thick with desire, his arms closing around her and pulling her back onto the bed with him. "My turn to undress you."

"Do you remember the headboard?" she whispered to him. "There's a wooden rail across the top. I want you to hold on and not let go."

"Hey," he objected, "the deal was I couldn't see but my hands would be my eyes. I want to touch you all over."

That was what was worrying her. That he might find curves where previously there had been none.

"Hold the bar," she whispered, more insistent now.

He groaned. "And you mock me by calling me 'Master'?" But she heard him shift to grab the rail.

Jessica smiled slowly into the blackness. "I'm finding it's nice to be in control for a change." She straddled him and warned, "Don't move your hands."

"I want to see this." He flicked on the bedside light. The dull gold light bathed the room. Then he reached for the rail again.

"Aren't you going to take off that dress?"

"No!" Her gaze flickered to the lamp. Then she abandoned her anxiety and gave him a slow smile. "I've never made love to you fully clothed. And this dress is so beautiful, it makes me feel like Cinderella." *Just for tonight.*

"From where I'm lying, it's as sexy as hell."

She stroked him slowly, running her hands over his smooth golden skin until he writhed under her touch. But he didn't let go. There was something utterly compelling about having him stretched out on her bed, naked, while she, fully dressed, touched him to her heart's content.

Finally, when his breathing was ragged, she remained poised above him and then sank down. His hardness slid into the softness of her body, his heat warming her.

The feeling was incredible. Jessica found that she was already so wildly turned on by a combination of abstinence, hormones and Ryan's hard, naked body between her thighs.

She rose and sank again, until Ryan was panting out loud. "I can't hold on anymore."

Before she could protest, he'd let go of the rail and grabbed her hips, yanking her to him, then one arm came round her and pulled her down, so that her breasts brushed against his torso. "I want you closer." His voice was hoarse. "Damn, this is good."

And then they were both shuddering and pleasure streaked through Jessica in sharp electric bursts. For a moment she was shocked at her wildness, at the wanton way she'd taken charge.

There had been something curiously liberating about playing the mistress, teasing him and watching him lose total control.

Even if it was only for one night.

Dressed in last night's clothes, Ryan drew open the long curtains covering the floor-to-ceiling windows that over-looked the city. In the east, splashes of gold and a rosy pink signalled the dawn of another day. He turned back to the woman lying in the hotel bed. Sometime after he'd fallen asleep she'd changed out of her dress and slipped on a nightie.

She'd kicked off the covers and the nightie had ridden up, revealing long, bare tanned legs.

Those legs had been locked around his waist last night. Ryan shut his eyes and resisted the urge to sit down on the edge of the bed and stroke those long limbs.

The last time she'd lain in his bed had been the day of his father's funeral. By nightfall she'd been gone, driven away by his accusation that she was his father's lover.

Deep down, he no longer believed that. But he couldn't understand why she hadn't simply denied it.

Ryan's brows drew together. Her denial would have taken his doubts away in an instant. He would have believed her. Instead she'd walked away—and he'd been shocked at how much her leaving had devastated him.

He wanted her back.

Last night was another step in his careful campaign, and he'd gotten much more than he'd bargained for. At the memory of the wild night he started to harden. He considered waking her and indulging again.

Ryan's frown deepened at the sight of the digital clock on the bedstand. No time. He still needed to get back to his room for a shower and change of clothes, then he had to leave. Kimberley and Ric would be waiting for him at the airport. They'd arranged to fly to Sydney together in time for the weekly financial meeting.

Pale pink light filtered through the window, casting a rosy glow on Jessica's sleeping features. She looked so innocent, wholly at peace. Then he caught sight of the dress draped over the bottom of the bed—the innocent-looking dress that had transformed her into a wicked seductress last night.

For a moment he was tempted to give in to the urge to climb back into bed, to pull her into his arms, and forget about work, about Blackstone's.

Hell, how could he even be thinking that? After all the years he'd striven to get where he was? He sucked in a shaky breath.

Ric and Kimberley were waiting for him.

The snippet of conversation that was lodged in the forefront of his mind replayed itself again. He could hear Jessica's voice. "We shouldn't be doing this."

And his own response, "Why not?"

She'd stiffened in his arms and he'd heard her resistance. "Everyone will think we're a couple."

He'd responded by holding her tighter, knowing that she was slipping away from him. "Maybe we should be."

"No!" Jessica's answer had been very final. "It's too late for that."

He suspected that, unlike him, Jessica was going to regret the night they'd shared when she woke.

Resisting the urge to kiss her goodbye, he let himself quietly out of the room.

Before she awoke and he read regret in her eyes.

* * *

Jessica opened her eyes and blinked at the flood of bright February sunshine that streamed through the open curtains. The room was quiet. No water splashed. No electric razor buzzed. Nothing moved.

"Ryan?" Her voice echoed emptily through the hotel room and the adjoining bathroom. No answer. Her body slumped.

Ryan had gone.

She was alone again.

Dragging herself out the bed, she made her way to the dressing table. No message waited for her. She tried the empty surface beside the television. Nothing there. And nothing on the coffee table.

Her heart hollow, she made for the shower and turned the jets on full. After a few minutes of standing like a zombie, she washed and hauled herself out again.

Back in the room, Jessica reached for the first thing that came to hand from her suitcase—a pair of dark chocolate-coloured trousers. She pulled them on and added a filmy top with bold lime and taupe and white geometric patterns. Damp hair slicked back from her face, she quickly shoved the balance of her clothes into her bag. She was ready to go.

Downstairs at the checkout desk a queue of business folk waited to check out, briefcases at their feet, chatting among themselves. A pile of Melbourne morning newspapers lay in a stack beside a tray filled with small glasses of complimentary orange juice. Jessica helped herself to the juice and gulped it down. Setting down the empty glass, she picked up a paper and flipped through it. She reached the lifestyle supplement and found herself staring into her own laughing face.

Ryan's Racetrack Romance. She glared at the headline. Then at her photo. Idiot! Why had she been grinning up at

Ryan like a love-struck fool? Hardly surprising that the society reporter had gotten her facts wrong.

This was just what she didn't need. She hoped that no one who knew her would see it. But there was little chance of that.

Briana lived in Melbourne. Then there were the people who worked at the Melbourne Blackstone store. A few designers she worked with lived in the city.

Oh, dear! When she started showing and the news broke that she was pregnant, how many would put two and two together and come up with "Ryan's baby"? She could only pray for a reprieve.

A quick skim through the rest of the text revealed lots of speculation about her and the fact that she worked for Ryan. Howard Blackstone's recent death and the shocks contained in his will were rehashed. The reporter laboured over the fact that Ryan had lost Miramare. And down at the bottom of the article there was a faded colour photo of James, Ryan and their mother holding baby Kimberley outside Miramare.

Ryan would hate that.

Of course there was also a rundown of the previous women Ryan had dated—most of them daughters of Howard's golf club cronies. No surprises there. Then there was a snarky comment about his single state for the last two years.

If they only knew…

Jessica was even less pleased when she took in the inset photo showing him attending an event at the National Gallery of Victoria in St Kilda Road earlier in the year, a redhead plastered to his side wearing a skimpy dress and a wide smile.

Jessica frowned. She remembered that weekend. Ryan had gone to Melbourne on business. He'd mentioned the exhibition…but she'd assumed that he'd gone alone. She accepted that he had his own friends, his own social life. But *this*—she glared at the redhead—was not what they'd agr—

"Miss?" Jessica jerked around. The reception clerk was staring at her. No one stood in the queue ahead of her.

"Sorry." She grabbed her bag and rushed forward. "Name is Jessica Cotter." She handed over her access card. "I'd like to settle my bill and check out."

The keyboard tapped. The printer whirred. The reception clerk pulled out the bill and handed it to Jessica. "The account is already settled."

"There must be some mistake…" Jessica scanned the bill. Definitely all paid.

"It was paid a little over an hour ago," the clerk said helpfully.

Ryan. Damn him, she could've settled it herself.

"And there's a message for you, Ms Cotter." The clerk handed her an envelope. Jessica moved to one side of the counter and slit it open with her index finger.

The note said:

Thanks for a sensational night. Had to leave for a meeting. See you at work.

He'd scrawled his name at the bottom and added:

P.S. Have that wicked dress charged to my account. I want you to think of me every time you see it or wear it.

Anger surged inside her, and all over again, she felt like a mistress. Nothing more than a night of passion. Unimportant. Paid for and discarded.

Her own stupid fault.

She'd played into the fantasy too well last night. Of course Ryan would regard her as nothing more than a mistress.

* * *

By the time Ryan sauntered into the first-floor showroom of Blackstone's, it was nearly midday and he hoped that Jessica would not read the fury of emotions stewing under his confident exterior.

He was eager to see her again. Yet he hardly knew how she would react. Would she want to turn their one night into more nights? Or would she regret the night they had shared?

Ryan searched for Jessica and found her pale blonde head shining like a beacon on the other side of the showroom, where she was helping a young couple. As Ryan drew nearer he saw that they were studying rings.

Diamond rings. Ryan hesitated. He heard her say, "What about narrowing it down to four or five that you like?"

"That will be hard," the young woman said. "They're all so beautiful. How would you choose?"

"I'd look for what fits with my personal style." Jessica drew a tray out from the locked drawers beneath the counter where some of the more valuable pieces were kept, in case any of Blackstone's favourite customers arrived without an appointment. "See this ring? It's a superb stone. But it's not ostentatious. I see a lot of very fine diamonds, but for me this one is special. I love the pale pink colour, the simplicity of the cut—it's an emerald cut, which is unusual for a coloured diamond. I like things very plain. It suits my style."

"That's an idea," the young woman said enthusiastically. She glanced at the man at her side. "Colin, let's each pick out a ring that appeals to us and see if we can find any that we both like."

"We want a stone that will be an investment. That's why we came to Blackstone's," said Colin, looking longingly at the ring that Jessica had pointed out. Ryan suspected it was the size of the stone that he liked, rather than the cut and style of the ring.

"I like that one." The woman pointed to a stone in an unusual shade of rich gold, set in a wide band with a design resembling leaves etched into the gold band. It was startlingly modern, very feminine and very different from the rest of the rings on the tray. "I love the warmth, the fire."

"A good choice," Jessica said, nodding in approval. "It's designed by one of our new designers, Dani Hammond. People will be killing for her designs after the launch of her new collection later this month."

"Does that mean the value will go up?"

"Oh, Colin." The young woman swatted her partner's arm and laughed. "Excuse him, he's a typical accountant, everything comes down to value. I won't be selling the ring, so it doesn't matter."

"Petra, the stone is not that big. With diamonds size really does matter."

"Carats aren't the only consideration." Ryan stepped forward. "There are other considerations."

"Like what?" Colin swivelled, clearly welcoming a male perspective.

"Cut. Dani Hammond is a top-class craftswoman. This gem has a unique facet pattern, she has used two different cuts, which shows off the reflected light brilliantly."

"It's different," Petra said. "That's what I love about it."

"And what else?" Colin asked Ryan, clearly not convinced yet.

"Clarity. And finally there's colour."

"Blue whites," said the young accountant. "That's what to buy. I was told to stay far away from brown diamonds. They're less valuable—and once cut they can turn orange or gold, so that they don't even look like brown diamonds." He cast a suspicious glance at the ring that Petra had admired.

"Yes," agreed Ryan. "But even brown can be beautiful."

He searched Jessica's startled gaze. "Some browns have warmth and glow with inner fire." A tinge of colour crept up under Jessica's fine-grained skin. She glanced down, her lashes dark against her cheeks. Ryan turned his attention back to the ring that Petra held. "That stone comes from Janderra, a mine deep in the outback Kimberley region. Janderra is famous for the candy-coloured stones it produces. Because of the intensity of the colour, that stone will be particularly rare. The rich deep yellow is unusual. It will always be a talking point."

The accountant started to look a little more interested. "Won't everyone think it is only a topaz?"

Jessica lifted the ring off Petra's palm and tipped it back and forth. "Topaz? With that inner fire? I think not. Look at the way it flashes and reflects the light."

"Is that what you really want, darling?"

Petra nodded enthusiastically. "It's beautiful."

"You'll be wearing it every day of your life, so it's important that you love it."

She stood on tiptoe. "What's important is that I love you and you love me." Their lips met.

The emptiness returned like a kick in the stomach. Ryan glanced at Jessica to see what she was thinking. But she was looking down, fiddling with the jeweller's trays. For an instant he felt devastatingly envious of the young couple, so secure, so in love.

Then he thrust the feeling aside.

Seven

Ryan couldn't help noticing Jessica's pensive expression as she watched the couple walking away, their fingers linked, the stunning yellow diamond ring firmly on Petra's left hand.

Despite her apparent happiness with the arrangement they'd had, and her denials that she didn't want marriage from him, did Jessica long to wear a diamond ring on her left finger?

"What are you thinking?" he asked.

"Moments like that are the highlights of my job. Two people, brave enough to give life together a go, who come into Blackstone's looking for a permanent symbol of their love."

"Jessica—" Ryan broke off.

She smiled up at him, a sweet curve of pale pink lips that he'd kissed to death last night. But her eyes held a wary light. "Yes?"

"About last night—"

"Last night was one night. Only one night. That's what we agreed." She turned away, locked the display counter and flicked a nonexistent fleck of dust off the top of the glass.

Clearly she didn't want to talk about the experience that had been utterly mind-blowing for him. He suppressed the disappointment that blasted through him. "It was. But I've been thinking—"

"Ryan, what are you doing here?"

Ryan bit back a curse as his sister's surprised voice sounded behind him.

"I thought you, Garth and Uncle Vincent were flying up to Janderra today?"

He turned to face his sister. "We postponed the trip. With the launch so close I decided it's better to stay close to Sydney." Near Jessica.

Kim glanced at him. Then back at Jessica. "I see."

Ryan frowned at his sister—a pointed sibling frown aimed at separating her from her erroneous conclusion as quickly as possible. She simply raised her eyebrows at him.

Despite whatever Kim's pensive green eyes saw, according to Jessica, he and she were finished. They'd had their one night.

"Holly can't join us for lunch, I'm afraid," Kimberley said to Jessica. "But I'll take notes of anything she needs to know."

"You two are having a lunch meeting?" Ryan asked.

Kimberley nodded. "At Flavio's across the road, to go over the final arrangements for the jewellery showing, before Monday morning's breakfast meeting with the event coordinator."

"I know about that," Ryan said. "I'm diarised to attend."

"Be warned." Kimberley gave him an evil grin. "If you attend Monday's meeting, I'll be spending some time talking to the coordinator about the ceremony Ric and I are having to renew our vows."

Ryan gave an exaggerated sigh. "Best thing I ever did was move down here. Head office was starting to feel like a bridal shower. Now let me get my jacket, and join you ladies for lunch. It sounds like I need to be there if it's about the show."

Kimberley narrowed her eyes, giving him a sly little look of amusement from under her lashes. But Ryan couldn't help noticing that Jessica didn't look nearly as amused.

Flavio's was smart and fashionable, the walls washed with an ochre shade reminiscent of a Tuscan villa. The wooden refractory-style tables were dark and narrow, and large oil paintings of village scenes hung on the walls. When the waiter came, Jessica ordered linguine Alfredo. The morning sickness had subsided at last, and she had acquired the appetite of a sumo wrestler. Kim elected to have grilled barramundi that the blackboard on the wall promised had been freshly flown in from Queensland.

While Ryan scrutinized the wine list, Jessica ordered a cola and thanked the heavens that she didn't often drink alcohol. Ryan had no reason to raise an eyebrow at her abstinence.

"And a bottle of Saxon's sauvignon blanc, please," Ryan said. After the waiter had departed, he turned to his sister. "I have it on best authority that the sauvignon blanc tastes of grapefruit, a hint of melon and a whole lot of summer."

"That sounds like it came from the mouth of a PR expert." Kimberley laughed. "Megan perhaps?"

Ryan nodded. "Spot on, sister. More cousins," he explained to Jessica. "But the Saxons never caught the gem bug. They make wine."

"Poor Megan is the younger sister to three brothers," Kimberley expanded. She nudged Ryan's arm. "It's bad enough having only one baby brother."

"Baby?" Ryan snorted and gave her a hard stare. "I'm taller than you, sister!"

Jessica flinched at the word *baby*. It must be worse for Kimberley, she decided. The renewed happiness between Kimberley and Ric had come at a price. Jessica had heard that Kimberley couldn't ever have children. It was so sad. So final. She touched her own stomach. She might not have Ryan's love, but she'd been fortunate enough to be blessed with a baby. She caught Ryan watching her.

Hurriedly Jessica produced the list of items she wanted to discuss and started to talk. The next half hour passed in a blur of discussion about security, models, stylists and jewellery while they ate. Only to be interrupted when Ryan's cell phone shrilled.

He picked it up and squinted at the number. "Caller ID blocked. I'm tempted not to answer it."

"Oh, go on, you know that you can't resist!" Kimberley scoffed. "And you'll only have to ring back later. Take the call, we'll forgive you. This time."

"Excuse me." Ryan rose to his feet and took the call a little way from their table. His answers were brief. Uncommunicative.

Jessica watched him out the corner of her eye as Kimberley checked through the points that had to be discussed at Monday's meeting.

"I'm not prepared to comment until we meet." Ryan's voice went up a notch. Kimberley's head shot up. Jessica watched him terminate the call with worried eyes.

"It never ends." Ryan sat down heavily. "That was one Tom Macnamara."

"If he's a journalist, you should've referred him to me, not agreed to meet him yourself," Kimberley rebuked her brother.

Ryan's mouth slanted. "He's not a journalist. He's a private investigator—from Macnamara Investigations."

Kimberley's breath caught in an audible gasp. "What does he want?"

Ryan's smile grew feral. "Money. What else?"

"Oh, no. Not another scandal." Kim paled at the prospect. "I don't know how much more we can take. What will it do to the share price—"

"Wait." Ryan held up a hand. "I should've clarified that he's not looking for a payoff. Nor is he threatening to go to the newspapers with whatever information he has. He wants payment of a bill that he says is due to him."

"What bill?" Kim asked. "And who retained him?"

Jessica's stomach cramped at the silence that followed. She glanced from Kimberley to Ryan's inscrutable face.

"It appears that our father did." Ryan directed the statement at Kim. "He claims that Dad hired him to find James—"

Kim waved a dismissive hand. "He's hardly the first."

"But he says that he's got a lead—" Ryan broke off as the waiter arrived with coffee. "He wants to meet with us. But first we have to pay him what he says he's due. Apparently the bill was sent to Ian Van Dyke, the lawyer killed in the crash."

"Oh," murmured Kimberley. "Of course, we'll pay him. But we want to hear what he has to say first."

"Exactly!" Ryan agreed. "I offered to meet him tomorrow. He says he's away, but he'll be back in Sydney in a couple of weeks. If he's a fraud, we'll expose him."

"But what if he's the real thing?" Kim whispered. "What if James is still alive?"

Jessica's eyes darted from one to the other.

Ryan's hand tightened around his coffee cup. Tension sizzled in the air.

"We'll deal with that when it happens." Ryan looked across at his sister.

"You should know that Ric told me this morning that there's a rumour that Matt Hammond caught a flight to Alice Springs."

"Hell." Ryan banged a fist on the table. "That's the last thing we need."

Jessica jumped. "What does that mean?" It was the first time she'd spoken. The other two turned to look at her, their expressions startled. She shrank back into her chair and resisted the urge to apologise. No, darn it. There was no need to apologise. Kimberley had invited her to talk about work, and Ryan had gate-crashed their meeting. She had every right to join in the conversation. She straightened her spine. She was every bit as good as a Blackstone.

"I'm sorry." Ryan thrust a hand through his hair, ruffling it. "I forgot that not everyone knows the dynamics of the rather complicated Blackstone family. Vincent lives in Coober Pedy, but he's in Alice Springs at present. If Matt's flown to Alice, it means he's after Vincent's shareholding."

"Oh." Jessica thought about that. "Would your Uncle Vincent sell?"

"That's the million-dollar question. Under normal circumstances, probably not." Ryan shrugged. "But opal prices have taken a hammering lately, and Vincent is no longer a young man. He may be ready to sell."

"The cousins won't let him sell," Kimberley said firmly.

"We can only hope that. But their main concern is their opal empire," Ryan responded.

"What happens if Matt gets those shares?" Jessica had a feeling that she wouldn't like the answer. She couldn't help thinking of Dani Hammond's fervent wish that the Hammond-Blackstone feud would end.

Kimberley leaned forward, a fine frown line marring her brow beneath a widow's peak. "Matt already has ten per cent he bought off Uncle William—"

Ryan muttered a less than complimentary assessment of dear Uncle William's parentage. Then added, "But with Vincent's shares, Matt would be looking dangerous. A couple more pockets of shares and he'd be in a very strong position to launch a hostile takeover of Blackstone's."

Jessica felt her mouth rounding into a startled *O*.

Ryan took another sip of coffee. "Some of my father's estate planning was less than perfect. The old bastard never thought he'd die so soon. He thought he had lots of time."

"Ryan!" Kim scolded.

Jessica looked from one to the other.

"It's the truth." Ryan spread his hands. "He thought he was immortal."

Like Ryan did.

It struck Jessica that Ryan had the same proud belief in his own infallibility that his father had held. Enough to verge on arrogance. Would Ryan follow in his father's footsteps?

"We need to make Vincent an offer. Beat Matt to it if we can."

"With Dad's personal fortune frozen until probate it will be difficult to stop Matt." Kimberley looked worried. "It will take a huge sum of money—more than we can spare right now—to buy more shares. We need to keep reserves on hand to run the business."

"You could raise a loan," Jessica suggested tentatively.

"Isn't that a contravention—"

"No." Ryan cut across Kim's protest. "Great idea, Jess." He gave her a smile of approval that made her shiver with delight. "But not from the company to buy its own shares. A loan from the bank—to one of us. Or several of us. We have enough assets in our own right to secure funds. I have shares and my penthouse, and there's the property you and Ric own."

Kim bit her lip. "I'll need to discuss it with Ric. The property is—"

Ryan didn't allow the protest to take hold. "We need to stop Matt before he destroys Blackstone's."

Jessica flinched at Ryan's steely tone. He sounded just like his father. A chip off the old block.

"We could also raise a loan against Miramare," Ryan said slowly.

"Miramare?" Kimberley's eyes widened.

"The first time I ever saw it was after the funeral. Before that I'd only ever seen photos of it," Jessica said.

"It's worth a millions," Kim said slowly.

"And as long as the executor of the estate is prepared to authorise the loan it shouldn't be too hard." Ryan put his coffee cup down and sat back. "Garth won't have a problem. With all our other combined assets, we shouldn't need to use the funds. We just want to make sure we have that extra line of credit available—in case we need it to fight Matt Hammond. I'll talk to the bank."

Kim looked anxious and although he patted her shoulder reassuringly, it was Jessica's gaze that Ryan sought.

"No photo could ever do Miramare justice," Ryan announced on Monday morning as the powerful BMW M6 braked in front of the glamorous triple-storey Italianate mansion. "Or Pemberley, as my mother apparently sometimes used to call this place. A joke, I think."

Jessica climbed out the car and looked around. Ryan had swept into the store an hour ago, after meeting with the event coordinator organising the jewellery show, and whisked her away to give her a tour of Miramare—all because of her casual comment at lunch last Friday that she'd never seen Miramare before the funeral.

He'd called over the weekend, told her he was at a loose end, and offered her a tour of Miramare, there and then.

Feeling besieged, she'd refused. He hadn't taken affront. Instead he'd invited her to come today while he met with the valuator. Compelled by curiosity for another glimpse at the house where he'd grown up, she'd accepted, deciding that it would be safe enough with a third person to keep them company.

Empty of the hordes that had been at the wake, the mansion looked so much bigger, so much grander than she remembered. It loomed over her and Ryan, emphasising the vast difference between her background and the manner in which Ryan had been raised.

A world apart.

Beyond the house lay a stunning view of the Sydney Harbour. Ryan headed for the front door and Jessica followed more slowly, her eyes scanning her surroundings, taking in the outbuildings with space to garage a dozen cars, the precisely clipped hedges that lined the street, the established trees and the manicured green lawns that spoke of the attention of full-time gardeners. Before Ryan could insert his key into the lock, the door swung open.

"About time you came to visit, Ryan."

Ryan shepherded Jessica through the door. "Jessica, meet Marcie, the most indispensable person in the entire household."

"Nice to meet you, Jessica. I'm the housekeeper," Marcie said in response to Jessica's smiled greeting. "Not his aunt, in case his introduction gave you that idea."

Bright white light spilled into the entrance hall from high-set windows. Jessica blinked. Then her eyes adjusted to the interior and she saw the double stairway with its intricate black wrought-iron balustrade that curved up to the next floor.

"Is Sonya at home?" Ryan asked from behind Jessica.

"She's meeting a friend this morning for tea," Marcie said, stopping and turning around.

"No worries, we're early for an appointment." Ryan grinned down at the older woman. "We don't need a hostess. But can I ask you to brew a pot of tea and bring it to the balcony?"

"I'll do better," Marcie replied with easy familiarity. "I'll bring out those freshly baked scones you love, too."

"Come," Ryan said, gesturing to Jessica. "I'll give you a quick tour of the house and then we'll go sit outside and have a cup of tea and a scone. The views are truly splendid from the balcony. We might as well take advantage of the sunshine while we wait for the valuator to arrive."

He led her from one room to another. Everything about Miramare was ornate and grand, beautiful to look at. But it was far removed from the comfortable, touchable kind of home Jessica's heart craved.

"Tea, I think," Ryan said at last and led her back to the living room.

As they stepped through the French doors, Jessica's breath caught at the view spread before them. "Gosh, you can even see the Sydney Harbour Bridge from here." The instantly recognisable arched structure dominated the skyline. "Who did you say inherits this place under the new will?"

"James, as the eldest son." Ryan's voice held a hint of self-mockery.

A rush of sympathy for Ryan engulfed her. Up until now she hadn't considered that Ryan and Kim might both lose the home where they had grown up. "But James is dead, so that makes you the eldest son. And Kim's left out completely?" She shook her head. "Your father never had much of an appreciation for women."

They headed over to a white wrought-iron table and chairs

perched near the edge of the balcony overlooking the swimming pool. Ryan pulled out a chair for Jessica. "My father was hard on both his offspring. But I might still inherit Miramare as the eldest son when James fails to show before August."

"But you're the one who's spent all these years working for your father." She sank down onto the chair and tilted her head to look at him, her hand shading her eyes from the sun.

Ryan dropped into the chair beside her and shrugged. "He never really forgave me for going off to South Africa after he brought Ric on board."

"He was too hard on his children. At least you won't repeat those mistakes with your own children." Jessica's lips curled into an ironic smile.

"Oh, no." He held up his hands as if warding off an attack. "I don't want children."

"I know—you told me. No cats. No kids. No press. No diamond rings."

"You remember."

Jessica couldn't decipher his expression. She decided it had to be relief. "How could I ever forget? But if you inherit Miramare," she said, the irony not lost on her, "then you'll have to rethink. You'll need a wife."

"Why would I need a wife?" Ryan shot her a look she couldn't read.

"Well, you'd have a mansion—not a jet-set penthouse— and you'd be in possession of a fortune. So you'd be in want of a wife."

He raised an eyebrow. "I'm not some Jane Austen hero."

And she was hardly Elizabeth Bennet. Jessica thought of what she'd overheard at the wake, when he'd said to Kimberley, not realising she'd come to offer comfort, *What makes you so certain that I'd want a wife like Jessica?* The words had sent her scuttling back across the room.

"No, you're not the marrying kind."

He looked startled for a moment. Then he said, "That was one thing about you, Jess, you always knew the score."

Ouch. "Yep, I knew the score. And after seeing this place, if I suspected it might be part of the marriage deal, it would most likely scare me away. So no pressure, Mr. Darcy!"

Ryan didn't laugh as she'd intended. After a moment's thought he said, "Not long ago I might've preferred that charlatan of an investigator to find James rather than to contemplate marriage."

It hurt that the idea of marrying her was so repugnant. Jessica looked away, determined not to let him see how much he'd gotten to her. Fortunately Marcie arrived with the tea and scones spread with butter and jam before the pause could become too pointed.

"Will you pour?" Ryan asked after Marcie had gone.

"Sure." Jessica filled two cups, topped them with milk and handed one cup to Ryan. He helped himself to a scone and took a bite. In the garden a gang of noisy sulphur-crested cockatoos landed in the trees on the boundary.

After a moment Jessica said, "I can imagine the pain that information from cranks and hoax calls must have brought your family."

"My father would run every lead down." Ryan brushed the crumbs off his fingers. "Even calls from fake psychics who claimed to have been in touch with James, to have talked to him and have messages from him for Mother. In every other aspect of his life he was totally in control—except when it came to James."

Howard's obsession must've been very hard for Kimberley and Ryan to live with. No wonder Ryan believed he'd never measured up to his dead brother. But she could also understand Howard's grief at losing a child. And, as the mother who had carried the baby in her body for nine months, Ursula must've been devastated, too. Jessica resisted the urge to touch her stomach, to stroke the swelling curve under her loose-fitting top. Just the thought of losing her unborn baby was enough to make her shudder.

She stared at the uneaten scone on her plate, then glanced back at Ryan. "It must've been terrible for your mother to be given fresh hope with each crank call and then be disappointed again."

"Mother wanted closure. She was responsible for commissioning a plaque in memory of James at Rookwood near where my grandfather is buried, but Howard would only let her put a date of birth on it. No date of death. In case James was still alive." The grooves beside Ryan's mouth deepened. "But at least Dad had a quest that kept him going. To build Blackstone's…and to find James. Mother had nothing—except her weekly Sunday afternoon visit to tend the rosebushes she'd planted around the plaque. In the end she gave up hope."

"She had two other children," Jessica pointed out softly, suddenly understanding why Blackstone's was so vitally important to Ryan. He didn't believe that James was alive, so he couldn't pursue that quest on his father's behalf. But he could continue to build Blackstone Diamonds. To make it richer, more powerful.

"She drowned herself, you know."

Before she could control it, Jessica's gaze flitted to the pool that lay blue and seemingly innocuous below the balcony.

"No, not here. At the beach house at Byron Bay."

"You were on *holiday* when your mother drowned herself?" What had made his mother do that?

Ryan nodded, his face closed. "A three-week getaway for Mother, Kimberley and me. Aunt Sonya was there, too—pregnant, I think, with Dani."

Picking up her teacup, Jessica took a sip. "Where was Howard?"

"Working."

Typical. She watched him over the edge of the teacup. "Oh."

Ryan must've caught the note of censure in her unguarded comment because he said quickly, a touch defensively, "He planned to arrive the day before Mother's birthday."

The information came in meagre drips, like water being extracted from a stone. Jessica felt guilty asking for more. but she'd never heard Ryan talk about his mother's death before. She doubted he ever had—even as a child. As he grew older she could imagine him trying not to do or say anything that his father might consider a sign of weakness. So he'd probably never discussed it at all. All that suppression could not have been healthy. She persisted. "Your mother drowned herself on her birthday?"

"No. Two weeks before. So Dad had to come early anyway."

There would've been no birthday party for his mother that year. Yet only a year earlier Ursula had celebrated her thirtieth birthday, here at Miramare. That night Ursula had fallen in the swimming pool in front of her guests—an uncanny portent of her suicide. And the night that had started as a birthday celebration had ended with the theft of the legendary Blackstone necklace.

"How…" Jessica's voice trailed away. She was going to ask how old had he been. Little more than a baby, she reasoned.

"How? Mother used to go for a swim alone in the sea each morning. One dawn she walked into the sea and never came back. At first we thought she'd gone for a swim and drowned by accident. But Aunt Sonya found the note. It was all hushed up. Dad liked to pretend that it was all a horrible mistake, an accident."

But the newspapers had not allowed Howard to continue

that fiction. Even now there was still wild speculation about Ursula Blackstone's death.

"No, no." Jessica was horrified that he might think she'd wanted all the gory details. "I was going to ask how old you were when it happened."

"I was three, so I don't remember it at all. It's more like a feeling of emptiness. And sometimes I smell things or hear a sound and get a flash of something I can barely remember."

In the tall trees a cockatoo screeched.

"How horribly sad."

"Kimberley was four when Mother died. She remembers more about Mother."

There was a touch of longing in Ryan's voice that caused Jessica's throat to close. She had a sudden picture of a lonely little boy standing at the front gate, waiting for his mother, or the memories of her to come back.

"Ryan." The housekeeper's call broke in. "Your visitors have just driven in. "I'll let them in and then I'm going to chase those cockatoos before they descend on the blueberry bushes."

"Visitors? I thought there was only a valuator?" Ryan rose to his feet. To Jessica he said, "Stay here, enjoy the sunshine. You haven't touched your scone. Marcie will scold you if you don't eat up. This shouldn't take long."

The hot sun was warm on her skin. Looking over the garden which Ryan would've played in as a child, Jessica shifted in her chair, uncomfortably conscious of his baby growing inside her body. Guilt niggled at her.

With each passing day, it became more pressing for her to tell him about the baby before he saw from the changes in her body. She'd delayed, frightened that he would demand that she get an abortion, but that deadline had now passed. It would no longer be safe.

But the thought of telling him, of losing the amiability that had been growing between them, distressed her.

By the time Ryan returned, Jessica was feeling drowsy from the hot sun. The cockatoos had vanished at the sight of Marcie brandishing a broom, and she'd eaten not one but two of the delicious scones and was dreading the thought of climbing onto the scale tomorrow morning. Right now her weight was rocketing up like the mercury on a sweltering day. If she didn't stop eating so much, she was going to look like a whale by the time she started to show.

"That's taken care of. The valuator brought a banker along who thinks the bank may not grant the loan unless James comes to life and consents to the application." Ryan frowned a little. "Or we wait until August when that provision expires."

"How crucial is it to get the loan in place?" Jessica asked.

"Ric and I are simply being cautious in case we need funds available to fight Matt on a takeover bid. And there's still the security of the Byron Bay property, as well as my penthouse and Ric and Kim's new home."

"Surely you won't need to be present for those valuations, will you?"

"Not really—certainly not for the valuation of Ric and Kim's home. But I'd like to make sure that the valuator gives each property the most favourable value. My presence will do that."

Ryan was definitely a control freak. But he was probably right. His presence would make a difference. Yet Jessica couldn't help thinking of Ryan returning to the house in Byron Bay that must hold painful memories of his mother.

"When will you go up to Byron Bay?"

"Wednesday, I think. My diary can be cleared. I'll probably fly up and back in the same day."

He'd be all alone. Jessica's heart melted at the thought of him confronting the ghostly memories that must lurk in the beach house. It would be the first time that he had visited since his father died. And she couldn't help thinking that seeing the beach house might give her some insight into the man who'd been her lover…the man who would be the father of her child.

Jessica rapidly considered her own schedule. "I've got a lot of leave due to me. I could take a day off—if my boss approves." She hesitated. "Would you like me to come and keep you company?"

The look Ryan gave her was impenetrable. "I would. And don't worry about taking leave. You work hard enough as it is. I have an early appointment with the security contractors for the show, so I'll be in the store a little later than normal. I'll pick you up midmorning."

Eight

Jessica was keeping an eye open for Ryan on Wednesday morning when Kimberley Perrini twirled into the showroom and did a little dance around the floor. "Jarrod Hammond is coming."

The show to unveil the new collections was now less than ten days away. Instantly Jessica got the significance of Matt Hammond's brother's attendance—and Kim's exhilaration. "Does this mean Matt is coming, too?" More importantly, did it herald the beginning of the end of the Blackstone-Hammond feud?

Kimberley stopped dancing and flung her hands out wide. "Who knows? He certainly hasn't replied to the invitation I asked Holly to send him. And he's not talking to me."

"So probably not."

Kimberley's eyes darkened. "I don't like being at odds with Matt. As well as being great to work for, he was a great friend."

"Then I need tips from you," Jessica said cryptically.

"On what? How to keep your boss as a friend? I don't think I've done too well in that department." Kimberley put a slim hand on Jessica's arm, her diamond engagement ring scintillating in the light. "My brother is a tough guy, a man of few words, but I'm certain you mean a lot to him."

Jessica sighed. "Not nearly enough."

"Jessica." Kimberley leaned forward. "I know my brother can be—" she paused, searching for the right word "—uncommunicative. But he's been through plenty in the last two months. Dad's disappearance. The recovery of his body. Then he had to identify Dad's remains. That must have been hell. And he's recently buried those remains. On the same day that it became public knowledge that Dad had left a fortune to Marise, a very stunning, much younger woman. And her son is now pretty much set up for life, too. God knows what Ryan thought of that! And that's before you remember that Uncle William's selling his shares to Matt...and Matt's threat to go all out for revenge is making it incredibly tough on the work front. It's been truly awful. I know how much it's affected me—and I'm not as self-contained as Ryan. Give him time."

Put like that, his problems made her own seem suddenly trivial. But then Jessica thought of the baby. Of the days— weeks—ticking by. Her body was swelling, growing ripe. Any day now she'd start to show. The flowing dressy tops she'd been wearing lately teamed with black trousers would soon attract comment. "Time is the one luxury I don't have."

But Kimberley's words stayed with her and when Ryan arrived to pick her up for their day trip to Byron Bay, she found herself searching his face for signs of strain. And forgiving him when he seemed a little distracted.

A car was waiting for them at the airport, and the drive to the town centre took less than thirty minutes.

The beach house turned out to be a historic five-bedroom

house sited a little below Australia's most easterly lighthouse on Wategos Beach. The boundary on the street frontage was edged with Norfolk pines and when the car turned into the drive, Jessica caught her breath at the immaculately maintained tropical garden dominated by palms and lush plantings. *Beach house* was definitely a misnomer.

"It's beautiful."

"I've come here often over the years," Ryan said. "My father used to spend most of his time away from work here. It was the only time he and I ever had alone. Kimberley never visits—the memories are too bad. She doesn't even swim." A glimpse of pain flared in Ryan's eyes, then it was gone. "Come, let's go in. The valuator should be here by now."

The valuator was already skirting the outside taking notes. Jessica went into the house that Ryan had unlocked to give Ryan the opportunity to talk freely. From the large wooden windows she could see that the house had been positioned to maximise the impact of the view from inside the house. The living room faced over rolling green lawns to a wide vista of blue sea. She didn't know how long she stood there, just soaking in the beauty.

"There are quite a few pods of dolphins who make Byron Bay their home." Ryan had come up soundlessly behind her. Jessica struggled to keep her composure as his warm breath winnowed her hair as he spoke. "And in winter the humpback whales come to visit. The bay is full of stingrays." His arms slid around her from behind, and his chin rested on her shoulder, his cheek against her hair.

Jessica heard a car starting as the valuator departed. "Your holidays were very different from mine, although we also went to the beach. When I was growing up, we used to go camping every Christmas. And when I was about seven my parents bought a battered secondhand caravan that they towed down to Lakes Entrance and left there during the year. My father was a mechanic so he was good at fixing things up. Every holiday we'd go down there, just the three of us." She leaned back in the circle of his arms, breathed in his warm manly scent and looked up at him with a nostalgic smile. "That was our beach house. Yet that's where I spent some of the happiest times of my life."

"What happened to change that?"

"When I was ten years old my father had an accident at work." Jessica looked down, veiling her eyes.

"At the funeral I couldn't help wondering why he was in a wheelchair. But I didn't want to pry. You must get sick of endless questions."

"I don't mind. I'm so proud of my father." She paused, then added, "Ironically enough, after his accident things got a little easier financially and we used to hire a holiday apartment after that, one with ramps for wheelchairs." She tried not to stiffen in his arms, not to withdraw.

"At least your parents had insurance."

Jessica didn't contradict him. It was better for Ryan to believe that. She freed herself from his arms and took a step away. "And I went to boarding school. I got awfully homesick. I missed home, my mum and my dad."

"Which one did they send you to?"

"Pymble Ladies' College."

Ryan looked startled. "That's where Kimberley went to school."

"I know." Jessica knew he must be wondering how a mechanic could justify such expensive school fees—even with an insurance payout. "She was a senior when I arrived. I was very much in awe of her especially when she became head girl."

"It's not something I often admit out aloud, but my sister

is a very special person." He gave her a conspiratorial grin. But then his eyes became serious. "What did we talk about for the last two years? How much more is there that I don't know about you? I don't think it's only me who talks too little. It wasn't only me avoiding intimacy in our relationship, was it, Jess?" He raised an eyebrow.

It was true. They'd both avoided intimacy, Jessica thought. It had been convenient to tell herself that all the faults lay on his side—his lack of commitment, his ruthless inflexibility, his Blackstone pride.

But she'd been so careful to hide so much of herself, too. If she wanted this burgeoning relationship between them to continue, she was going to have to open herself up to him. As difficult as that might be.

At last the lack of communication between them was emerging, the hurts, the disappointments, the unspoken dreams. And it gave her hope, hope that they could both change the parts of themselves that had blocked their chances at happiness before.

When he suggested that they go for a drive to see the lighthouse, Jessica jumped at it. They were too alone here in this place. Too secluded. And she had some thinking to do before she shared all the secrets.

An hour later after a climb to the top of the headland where the lighthouse was located, they made their way back down again and Ryan produced a picnic hamper.

"You think of everything," Jessica sighed in bliss as she drew out a bottle of Bundaberg ginger beer. From where they sat on the sunlit grass below the lighthouse, the bay stretched out in front of them. And, except for the shrill calls of the silver gulls and the whisper of the sea wind, there was absolute silence.

After they'd eaten the dainty smoked salmon sandwiches

and snacked on biscuits with wedges of camembert, Jessica asked, "What will happen to the beach house now that your father is gone?"

Ryan lay on his back with his arms folded behind his head. "In terms of the will it comes to me. I'll sell it as soon as I can."

"Oh."

He turned his head. "You wouldn't sell it in my place?"

"I don't know. I can understand the terrible memories it brings. But it was also a place where your mum spent time with you and your sister. Where you spent time with your father. Maybe you should wait before you rush to sell."

There was a moment's charged silence. Then he said, "Maybe I will. Unless we need to raise funds in a hurry to fend off Matt."

Matt Hammond again. Jessica looked down at the face she'd grown to love so much and wished that he was less like his father. "Don't you think that the Blackstones and the Hammonds should try and end this feud before it causes more unhappiness?"

"I'd be happy to end it."

Jessica felt a surge of relief. Perhaps Ryan was different from his father after all.

"But only if Matt Hammond backs off from buying our stock—and his father apologises for stealing the Blackstone Rose. Matt Hammond needs to make the first move."

Or perhaps, Jessica thought, not so much had changed at all.

Matt Hammond needs to make the first move.

The words stayed with Jessica, keeping her awake deep into the night. So the following morning, as soon as she reached her office in the Blackstone's store, Jessica picked up the telephone before she could chicken out. Ryan *would* appreciate what she was about to do, Jessica assured herself, her heart knocking against her ribs, as she dialled the number. "Matt Hammond, please."

If only Matt would come to the launch, that might be the first conciliatory step toward bridging the feud. And maybe then Ryan would not be quite so intransigent in his demands of what was required to end this ridiculous feud—especially if Kim could convince him.

Jessica almost fainted with relief on being told that Matt was in a meeting.

Struggling for composure, she left a message asking him to call her back. After she set the handset down she started to shake. What on earth was she thinking? Ryan would not welcome her interference.

But then she picked up the brochure for the launch that lay on the counter and started leafing through the pages. She saw the work of all the talented designers that Blackstone's used, and of the new designers, like Dani Hammond, who were being groomed to become big names.

She thought about the lustrous pearls that Matt was famed for sourcing. A vision that had started out as insignificant as a grain of sand in an oyster grew clearer in her mind. The excitement that churned in her stomach whenever she had an idea that the market later caught on to told her that it would work. And Xander Safin would be the perfect person to bring the vision to crafted life.

The morning passed in a rush. Jessica was talking to her mother on the phone, arranging to have dinner with her parents, when Ryan walked into her office and turned the chair in front of her desk around before straddling it. Folding his arms across the top, he rested his chin on it and smiled at her.

It was a smile full of charm and affection. It did strange

things to her and caused her heartbeat to speed up. Jessica cut short her conversation with her mother. But before she could greet him the ringing phone cut in, stalling a reply. She signalled for him to stay.

This was the relaxed version of Ryan she'd fallen in love with in Adelaide. But in the time she'd lived with him she'd discovered there was so much more depth and character under the superficial charm and wonderful manners that always made her feel like a woman in a million.

"Ms Cotter?" The voice was deep, with a hint of Trans-Tasman accent.

Her breath caught. "Jessica, please. May I call you back a little later?" She sent Ryan a guarded glance. He slanted her a wicked smile.

"I'm afraid I'll be out for the rest of the day and tomorrow. So it will be a couple of days before you will reach me."

Jessica fought an unfamiliar urge to swear. Of all the hours in the day why did Matt Hammond have to call now?

Drawing a deep breath, she launched into speech. "I've a proposition to put to you. I've heard you source amazing pearls."

"I like to think so." There was a hint of humour in Matt's voice and Jessica relaxed a little. Maybe this would not be as difficult as she had anticipated.

"I'd like to be frank with you. I've been struggling to find the kind of pearls Blackstone's need."

Over the line she could feel the sudden chill at the introduction of the Blackstone name. Jessica told herself she was being oversensitive. She rushed on. "I'd like to use House of Hammond pearls in a range of jewellery designed by Xander Safin to be available for next year's northern summer."

"I take it these designs will be carried by Blackstone's stores?"

"Yes, as part of a new collection to be launched next year—a whole new take on the Sea Meets Sky collection Xander Safin has crafted."

"Is the board aware of your proposition, Ms Cotter?"

Across the desk her gaze tangled with Ryan's. He was shaking his head and motioning that he wanted her to end the conversation. Without a doubt, Ryan knew who was on the other end of the line. "No."

"Perhaps you should discuss this with the directors first. You may find that what you propose is not welcome."

Jessica looked away from Ryan's irate face and chewed at the inside of her cheeks. "I needed to know that you would be willing to supply Blackstone's first. I was hoping that we could discuss this further at the launch."

Jessica's pulse was racing. She'd come this far, she wasn't backing off now. She thought about Kim. About how Matt Hammond's remoteness was hurting her. She thought about Ryan. About the feud and its effect on him.

"You will be coming, won't you?"

Ryan was saying something to her now, his voice fierce. She blocked it out.

"No, I won't be attending," Matt Hammond said with a finality that indicated that the conversation was over.

Jessica rushed on. "But your brother is coming."

She sneaked a glace at Ryan. His face was even blacker than before. Jessica forced herself not to let his displeasure sway her. She told herself that it was for his own good. She tried to convince herself that he would one day thank her. She nearly succeeded—until she heard the sputtering sound coming from his direction.

"Jarrod?" For the first time she caught a hint of uncertainty in Matt's voice. Apparently he hadn't known that. "Jarrod will be there?"

"Yes, he contacted Kim for an invitation." Jessica didn't dare look at Ryan.

A moment later Matt responded. No chinks in that hard voice remained. "That's his concern. And, Ms. Cotter?"

"Yes?" Jessica had a feeling she wouldn't like what was coming next.

"It won't be long before all the pearls in Blackstone pieces will come from the House of Hammond."

It was a threat. A threat of a man who had vowed to take over the empire Howard Blackstone had built. Was Ryan correct? Did Matt want to destroy everything that the Blackstones had built?

When Jessica set down the handset she discovered that her hands were shaking. She couldn't decide which of the two men was harder or more proud.

"That was Matt Hammond, wasn't it? Did you call him first?"

Jessica gave a start. Ryan stood beside her, his mouth drawn tight, his shoulders tense. Despite his deceptively mild tone, Jessica realized he was seething with rage.

"Does it matter? He won't supply the pearls I need for next season's designs, nor is he coming to the launch."

Softly, dangerously, Ryan said between his teeth, "If I hadn't been sitting here when the call came in, you would never have told me that you'd contacted him."

"What was the point? He refused." Jessica felt overwhelmed by a deflating sense of failure.

"You would have lied to me by omission."

Jessica's gaze leaped to his.

"Like you lied before," he continued.

Her heart started to pound with apprehension. "When?"

"You never told me you were going to Auckland in my father's jet."

That again. "I missed my plane to Auckland. I didn't see

any need to let you know. You and I weren't talking, remember?" The memory of the argument they'd had seemed like a lifetime ago.

Desperate for a sign that she wasn't wasting her time in a dead-end relationship, Jessica had pushed for an invitation to spend Christmas and New Year with him. It would've been their second Christmas together and she'd wanted more than separate vacations. As little as Jessica wanted to spend vacation time with Howard Blackstone at Byron Bay, she'd needed Ryan to prove his commitment to her by spending Christmas together, to be reassured that she'd be more than his secret mistress for the coming year.

But Ryan had made it icily clear that Christmas at Byron Bay was off-limits. She'd been wounded and she'd lashed out. They'd fought and parted in anger. Then two days before New Year's Day Jessica had discovered she was pregnant—and her whole life had swung upside down. It had been the final nail in the coffin of their precarious affair.

"I don't like you keeping secrets, Jessica."

The baby. Her gaze slid away from his. Guilt surged in her chest, along with a tight, uncomfortable feeling of regret.

He'd had his chance.

"Look at me." She met the dark jade eyes, heard the ragged breath he drew. "I want to start over…with everything out in the open."

"Make me your public mistress?" She heard the distaste in her voice and knew he must have, too. "I don't think so, Ryan."

Slowly he came towards her. She had lots of time to turn her head away, but she didn't. Instead she held his gaze.

When his lips took hers, she let herself open up like the petals of a flower unfurling to the sun, kissing him back with all the emotion and intensity she could dredge up, trying to communicate her feelings about him.

He drew back, confusion written all over his handsome features. "You respond to me like that? But you refuse to be my lover. What do you want?"

She bit her lip. "A couple of months ago a little commitment would've been good. But now I'm not sure if that's what you really want or if you're only making the noises you think I want to hear."

"I want to make our relationship public."

"Because the biggest critic is dead?"

"This is not about my father." Now there was annoyance in his tone; the softness had vanished. "Everyone knows I'm against workplace relationships."

Making their relationship public would be a huge concession for him, Jessica realised. But she wanted more. She would no longer be satisfied with anything less than his love.

Slowly she shook her head. "I'm sorry, Ryan, it's no longer enough."

"Is this about marriage? Because I don't want—"

"Relax, this isn't about marriage. It's about me. About what I want. And I don't want to be your lover, nor do I want to marry you." At least, not while things stood so badly between them. Not while he didn't love her. And certainly not while she was lying to him.

Ryan was right, she was keeping secrets. Well, no more.

She drew a deep breath. "I'm pregnant, Ryan."

Whatever he'd been about to say escaped in a whoosh of air. He stared at her, clearly stunned.

"And, before you ask, yes, it is your baby."

"I wasn't going to dispute that." A frown gouged deep lines between his eyes. "When did you find—"

"And, no, I won't be working after the baby is born—"

"Nor did I ask that," he interrupted, the lines of irritation marring his features.

"At least not for a while," Jessica continued as if he hadn't spoken. "I'll get through the launch and then I'll work my notice. You'll need to find someone else to run the Sydney store. I'm resigning."

"You can't leave!" He looked poleaxed. "You love the store."

"The baby will come first. I can't do justice to a high-flyer job and be a single parent. I want to spend time with my baby." A softening filled her as she spoke the words and she realised that was what she truly wanted. To spend time with the baby she and Ryan had created. She had no future with a man who was following in the footsteps of a man she despised. And she had no intention of spending her life with a man who was never at home.

"You've thought it all through," he said slowly. "You've got it all planned." He didn't look thrilled at the prospect. Jessica could see the wheels turning in his mind. "What about me? Where's my place in all this?"

The first twinge of uncertainty pierced her. He'd never wanted children, so why did he look so unhappy? "You'll always be my baby's father, Ryan. You're welcome to visit whenever you want." She'd made her choice. And Ryan's life, his priorities, were too different from hers. Jessica doubted she'd see much of him after the baby was born. But she knew he'd get a team of lawyers onto it, that his rights would be spelled out, that the baby would be given all the financial support he or she would ever need. "And don't worry that I'll be looking for support for myself. I've always been a careful saver and I've a healthy nest egg built up which will allow me time before I need to go back to work."

"Of course I'll contribute." His teeth snapped shut. "What if I want joint custody?"

Jessica laughed. She couldn't help herself. "Oh, Ryan! There's no space in your executive bachelor lifestyle for a cat.

Where would you fit a baby?" *No cats. No kids. No press. No diamond rings.* She knew his creed by rote.

He swallowed, slid off the chair and headed for the door, his haste revealing his desperation to escape. "This is a huge shock. I need to think about it."

"Don't worry about it." She watched him freeze in the doorway, his shoulders hunched. "You have enough on your mind with Matt's takeover bid."

In the course of the morning, despite being incredibly busy, Jessica found herself mulling over Ryan's unexpected reaction to the announcement of her pregnancy.

She'd expected him to feel trapped. He'd never wanted a family. Already he was trapped in the obligations to his family, to the company. She had expected him to be shocked. What she hadn't expected was his apparent desire to be involved in the baby's life beyond superficial financial support—his remark about joint custody had shocked her to the core.

But with the launch getting closer by the day, Jessica barely had time to breathe, much less think about custody arrangements as she fielded calls from Kimberley, as well as Holly and a host of caterers and security contractors and designers to finalise the finer details.

A couple of hours later, with Kimberley in a meeting and not taking calls, Jessica found herself on the phone to Ryan, stiltedly arranging to pay a quick visit to Miramare to make the final selection of paintings from Howard's collection. The paintings would be hung downstairs in the gallery-style lobby for the launch.

"I'll meet you at Miramare in an hour," Ryan stated, without mentioning the baby bombshell she'd dropped earlier.

"No, no." The last thing she wanted was to see him again

today. She needed time to think his reaction through. "Just let Marcie know I'm coming."

"I'll be there."

And the line went dead.

Jessica was apprehensive when she parked her Toyota in front of the mansion for the second time that week. To top it all, she was hot, irritated and totally out of sorts.

And of course, Ryan looked gorgeous, groomed and totally together, not a hair out of place, no sign of sweat from the sweltering Sydney heat.

Keeping her spine stiff to conceal that the heat was causing her to wilt, she strode beside him through the downstairs reception rooms, once again struck by the opulence, the grandeur. In the grand salon she picked out two modern paintings that would fit in with the mood of the launch. Ryan promised to have them sent over. The insurance for the transfer was already in place.

In the air-conditioned living room a large family oil portrait dominated one wall. Jessica stopped to admire it. A young and very beautiful Ursula, dressed in flowing white, knelt on a carpet of grass studded with white daisies under the wide branches of an oak tree. Beside her stood a small boy—James?—clutching a teddy bear and a baby clad in a pale pink dress in a bassinet. Howard stood behind the family, while, in the background, horses grazed on the hillside.

It was a picture of wealthy pastoral bliss. Jessica searched the painting. "You're not there."

Ryan barely spared the painting a glance. "I wasn't born yet. Mother was pregnant with me at the time." For a moment she thought he was going to add something about her own pregnancy, then to her intense relief, he said, "Look, why don't you use this picture over on this wall in the show?"

"I'll look now." But Jessica didn't move. Her attention

was fixed on Ursula Blackstone. Now she noticed the rounded belly that the dress's fullness concealed so cleverly. "Your mother looks so happy."

"That was painted before James…disappeared. After that she became very depressed, and when I was born, the depression worsened."

"Some women do feel blue after the birth." Jessica had been reading about the baby blues. In fact, she'd been reading everything she could lay her hands on to do with pregnancy and birth. Jessica-the-mother-to-be would bore Ryan to tears.

"Her depression pushed my father away. But he stood by her. It was only after her death that he started to have affairs."

She could see that the admission cost him. "Your father never brought his mistresses here, did he?"

"What?"

"Your father kept his affairs at work, separate from his family."

"If you mean that he had affairs with secretaries then yes, he kept his affairs at work." He glanced at her. "Although Marise wasn't strictly a secretary—"

"This isn't about Marise. It's about you. Until the funeral I'd never seen Miramare, much less set foot inside. You were following the patterns of behaviour your father had set. You would never have brought me here while I was your lover."

"Jess—"

"You didn't want your mistress to cross the threshold."

"You're wrong about that! It wasn't because you were my lover that I didn't want our relationship made public." He pushed a hand through his hair in a harassed manner. "It was because I didn't want to follow in my father's footsteps, sleeping with the staff. I've always been appalled by that."

"Sleeping with the staff?" she repeated.

"God, that sounds awful. Makes me sound like a total

snob. And that's not the reason why I'm against work relationships. They're disruptive, bad for the company."

"So why did you ever have an affair with me?"

"Because—" He stopped and shook his head. "It's too hard to explain. I'm not sure I know the answer myself. Except that I didn't seem capable of resisting you."

So he thought her irresistible. What did that mean? "But you have very firm ideas about what kind of woman you would not marry. A woman like me. I heard you at the wake telling your sister you wouldn't marry a woman like me."

He caught her hands. "Jessica, I've been an arrogant jerk. Your value is beyond—"

"My value as a staff member to Blackstone's?"

He paused. "Yes." Then he saw her face. "But that's not all. You mean a lot to me as…" His voice trailed away.

"As a lover?"

"Yes!" He looked relieved.

"But never as a wife."

He didn't answer, and his eyes held shadows that made it impossible to fathom what he was thinking. With a sigh, Jessica turned on her heel and walked away to the French doors. She stared out absently, noting how the sky reflected in the sea, making the harbour appear even bluer than usual. "You know, when I stayed with Mother over the Christmas holidays, I told her there was someone I was seeing. She's wanted me to get married for a long time. Finally, on New Year's Day, I told her it was you." Her mother had been conflicted—partly thrilled, partly fearful that Jessica would be hurt.

"So you wanted me to propose for your mother's sake?"

Jessica wished she'd never started this conversation. She pushed the door open. Ryan followed, his hands shoved deep into the pockets of his trousers. Before she knew it, she was standing beside the broad expanse of the swimming pool. "My mother said a Blackstone would never marry someone like me." And she'd been right.

"What made your mother think she knew how I would react?" He pulled his hand out of his pocket. In the palm lay a ring box covered in midnight blue velvet. "Jessica—"

"Don't!" Jessica shut her eyes in horror. How had this happened? She didn't want his proposal now. It was much too late. She'd never be sure why he married her. Heck, it couldn't be for love.

"Why not?"

He was only asking her to marry him out of some chivalrous impulse because of the baby. "I can't. My mother is right. You…me…it wouldn't work."

"Now who's the snob?"

She shook her head frantically. *"I can't.* I don't want to be married to a carbon copy of Howard Blackstone. I want a husband, a family—not a megalomaniac intent on building an empire without thought of the cost to his humanity."

He stepped closer. She fended him off. He came closer still. Desperately Jessica gave him a push to hold him at bay. She couldn't cope with his kisses. Not now. Her eyes widened as he reeled backward. "Look out!"

Ryan hit the water with a splash, his arms flailing as he tried in vain to keep his balance. When he rose, his hair was plastered against his head, the water streaming off the shoulders of his suit jacket. He pulled it off and hoisted himself onto the side of the pool. His shirt clung to muscles she knew were every bit as hard as they looked. In one movement he unbuttoned the top buttons and yanked the shirt over his head.

Jessica made a strangled noise in her throat and gave his naked torso a furtive once-over. *Goodness, but he was beautiful.* "Have you still got the ring?"

"You want to reconsider?"

"No, but I'd hate for you to lose it." That sounded flippant. Jessica tore her eyes away from the glorious view of skin and muscle before she said something even more stupid.

He shifted, and, unable to resist, she took another peek. He was dabbing the wet shirt at the rivulets of water on his chest, trying to mop up the excess. She suppressed an offer to help.

"You haven't even seen what I was going to offer you."

"I can't accept it." She turned away from his sheer over-whelming masculinity. She needed to get out of here before she was tempted to give in to a bunch of crazy impulses. To touch him. To marry him. To do whatever he asked, even though she knew it wasn't what he'd planned for his life.

He'd be marrying her for all the wrong reasons.

"Dinner was scrummy tonight, thanks, Mum."

Sally Cotter turned from where she was packing the dirty dinner dishes into the dishwasher and smiled with pleasure. "Scrummy? It's years since I've heard you use that word."

Jessica had craved the familiarity of her parent's company tonight, and comfort food was precisely what she'd needed.

"Where can I put these?" The empty lasagne dish balanced precariously on top of the plate she held.

"Give it to me, love."

"Mum…" Jessica paused. "I wanted to tell you Ryan asked me to marry him today."

Her mother straightened. "Oh, Jessica! That's wond—"

"I turned him down." Jessica didn't want her mother getting her hopes up.

"You turned him down? But why?" Confusion churned in her mother's eyes. "It's your dream come true."

"No, Mother. It's *your* dream come true."

Her mother gave a start of surprise.

Jessica sighed. "I only wanted Ryan's love. I wanted him to be proud to proclaim it to the world, not keep me hidden away like some sordid secret. Without his love, a diamond ring—even the finest Blackstone fancy pink—is worthless."

Dishtowel in hand, Sally stood staring at Jessica. "But you love him. You admitted that on New Year's Day."

"If you remember, I also said it was all one-sided—all on my side—and that I was going to go back and break it off."

"But you didn't. So I thought—"

"Because only a few hours later, Ryan's father's plane went missing."

Sally tossed the dishtowel down and came toward her. "Maybe your love will be enough—"

"No, Mum. It can never be enough. You should know that." Her mother paled, her lips whiter than the tall lilies in the vase on the table. Instantly Jessica felt dreadful. She reached out and touched her mother's arm. "I'm sorry. I shouldn't have said that."

"Shouldn't have said what?" The whirr of wheels heralded Peter Cotter's arrival.

"Hello, Dad." Jessica withdrew her hand.

"I'll get us all a cup of tea." Her mother rushed into the pantry.

Jessica forced a stiff smile. "Do you want some French vanilla ice cream?"

"Maybe later." Peter Cotter's gaze was watchful. "You're not giving your mother a hard time are you, Jess?"

Jessica drew a deep breath. "I came to tell her that Ryan Blackstone asked me to marry him and I refused."

"Probably for the best."

"You're right." So why did it ache so much? "But Daddy, I wish I had said yes."

"Come here." Her father opened his arms and Jessica flew to

him. She hugged him awkwardly, the armrest of the wheelchair digging into her side. He smelt of the aftershave her mother bought him every Christmas and faintly of cigarette smoke.

"You've been smoking."

"Hush, don't tell your mother."

Jessica wagged her finger at him. "Daddy, you shouldn't be keeping secrets."

All humour disappeared when she read the knowledge that lay in her father's gaze. "Good advice, Jessica. So when are you intending to tell us about the baby?"

"Baby?" She could feel the blood draining from her face.

"Yes. Your and Ryan Blackstone's baby."

"How did you know?"

"A little observation. You were ill at the funeral. You've been complaining of nausea. You're not drinking coffee. Your mother was the same when she was pregnant with you."

The sound of china shattering caused them both to look up.

"You're pregnant?" Shock silvered her mother's eyes. "Is your father right? Is it Ryan's baby?"

Jessica nodded.

"Have you told Ryan?" her mother was asking.

"Yes."

"Is that why he asked you to marry him?"

Jessica hesitated. "Maybe. I think so. I don't know. Oh, Mum, my head is a mess!"

"I should've known a Blackstone would never bring you anything but pain."

"I've already broken it off."

Her mother slumped down onto a kitchen chair. "You need to leave Blackstone's."

"I've resigned. But I'm going to miss Blackstone's." And Ryan. Unbearably.

Her mother had struck the heart of her dilemma. She loved

working at Blackstone's—and hated the idea of leaving. An image of Kimberley Perrini flashed into her mind. Kim had left Blackstone's and gone to work for House of Hammond but it had been a time of drought for her. And Jessica knew she would feel a similar sense of loss.

But she had no choice.

She wanted a clean break. From Ryan. From Blackstone's. She stepped away from her father's wheelchair. She would see the show through. When the baby was older she would start looking for another job. She'd told Howard Blackstone that she'd quit after their terrible confrontation, only hours before his jet disappeared.

She should've cut her losses then, walked away and never come back. As much as she loved Ryan Blackstone, their relationship could never have a happy ending.

Later, as her mother came to see her off, Sally said, "Your father has forgiven me, Jessica. Why can't you?"

Jessica halted just short of the garden gate, and before she could stop herself, the words escaped. "How could have you let Howard Blackstone seduce you?"

Her mother's hand dropped away from the latch and the gate clicked shut again. "It's so hard to explain. Howard was so compelling. Attractive, successful, wealthy. A widower. He appreciated me." Sally drew a shuddering breath. "It started off as a light flirtation—"

Jessica raised an eyebrow. "With your boss?"

"I was a temp—everything was so tough back then. Before I knew it, I was in his bed." Sadness clouded her mother's eyes. "Your father was in a bad way after the accident. You were only ten when it happened—when that car fell off the jack on top of him mangling his legs. Things were hard. Without my job, without Howard Blackstone, everything would have been a lot worse. Howard was my escape. He gave me a job, took me to places I'd never seen, bought me clothes I could not afford. He gave me a glimpse of another world and made me feel like a princess."

"But you were married, Mum."

"I know." Her mother sucked in her cheeks and leaned against the gate. "And I hurt your father. But even worse, you found out and you disapproved. Your disapproval made me feel so guilty, I was almost relieved when Howard arranged for you to go board at Pymble Ladies' College, and offered to pay for you. Your father and I would never have been able to give you such a wonderful education."

Jessica had always suspected Howard had wanted her out of the way while he conducted a raging affair with her mother. He had disliked her intensely and had hated it when her mother had taken her along to meet him at out-of-the way cafes on those Friday afternoons. Of course, her mother had sworn her to silence about those trysts, and she'd felt like a silent accomplice.

Worst of all, as a teenager Jessica had read Howard's notes and letters to her mother. She'd found the box where her mother had hidden them on the top shelf of her closet and read them all. Some of them were seductive. Some were romantic. And some were downright frightening. Like the note that must've been sent after a pregnancy scare where Howard had made it clear that if Sally ever fell pregnant, she would have to get an abortion.

"Will you ever forgive me?" Her mother's eyes were bleak and troubled.

Jessica blinked back the moisture in her eyes. "Oh, Mum, I *do* forgive you. Maybe because I understand more than you think. I've made the same mistake. I've fallen in love with my boss. But I've been even more stupid than you ever were. I fell pregnant."

"At least you're not married to another man—a man who is injured and needs you—nor do you have a young daughter at home waiting for you to come home while you attend illicit meetings with your lover." Her mother's eyes were full of self-loathing. "And at least Ryan Blackstone has offered to marry you."

"Oh, Mum." Jessica stared blindly over Sally's shoulder to where a car droned past on the suburban road. She remembered how frigid she'd been when years ago she'd discovered what those out-of-the-way encounters meant. That her mother was Howard Blackstone's lover. How she'd hated discovering halfway through her schooling where the money for her fancy girls' school funding came from.

Despite her reluctance to maintain any ties with Howard, she'd taken the job he had arranged for her when she turned seventeen only because it offered an escape to Melbourne. She'd been relieved to escape the strange relationship her parents shared, to gain financial independence. Ironically, driving her away had brought Sally to her senses and caused her mother to break off her relationship with Howard and leave his employ. But Jessica had already been gone; she hadn't been there to help her mother pick up the pieces and put her life back together again.

She put a hand over her mother's where it rested on her arm and clasped it tightly. "I was a right royal brat, wasn't I?"

"You had every right to be. I should never have had an affair. I put you into an impossible position. You were very loyal to your father."

"It must've been hard for you."

"It was. But Howard gave me an escape, some time away from home, where I could pretend your father's accident never happened."

"Oh, Mum. I love you."

Sally's smile was bittersweet. "The Blackstones are fabulously wealthy. Ryan was always a very nice youth. Polite. But all I want for you is to find someone to love you."

Jessica threw her arms around her mother. "With you and Dad to love me—and the baby—why do I need a husband?"

Nine

After the upheavals of the week, Jessica slept most of the weekend away. There was no doubt that her body was changing, swelling, growing fuller each passing day. Driving to work on Monday morning she told herself that once the launch was past, she would make up for all the stress by sleeping for a week.

Her work day did not start well. She walked into the showroom to be met with the news that Emma, one of the salesladies, had called in sick, leaving them short-staffed for the day. And then, with a great delighted smile, Candy broke the news that the emerald-cut pink that Jessica loved so much had been sold.

But the message that Ryan had already been in and left to attend a board meeting at the Pitt Street offices drained some of the unrelenting tension from her. Jessica gave a silent sigh of relief. At least she would have a while to prepare herself to face him again.

By midmorning, after a rush of customers, and several hours on her feet, Jessica needed a break. She made herself a cup of herb tea and retreated to her office to catch up with her latest batch of e-mails. That was where Ryan found her.

He entered her office, closed the door softly behind him and leaned against it. Jessica tensed, fearful of a confrontation after their last meeting, where she'd turned down his proposal before he'd even begun.

But she need not have worried.

"Hi. How are you feeling?" The eyes that scanned her held concern and something curiously like tenderness.

Jessica relaxed a little. "Tired. I'm gaining more weight than I should be."

He took a step forward and suddenly the space between the four walls seemed to shrink. "Can you feel the baby moving yet?"

"No, but my tummy is growing." Driven by the longing she read in his eyes, she said, "Do you want to feel?"

His face lit up. "I'll be gentle."

And Jessica felt a lump growing in her throat as he knelt before her and carefully put his hands on her belly.

"There is already a bit of a curve here," he said in surprise, his hand stroking her.

"I'm getting fat."

"You'll never be fat. You're gorgeous, Jess."

"Thank you." She beamed down at him. In a dark formal suit and old school tie he looked a little out of place on his knees. But he didn't seem to care. His large tanned hands were gentle on her body and Jessica could feel the caring in the tender touch of his fingers. Suddenly she didn't feel so tired, her body didn't feel so heavy. All because Ryan thought she was gorgeous, because he was touching her awkward belly with reverence.

"During my lunchtime I've got an appointment for my first

scan." She hesitated for a fraction of a second, then she plunged on. "Would you like to come?"

Ryan's eyes glowed with pleasure. "Wild horses wouldn't stop me."

And he was good at his word. In the doctor's reception, he held her hand tightly in his. When their time came to go in, Jessica introduced him to Dr. Waite and saw the doctor's eyes widen in recognition, before his surprise vanished and he bustled around while Jessica changed into a gown in a curtained cubicle.

"You can lie here," a nurse told her when she returned.

She lay down on the bed, wrinkling her nose at the smell of antiseptic, and Ryan sat in the chair beside her and took her hand again, while the nurse smeared her belly with a gel that was cool enough to make her gasp.

Seconds later Dr. Waite pointed at the screen. "See, there's the fetus."

Ryan's hand tightened around hers. "I can see it." His voice sounded hoarse, as though his throat, too, was burning with suppressed emotion.

Jessica peeped sideways at him. He sat hunched forward, staring at the monitor with an intensity he usually reserved for balance sheets.

"And, Jessica, here's the reason why you've been so tired and hungry. And the reason for your more than expected weight gain."

A pang of anxiety pierced Jessica. She stared at the blipping movement Dr. Waite had indicated. "What is it? What's wrong?"

"It's another beating heart."

"Another?" she said, bewildered, trying to make sense of the movement on the screen.

"Twins?" Ryan caught on quicker. "For Pete's sake, that's the last thing I ever expected."

Jessica flinched.

Not one baby. Twins. A ready-made family.

Ryan was going to regret that he'd ever started to propose to her and turn and run as far as his long, strong legs could take him. And she couldn't blame him one little bit. Why should he settle for a pregnant mechanic's daughter with twins on the way, when he could have his pick of Sydney's best-connected and most beautiful women?

"Are there twins in your family, Jessica? Fraternal twins can be hereditary on the mother's side," Dr. Waite was saying.

Her brain felt like it was made of warm wet noodles. She tried to concentrate. "My mother is a twin," she said slowly, still trying to come to terms with the shock, and thinking about the upheaval the discovery would cause her and Ryan.

But the look Ryan turned on her wasn't the look of a man about to run for his life. If Jessica hadn't known better, hadn't known how wary he was of losing the freedom of his bachelor/executive lifestyle, she might have been foolish enough to think that the glow in his eyes, the emotion she glimpsed there, might be love.

That evening, Ryan insisted on picking Jessica up from her apartment and taking her to dinner. "To celebrate," he told her firmly when she started to protest.

But it was more than that, he admitted to himself as he helped her into his car. He wasn't letting Jessica out of his sight. He wasn't giving her a chance to disappear, to take the joy out his life again.

He pulled in to the undercover parking ground and heard her breath catch.

"We're going to your penthouse? I thought we were going out."

"Don't worry. You won't need to cook." He gave her a wry smile. "I've arranged for Le Marquis to do takeout."

His comment had the desired effect. She gave a breathy laugh of surprise. "Le Marquis does takeout?"

"Well, not take out exactly." He cut the engine of the M6. "They've provided a chef to make it an authentic Le Marquis experience."

"A takeout chef? You shouldn't have gone to so much trouble." She turned wide brown eyes on him that held a hint of uncertainty in their depths.

"I thought rather than going out, you might want to relax," he said quietly. "So come upstairs, sit back, put your feet up and enjoy. No pressure."

"No pressure?"

"I'm not going to seduce you."

"Oh." Something like disappointment flitted across her expressive features.

Ryan refused to let himself think about what that non-committal little sound might mean as he went around and opened the passenger door for her. Tonight was not about sex.

Tonight was about Jessica.

To show her how special she was.

Upstairs in the living area the French doors onto the deck had been flung open to let in the warm summer evening. The gold of the setting sun cast a glow over the harbour beyond, while a French chef was setting the finishing touches to the first course, a masterly arrangement of iceberg lettuce, smoked salmon and dill. As they approached the table, he came forward and took Jessica's wrap with a flourish while Ryan pulled out her chair.

Once seated, the chef, who introduced himself as Pierre, rattled off the choices for the main course. Jessica selected sliced fillet of chicken with a creamy Roquefort sauce and Ryan chose Boeuf Bourguignon. Pierre made for the kitchen, leaving them alone.

For a couple of seconds silence hung between them. Then Jessica asked in a subdued voice, "How do you really feel about the babies?"

"Stunned. I've never thought of myself as a father." His whole identity had been built around being Howard Blackstone's only surviving son. "And certainly not as the father to twins."

Yet now both the prospect of marriage to Jessica and the idea of being a father to two flesh-and-blood miniatures of himself and Jessica intrigued him enough for him to want to convince Jessica that she *had* to marry him. Sooner rather than later. He didn't want to miss a moment of the roller-coaster experience.

"Are you furious?" she asked in that same low voice.

He stared at her in amazement. "Why should I be furious?"

"Because I fell pregnant?"

"It takes two." He gave her a wolfish grin, but she didn't smile back.

"You never thought I'd tried to trap you into marrying me?"

He tilted his head to one side. "Is that what's worrying you? You're thinking that I might be blaming you? That I might consider you did it deliberately?" He shook his head. "I don't."

Jessica let out a soft sigh, and Ryan's gaze sharpened. "What are you worrying about, Jess?"

"I'm not sure that you'll understand."

"Spit it out. We can work it out. Are you worried that the babies might sap everything out of you? That you're going to lose your identity? Don't be. If you want to work, we can arrange something. I know how important your career is to you."

She looked down. "It's strange. I always thought my job was everything to me. Then a couple of months ago some-thing changed. Suddenly I realised I could walk away from

Blackstone's, from my career, and it wouldn't change who I was, what I believed."

"You mean when you discovered you were pregnant?"

"That was part of it." She met his gaze. "But not all of it. Remember we fought because I wanted us to spend Christmas together?"

He frowned. "Jess, we don't need to talk about past friction. Not tonight. Let's celebrate the baby…babies," he corrected himself.

She played with the napkin, unfolding it and balling it in her hand. "I *need* to tell you this. I wanted to spend that holiday with you because I needed reassurance from you that our relationship was heading somewhere."

He stretched his hand across the table and covered hers. "I'm sorry. I was selfish."

"But I didn't understand how important it was for you to spend time with your father at Byron Bay. Not back then. I felt hurt that you never invited me to share your family occasions. I thought you were ashamed of me."

"I was never ashamed of you. But I didn't want anyone knowing that I was having an affair with someone who worked for me." He'd lost Jessica because of his stupidity. "If I'm ashamed of anyone, it should be of myself. I should have been more considerate."

"I should've told you what I wanted." She dropped the napkin and threaded her fingers through his. "But I was torn apart. On the one hand, I was afraid of driving you away, that you would break off our relationship if I forced the issue—after all, I knew your stance. On the other hand, I wanted to force the issue. I wanted a commitment from you."

"Which I wasn't ready to give."

She glanced down, and her extravagantly long lashes covered her eyes. "Then I found out I was pregnant. It was a shock. But I discovered I liked the idea of having a baby. I was ready for it. But you'd said—"

"No cats, no kids, no press, and certainly no diamond rings!"

That got her attention. She stared at him, a little startled at his self-deprecation. "Well, yes. So when the test stick changed colour, I knew it was over."

"I wasn't ready for marriage," he admitted quietly. "I'm so sorry, Jess."

"Okay, so I came back with this New Year's resolution to end our relationship. I was going to be very staunch about it. I wasn't going to tell you about the baby until I'd come to terms with it myself."

"But you didn't tell me."

Pressing her hands against her cheeks, she confessed, "Because I was angry with you for not giving me the commitment I wanted. I decided to fly straight to Auckland for the opening of the new jewellery store in the city. But I missed my plane and I couldn't get another flight. I called Vina, Ric's secretary, and she arranged for me to catch a ride with your father on the chartered jet—even though normally I tried to stay as far out his way as possible."

"Why?"

Jessica dropped her hands and looked away. "That's a long story."

"I've got all night." Ryan had a feeling that whatever she had to tell him was important to their future together.

But Pierre chose that instant to emerge from the kitchen with their meals.

"Crème brûlée for dessert, *oui*?" Pierre asked, looking from one to the other.

They both nodded.

When Pierre had vanished back into the kitchen and shut

the door again, Jessica picked up her knife and fork. For a few minutes they ate in silence, then she said, "My mother worked for your father. First as a temp and later probably as what is euphemistically called a 'travel escort' for years."

Ryan knew he should've been more surprised. But he wasn't. Nor did he doubt what she was telling him. The pieces fitted. Her strange behaviour around his father had been tension. It also explained why he'd vaguely remembered her mother when he'd met her at the cemetery. He must've met her in his father's office years ago.

"That's why you avoided my father, why you told me you despised him."

"Yes." Jessica drew a deep breath. "I once snooped in my mother's things and read a note Howard had sent my mother. It must've been after a scare that she might've fallen pregnant. It scared me."

"What did it say?"

"That if she ever fell pregnant, she would have to get an abortion."

Ryan paled. "Oh, my God."

If she was honest, that note had coloured her view of Ryan, too. "Deep in my heart I thought you might expect the same of me."

"That's why you never told me about your pregnancy when you first found out." Now his skin was almost grey, and he looked haggard. "I would *never* have asked that of you. I can hardly believe that he expected that of your mother."

She breathed a deep sigh of thanks. Ryan was nothing like his father. "I'm sorry I doubted you. And, Ryan, I know he's your father, that you say he loved your mother and mourned your brother's disappearance. I know that you admire him. But I never saw that side of him. I only saw the ruthless businessman and the womaniser. I was terrified that my mother's affair with him would break up my parents' marriage."

He chewed and swallowed, barely tasting the last mouthfuls of the fine meal. "I can understand that. It must have been very difficult for you to become my lover with all that baggage."

She gave him a small smile. "The day at Miramare, you said that you didn't seem capable of resisting me." Her smile widened. "Well, it's mutual. What chance did I have? You were gorgeous, clever and you could charm birds out of trees. I tried very hard not to fall for you, but how could I resist?"

Colour stained the slash of his cheekbones. "You exaggerate." A moment later he asked, "Was that what you argued about with my father in the airport? His treatment of your mother?"

"No." Her gaze held his. "We argued about you."

About him? Given her relationship with his father, it could not have been good. "Tell me, Jess."

"He'd found out about…us. That we were having an affair, that I was living in your apartment."

Ryan sat back. His father must have used a detective. That, too, would not surprise him. "And?"

"He wanted me to break it off with you. He told me I wasn't fit to be a Blackstone consort. An escort maybe, a consort never. 'Like mother, like daughter' were his exact words."

Ryan bit back a stream of curses. They wouldn't wipe the grief out of Jessica's eyes. The pain that his own flesh and blood had put there.

"He only reinforced that I would never be good enough for you, that I would always be the mistress's daughter."

"Bollocks," Ryan said. "No one thinks of you as that. My sister admires you, so does Ric. And Dani likes you, too. People respect you for the smart, clever woman you are. Don't let my father strip you of your confidence. He was a master of that."

"That wasn't all." Her mouth barely moved and her lips were pale.

Ryan had to crane his neck to hear her. Again he felt a stab of anger that his father could've hurt her so much. "I want to know every detail, however minor you might consider it."

"We boarded the jet, then he threatened me. He told me that if I refused to break it off with you, he would fire me and disinherit you." Jessica's eyes were dark with remembered pain. "But if I did what he wanted, I'd get to keep my job *and* he'd consider not leaving all his shares to his eldest child. I thought he meant Kimberley. It never occurred to me that he might be speaking about James."

"What did you say?" Ryan's voice was rough with fury.

"I'd already decided to break it off with you so I told him that I quit and I walked off the jet."

"Good for you." But already he was trying to make sense of this new revelation. Jessica had never told him she'd quit.

"I was furious and upset. And on my way out, I nearly ran down Marise boarding the jet. I was way too uptight to go to the penthouse. I knew I was going to have to see you to tell you it was all over, and I wanted to think it all out. I'd quit, so I couldn't go back to work the next morning—everyone thought I was in Auckland."

"So where did you go?"

"It was getting late, so I went to my apartment. I knew I would be moving back soon. I ended up spending the night there. I figured that you would think I was already in Auckland, so I had a day's grace."

"After the jet went missing in the dark hours of the following morning, a passenger list was faxed through that still had your name on it. I nearly died myself." It had been the worst moment of his life. Coming on top of the shock that his father was missing, too, he'd gone wild with grief. "I tried to call you in the vain hope that you'd caught another carrier. But you weren't answering." He'd thought she was dead. He'd been distraught. And then guilt had kicked in because he was less concerned about his father than his lover. He'd thrown himself into tracking the search-and-rescue operation and the funeral preparations. Anything to avoid the alarming suspicion that he might be vulnerable to an emotion he'd never sought.

"My cell phone was off," she explained. "I didn't want to speak to you. Not until I'd decided what I was going to say to end it. Then it was too late. I heard on the news that your father's plane had gone missing. So I went to your penthouse. I thought you might need me." Jessica looked shattered. "Why didn't you ever tell me all this? That you thought I'd died?"

Ryan shook his head. "I got back to the town house, after an appalling day, to find you watching the news of my father's disappearance on TV. There was so much to be done, I had to stay focused, do what needed to be done. There would be enough time to come to terms with the emptiness later." There'd been a treacherous moment when he'd wondered what she'd been doing booked to travel on his father's chartered jet…and why she'd kept quiet about it. It had been a horrible suspicion that had lasted only for a fraction of a second and he'd thrust it out of his mind until Kitty Lang had stirred it all up again.

Something in his expression must have alerted Jessica to his thoughts. "That's when the suspicion began that there was something going on between Howard and me," she said slowly with a sense of dawning realisation.

"It didn't help that you grew increasingly pale and withdrawn over the past month." His mouth kinked. "That did little to reassure me."

Jessica pushed her plate aside. "I was unhappy…and

pregnant. I needed to end our relationship, but you were hurting. How could I be so unfeeling as to walk out during a time of such grief?"

"And I didn't make it any easier for you." He'd been so focused on the search-and-rescue effort last month, and this month his attention had been concentrated on the fallout from the will, compounded by his puerile resentment of Ric and the blazing animosity from Matt Hammond. Yet, startlingly, somewhere in the past couple of days since discovering that Jessica was pregnant, he'd discovered that he *did* want to get married. Nothing would make him happier than a future with Jessica and their children.

He loved Jessica. The discovery hadn't hit him suddenly. Instead it had sneaked up on him gradually, like the silvery early-morning mists that sometimes crept up from the sea over the beach house at Byron Bay.

It had taken him a while to realize that what he felt for her was love. Partially because he'd been so resistant to the idea of committing to a woman and giving up his independence. But mostly because he hadn't been able to see beyond the incredibly fierce passion she aroused in him, to the tender emotion that lay beyond.

He wanted Jessica to share the rest of his life.

As his wife.

Yet he could hardly blame her for refusing him. She'd lived with him, and he'd never attempted to make her more than a mistress, unknowingly echoing his father's treatment of her mother. How could he blame her for thinking that he was no better than his father? How could he ever convince her how much he needed her?

He stretched out a hand. "Jessica—"

"Dessert is splendid." Pierre burst from the kitchen. He set the ramekins down and kissed his fingertips. "Splendid."

Ryan drew back his hand, suppressing his urge to reach for Jessica, hold her and protect her from anything that might harm her.

"Thank you, Pierre."

"I have brewed the coffee. It is in the kitchen with two cups. Now it is time for me to go, *oui?*"

"*Oui,*" Ryan agreed, giving the chef a man-to-man look. And, in a magically short time, Pierre had packed up his utensils and tiptoed into the elevator, leaving Ryan alone with Jessica.

Ten

After Pierre had left, they finished the rich creamy desserts before making their way to the living area. Jessica plopped herself down, kicked her sandals off and wriggled her toes.

"Feet sore?" Ryan asked.

"Not really."

He lifted them and propped them on the arm of the sofa. "Lie back, relax."

"Right now I feel replete." She closed her eyes with a contented sigh until, unable to bear the silence that had fallen, her lashes fluttered upward to see what Ryan was doing. He stood beside her, staring down at her with an odd expression.

"What are you thinking?" she probed.

He hesitated.

"Tell me," she demanded.

"I'm thinking of all the mornings I've woken and watched you sleeping in my bed. The crescent shadows your lashes form on your skin, how you always kick your legs free of the covers, the way you sleep with your hand under your cheek."

She blinked. "You've studied me sleeping?"

"Often."

And she'd thought he barely noticed her, took her for granted. "Why?"

"You always look so at peace when you sleep, so beautiful. It gave me sense of pleasure. Something to carry with me all day long."

"I never knew." Strangely she didn't feel freaked out by the fact that he'd watched her sleep without her knowledge. The idea that he'd carried that memory with him every day was flattering.

"I've missed those minutes each morning." His jade eyes darkened.

Jessica stilled, barely daring to breathe as she absorbed his revelations. "I never knew. Although I remember sometimes waking to the sound of the door closing when you left in the morning." And feeling desperately alone.

"It was tough to leave without kissing you goodbye."

She gave him a glance from under her lashes. No humour glinted in his eyes. He was perfectly serious. "You should've kissed me."

"You looked so at peace, I didn't want to waken you."

"Well, you can make up for it by kissing me now."

He bent his head. His lips were gentle on hers, his breath warm. Her pulse quickened as it always did when he came near. His hand caressed her shoulder, drawing her toward him and deepening the kiss.

Jessica felt emotion surge deep within her heart. So strong. And so sweet. As his tongue pressed into her mouth, Ryan's hand stroked along her throat, down between her breasts… and stopped on her belly.

It lay there, motionless.

A frisson of expectation swept her.

He broke the kiss and lifted his head. "You're wearing too many clothes."

"Maybe I am."

"This time I'm taking them off." The look he gave her was hot enough to singe. "You're not hiding anything from me. And this time, not only do I look, I get to touch, too."

Before she could murmur a protest, he swung her up into his arms and carried her up the stairs, his breathing barely growing heavier. By the time he set her down carefully on the wide king-size bed, Jessica had lost any desire to object.

Her heart pounded as he knelt on the covers beside her, his shoulders broad under a white cotton shirt.

In the light of the bedside lamp, his face was all angles. The shadows gave his expression a sensual intensity, a passionate power that caught at her throat and increased her heartbeat to a drumroll.

Her skirt came off in one sweep of his hand; the silver top took only a moment more and he dealt with her lacy bra and briefs with the same ruthless efficiency.

Jessica felt a brief flare of self-consciousness as she lay naked across the covers, while he loomed over her still fully clothed, until his head tilted so that the lamplight fell directly across his face and she read the expression in his eyes.

Sensation rushed through her. Warm. Supple. Like honey melting in the sun. So very sweet. And making her feel all woman.

"I've been a fool." He said it so softly, she barely heard. "The greatest jewel of all lay in my possession all the time. I nearly lost it."

"Oh, Ryan."

"I love you, Jess."

The poignant openness in his usually closed expression revealed the truth. He loved her!

"I'm sorry I never realised what you meant…what you were worth to me. I'll make it up to you, I promise. If you'll let me."

Let him? As if she'd be fool enough to turn him away.…

"All I ever wanted from you was your love." She opened her arms wide.

And then he was shucking off his clothes. As always, Jessica couldn't stop admiring the sheer beauty of his nude body. His hips were lean and his flanks smooth. He came down on the bed beside her, his stomach muscles rippling in the lamplight, the light dusting of hair tapering down to where his erection jutted out, revealing how much he desired her.

But when he touched her, the ravenous hunger she'd anticipated was tempered and his hands were tender. On her face, her breasts, her stomach.

His lips followed the trail his fingers had carved out. He pressed his lips against the rise of her belly. "Mine."

She smiled at the possessive declaration. "There'll be much more there in the months to come."

"I'll relish every moment." His eyes glinted. "I like your curves…your lush breasts…the voluptuousness. Very sexy. I can't believe I didn't realise you were pregnant sooner."

"I can. You've had a lot on your mind."

"Not so much that you shouldn't have been at the forefront. But I swear I'll make it up to you." His hand stroked lower.

Jessica gasped as his fingers touched the soft, wet core of her. Her body shivered as his touch became more insistent, sensation shafted through her. "Oh, goodness!"

His fingers moved more slickly as the heat of her body lubricated his hand.

Ripples raged through her in widening rings, consuming her. She arched her back and moaned out loud.

Instantly Ryan shifted himself over her, propping himself on his elbows, holding his weight off her, and Jessica went liquid at the caring in his eyes.

When he sank into her, it felt different from ever before. The white-hot passion was still there, bubbling through her bloodstream. But as the ripples started all over again, she felt even more. A warmth, a feeling of being cherished and protected. Of being special beyond price.

Afterwards he couldn't keep his hands off her. He stroked her hair off her face, stroked her breasts, and, as if drawn by a compulsion stronger than he could control, he touched her stomach again. "I still can't believe it."

Jessica raised her head. The eyes that met hers held a heart-stopping tenderness. Her breath caught.

Disbelief shot through her. "You're pleased about the babies!"

The smile that curved his mouth was more than a little sheepish. "And proud. I can't wait to tell the whole world that you're pregnant."

Tell everyone? Ryan wanted the world to know that she was pregnant? She had never expected that. "Wait a moment…"

"You will marry me, won't you, Jess?" Concern flitted through his glorious green eyes before he suppressed it.

Jessica could barely assimilate it all. He said he loved her. He still wanted to marry her. The delight and joy was back stronger than before.

"Don't answer now. Think about it. I'll give you until the night of the jewellery showing to absorb it." This time his smile was slow and sure.

The rest of the days leading up to the launch of the Something Old, Something New collection flashed past in a mad rush. On Friday afternoon, Jessica stood back to find that everything had somehow miraculously come together. All the details were under control and there was nothing left for her to do.

Confident that everything was running smoothly for the evening to come, Jessica left to have a manicure and her hair done. Then she returned to her apartment to take a cool shower to rid herself of the afternoon heat.

Once showered, Jessica dressed in a summery creation the colour of watermelon and embroidered with fine, clear beads that gave an added shimmer. The dress had a deep halter neckline and a fitted top that showed off her lush, newly acquired cleavage, and the full skirt swirled around her legs.

Staring into the mirror, Jessica knew that tonight no one could doubt that she was pregnant. There was a fullness to her breasts, a ripeness to the curve of her stomach that the bodice couldn't possibly hide, unlike the flowing tops she'd been wearing to work.

She couldn't help wondering what Ryan was doing, what he'd be wearing tonight.

When the doorbell rang, Jessica frowned, tempted to ignore it. A cab was coming to pick her up. If she dallied she would be late. The bell rang again. She wrenched the door open and her mouth went dry.

Ryan stood there in a black tuxedo, looking utterly devastating.

"What are you doing here?"

"I've come to take you to the event of the year."

"I thought I was meeting you there."

"So did I. But then I realised you have to go with me."

Curiosity got the better of her. "Why?"

"So that by tomorrow no one in Sydney will have any doubt of how I feel about you." Ryan rocked back on his heels. "You've always intimated that I hide you away. I've vowed that you'll never again be my secret mistress. After tonight there will be no doubt exactly what our relationship is and how much you mean to me. Now finish getting ready and let's go."

Jessica quickly fastened her pearls around her neck, clasped a thick gold bangle around her wrist and slid into a pair of silver sandals. A light spray of perfume, a final application of lipgloss and she was ready to go.

She and Ryan were among the first to arrive. Jessica slipped upstairs to check that the models, stylists and jewellery designers were all there among the organized chaos. Satisfied that everything was running as smoothly as could be expected, she returned downstairs to Ryan's side.

The space had filled up with Sydney's glamorous, A-list crowd. Some were already seated and were chatting among themselves. A T-ramp carpeted in crimson had been erected at the bottom of the stairs that led to the floor where the showroom was situated. Overhead the chandeliers glittered and light scintillated off the jewels worn by the guests. Waiters circulated with trays loaded with glasses of champagne, cosmopolitans and an assortment of hors d'oeuvres.

"It's going to be a full house." Jessica tipped her head up to Ryan. "Everything looks wonderful."

"It certainly does." Ryan gave her a slow smile.

Jessica felt herself flush at the concentration of his attention on her. "I meant, all your planning and hard work is paying off."

"Your hard work, too," he said. "And don't forget all the other people who played a part. It's been a team effort."

"Jessica...Ryan." Briana's gaze was very interested as she took in how close Ryan stood to Jessica.

Jessica turned and gave her friend a hug. "Are you all ready?"

"I'm about to go and do a lightning-fast change into what

I'll be modelling first. I shouldn't even be down here. I just wanted to make sure Jake didn't feel lost."

"Jake Vance?" Jessica started to smile. "He's here with you tonight?"

Briana shook her head. "I told you, Jess, it's not serious." And then she was gone.

Ryan led Jessica to the front row where seats had been reserved for them. A little distance back Jessica caught a glimpse of Dani Hammond, elegantly clad in a sleek black dress, her curls fiercely pulled back from a face pale with nerves, the severity of the style broken by a spray of twinkling gems in her hair. Beside her sat her mother, Sonya, elegant and restrained. Jessica gave them both a quick wave and again watched the quickly masked astonishment as they took in Ryan hovering beside her.

Jessica suppressed a smile. Ryan had been right. By the end of the night everyone would know what the relationship between Ryan Blackstone and his store manager was.

When Ryan got up onto the red carpet, the capacity crowd stilled. On the large screen that formed a backdrop, pictures flashed as he spoke. Of Janderra. Of fancy-hued diamonds. Of the designers involved in the collections being launched tonight.

An image of the Desert Star flashed up, the first significant diamond find at Janderra. Ryan spoke of the wealth of talent that Blackstone's Jewellery had developed; he introduced the designers and welcomed Dani Hammond as the newest star. Jessica glanced across to see his cousin blushing furiously, while Sonya smiled proudly.

Then Jessica heard her name, saw a picture of herself flash up as Ryan introduced her as the hard-working manager of the Sydney store. Her cheeks went hot. Now how was she ever going to be able to resign? Perhaps they could work out something that allowed her shorter hours in the store after the birth of the twins.

When he'd finished, one of Australia's favourite female pop icons appeared at the top of the stairs and sashayed down singing the seventies hit "Diamonds Are Forever," her voice pure and true. She was closely followed by Briana wearing a fabulous ballgown and a collar of dazzling diamonds. On the giant screen a close-up of the collar made the crowd gasp.

The show had begun. The newest series of famed Blackstone's collections had arrived.

"Who's that?" Jessica leaned toward Ryan and he bent his head to catch her whisper. As promised, he stood at her side, his hand possessively wrapped around her waist, making it clear to everyone that she was with him.

"Who?"

"That tall, very handsome, dark-haired stranger who has been staring at Briana like he's been hit by lightning. The one whom one or two of the newshounds seem to be sniffing around with keen interest."

Ryan followed her gaze and started to frown. "That's Jarrod Hammond. And the reporters are fascinated by a Hammond turning up. They're waiting to see if there will be any more scandal tonight."

"That's Jarrod Hammond?" Jessica looked at him curiously. "Funny, he doesn't look at all like what I expected. He's quite different from Matt, although I have to admit I only caught the briefest glimpse of Matt at the funeral."

"They're not related by birth. My Aunt Katherine and Uncle Oliver weren't able to have any children. That's why it was such a bitter blow when old granddad Jeb gave the Heart of the Outback to my mother when James was born."

Jessica studied the features of the man who appeared to be

oblivious to everyone in the room except for Briana. "So Jarrod Hammond is adopted?"

"Yep. But he was still brought up a Hammond, so warn Briana to watch every move he makes," Ryan growled darkly.

A tall, very slim model was showing off a pair of spectacular diamond-drop earrings to oohs and aahs from the crowd.

As each new model came on, the pieces became more and more spectacular. "Judging from the appreciative sounds, I'd say that the launch is a runaway success," Ryan said softly in her ear.

She nodded. "I think you're right."

"Well done. A large part of this is because of you."

Ryan was proud of her, pleased with the success of the launch, and for the first time Jessica realized that Ryan viewed her as his equal. She was more than a match for him.

The music started to build. "The finale is coming."

And then Briana was coming down the stairs, wearing an exquisitely simple wedding dress that left her shoulders bare and fell around her feet in soft folds. Behind her walked three models dressed as bridesmaids, their hair braided into plaits and wound around their heads, diamonds dripping from their arms, which held baskets filled with white roses.

By contrast Briana's hair hung loose and she wore a crown of white rosebuds. Around her neck glittered a single suspended pendant.

"The Desert Star," someone gasped beside them. Applause thundered through the room.

"Look at Jarrod Hammond's expression," Jessica whispered to Ryan. "He's a goner."

"Not if Briana has any sense. He's a Hammond."

"Oh, Ryan! You never change."

"You know, I think I am changing," he murmured enigmatically. "It won't be easy for Jarrod. Don't forget who his brother is and who Briana's sister was."

"Oh, good grief. Matt and Marise."

"I wouldn't bet on Jarrod managing to surmount those obstacles."

"Then it's just as well I don't bet," said Jessica primly.

Ryan laughed out loud, pulled her closer to his side and dropped a kiss on her hair.

"Hush," she said, "it's the big moment."

He turned his head to see that Briana and her bridesmaids had arrayed themselves along the ramp and started to toss the long-stemmed white roses into the audience. One landed in Ryan's hands and, with a flourish, he handed it to Jessica.

"For you."

She took it from him, flushing with pleasure.

With the departure of the bride and her attendants, the show came to an end. Ric Perrini spoke a few words in closing. The crowd rose to their feet for a moment of silence in memory of Howard Blackstone and all who had died aboard the jet with him.

Ryan shut his eyes and felt each second pass in time to his heartbeat. *Goodbye, Dad. Rest in peace.* He felt an unexpected and appalling sense of loss. His father was gone, forever.

But Jessica had been spared.

His love was alive. He pulled her into his arms, heard her soft gasp and tightened his arms around her, oblivious to the stares they were attracting.

He bent his head, so that his mouth was beside her ear. "You know, the worst hours of my life were when I thought you'd died in that crash with my father." He brushed a tender kiss against her temple, uncaring of what anyone thought. "I have changed. I will never be like my father."

He put a finger under her chin and tipped it up so he could

look down into her delicate features. "I love you, Jess. Please marry me."

"Even though it will mean the end of your executive bachelor status?" Joy danced in her eyes. "Even though you'll have a wife and two children before the year is out?"

"That's not going to scare me off."

"Is this the same man who always vowed, 'No cats, no kids, no press, no diamond rings'?"

"Hey, that started crumbling a while ago. I told you, as long as you come back, I don't mind if you bring that damn cat with you."

"His name is Picasso."

"Right. And I already asked you to marry me *after* you told me about the baby. So there goes *no kids*."

"That was when there was only one baby under discussion, there are now two. I won't blame you if you head for the hills."

"I won't be heading for the hills." He wound his arms around her. "I won't be going anywhere far from you. The *no press* thing was already blown out the water after the races at Flemington."

"I didn't realise you'd seen that photo in the paper."

"How could I miss it?" He pulled a face at her. "My sister thrust it under my nose the moment I set foot on the jet that morning. She thinks you're good for me."

"Oh," said Jessica, lost for words.

"The only one left on the list is the diamond ring. And I've already tried to give it to you, but you refused to let me."

Jessica caught her breath. She grabbed Ryan's hand and placed it on her stomach with trembling hands. "I don't think I'm going to be allowed to refuse this time round."

"What was that?"

Her powerful corporate warrior sounded utterly terrified.

"I think one of our babies just decided to rock our world."

"Wow." Under their hands one of the babies moved again, a tiny flutter of life. Ryan's eyes lit up with wonder.

And in that moment, Jessica realised that Ryan wanted them all, her and her babies. The whole ready-made family.

"Yes, I'll marry you."

"Because of the babies?" His smile was wry.

"No, because I love you."

The ring box he took from his pocket showed no sign of being soaked in the swimming pool. But when he flipped it open, Jessica's breath left her lungs. "You remembered."

She stared at the ring she'd spent the months admiring, talking people out of buying. "Candy told me it had been sold. I was so disappointed. I thought that was a sign that marriage and me were not meant to be."

Ryan laughed. Before she could say another word he slipped the ring on her finger and stopped a passing waiter to snag two glasses of mineral water from the tray.

"To us."

"To us."

They stared at each other in wonder.

Somewhere behind her, Dani gave a shriek. "Jessica, lift up your hand! Is that an engagement ring? Ryan, you sneaky thing, no one even knew!"

Champagne corks started to pop. Everyone crowded around, giving congratulations. Kimberley and Ric. Briana with Jake. Vincent and the rest of the Blackstone cousins. As well as Sonya and Garth, who were a little more restrained in their delight. Then everyone raised their glasses and toasted, "To Ryan and Jessica."

"You do realise we'll have to contact a Realtor. I'm going to need to put the penthouse on the market," he murmured in her ear when the hullabaloo had subsided. "I have it on good authority it's not the kind of place where twins can leave sticky fingers."

A flash of blonde ringlets and the dangle of gold earrings across the room caused Jessica to whisper, "I know she's a top-notch Realtor, but we're not retaining Kitty Lang."

"Earlier Kitty looked like she's snaring herself a rich man. She may not be available." Ryan grinned. "All I care about is finding a house where you and the kids can be happy."

"And the cat. Don't forget about Picasso." Jessica peered at him from under her eyelashes as he threw his head back and laughed out loud. "And, of course, you need to be happy, too."

Ryan bent toward her, "I'll be a happy man—and our house will be filled with the sound of laughter—as long as I have you by my side." And then his mouth closed over hers in a loving kiss.

* * * * *

MISTRESS & A
MILLION DOLLARS

MAXINE SULLIVAN

Maxine Sullivan credits her mother for her lifelong love of romance novels, so it was a natural extension for Maxine to want to write her own romances. She's very excited about seeing her work in print. Maxine lives in Melbourne, Australia, and over the years has traveled to New Zealand, the UK and the USA In her own backyard, her husband's job ensured they saw the diversity of the countryside, including spending many years in Darwin in the tropical north, where some of her books are set. She is married to Geoff, who has proven his hero status many times over the years. They have two handsome sons and an assortment of much-loved, previously abandoned animals. Maxine would love to hear from you and can be contacted through her website at www.maxinesullivan.com.

To Melissa Jeglinski for 'everything.'
To the Down Under Desire authors—
with admiration.

One

"*We are gathered here today in the face of this company to join together Kimberley Blackstone and Ricardo Perrini in matrimony....*"

Jarrod Hammond heard the words of the female marriage celebrant, but his eyes were drawn not to the bride, but to the woman sitting opposite him in the horseshoe circle surrounding his cousin Kim and her soon-to-be husband, Ric Perrini.

Adrenaline kicked in as he leaned back in his chair and let his gaze rake over Briana Davenport, the Australian supermodel who was the face of Blackstone Diamonds. Through the massive yacht's large windows behind her, the late-afternoon sun highlighted the most glorious harbor in the world and created a picture-perfect backdrop for her beauty.

Framed by the Opera House and Sydney Harbour Bridge, and dressed in a silky, pale blue pantsuit that flowed as she moved, she was elegance and sophistication. The epitome of glamour. A crowning glory for the diamond company she symbolized. He could see why Howard Blackstone had chosen her to represent his business.

And just as expensive, Jarrod mused rather cynically, noting with satisfaction the exact moment she saw him looking at her. Her eyelids flickered just a bit before she looked away, but only someone with an internal radar for this woman would pick up on it.

Someone like him.

"If anyone can show just cause—" the celebrant continued.

Much to Jarrod's displeasure, his internal radar was constantly tuned on Briana. It had been that way from the moment he'd set eyes on her at his brother's marriage to her sister four years ago. It had been on high ever since, even though he knew Briana had a serious flaw. An *expensive* serious flaw. She liked money, and plenty of it, and went through it like it was going out of fashion, according to her now-dead sister, Marise.

Of course, being attuned to Briana didn't help when everywhere he turned she was there in front of him: up on billboards…on television…in glossy magazines. Nor was it easy knowing they lived in the same city in another part of the country. Thankfully with her jet-setting around the world as a supermodel, and him with his law practice, Melbourne was big enough for the two of them not to run into each other.

"Ric, do you take Kimberley for your lawful wedded wife, to live in the holy estate of matrimony? Will you love, honor, comfort and…"

But now, seeing Briana in the flesh again—her oh-so-delicious flesh—reminded him why he'd inveigled an invitation to the Blackstone Jewellery launch here in Sydney last Friday and flown up from Melbourne. And why he was glad he'd accepted Kim's invitation today. Being a Hammond at a Blackstone wedding was never going to be easy, but with Briana here, the day suddenly seemed full of sensual possibilities, despite the presence of millionaire Jake Vance, who once again partnered her.

"Kimberley, do you take Ric for your lawful wedded husband, to live in the holy estate of matrimony? Will you love, honor, comfort and…"

Jarrod's mouth tightened as he looked at the man sitting beside Briana. The pair had been photographed together in the Melbourne papers at the St. Valentine's Day races a few weeks ago. And again last Friday at the jewelry launch. Were the two of them lovers? Probably, he decided, not pleased by the burst of irrational jealousy he felt at the thought of her in the other man's bed.

"May this ring be blessed so that he who gives it…" the woman continued.

Dammit, was he being a glutton for punishment by going after her? Hadn't he already made his decision to bed her? A decision based on wanting to find out all he could about her sister for his brother's sake. He'd seen

Matt only two weeks ago and had been shocked at how worn and bitter he'd become. Jarrod and Matt may have been adopted, but they were closer than blood brothers, and he'd do everything in his power to make sure Matt found some inner peace—no matter what it took.

Or whom.

But he couldn't blame his brother for being bitter when his wife, Marise, had died from injuries sustained in a plane crash almost two months ago, along with Howard Blackstone and four others. It had conjured up a myriad of questions: questions that no one had any answers to, except maybe Briana Davenport.

"Wear it as a symbol of love and commitment…"

Surely Briana knew why her sister had been on Howard's plane before it crashed. And she knew if her own sister was having an affair with Howard, the enemy of the Hammond family ever since his greed parted the two family factions many years ago. She just wasn't saying.

And then there'd been the shock of Marise having been named as a beneficiary in Howard's will. A seven-sum figure and the Blackstone jewelry collection was a considerable inheritance for a young mistress. And that begged the question as to whether Blake was really Howard's son and not Matt's. Blake certainly had the same dark hair as Howard, unlike Matt's sandy-blond head. It made Jarrod sick to his stomach to think about it.

"You may now seal the promises you have made with each other with a kiss."

Dammit, the Blackstones had caused enough pain for his family. His parents would be devastated if they found out that Blake was not their grandson, but their great-nephew, instead. Not that it would make any difference to the way they felt about the child. They'd proven that by adopting him and Matt all those years ago. As for Matt and how he would feel about Blake not being his own…

"Ladies and gentlemen, I present to you Mr. and Mrs. Ricardo Perrini."

Just then, as if his angry thoughts had drawn Briana's blue eyes back to him, Jarrod held her gaze among the clapping and the cheers, and let her know with a look what he had decided. She was the woman he wanted.

She was the woman he would have.

While she was waiting to be seated for the wedding feast, Briana sipped champagne and listened with delight as the beaming and slender Jessica Cotter talked about her newly announced pregnancy. They'd spoken last Friday night at the jewelry launch, but it had been a busy night for both of them and their chat had only been brief. Now it was great to be able to catch up with each other.

"Ryan's thrilled," Jessica said, sending the man in question an adoring look across the deck where he stood talking to his just-married sister, Kim.

And the ruthless and handsome Ryan Blackstone smiled back. A warm, love-filled look that was meant for one woman and one woman only—his fiancée.

"You're one very lucky woman, Jess," Briana said with a smile, envious of Jessica's happiness but so very pleased for her.

"I know," Jessica said, grinning. Then her gaze slid to the woman standing next to Ryan, brother and sister clearly both Blackstones. "And doesn't Kim look absolutely gorgeous? That white gown is exquisite, but with her dark hair and green eyes, she looks stunning."

Briana's gaze slid over Kimberley Blackstone, now Kimberley Perrini, who wore an elegant couture wedding dress. "I've got to agree. She's stunning."

"I bet Ric thinks so, too." Jessica gave a dreamy sigh. "This must be so different from the first time they were married in Las Vegas. It just goes to prove that divorce isn't always final."

"I guess it all depends on the couple," Briana said, thinking about some of the people she knew in the modeling world. Her profession wasn't easy on a marriage. She'd seen some wonderful partnerships, as well as some horrors.

"By the way," Jessica said, interrupting her thoughts. "Did you contact Quinn Everard yet about those diamonds Marise left in your safe?"

At the thought of her dead sister, Briana's heart squeezed tight. "Yes, I phoned him the other day. I've been so busy lately that I just kept putting it off. What with work and trying to help Dad cope with Mum's death and now Marise's, it hasn't been a priority."

"That's understandable," Jessica said sympathetically. "You just make sure you take care of yourself, too."

"I will," Briana said, her eyes thanking her friend. "Anyway, Quinn said to drop the diamonds off at his office. He's away at the moment but I can leave them with his office manager. I'll do that tomorrow morning." She grimaced. "Frankly, I'll be glad to know their value so that I can decide what to do with them. Matt said he didn't want anything of Marise's, but I just can't keep them."

Jessica nodded. "Well, Quinn's the man. He's got an excellent reputation as a gem appraiser. He—" All at once her gaze focused on the men across the room and she scowled. "Oh no, I think I'm needed. Ric and Ryan look like they've had enough of each other for a while." She rolled her eyes. "Men!"

Briana chuckled as she watched Jessica hurry away, but she knew that tensions associated with members of the Blackstone family right now weren't anything to laugh about.

Knew it only too well, unfortunately.

Not that any of them held the controversial deaths of her sister and their father against her. They'd all been very considerate. Ric and Ryan had treated her with respect, and Jessica and Kim had become good friends. Not to mention the elegant Sonya Hammond and her charming daughter, Danielle. Though the latter two were not blood relations to Howard Blackstone, they were still related, and they'd shown her kindness at Howard's funeral, and welcomed her warmly today.

Of course, she couldn't think about the Blackstones without thinking about Matt Hammond. Her brother-in-law could be hardnosed but he was also a fine, upstanding man, and hadn't deserved the legacy of doubts her sister had left him and their young son, Blake. His adoptive parents, Katherine and Oliver Hammond, had been wonderful to Marise, too, but her sister hadn't really appreciated them.

As for the older adopted son…it was obvious to her that beneath Jarrod Hammond's veneer of sophistication, he fully believed she and Marise had shared the same liking for the good life that Marise had enjoyed as Matt's wife.

Only, nothing was further from the truth. Marise may have been flighty and always looking for something more, but *she* was happy with her lot in life. And for that she still felt guilty. If only she'd been closer to Marise, maybe then she'd understand why her sister had been keeping company with Howard Blackstone and why he'd left all his jewelry to Marise in his will. But no matter how she'd tried to breach the gap, they were poles apart. She didn't understand how Jarrod couldn't see that.

Just then, her eyes met the man in question across the breadth of the middle deck, and a hush seemed to descend upon everything in the room. An imaginary hush, obviously, though there was nothing imaginary about the hunger in Jarrod Hammond's eyes. The hunger had always been there, waiting…for what, she wasn't sure. He'd certainly made no move to further anything between them over the years.

Not that it would have done him any good. She wasn't getting involved with another high-powered male. Not after Patrick, her ex-business manager and lover, had invested most of her money in a "surefire" deal and had lost it.

No, she didn't need a man in her life.

And definitely not Jarrod Hammond.

Suddenly he started to walk toward her. She wanted to run as fast and as far away as she could, up the stairs and out on the top deck where the breeze off the harbor would cool her heated cheeks, but her strappy high heels seemed fixed to the floor.

And then he was standing in front of her, and she could do nothing but face him and try not to let him overwhelm her with his sheer presence.

"Hello, Briana," he murmured as he leaned in close and kissed her cheek, his firm lips lingering just a whisper too long. "We seem to be running into each other a lot lately."

She tingled. "Yes, we do," she said, then saw his eyes darken at her husky tone. Quickly she cleared her throat, trying not to show that she cared he had touched her. "Um…but I didn't expect to see you here, Jarrod."

"Really?" A cool light came into his eyes. "Why not? Kim is my cousin."

"Yes." And one he must know more than the others, seeing that Kim had worked for the Hammonds until recently.

But that was merely a reason for his presence, not an explanation. The Hammonds and the Blackstones, despite being related, had thrown some pretty wild accusations at each other's dynasties over the years. Marise had once briefly mentioned how Jarrod's father, Oliver, had accused Howard Blackstone of some pretty dastardly things, including marrying Oliver's sister for monetary gain. In retaliation, Howard had accused Oliver of arranging the kidnapping of his two-year-old son, James Blackstone. The child had never been seen again.

"Maybe I'm surprised to see *you* here," Jarrod said, cutting across her thoughts, and she knew nothing much would surprise this man. She had the feeling he'd known she'd be here today.

"Kim and I have been working together on some of the Blackstone events," she said, a touch defensively. "We've become friends."

"Good. She could do with another friend right now."

For a moment, Briana thought he was being sarcastic, but then she realized he was sincere. Something inside her softened. Kim had certainly had it tough these past few months, but coming from him—a Hammond who on his brother's behalf now had another reason to hate any Blackstone—the comment was even more surprising. Perhaps he wasn't as coldhearted as she'd thought?

"She looks beautiful, doesn't she?" Briana said, turning away from him to look at her friend, mainly so she didn't have to look at Jarrod.

"Yes, she does," he said in a seductive voice that made her spin back toward him. He was staring at *her.*

Whatever had softened inside her now turned to mush. She had to force herself not to redden, her years of modeling doing nothing to stop the faint warmth rising up her neck.

She took a sip of champagne, then, "What did you think of the ceremony?" she asked for something to say.

His knowing blue eyes held hers a moment longer before breaking contact. He shrugged. "A wedding's a wedding."

It was such a typical male reaction that she had to

smile. "Really? We're at a lavish affair on a luxury cruiser in the middle of Sydney Harbour on a perfect autumn day, and the daughter of one of Australia's richest men has just re-married her late father's right-hand man." She gave a rueful smile. "No, this wedding isn't just any wedding. This is a *Blackstone* wedding in all its glory."

The corners of his mouth curved with the beginnings of a sexy smile. "Do Blackstones pay you to promote them like this?"

She laughed. "I'd be stupid *not* to promote them, don't you think?"

He paused, his eyes hardening as they swept over her features. "And you're definitely not stupid, are you?"

Her smile disappeared. "That doesn't sound like a compliment."

Something came and went in his eyes. "I admire how far you've come in this business."

She tried not to stiffen, but she did anyway. What was he implying? "It still doesn't sound very flattering," she challenged.

His lips twisted, then he appeared to mentally back off. "So you like to be flattered, do you?"

She realized he'd backed off only because he chose to. "Didn't you know? I need to be flattered at least once every hour," she mocked, then arched a slim eyebrow. "After all, isn't that what all models are about?"

His eyes narrowed slightly, but there was a sardonic tilt to his mouth. "But you're a *super*model."

"So I need to be *super*-flattered," she returned as a waiter offered to refill her half-empty glass of champagne. She put her hand over the glass and shook her head. She didn't need more to drink. She needed her wits about her.

"I'm told I'm usually good at *super*-flattering a woman," Jarrod murmured, once the waiter moved away.

Her gaze flew back to the man beside her and panic stirred in her chest. "I'm sure you are. Usually." In a deliberate movement, she looked around for her date. Where on earth was Jake when she needed him?

And then she saw him listening with mild amusement to Danielle Hammond. The other woman's coppery curls bounced as she moved her head animatedly, her full mouth wide and smiling in a friendly fashion.

"Looks like your date is occupied," Jarrod said pointedly.

She glanced sideways at him and shrugged.

"So you're not the jealous type?"

"Not in the least." She enjoyed Jake's company but, as handsome and charming as he was, he was only a friend. And thankfully he was someone who had nothing to do with the Blackstone dynasty and all its associated problems. But she wasn't about to tell Jarrod any of that. "Danielle's such a sweetie," she added to show her non-jealousy.

"That she is," he agreed slowly, but she could hear in his voice that he was still looking at her, trying to get inside her head and figure her out.

Pretending not to notice, Briana let her gaze wander around the room, forcing herself to concentrate on the other guests. Anything but concentrate on Jarrod Hammond…or let him concentrate on her.

There were about sixty guests and most of the faces were strangers to her, but she did see Sonya Hammond talking to Garth Buick, an urbane and charming man who'd been Howard Blackstone's company secretary. They were only a few feet away and Briana could hear them talking about going sailing together. Something about the way they looked at each other—or perhaps it was the way they were trying *not* to look at each other— made Briana wonder if there was something between the two of them. If so, they were a good match. In her late forties, Sonya had a tall, willowy elegance that comple- mented the trim and well-toned Garth, who was just a few years older.

"Are you always so trusting?" Jarrod said, bringing her focus back on him.

She'd grimaced. "Unfortunately, no."

His glance sharpened. "What happened to rob you of your trust?"

Heavens, how was she going to get out of this one? She only had to look at that firm jaw to know he wasn't a man to give up when he wanted something.

"Nothing of interest," she said airily, but her heart was pounding in her chest.

"Oh, but I think there is," he said, confirming her suspicions.

"Let it go, Jarrod. It's nothing important." And to prove it, she scooped a canapé off a tray as a waiter passed by.

"Let me be the judge of that."

"Ahh, but I thought you were a property lawyer, not a judge."

His lips began to twitch. "And you're obstructing the course of justice, Briana."

"Or guilty of contempt," she mocked, then popped the canapé into her mouth, feeling pleased with herself.

He laughed out loud, taking her unawares. "I didn't realize you had such a smart mouth."

Because she'd never let him know it before, that's why, she mused, chewing the delicate morsel. She'd never let him get close enough.

So why was she letting him get close now? More importantly, why was he *trying* to get close now, she wondered, watching as his gaze fell to her lips and darkened, as if he were thinking about kissing her. She quickly swallowed, then took another sip of champagne.

Just then, the sound of a helicopter rent through the air as it came close and swooped the yacht. Far too close for Briana's piece of mind.

And obviously for Ric Perrini's.

"Damn the media!" Ric growled, striding across the middle deck to look out the side window of the cruiser right near Briana. "Can't they leave us in peace for one day?"

It broke the moment between her and Jarrod, for which she should have been grateful but wasn't. Instead she kept remembering that gorgeous laugh of his. It sent shivers of desire down her spine.

"I'm already on it," Kim said, coming over to her new husband and slipping her arm inside his. "The captain should be on the phone right now to the water police. They'll sort it out."

"They'd better," Ric warned.

"Anyway, we have more immediate problems. The photographer's about to have chickens if we don't let him take some pictures of us with our guests." She smiled at Briana and Jarrod. "You two will have your photo taken with us, won't you?"

Briana's fingers tightened around her glass. She knew it hadn't been Kim's intention, but even a small mention of her and Jarrod doing something together made her uncomfortable.

"Perhaps later, Kim," Jarrod said with a tight smile, then excused himself and headed to where an older couple stood looking out the back of the cruiser.

There was a flash of disappointment in Kim's eyes and Ric stiffened beside his wife, before she quickly gave his arm a squeeze. For all that Jarrod was here today, it was apparent Kim's falling out with his brother was still an issue between the Hammonds and the Blackstones.

For the Hammonds anyway.

To cover the awkward moment, Briana pasted on her best smile for the new bride. "Hey, that's all the more coverage for me then. You know how I love being in front of the camera."

Kim smiled with gratitude. "Thanks," she murmured, just as the photographer appeared.

Later, when everyone sat down to dinner, Sonya asked Briana how she managed to look so good in front of a camera when it was such hard work.

"You don't know the half of it," Briana said, smiling across the table at the other woman.

"I'd love to hear about it," Sonya said, the warmth in her eyes belying her cool reserve.

Briana obligingly chatted about some of the more obvious facets of modeling, yet she knew they'd all be surprised if she told them the truth. She'd fallen into modeling as a teenager but much preferred being behind the camera than in front of it.

Perhaps one day after she'd made enough money to recoup the money Patrick had lost, she'd further her dream. Until then it really wasn't such a hardship smiling for the camera or showcasing Blackstone jewelry. And it certainly wasn't a hardship attending a Blackstone wedding like this one.

Except for Jarrod.

She groaned inwardly. Lately he was turning up everywhere she went. At the jewelry launch the other night she'd never felt so self-conscious being on show before, but seeing him there in the audience, feeling his eyes upon her, she felt as if she was showcasing *herself,* not the Blackstone jewelry.

And now here he was at the wedding, sitting next to Vincent Blackstone, the late Howard Blackstone's older brother, deep in conversation. From time to time, though, his eyes were on *her.*

"You seem to be pretty cozy with Jarrod Hammond," Jake murmured in her ear, startling her when she must have looked at Jarrod once too often.

Trying to appear nonchalant, she glanced at Jake and

saw a very male look in his eyes that reminded her too much of Jarrod. This guy hadn't missed a thing going on around him. No doubt such ability was part of the reason he was now a rich and successful businessman.

But at least he wasn't the jealous type, she mused. "We're distant in-laws, that's all. Nothing special."

"Really?" he mocked in an arrogant way that said she wasn't fooling him.

"You know, Jake," she said, getting a little irritated being surrounded by males who thought they knew everything. "I think all the testosterone on this boat must be keeping it afloat."

A surprised look entered his eyes then he burst out laughing. For a moment she stared at him, then began to smile in return. It *was* quite funny, now she came to think about it.

"I'd have thought a beautiful woman like yourself would be used to being surrounded by testosterone," Jake teased.

"In the modeling world?" she jokingly scoffed, and received a chuckle from Jake.

"No, I guess not," he agreed with a rueful grin.

Suddenly she caught Jarrod looking at the two of them. A slither went over her skin and quickly she looked away just as the waiter brought the next course. Once the food was served, talk at the table turned to other things.

Briana deliberately didn't look at Jarrod after that, preferring instead to concentrate on the speeches and proceedings, though she was aware of him. Afterward, dark descended and they all moved to the well-lit top deck where the bride and groom began their first dance. Before too long, others had joined them, including her and Jake.

As for Jarrod, he seemed to have disappeared. She remained on edge, at first expecting him to show up at any tick of the clock, but when he didn't, she quickly pushed aside the disappointment that filled her. She wasn't going to let herself be disappointed by a man again, she reminded herself, then promptly did the opposite when she saw the lights from a small boat moving away from the cruiser, taking Jarrod back to shore.

He hadn't even said goodbye, she thought, then something on the shoreline caught her attention. Myriad lights began to flash as the small boat approached them.

The media.

Not that Jarrod would give them a second thought. No doubt he'd stride through the pack to a waiting car like he was parting the Red Sea.

After that the evening seemed flat. Briana smiled and talked, and when it came time for the yacht to return to shore, she was glad that the security people held back the media circus while they made their way into a fleet of cars.

Lights flashed in her eyes as Jake guided her into the back of a limousine, but the media's attention soon focused back on Kim and Ric, who had insisted they would only leave the boat after all their guests had alighted.

"They're a brave couple," Jake said, shaking his head as a shower of flashes seemed to light up the night sky through the back window of the car.

"Yes," Briana agreed. "And very determined to show the world a united front."

His smile disappeared. "I can understand that."

The limousine drove off but they didn't talk much while it weaved through the streets of Sydney to her apartment building. Then Jake walked her to her door.

"I had a good time," he said, moving in closer, pushing a strand of hair off her cheek.

Briana knew it was a prelude to a kiss and she moved in closer, too. Jake had kissed her before and it had always been nice, but tonight she suddenly wanted him to kiss her like he meant it. As if she was the only woman in the world he wanted.

Only, when the kiss finished, one thing was clear. Jake's kiss had been just a kiss. And by the wry glint in his eye he knew it, too.

"I think you'd better get some sleep," he said, tapping her on the end of her nose with his index finger. And then he pivoted and headed back to the elevator.

Briana watched him go with a sinking feeling in her stomach. Jake was an extremely handsome man who knew how to treat a woman right. And he knew how to kiss. It was just a pity she hadn't felt anything when his lips were on hers. Not like she would if Jarrod Hammond had kissed her.

Of that she was certain.

Two

The next morning Briana caught a taxi to Quinn Everard's office and left the diamonds with his office manager. Then, after another couple of days in Sydney, including lunching with her agent, she caught a plane back to Melbourne on the Wednesday, and drove to her father's house to check on him first. Then she'd go home to her apartment on the other side of the city. She still had to prepare for the Moomba Fashion Show this coming Labor Day weekend at the casino.

So it was mid-afternoon by the time Briana parked in the driveway of the solid brick home that her parents bought when they'd moved to Melbourne from Sydney nearly thirty years ago. They'd never been rich but had been comfortable. Her mother had even insisted on sending her and Marise to one of the top private schools here in Melbourne, after a spinster aunt had left her some money.

Now, when Ray Davenport opened the front door to her, Briana noted with concern that her father was looking tired. He'd been through so much, having kept her mother's secret of the cancer that ravaged her body, until the end, when her mother had become so ill he'd finally told their daughters she was dying.

"Want some coffee, honey?" he asked, walking ahead of her into the kitchen.

"Thanks, Dad. That would be lovely." She followed him, noting the stoop to his shoulders. "By the way, I dropped those diamonds off for an appraisal."

He looked over his shoulder with a frown. "Diamonds?"

"The ones Marise left in my safe."

His face cleared. "Oh, that's right. You found them in your safe after the plane crash, didn't you?"

"Yes." Overcome with grief, she'd nearly forgotten Marise asking for the safe combination to keep some jewelry in there.

Briana had thought nothing of giving the combination to her sister. She'd also let Marise stay in her Sydney apartment once she and her father returned to Melbourne, after Barbara Davenport had been buried next to her own parents in Waverley Cemetery. It was then that Marise seemed to go off the rails, those last few weeks before the plane crash. Their mother's death had devastated Marise, but for her sister to remain in Sydney had been unwarranted.

Especially after she'd started to be seen around town with Howard Blackstone.

Especially when she had a husband and a small son back in New Zealand waiting for her.

No wonder Matt had said he didn't give a damn about any jewelry belonging to Marise. But she knew her brother-in-law wasn't thinking straight, and that was part of the reason she'd decided to get them appraised. Perhaps if they were valuable they'd be worth keeping for Blake as a memento of his mother. Or maybe one day Matt would forgive his late wife and want the diamonds back. In the meantime, getting the diamonds valued was something *she* could do for her dead sister.

"So you're getting them appraised, you say?" her father said now, bringing her back to the moment. Again she noticed he didn't look well.

She stood in the kitchen doorway, her forehead creasing. "Dad, are you okay?"

A moment crept by.

"Dad?"

He looked up at her then, and there was a despairing look in his eyes that had her sucking in a sharp breath. "I'm a thief, Briana. I've stolen some money."

The breath caught in her lungs. "Wh-what?"

"I stole from Howard Blackstone."

She stared in astonishment. "My God! How much?"

He paused, then let out a shaky sigh. "One million dollars."

* * *

Briana was still reeling from her father's confession as she sat at the roulette table at the casino on Saturday evening. It had taken such an effort to keep her mind on the fashion show today, then again at the cocktail party this evening, but somehow she'd put a professional smile on her face. Afterward, not ready to go home to an empty apartment, she had stayed on.

It wasn't every week a daughter learned her father had stolen a million dollars. And from a "secret" account he'd been told about while working as an accountant for one of Australia's richest men thirty years ago, after Howard's previous accountant had passed on that bit of information.

Nor was the reason her father had taken the money in the first place enough to stop Ray Davenport from going to jail. Medical expenses for his wife's cancer, then a world cruise after a terminal diagnosis would garner immense sympathy, but in the end, the law would not condone embezzlement.

A lump wedged in her throat. With the newspapers continuing to report on the anonymous buy-up of Blackstone shares, she could just imagine how the media would hound her poor father, not to mention herself. They'd already gone through that after the plane crash. She didn't want to go through it again.

Besides, it wouldn't look good that her father had never forgiven Howard for firing Barbara when she'd become pregnant with Marise. Yet even after the Davenports had pulled up roots and moved from Sydney to

Melbourne, the Blackstones had ended up an intrinsic part of their lives. In the latter years, Marise had worked for Blackstone Diamonds in sales and marketing, then Briana had found herself a model and the face of Blackstone Diamonds. And then Marise had been with Howard on the flight to New Zealand, and had died in the aftermath of the crash. It was crazy, but it was as if destiny had somehow wanted the Davenports and the Blackstones to keep a connection.

And how ironic that his supermodel daughter couldn't help Ray out with money when he needed it. Her new million-dollar contract with Blackstone's was due to be renewed in three months' time, but nothing was ever certain until it was signed. Until then she had just enough to live on, thanks to her ex-business manager and lover, Patrick, who had convinced her to invest nearly all her money in an unbuilt apartment complex. It had sounded like a good investment at the time, until the developers had gone bust and she'd lost the lot.

She'd never told her parents about it, feeling like a sucker. They'd known she'd invested her money. They just hadn't known she'd lost it.

All at once someone sat down on the seat beside her, and the hairs on the back of her neck stood up. She turned toward the man who suddenly and completely filled her vision.

"Jarrod!"

"Briana," he murmured, his blue eyes trapping hers for a heart-stopping second.

She moistened her mouth even as she realized something. "You knew I'd be here, didn't you?"

One brow rose. "Did I?"

"It's too much of a coincidence otherwise," she said, letting him know she wasn't being hoodwinked.

He shrugged. "Perhaps."

Her forehead creased. "You want to see me?"

"Oh yes," he drawled, his gaze going over her long, blond wavy hair that tumbled around her head, before dipping to the creamy expanse of her neck and shoulders above the black cocktail dress, then further down and over the gathered bust held together by a diamond center clasp.

Her heart dropped to her toes but she managed a glare. "I meant that you wanted to *talk* to me?" she said, in no frame of mind to fend off his seduction.

He paused, his face turning unreadable now. "Yes."

She waited for him to speak, and when he didn't, she said, "Then talk."

"Not here." He got to his feet, his hand cupping her bare elbow, sending a warming shiver through her. "Come have a drink with me in the lounge."

She looked up at him standing so close beside her, an air of command exuding from him, threatening to engulf her. She wanted to say no, but couldn't think up a suitable excuse. "Just for a moment."

Then she stood up too and his eyes approved the short, glamorous dress. Heat curled in her stomach, before he led her away from the crowds and into one of the lounges. It was quieter in here with plenty of small tables circled by large comfortable leather chairs.

He took her to some seats in a secluded corner that was much too intimate for Briana's peace of mind, but when she saw some of the other patrons looking their way she was rather thankful no one could listen in on their conversation.

A waiter immediately came over to them, and she agreed to join Jarrod in a brandy. It would calm her nerves, she decided, watching him place their order, his self-confidence and sophistication an attraction many women would find appealing.

Dressed in dark trousers and a sports blazer with a white T-shirt underneath, he could have been a male model himself if there hadn't been such a hard edge to him. Those blue eyes clearly showed that hardness, an arrogance that would never let anyone dictate to him, let alone a camera.

"No Jake Vance today?" he said once the waiter left.

"I gave him the day off," she quipped.

The edges of that firm, sensual mouth tilted. "I doubt Jake would think of it that way."

She doubted it, too, but she didn't say so.

His smile disappeared and he fixed her with a candid gaze. "You and Jake are an item then?"

She lifted her chin. "I don't think that's any of your business."

He considered her for a moment, a pulse beating in his cheekbone. "The two of you were having a good laugh together at Kim's wedding."

For a moment she didn't know what he was talking

about. Then she remembered her comment about testosterone keeping the boat afloat and a bubble of laughter rose in her throat.

His eyes narrowed. "So there *is* something going on between you two."

She lost her amusement, not sure why he was being so insistent. "You wanted to talk," she reminded him, crossing her legs, pretending this line of questioning wasn't getting to her.

His eyes plunged to her legs in the ultrasheer silk stockings revealed by the ruffled hem, admired them, then rose back up to her face. "Are the two of you lovers?"

Her own eyes widened in dismay. "I don't believe I'm hearing this."

He held her gaze. "Tell me the truth, Briana."

Panic stirred in her chest but she kept it at bay. "Why, Jarrod? Why do you want to know about Jake and me?"

"Because if he doesn't want you, *I* do."

Her head reeled back. "What?"

"I want you to be my lover," he repeated firmly, leaving no doubt this time.

She gave him a glance of utter disbelief. "You can't be serious!"

"You deny you want me, too?"

She swallowed past her suddenly dry throat, tried to speak and had to swallow again. "I *can* deny it and I do," she lied, knowing she couldn't admit wanting him. It would give him an unfair advantage over her. One he wouldn't hesitate to use.

"Why sound so shocked? I'd have thought a woman

like yourself—" he gave a tiny pause "—would be used to such propositions."

Her blood pressure began to rise. "You mean because I'm a model?"

He inclined his dark head. "What other reason would there be?" he said silkily, as the waiter arrived with their brandy.

Her lips flattened with anger. At the wedding, Jarrod had made a similar comment about how far she'd come in the business. It hadn't sounded like a compliment back then, and neither did this comment. Had he thought she'd slept her way to the top? It sickened her to think that, yet why she cared she didn't know. It would serve him right if she called his bluff.

Why not?

"Okay, I'll sleep with you," she said, once the waiter left. "For a million dollars."

His eyes flickered then became shuttered. "That can be arranged."

Her brain stumbled. "What?"

He shot her a dry look. "Sleep with me and I'll give you a million dollars."

He'd well and truly called her bluff. "But—but you don't have that kind of money to give away."

His brows lifted. "You know that for a fact, do you?"

Oh heavens. Was she stupid or what? Apart from coming from a wealthy family, he'd made a name for himself as a property lawyer. Of course he'd have a million dollars to spare. What an idiot she was!

From somewhere she managed to scoff, "Ill-gotten gains, Jarrod?"

Contempt flashed in his eyes. "No. I'll leave that to the Blackstones."

"That's my employer you're talking about," she said coolly.

"Doesn't change a thing. The Blackstones are far from saints." He picked up the two glasses and passed one to her. "Now, about our agreement—"

She took the brandy glass from him, but an acute sense of panic raced through her again. "Keep your money. I don't want it. I—" She stopped.

She *did* need the money.

Needed it more than he could ever know.

"Having second thoughts?" he asked.

"No." She took a sip of brandy, and wished her denial carried the same strength as the alcohol now burning her throat.

"We can always do with more money," he pointed out, watching her as if knowing all along it would come back to this.

This being money.

Of course, she now realized that by even suggesting the million dollars she was playing into his belief that she was cut from the same cloth as her sister. Marise had said she'd fallen in love with Matt, but Briana suspected Matt's wealth hadn't hurt, either. And then there was Marise and Howard….

"A million dollars, Briana," he reminded her.

No, she couldn't do it. She wasn't for sale.

Then she forced her heart to steady itself. What if she looked upon it as a loan, asked a small voice inside her. A loan she would pay back once her contract with Blackstones was renewed.

A million-dollar contract.

But if it wasn't renewed? What if they got someone else to replace her as the face of Blackstone Diamonds? What if—

No, she wouldn't think about "what if's". Nor would she think about not repaying the money to him at all. It just wasn't in her to be underhanded.

But could she make love to Jarrod Hammond?

Oh God. How much of a hardship would that really be? She was attracted to him, no doubt about it. Intensely attracted, if she were to be honest with herself. It wasn't like she would be making a huge sacrifice and giving her body to someone who was revolting and wouldn't appreciate her. Jarrod would definitely appreciate her. Oh yes. She didn't know a man who would appreciate her better.

"Briana?"

She glanced at him then. He looked cool and calm, yet she sensed he was anything but. He wanted her just as much as she wanted him. So what harm would she do in sleeping with him? It wasn't as though she would be doing anything against her will.

On the contrary...

"It's a deal," she heard herself say.

He scowled. "It is?"

"You don't have the money?" she said with a rush of

disappointment that was about more than just getting her father out of trouble.

His dark brows straightened. "I have it." Just as quickly a considering light came into his eyes. "But now that I think of it," he drawled, "a million dollars for one night *is* a bit too much money—even for the face of Blackstone's."

Her lips tightened. He'd been playing with her. "Fine. That's it then."

"No, I'd say it's worth a month of nights together, don't you?"

She stiffened in shock. "No! I can't. A month is too long."

He shrugged his broad shoulders. "That's my offer. Become my mistress for one month and I'll give you a million dollars."

She swallowed hard. "That wasn't what I agreed to, Jarrod, and you know it."

"You agreed to sleep with me. True. But we didn't mention a timeframe."

She shook her head, not understanding him. "Why can't you be satisfied with one night?"

He didn't move a muscle. "Can you?"

She winced inwardly. Could she do it for one whole month? One night was so different. Or was it? Wouldn't only one night make her feel as if she really were selling herself? Wouldn't being his mistress for a month make her feel better about it all? Or was she just kidding herself?

"Briana, you want the money. Don't deny it." He waited a moment. "And I want you."

She cleared her throat and ignored an inward shudder of heat that couldn't be attributed to the brandy. "Who said I want the money?" she asked, trying to put him off the scent of her father's trail.

"You don't? Then it must be *me* you want," he mocked, his smirk saying he'd backed her into a corner.

Mentally kicking herself, she raised her chin. "I'm not denying the money wouldn't come in handy." She saw the hard look that entered his eyes. "And I don't deny that sleeping with a man such as yourself wouldn't be a—nice experience."

He smiled sardonically. "I'm glad you think so."

"But a month does seem a bit too long."

He swirled the brandy in his glass, then looked up at her. "Take it or leave it. But let me tell you, if you leave it, there won't be another chance."

Suddenly a feminine power settled over her, giving her confidence. "You might want to rethink that, Jarrod. After all, I've got something you want—my body. And if in a month's time I say I want you, I'm pretty sure I won't have to beg."

His nod acknowledged her words. "Oh, I don't deny that. But next time there won't be any money involved, sweetheart. It'll be just you and me. I won't be offering a million dollars again."

She gritted her teeth. He was a clever devil. Somehow he sensed she wouldn't walk away from the money. What he didn't know was that she *couldn't* walk away from it. Not if she wanted to help save her father.

So what if she accepted Jarrod's extended offer? The month would go fast. She had quite a few modeling engagements around the country to give her a break from Jarrod's overwhelming presence. At least there was that.

And perhaps she could even prove to him that she *wasn't* like her sister, she thought, then immediately rebuked herself. Why would she even want to? She owed Jarrod Hammond nothing.

She placed her glass of brandy on the coffee table in front of her. "I'll give you until the end of the month. That's three weeks. Take it or leave it," she said, putting the ball back into his court.

A moment crept by.

Static crackled the air between them.

Then he drained his glass and put it down next to hers. "I'll book a room," he said, about to get to his feet.

Her eyes widened. "What? Here?"

He stopped with a frown. "I thought it might be easier for our first night together."

"For whom?"

"You." He watched her in silence for a moment. "If you like, we can go back to my apartment…or to yours."

That was the last thing she wanted. "No," she said quickly. "A room here will be fine."

"Good." He stood up. "Wait here. I'll send you a note to say what suite I'll be in." He glanced around at the other patrons, then back at her. "I'm sure you don't want your reputation to suffer if somebody sees us going up together."

"Not to mention yours," she managed to say, still reeling from what tonight's outcome would be.

His eyes darkened. "I don't give a damn about my reputation, Briana. It might be wise to remember that." He strode off.

Three

It was silly to feel so nervous, Briana told herself as she tapped lightly on the door to the room fifteen minutes later. Heavens, she'd paraded in front of prime ministers and heads of state, done photo shoots in the middle of huge crowds, stood practically naked backstage at fashion shows, yet nothing made her feel as exposed as she did right now.

And was it any wonder, she decided when Jarrod opened the door to the deluxe suite and she met the full power of those intense blue eyes. Her stomach did a slow somersault.

And just as slowly, he reached out and curled his hand around her wrist, drawing her into the room before closing the door behind them. There he stood looking down at her, his hand still holding her, his palm warmly touching her skin, his thumb resting against the tender inside of her wrist where her pulse raced. She could feel him through every living cell in her body.

And then his gaze dropped to her mouth. He was going to kiss her. She could even feel herself lean just the barest hint toward him. Suddenly she wanted those lips on hers…wanted that body against hers.

"Have you eaten?"

His words snapped her out of her trance. Dismayed at how easily she would have succumbed, she stepped back, letting his hand drop away from her. "Just some finger food at the cocktail party," she said, walking casually into the suite. A wall of floor-to-ceiling glass drew her attention to the city lights below, but Briana only gave the view a quick glance. The world was out there but tonight that's where it would stay.

"You look disappointed a moment ago."

Her heart slammed against her ribs as she glanced across at him. "I did?" She shrugged. "I thought—"

"That I wouldn't waste any time getting you into bed?" A seductive glint entered his eyes. "Briana, being in your company, looking at you, isn't wasting time. Far from it." A smile touched his lips. "The ravishing comes later."

Her breath quickened. He made it sound so… ravishing! "Yes—well—"

"Unless you'd like me to start now instead of ordering you some food?" he drawled.

She sent him a wry look. "No thanks. I'd prefer soup."

His lips twitched. And then his gaze swept over her and awareness danced between them again, and for a moment she thought he really was going to come over to her and ravish her on the spot. And she wanted him to. Dear Lord, she did.

He broke eye contact and strode toward the phone. "I'll order room service," he said, his voice sounding gruff.

Knowing she had affected him, her heart skipped a beat. "I'll just go and freshen up."

He indicated across the width of the room. "The bedroom's that way."

The bedroom.

Carrying her small purse, she took her time to walk across the room, while fighting every instinct to break into a run and lock the door behind her like some frightened virgin. Wouldn't that go down well, she mused with a dash of humor.

The problem was that's exactly how she felt. This was her first time with Jarrod and she was feeling overwhelmed. Despite knowing him for years, despite now acknowledging to herself that she had wanted him for years, there was a difference in the *doing.* A huge difference. She doubted she could ever have prepared herself for this.

Needless to say, seducing women was par for the course for him. He would have done all this before. He certainly seemed to know his way about the suite. He'd probably even met some other women here, just like he'd met her tonight. Had he brought them up here, too?

No, she wasn't going to think about that. She had enough to worry about tonight, she decided as she entered the lavish bedroom, her eyes immediately fastening on the huge bed and her heartbeat skidding to a screeching stop. She and Jarrod would make love on that bed tonight. The thought made her go weak at the knees.

She hurried into the equally giant bathroom and freshened her lipstick. Then she combed through her wavy tresses that bounced along her shoulders as she moved, though why she bothered she wasn't sure. Jarrod would only mess her hair up, just like he would mess with her dress and…

Help!

She took some deep breaths. Okay, so she could stay in here and act like a coward, or she could go out there and face the music. She'd made a deal with the devil, but that deal still stood. And unfortunately so did the devil.

She didn't stay in there long. There was no reason to hide from him or their situation, though she had a few things to say to him first.

"I hope I can count on you not to tell anyone about this," she said, once back in the main area, her chin held high.

He scowled as he stepped away from the bar, carrying two glasses of wine. "Why would I? What we do is our own business."

"As long as we're clear on that."

He handed her a glass and gestured for her to sit on the sofa. "I'm a grown man, not some high-school kid. I don't need to prove anything by telling the world."

She sank down on the soft leather lounge and hoped she could believe him. Patrick had been different, a fact she'd only found out after she'd ended their affair. Apparently he'd often boasted about bedding the face of

Blackstone's. She wished Jarrod was the same type, then she might have the strength to leave right now, but she instinctively knew he wasn't.

He sat down on the chair opposite. "But first, tell me why."

Her throat almost closed up, knowing instantly what he meant. "Er...why?"

His eyes said she wasn't deceiving him. "Why you're willing to sleep with me now and not in the last four years."

She took a sip of her wine before answering. "You never asked before."

And she knew the reason for it. He considered her the same as Marise and hadn't wanted a bar of her. She knew that, and had felt protected by it. Until today.

"Oh, I wanted to ask. But you knew that, didn't you? There's always been an attraction between us."

Her mouth went dry. "You're imagining things."

"The only thing I'm imagining is you in bed with me. And soon I won't need my imagination for that."

Her breath suspended for a full five seconds.

His eyes held hers captive. "Why now, Briana?"

She slowly released her breath and pasted on a cynical smile. "How can I refuse a million dollars *and* the chance to have sex with a man like you?"

He sent her a measured look. "Don't try and pick a fight by insulting me. You're here of your own free will. If you don't want to go through with it, then say so now." A heartbeat passed. "I want you with every breath I take, but I won't force you."

Her heart bumped against her ribs. Oh, how she

wished she could blame him for all this. But he was right. She'd made the choice to be here tonight, if only for her father's sake.

"It won't be force," she agreed, then saw him visibly relax, but he kept his eyes trained on her.

"Tonight is the beginning of our three weeks together, Briana. Nothing more. Are you clear about that?"

Her body immediately tensed. "Very clear. And by the way, *you* were the one who wanted the full month together," she reminded him. Oh, how she'd love to tell him where to shove his money.

"I'm not talking about a month. I'm talking about anything beyond that. I'm not after a long-term relationship."

She gave a derisive snort. "Long-term relationship? With you? I'd rather put my head in an oven."

His hard sensual mouth lifted at the corners. "Now, that would be such a waste."

"Not from where I'm sitting."

He gave a light chuckle as someone knocked lightly on the door and called out, "Room service."

Jarrod pushed himself to his feet and went to let the waiter in. Briana got a good look at the cut of his tailored trousers and blazer from behind. Superb. And so was the masculine body beneath it, she grudgingly admitted, even as she realized something else.

"Wait!" she hissed just as he went to open the door. She jumped up and almost ran across the room to the bedroom and out of sight. She didn't want anyone seeing her there.

A couple of minutes later, Jarrod called to her, "You can come out now."

Feeling slightly foolish, she straightened her shoulders and calmly walked back into the living area, constantly aware of his eyes on her every movement, and trying to keep her own eyes off him. He'd taken off the blazer, and the white T-shirt underneath exposed the muscles of his upper torso.

"Ashamed to be seen with me?" he mocked, holding out a chair for her at the small dining table.

She shrugged. "Don't take it personally. I'd do the same with any man."

His eyes hardened. "Is that so?"

She ignored the implication in his eyes and sat on the offered chair. "Don't you know? The media would love to catch me in a compromising situation such as this."

He walked around the table and sat opposite her. "I'd have thought you'd revel in media attention," he said, showing his low opinion of her.

She flinched inwardly but on the outside, she arched a brow. "You really think I would welcome bad publicity?"

"No, I guess not," he admitted, and she felt the tightness inside her unwind a little. "No doubt bad publicity wouldn't look too good for the face of Blackstone's," he said, lifting the lid off his plate of food.

Briana felt the words sting.

Then he looked up and caught her staring at him. "Aren't you going to eat?"

She shook her head.

He watched her with an observant eye. "Are you okay?"

Suddenly it all got the better of her. "Okay?" she choked, throwing her napkin aside. "I'm about to make love with a stranger, Jarrod. Is it any wonder I'm on edge?"

"I'm not a stranger, Briana," he corrected calmly.

"For all intents and purposes, you are." Unable to sit still a moment longer, and knowing she couldn't eat now anyway, she walked over to the windows. "Can we please get this over and done with?"

Silence hung in the air behind her.

"Don't sound so eager," he drawled, but a moment later she heard movement. "Let's have some privacy, shall we?"

Tension rattled inside her as the suite flooded in darkness, leaving only a faint glow from the city lights beyond the glass. She still didn't turn around. She needed to focus on those city lights, to remember she was here for a purpose.

"Will you respect me in the morning, Jarrod?" She heard herself mutter the cliché, but needed to say it all the same.

"Yes," he said quietly, close behind her, so close his breath stirred strands of her hair. "But will *you* respect you in the morning?"

She thought about that, surprised by his astuteness. His question had dispelled any hint she was selling herself, and she was grateful to him for that. "Yes," she murmured.

And then his hands cupped her bare shoulders, the thin straps of her dress were little protection against him. "I'll make this special for you, Briana."

She could see his reflection as if they were standing in

front of a mirror, the gleam in his eyes seeming to pierce the glass to reach her, seeming to suspend them in time.

Her throat thickened. "I know."

All at once he slid his hand under her golden-blond hair, held it up as if loving the feel of it, then letting it fall like sparkling champagne over her shoulders.

"You're stunning," he murmured, admiration in his voice as he pushed some strands aside to kiss her nape in a gesture that was simply and deliciously sensuous. "A natural beauty."

For a split second she tried to stay in control…tried but soon weakened when his kisses continued to caress her skin. She lowered her lashes, silently shocked at how easy she was succumbing to his touch.

Yet it wasn't just this moment between them. Jarrod was right about there having always been an attraction between them. And that attraction had been unrelenting in its pursuit of them. Tonight, right now, was the culmination of it all.

She couldn't help herself. She tilted her head to the side to allow him easier access—and she gave in. There was no going back now. Nor did she want to. She wanted to be in his arms.

Slowly he undid the zipper at the back of her dress, his lips whispers of sensation as they followed the lowering zipper, making their way down her spine, kissing her where no man had ever kissed before. It was a seduction of the senses that made her head spin.

At the base of her spine he let go of the zipper, and her dress plummeted to the floor and pooled around her ankles. She held her breath, frozen in this instant, watching in the glass as he straightened behind her, all the while admiring her lacy black bra, matching high-cut panties and thigh-high silk stockings.

"My very own model." His hands splayed over her hips as he moved closer, letting her feel his arousal.

A moan escaped her but she managed to say, "Supermodel," and was proud of herself for still having some sort of fight left in her.

He gave a husky chuckle, then lowered his head. He placed his lips against her shoulder and began to nibble at even more pleasure points she never knew she had. When his hands slid around to capture her lace-covered breasts and his fingers lightly squeezed her nipples with the sweetest torment, she moaned with wanting him.

"Too much?" he muttered.

"Yes."

"Good."

He scooped her up and carried her into the bedroom, spreading her across the thick bedspread as if she were a pleasure to be savored. She lay there in the lamplight and stared up at him. His eyes glittered as he took in her half-naked state, her breasts eagerly straining against the lace, the V-shape of her high-cut panties a sensual delight.

His gaze soaked her up, then landed on her face. "Do you realize I've never kissed you?" he muttered roughly, his eyes focusing on her mouth.

She inadvertently moistened her lips. "Same here."

Neither of them smiled. The moment was too intense.

He pulled the T-shirt over his head, his chest bronzed

and sprinkled with hair. He kicked off his shoes and slid onto the bed next to her. And then he claimed her mouth in a kiss that was so passionate it made her head spin. This first touch of his firm lips against her softer ones was more than she had ever expected, more than she'd ever wanted from a man—until now.

And then his tongue parted her lips and stole into her mouth, stole the breath from her, demanding she give him everything of herself. When she capitulated, his groan of appreciation sent a thrill through her as she clung to him like there was no tomorrow.

Right now there *was* no tomorrow. There was only him and her, and the wonderful sensations he was stirring inside her. He undid her bra and eased back, the lace falling away, and she quivered when his fingertips brushed her bare breasts.

"Aah, something else that needs kissing," he murmured as he lowered his head and took a nipple in his mouth, playing with it with his tongue, then sucking in the sweetest of tortures.

Needing to touch him, to be a partner in this, her hands cupped the back of his head and held him to her. She loved spreading her fingers through the short hair, loved it even better when she slipped her hands down to his sculpted shoulders, then the length of his back to the waistband of his trousers.

He shuddered and muttered low in his throat, "You're distracting me." Then he took a deep breath and got to his knees beside her. "Now, what else needs my attention?" he teased, though his eyes were dark with desire as his palm glided down over her stomach, farther down where he dallied and stroked her through her panties, until heat washed over her and made her limbs tremble.

And then his gaze dropped to those trembling limbs, covered by the sheer silk stockings. "I love these things on you," he rasped, slipping his finger under the band of one stocking, and ever so slowly peeling it down her smooth leg. His lips followed the trail until she breathed his name through parted lips.

He repeated the process with the other leg, and when she breathed his name again, his lips trailed back up to her thighs, up the center of her panties where he paused to inhale her.

He turned his head and looked up at her. "Are you sure?"

Tender warmth entered her heart. He was giving her another chance to back out, another chance to say no to all this. As if she could now.

"Yes, I'm sure," she said on a whisper, and that was all the encouragement he needed.

He rolled off the bed and shed the rest of his clothes, and he was suddenly, magnificently, naked. She stared at his unashamed erection, the hardness of him, the powerful male perfection, and she knew that she had to have him inside her. She put out her hand to reach for him, then stopped.

Instead, she lifted her bottom off the bed, pushing her panties down and off herself. Her eyes connected with his as she held them in the air with one finger before dropping them on the floor like a flag of surrender. It was a surrender she willingly made tonight. There was no tomorrow after all.

Something smoldered in the depths of his eyes, and a pulse leaped along his jaw, making her hold her breath. A moment later, he didn't say a word as he reached for the condom from the bedside table and sheathed himself, before coming back to her, kissing her deeply, the full length of his body pressing her down against the mattress.

She kissed him back, loving the feel of his hair-roughened chest against her own tender breasts, the heat of his arousal as he melded into her femininity, filling her completely. She felt like she had never made love before. Not like this.

And then he stopped kissing her, and his eyes captured hers with a look that was undeniably male. It was a triumphant look that said he was here, he had conquered and now he would take.

She thrilled to the silent communication, allowing him his moment of masculinity. And then he began to move his body inside her with long, slow strokes that had her own body raising to meet him with a feminine power of her own. Together they built pleasure upon pleasure, until slow was no longer enough, and fast and deep became a necessity, an essential part of their love-making. Of them.

And together they came as one.

If any woman in the world had been worth a million dollars, it was the woman next to him, Jarrod reflected the next morning as he lay facing Briana sleeping on the pillow next to him. They'd made love three times throughout the night. Three times and he still hadn't had enough of her.

She was dazzling, this golden glamour girl with her velvet eyelashes fanning her smooth cheeks, and her blond hair tousled so sexily over her naked shoulders. The sweet scent of her gorgeous body drifted up beneath the sheet and reeled him in, making the blood pulse in his temples, rush through his body.

Suddenly he wanted her a fourth time.

And a fifth.

And he would have her, too.

Just not right now, he thought regretfully as he glanced at the clock and saw the time. Dammit. He had a meeting with a client in an hour. A very important one, or he would cancel it. But the guy was going overseas later today, and needed a Sunday morning appointment.

Sighing with regret, he slid his hand off Briana's slim hip. It was probably for the best anyway. Despite his body's urges, he needed a moment to himself. Why, he wasn't sure, except that having Briana in his arms had been fulfilling in a way he'd never felt before. And that just didn't make sense. Why did he have to feel this way about a woman beautiful enough and sexy enough to eat?

Yet it was more than a physical sexiness. It was something in her. Something that drew him to her. Drew many men, no doubt, he thought as cynicism gnawed at his gut. How many lovers had seen her like this? Probably too many to count. She may have put on an act about accepting the money, but she'd still accepted his offer.

She was definitely a gold-digger, even if something wasn't quite right here. His lawyer's instincts told him there was more to her taking the money than she was letting on. But what?

His dark brows knitted together. Perhaps he just wanted to believe she had a motive that wasn't attached to the money. More fool him. In his experience, beautiful women couldn't be trusted. They'd always wanted something, always had an angle. The only exception was his adopted mother, Katherine Hammond. She was lovely inside and out.

But his birth mother, an ice-cold beauty whose looks had started to wear thin, was out for all she could get. She'd given him up for adoption to remain footloose and fancy-free. She'd told him so the first time she'd come looking for a handout. The times he'd seen her since hadn't changed his mind.

She and Briana would get on well.

Or would they, he wondered, his eyes resting on Briana, her sheer beauty making him doubt himself. But he had to remember she was the sister of his dead sister-in-law. She and Marise were the same breed of women. Out for all they could get. Marise had proved it with his brother. Briana had just proven it with him.

He slipped out of bed and reached for his checkbook, wrote out the million-dollar check and put it on the pillow he'd just vacated. Then he left Sleeping Beauty in the bedroom, closing the door behind him to go into the main suite to make a phone call. Soon he'd head home to shower and change before his meeting.

But as he hung up the phone, he heard a noise in the bedroom. He strode over and opened the door, but she must not have heard him. She was sitting up in bed, having wrapped the sheet around herself. In her hands was the check and she was looking down at it as if she was defeated rather than pleased.

Something twisted inside his gut, reminding him that there was more to this than met the eye. "Isn't that what you wanted, Briana?"

Her head shot up, her wide-eyed beauty latching on to him. "I thought you'd left," she accused, heat rushing into her cheeks.

Her reaction wasn't what he'd expected from such a woman of the world. For a moment she almost looked…guileless.

"You mean, you were *hoping* I'd left," he said, leaning against the doorjamb, fascinated by every aspect of her. What was going on in that mind of hers?

She angled a chin that was more defiant than delicate right now. "So you don't feel you got value for the money, Jarrod?"

"You know I did. And it's not over yet. We have three weeks of—getting to know each other."

Her lips briefly stretched in a fake smile, then not. "How nice."

"Yes, just like your 'nice' experience last night," he drawled, reminding her of her words last night down in the casino lounge. *Nice* didn't describe the half of it. "At least, I assume it was as 'nice' for you as it was for me."

"Searching for compliments, Jarrod?"

All at once he'd had enough. As much as he liked verbally sparring with her, he had other things to do this morning. "What do you have planned for the rest of the long-weekend?"

She blinked, then wariness clouded her eyes. "Why?"

"I want you to spend it with me."

"So soon?" she said with obvious dismay.

His mouth twisted. "Your enthusiasm is refreshing. Is that a problem?"

She took a ragged breath. "I guess not."

His mouth flattened in a grim line. Anyone would think he'd asked her to give up all her earthly possessions. "Do you have any further engagements this weekend?"

She shook her head. "No, just some things to do in the lead-up to the Grand Prix next weekend."

Yes, the papers were already advertising her attendance at the Melbourne Grand Prix. "Look, I've got an appointment with a client, but I'll be back in a couple of hours to take you to lunch. And tomorrow we can go to the Moomba Festival together."

"Oh, but—"

"I've asked them to send you up some new clothes to gad about in now," he said, preempting her.

Anger flared in her eyes. "I don't want a new set of clothes to gad about in."

"Then wear none," he mocked.

Her mouth thinned. "I prefer my own clothes, thank you."

He glanced at his watch then back at her. Time was running out. "Just relax, order some breakfast and take another nap. You didn't get much sleep last night. I'll be back at noon."

"And if I don't want to spend any more time with you?"

"Then I'll know you're not a woman of your word." He turned and walked out of the hotel room.

Four

After Jarrod left the suite, Briana wasn't sure how long she sat in the king-size bed, cursing him, cursing herself for being attracted to such a man. He'd made love to her last night as if she'd been meant to be in his arms all along. He'd made her feel special and complete, taken her to heights she'd never imagined. She could still feel the remnants of his lovemaking; her breasts were still tender from his touch, her mouth still swollen from his kisses, her lower body still sensitive from his possession.

And she *had* been possessed, there was no doubt about it. Possessed by him. Possessed by her desire for him.

The latter had been a shock.

She couldn't remember even coming close to this with Patrick. No, Patrick had taken what he'd wanted, when he'd wanted in bed, but had never really given her the same fulfillment. Because she'd been in love with him, she hadn't let herself think about it. Her love had covered up a multitude of his flaws…until her rose-colored glasses had been well and truly ripped off her.

And now Jarrod Hammond was making her feel special again, not because she'd fallen in love with him, but because he treated her as the woman he wanted.

She didn't fool herself that it was more than sex— for either of them. He'd wanted to possess her body and he had. She'd wanted him to make love to her, and that was the reason she was feeling fulfilled. Nothing more. It was only about sex. Good sex, admittedly.

All paid for and delivered, she reminded herself, making a half-choked sound as she looked down at the check in her hands. She still couldn't believe she'd given her body to a man for a million dollars. Her father would be horrified. *She* was horrified.

Yet, to be honest, Jarrod hadn't made her feel as if she'd sold her body to him. And that was totally crazy. Any other man would have made her feel cheap.

What was she going to tell her father about the money she'd suddenly acquired? She'd found it lying around in an old bank account? No, too far-fetched. Only Howard Blackstone had kept money in old, "secret" accounts, she mused cynically.

Then the answer came to her. The check was one of Jarrod's, so she would tell her father she'd asked Jarrod for a loan to buy more property. Yes, that was it! Her father probably wouldn't think anything out of the ordinary, not with Jarrod being a Hammond, and with Marise being married to Jarrod's brother.

Of course, loan or not, she still had to pay the money back. She just hoped to high heaven that Blackstone Diamonds wanted to continue their contract with her.

And if she couldn't pay it back? No, she wouldn't think about being beholden to Jarrod any longer than necessary. As it was, he had started to boss her around already, telling her to stay in bed and take a nap, buying her clothes, telling her to wait in the room until he got back, expecting she'd go to lunch with him.

Did that mean he expected her to do everything he asked? Would he expect her to be at his beck and call for the next three weeks?

She was no man's plaything. Not even for a million dollars, she told herself as she pushed aside a sense of trepidation and asked herself what to do next. Oh, she'd keep her word to spend the next three weeks with him, and she'd no doubt enjoy some of it. But she wasn't about to wait around this hotel room for him to return. If he wanted to take her to lunch, then she'd leave him a note and go home to her apartment until he called. She certainly wasn't chasing him. If necessary, she'd meet him at the restaurant.

And she would still be a woman of her word, she decided, throwing back the sheet and pushing her naked body out of bed.

Of course, as soon as her doorbell buzzed, Briana knew who it would be. Despite having a doorman who was harder to get past than a crocodile, somehow Jarrod had managed it.

And now he stood there, looking like a man should look—handsome, confident, charismatic—sending her pulse racing into overdrive. She had no idea how much she'd been wanting to see him until this moment. Correction, how much her *body* had wanted to see him.

"You left your new clothes behind," he drawled, empty-handed.

"I don't need you to buy me clothes," she said coolly as she turned into her apartment, only to find herself twirled back toward him.

Without warning, he kissed her. For heart-stopping seconds she tried to hold something of herself back, but he deepened the kiss. When a faint groan escaped from his throat, she slid into meltdown. Her lips parted.

Just as suddenly he let her go. "Not so cool, eh?" he murmured.

She forced her head to clear. "Talking about yourself?" she challenged.

"Talking about *both* of us."

The nerves in her stomach tightened and she quickly turned into the living room. "How much did you pay the doorman to let you in?"

"He happens to be the father of a friend."

She picked up her purse from the sofa and shot him a look of disbelief. "My, that's quite a coincidence."

He held her gaze. "Yes, it is."

She realized he was serious. Either way, she needed to have some discreet words with the doorman.

"Don't try and get him fired," Jarrod warned.

"Who said anything about getting him fired?" she said in astonishment.

"Oh, I don't know. There's a certain look of revenge in your eyes."

A smirk coated her lips. "That isn't for the doorman."

He gave a husky chuckle, taking her unawares. She wished he'd stop doing that. It was one thing knowing he was enigmatic, quite another to see his more human side. It was best she keep her distance.

She mentally straightened her shoulders. "I'm ready."

His gaze traveled down over her outfit. "I can see why you prefer your own clothes."

She glanced down at her sleeveless, slimline knit dress in vivid marigold, the material lightly rouched at the waist and harmonizing with her hips. It was sexy and flattering and she felt good in it, especially when she combined it with delicate high-heeled sandals in the same color. And heavens, she needed every bit of confidence she could find right now.

She looked back up at Jarrod. "Actually this was a gift from someone."

A cynical look entered his eyes. "A male, no doubt?"

Ah, so they were back to that again. He thought she had conned every man she'd ever met out of something or other.

"Who else?" she retorted, walking toward him. One of the designers had given it to her after a fashion shoot, but she'd let Jarrod think what he liked. It's what he *wanted* to think anyway.

Yet he frowned as she preceded him out of the apartment, and he was still frowning when she closed her door behind them. She hid a small burst of satisfaction. Good. Let him be the unsettled one for a change, even if she had no idea why. It would be too much to ask that he might think he was actually wrong about her.

Her inner poise restored, she headed toward the elevator. "Where are we having lunch?"

"Southbank."

She inclined her head. "Lovely." Lunch at a riverside restaurant would at least surround them with a multitude of people and would take an hour or two out of their day. She dare not think beyond that.

Only, once he'd parked his BMW Coupe in an underground car park in the city center and they rode up the elevator, she realized he was taking her to one of the top hotel restaurants, rather than one of the many places alongside the Yarra River.

Pity it wasn't as crowded as she wanted, she mused as the waiter walked them through luxurious surroundings and seated them at a table for two overlooking the river.

The picturesque city views beyond the glass gave a feeling of spaciousness that would have been delightful if she'd been with anyone else. In Jarrod's company, not even watching the slow-moving riverboats and the strolling couples along the promenade below could put her at ease. The world was still out there but it was hard to notice when she was seated intimately with a man who was now her lover and who intended to remain her lover for three more weeks.

"So," he said, leaning back in his chair once the waiter had departed after taking their order, "tell me about Briana Davenport."

"Read my bio," she quipped, leaning back in her chair, too, pretending to be relaxed.

A corner of his mouth twitched upward. "I want to know about Briana Davenport, the person. Not Briana, the model."

She shrugged her shoulders. "Same thing."

"No, different." He tilted his head, considering her with a slight frown. "I'm just not sure how yet."

"Don't tax yourself thinking about it."

His eyes suddenly narrowed. "So you think I'm only interested in you for your looks?"

She kept her gaze steady. "You mean you aren't?"

A muscle tightened at the edge of his jaw. "No."

Oddly enough, she believed him. But it probably wasn't a good thing to delve too deeply. It would mean having to consider why he was sleeping with her.

"It's a bit late asking me about myself, don't you think?"

He offered her a smile. "I knew enough to sleep with you."

"Hey, don't say that too loud," she whispered, straightening and looking around but seeing there was no danger of anyone's hearing. Thank goodness, she thought, her gaze returning to Jarrod's.

A smile reached his eyes, then was banked. "Okay, let's start again. What do I know about Briana Davenport?" He gave her a silent appraisal. "Hmm. You don't snore."

"I'm pleased."

"You like to snuggle up against a man."

"A natural reaction."

"And you like to be kissed all over."

"Shhh," she hissed.

"It's all true."

"So is the million dollars."

The amusement left his eyes and his gaze hardened, but just as quickly he arched a brow at her. "You don't want to know about me?"

She looked at him long and hard. "I know all there is to know."

"Really?"

She assumed a thoughtful expression. "You have no hesitation in taking what you want."

"True."

"You'll go to any means to get it."

"True."

"You're suspicious of beautiful women."

"True."

"Oh, I forgot. They have to be beautiful *and* greedy."

"Now you're getting there," he said in a dry tone, just as the waiter brought over their first course.

But Jarrod didn't seem fazed by her comment, and after that they ate in silence for a while. She used the time to recover from the constant barrage of awareness Jarrod's presence caused. In her job she was used to being constantly "on," but this was different. Being with Jarrod was being *turned* on.

They had just finished their appetizer when the waiter brought over a bottle of wine.

Jarrod frowned. "I didn't order this."

"No, sir, you didn't. It's compliments of the gentleman over there." The waiter's gaze went across the room to the gray-haired man sitting at a small table by himself, watching them. "For Briana," the waiter added as the older man raised his glass at her.

"Send it back," Jarrod snapped.

"No!" Briana exclaimed, horrified. She speared Jarrod a dark look then smiled at the waiter. "Please pour me a glass," she told him as she got to her feet. "I'll be back in a moment."

"Briana," Jarrod said through gritted teeth.

"Pour him one, too," she instructed the waiter, turning away but not before she saw the glint of humor in the waiter's eyes.

Laughter bubbling within her, her steps were light as she walked across the room with a natural smile on her lips. She couldn't help but feel good that she was winning this battle against Jarrod.

Then she thanked the older man and spent a few minutes talking to him. He turned out to be a fan of hers and was a thorough gentleman.

When she returned to the table, Jarrod's eyes burned through her. "Made an arrangement to meet later?" he snarled.

She shot him a dark glance. This was going too far. "No, but I can go back and ask him, if you like."

"How much did he offer you? One million or two?"

She sucked in a sharp breath. "Don't be ridiculous."

"Isn't that why you went to thank him?"

He sounded jealous, and the thought sent a weird thrill through her. Then she realized this wasn't about jealousy. This was about belonging to Jarrod Hammond, as temporary as that was.

"He was just being nice," she said firmly. "He's a gentleman."

"He wants to take you to bed."

"So does most of the male population, I imagine, including yourself."

A second ticked by, and a smug look crossed his face. "Ah, but *I* did, you see," he drawled, his voice silky-smooth now.

Her mouth tightened. "I hope you marked it on that belt of yours with all those other notches."

Sexy amusement flickered in his eyes. "You know something, Briana? I really like fighting with you."

She ignored that, even as she privately acknowledged enjoying a verbal victory with this man every now and then. "By the way, it's part of my job as the face of Blackstone's to maintain good public relations. I wouldn't want to offend him."

"As long as they are only *public* relations."

"If they weren't, it's none of your business."

"Don't bet on it, sweetheart."

So, she'd been right to be worried about his thinking he could boss her about. Her chin tilted in defiance. "You don't own me, despite the million-dollar check."

His eyes grew cool. "No, but I do own three weeks

of your time. And don't forget you're the one who suggested the million dollars. And you're the one who took the money. I would have just been happy to go to bed with you."

"Yes, and I'm the one who'll pay the price," she said, suddenly feeling sickened by it all. "I think I'd like to leave."

Jarrod's gaze swung across the room. "Won't your number-one fan over there be offended if you don't drink his wine?"

"Oh, you're so right." She picked up the glass and drank it in one go. Thankfully it was only half-full. "There." She put her empty glass back down on the table.

Jarrod's brow rose. "You can handle drinking it that fast, I presume?"

"It was only half a glass." She went to get to her feet but all at once he leaned across the table and put his hand over hers, his touch heating her skin.

"Unless you want our little tiff in tomorrow's papers, you'd better stay here and finish your lunch."

Her forehead creased. "What do you—"

"Here we are, madam," the waiter said, startling her as he slid a plate on the table in front of her. Not that she had much of an appetite by this time. Jarrod seemed to rob her of that once again.

The waiter walked around to Jarrod and did the same. "If there's anything else you would like—"

"No," Jarrod cut across him. "We're fine."

"Very good, sir." The younger man left them alone.

Jarrod waited a moment before speaking. "I saw your

fan talking to some guests at the table over there. They've been checking us out, so I wouldn't be surprised if he said something about the bottle of wine. If you get up and storm out it'll be in tomorrow's paper."

"Maybe you shouldn't have acted like a jealous husband, then," she said without thinking.

He actually looked surprised. "Is that what I sounded like?"

"Either that or a jerk," she said as the rush of wine made her feel a little light-headed.

He grinned. "I think that wine's gone straight to your head."

"No."

"Yes," he insisted.

"Okay, just a little," she acknowledged, finding it easier to give in this time. "But I'm used to it."

"Really?" he mocked.

"I don't have a drinking problem, if that's what you're implying." But somehow she couldn't seem to summon up much anger. She was beginning to feel relaxed and mellow. And, oh my, Jarrod Hammond really was a hunk. And that slow smile…combined with his expert hands…

"I think we'd better finish lunch," he said, breaking into her thoughts, "then I'll take you home."

Would he make love to her?

"Come on, eat. It'll soak up some of that wine. The media would have a field day if they heard the face of Blackstone's was drunk *off* her face."

That brought her out of her trance. He was right. It

could jeopardize her contract renewal. And then she wouldn't have the money to repay Jarrod....

She took a steadying breath, picked up her fork and started eating. Not long after, Jarrod began speaking of general things and she was glad to answer. Polite conversation she was used to. Personal, she was not.

She refused dessert but as they drank their coffee, he sat there looking at her. "How do you feel now?"

"Back to normal. The food helped."

"Good." His eyes took on a sudden sensual warmth that made her heart start hammering. "Now that you're no longer tipsy, I'm going to take you back to my apartment."

Her mouth turned dry. "Why?"

"I want to make love to you. I want you in my bed. Today. Tonight. Right now."

She gave a soft gasp. "Don't say things like that, Jarrod."

"Does it offend you?"

Unfortunately, no.

"It...unsettles me," she admitted, not knowing why she was even admitting that to him.

His gaze took on a piercing look. "I thought you'd be used to men saying they wanted you in their bed."

"Then you'd be wrong."

He gave her a sharp look, as if he had trouble believing that. Then he signaled to the waiter to bring over the check, and before too long they were walking back through the restaurant, through the diminishing crowd of people. The older gentleman had gone, and so had the other people, and that made her wonder if Jarrod had just made that up to keep her here.

But why keep her here when he wanted to take her to his home and make love to her?

And he proved that point as soon as they stepped inside his downtown apartment. She had a glimpse of luxurious surroundings before he swept her up in his arms and carried her into his bedroom.

"I almost hate to take this dress off you," he said in a gravelly voice, slipping it over her head anyway. "It's so very sexy." His gaze slid down over her bra and panties. "*You're* very sexy."

And then he pulled her toward him and his lips found hers, his kiss flooding her with want and need and must haves. Before too long she was aware of a mattress giving way beneath her, of his hands cupping her breasts, touching her secret parts. Then he entered her in one swift movement. When he started to move inside her, hard muscle against soft satin, desire exploded inside her. Finally…finally…he consumed her.

It was dark when she woke and she had to gather her bearings. Her job took her all over the place, so she was used to waking up in strange beds. Alone.

"It's eight-fifteen," a deep male voice rumbled in her ear.

Jarrod!

"At night?" She should move, instead of lying there in the curve of his shoulder, her face pressed against his warm skin.

"I suppose we could be having an eclipse," he joked in a husky voice, his sense of humor surprising her. It wasn't something that came to mind with this man.

She stayed where she was. She couldn't seem to find the energy to move. "Why didn't you wake me?"

"I've been asleep, too. Neither of us got much sleep last night, remember?"

Everything came flooding back. The casino. The million dollars. Being possessed by this man.

Suddenly panicked, she lifted her head. "I'd better get back to my apartment."

"Why?"

She looked up at him in the dim light, trying to focus, trying to think, but it was hard when "God's gift to women" was beneath her. "Um—so I can go to—"

"Bed? You're already in bed. With me."

She moistened her lips. "I need to shower and get something to eat."

"No problem. I'll order in pizza. We'll sit on the balcony and watch the Moomba fireworks light up the sky." All at once, he put her away from him and rolled out of bed. Naked. And then he pulled her up on her feet. Naked.

"What are you doing?"

He bent and scooped her up in his arms. Naked. "We're going to take a shower first."

"Together?"

His brow rose as he carried her into the bathroom. "You have a problem with that?" he said, his blue eyes sure she wouldn't object.

And for once she didn't. "No."

He gave her a look of mild surprise. "Sweet acquiescence?"

She nodded. "Maybe."

His eyes dropped to her mouth. "I think I like it."

Her heartbeat accelerated. "Don't get too used to it."

"That's good. Because I kind of like that snappy Briana Davenport, too, remember." He stood her inside the glass cubicle and picked up the soap. "And now, let's see what type of fireworks we can make for ourselves tonight."

She opened her mouth to jokingly point out that water would put out any fireworks, but his kiss stole her words away. Before too long she didn't care anyway. She went up in flames first, then he joined her, and it proved one thing. They were combustible together, wet or not.

Afterward, he left her on the bed and walked out of the room with a towel wrapped around his hips, saying he'd be back shortly. Satiated but trying not to show it too much, Briana pulled the edge of the comforter over her nakedness. It was silly to even consider hiding her body, but she was still tingling from his touch. She had been putty in his hands. And that wasn't good. Not good at all.

He was back in a few moments, carrying a woman's robe. He came over to the bed and held it open for her, but she stared at the oyster-colored silk as if it carried the bubonic plague.

"Don't worry. It's new."

"Order in a supply, did you?" she said, relieved not to be offered something worn by one of his previous lovers. Then she saw the label still attached to the sleeve.

She glanced up at him. "This is one of the pieces you bought at the casino."

"Yes."

She almost said something about his getting his money's worth, but she didn't want to bring that up. Not right now. Not after he'd made such wonderful love to her. Besides, her brain was tired from fighting.

She let her mouth ease into a smile. "I hope you don't plan on me wearing them all."

A surprised glint of amusement appeared in his eyes. "That was my intention."

"Good luck," she quipped, throwing the cover aside in an attempt to be blasé. Then she got up and slipped into the robe. "You're going to need it, mister."

A moment's silence met her ears, and she looked back at Jarrod behind her, only to find his eyes dark with desire.

He turned her in his arms to face him. "Lady, having you in that robe is all the luck I need," he murmured huskily, his gaze raking down her bare skin exposed by the open gown, making slow warmth heat her cheeks.

"Um…what about the pizza?"

"They deliver late."

He kissed her then and it turned her inside out, and soon he had slipped the robe back off her shoulders, slowly, slowly making love to her once more.

As Briana watched him enter her, she knew one thing. It was wonderful to be wanted by a man who wanted *her*. Not just Briana, the model.

Five

The sound of muffled voices out in the living room woke Briana the next morning, but it was the angry undertone in Jarrod's voice that made her sit up and listen. She hadn't quite heard that disdainful tone before. She'd been the recipient of his derision, but his voice held so much contempt she felt sorry for the other person.

"This is the last time, Anita," he was saying now, in a firm tone that brooked no argument.

"How can you say that, Jarrod? I'm your mother," a woman's voice said tearfully, making Briana gasp.

"You are *not* my mother. My mother is back in New Zealand looking after my sick father."

"And who gave you the opportunity to be a Hammond?" Anita said, her tone coldly unemotional now. "If it hadn't been for me, you would never have been given that silver spoon in your mouth."

He made a harsh sound. "Yes, I suppose that's the only decent thing you ever gave me."

"There you are, then. You should be grateful."

"Anita, don't pretend you gave me up for adoption for *my* sake. It was for *you,* and *you* alone."

Briana was out of bed by this time and slipping into the silk robe, curious in spite of herself. She had to see what Jarrod's real mother looked like.

"That may be so," Anita was saying as Briana tiptoed up to the bedroom doorway. "But I need money, Jarrod, otherwise I'll lose the house."

"That's not my concern," he snapped, as Briana carefully peeked around the doorframe and saw a petite, well-dressed blonde facing her hostile son. But even from here, Briana could see the hardness in her face. It was written clearly in her eyes and in the tight way she held her mouth. This woman was out for all she could get.

"You can spare ten thousand dollars for a loan, Jarrod. You probably make that much money every time you go to sleep."

"I work hard for my money. I invested it well."

"We're not all good money managers, son."

"Don't call me that," he growled, then swore and strode over to his briefcase and took out his checkbook. "This is it, Anita. This is all you're getting." He quickly wrote out the check, then shoved it at her. "Now here. Take it. And don't ever come back."

The woman greedily snatched the check, read the

amount, and her eyes widened with glee. She folded the paper and put it in her handbag. "I won't come back. I promise." A minute later, she left without a word of thanks, or regret, and Briana's heart squeezed with hurt for Jarrod. He didn't deserve a mother like that. No one did.

"You can come out now, Briana."

She stepped away from the door with as much aplomb as she could. "How did you know I was there?" she asked, moving into the living room.

"I heard the swish of your walk."

"Oh, you did not," she chided, slightly embarrassed. He'd been much too busy with Anita.

"I did." His eyes slid over her with lazy sensuality. "Like now."

The arm of the sofa was close by, so she casually sat herself down on it, her knees weak. Then she took a breath and concentrated on the woman who had angered him so much. "She'll come back, you know."

All at once, he turned toward the patio door, but not before she'd seen the bleakness in his eyes. "Yes, I know."

"Will you give her more money?"

His shoulders stiffened but he didn't turn around. "No. She's gotten enough out of me over the years."

She soaked up this information as she considered the tense line of his back beneath the gray polo shirt and black trousers. His clothes may be casual but their quality wasn't. Neither was the tumultuous feelings he must hold inside him.

"How long have you known her?" she asked, not sure he would share any information with her.

He remained where he was. Then, "Anita first came looking for money in my early twenties."

Her heart softened with sympathy. How terrible that his mother had come looking for money, and not her son. "Does she come often?"

"She turns up every couple of years and asks for a 'loan,'" he said, and this time he did spare her a look over his shoulder, his eyes filled with cynicism.

Briana stood up and went beside him. "You don't owe her anything," she said quietly.

"I know."

She put her hand on his arm. "But I guess it's hard to cut ties, no matter what she's done to you."

He glanced at her, put his hand over hers. "She never hesitated to give me up, you know," he said, surprising her with the admission. "She told me so the first time I met her. She said she'd been young and single, and a baby would have tied her down, and she'd had no intention of giving up her freedom."

Briana winced at the other woman's insensitivity. She hated thinking how he must have felt when he discovered she had so easily given him away. Up until then he had probably given his mother an excuse, some leeway, as to why she'd given him up. But to face the reality that she just hadn't wanted a baby, hadn't wanted *him*, and worse, that she hadn't cared, must have been a dreadful shock.

"She's just selfish, Jarrod. Lots of single mothers keep their babies, even back then."

He dropped his hand and turned to face her. "Exactly. If she'd given me up for *me*, then I could have forgiven her. But it was all for her." His jaw clenched. "I was better off without her."

"Absolutely." She paused, not sure whether to ask or not. "What about your real father?"

He shrugged. "Apparently he died years ago."

She arched a brow. "You were never curious about him?"

"No. Should I have been?" He grimaced. "Look, I was never curious about my birth parents. Never. I had a terrific upbringing and so did Matt. As far as I'm concerned, Katherine and Oliver Hammond are my real parents and Matt is my real brother."

Her throat almost closed up for a moment. "Good for you," she said huskily, and meant it. She was beginning to see a new side to the Hammond family that was no longer tarred by Marise's somewhat sarcastic comments. Not that she hadn't liked the Hammonds when she'd met them at Marise's wedding and the few times since. Only, now she could see a different dimension to them, and she liked what she saw.

She gave a slight smile. "It may sound crazy, but when I first heard how Howard believed his kidnapped son was alive, I thought for a moment it might have been you."

Jarrod snorted. "There's a thought. Son to Anita Stirling or Howard Blackstone? What a choice!" He shook his head. "No, I'm afraid I'm not the missing heir to the Blackstone fortune. Thank God!"

Briana had to agree with him. He'd been adopted by the Hammonds, raised by the Hammonds—he was a Hammond. To find out he actually belonged to his family's enemy would have been hard to take. And now that she knew how cruelly his mother had abandoned him, the blow would be doubly hard.

Not that he wouldn't rise above it, she knew, admiration stirring inside her with a new understanding of this man.

He put his hand under her chin, and for one heart-stopping moment held her gaze. Then he leaned forward and kissed her softly on the lips.

"Thank you," he said, lifting his head.

"For?"

"Listening. Understanding."

Her stomach fluttered like a butterfly's wings. "I'm told I have a good ear for listening."

He lifted a finger and ran it around her ear. "They're beautiful ears. Perfect." He placed his lips against it, then gently tugged at her lobe with this teeth.

She groaned as his lips began making their way down her throat. "Um—weren't we going to the—"

Where were they going?

Oh yes.

"—Moomba Festival?" she finished.

"After."

"After?" she murmured.

"After we make love."

Regardless of the way Jarrod made love to her—with a passion that hadn't diminished despite the numerous times he'd taken her in the last thirty-six hours—Briana didn't deceive herself that anything had changed.

And obviously he'd thought the same. He certainly seemed in a hurry to dress and leave the room afterward, saying he had some work to do before they went to the festival. That was probably so, but she suspected he needed some time to himself. It wasn't every day a man like him let a woman see his vulnerable side.

Still, she was relieved he had put up that wall of reserve again. It made her remember that the only reason they were together right now was the money.

So why fool herself that what she knew about him now made any difference? His dislike of the woman he thought she was hadn't changed. He still put her in the same category as Marise—and as his mother.

Having met the older woman, Briana felt doubly insulted. She got out of bed, showered and dressed in one of the outfits Jarrod had bought in the casino. It was either that or put on yesterday's clothes.

Then she left the bedroom and poured herself a much-needed cup of coffee. She was standing with her back against the black granite counter and sipping the hot liquid when Jarrod spoke from the doorway.

"You look great."

She glanced up into his approving gaze. "Thanks," she said somewhat sourly.

"I mean it," he said, obviously sensing her withdrawal.

"I know."

"And?"

"What do you want me to say, Jarrod? That I've been waiting all my life for you to come along and tell me how wonderful I look?"

His forehead creased in a deep scowl. "What's the matter with you?"

She took a deep breath and told herself to take things easy. Okay, so nothing had changed, but then had she really wanted it to? Besides, if he wanted to consider her a money-hungry gold-digger, then nothing she said or did would change his mind.

She pasted on a sickly sweet smile. "How can there be anything wrong when everything is so right?"

He shot her a wry look. "Yes, I can see that," he mocked, but there was also a guarded look in his eyes, as if he suspected she was feeling hurt because he'd shut her out after they'd made love.

Well, she wasn't.

She placed her cup on the sink and tried to sound casual as she said, "I know it's out of our way, but can we go to my apartment first? I'd like to get my camera so I can take some pictures of the festival."

His eyes gave a flicker of surprise. "I have a camera you can use."

"No, that's fine. I'd prefer to use my own camera. It's a very expensive one."

"And you think mine isn't?"

She conceded the point. "A camera's a rather— personal thing."

He scrutinized her response. "I never thought of it that way." Then studied her further. "You like taking pictures, do you?"

All at once she felt uncomfortable. "It's a change from being on the other side of the lens."

He stared hard for a moment longer. "Give me five minutes, then I'll be ready to go," he said, and turned and walked into his study.

An hour later, they'd found a good vantage point along Swanston Street. The Moomba Festival was Australia's biggest community festival and a Melbourne tradition for over fifty years, with firework shows, outdoor movies, the Moomba parade and lots of water-related activities on the Yarra River.

The parade was the highlight of the Moomba Festival and Melbourne families turned out in droves, creating a sea of color and excitement.

The celebrations continued in Alexandra Gardens and along the riverfront, with live entertainment, roving performers and water sports. Briana strolled next to Jarrod, clicking her camera whenever she saw something of interest. She particularly liked taking pictures of people's faces when they were unaware of it. She loved to capture the wondrous expression of a child watching a magician, or the parents watching that child with such love on their faces.

"Don't you get sick of people looking at you?" Jarrod asked after she'd taken a picture of a group of people who'd kicked off their shoes and were having dancing lessons.

She looked at him, startled. "Do they? I hadn't noticed."

"Everyone's recognizing you."

"Maybe it's the camera. Maybe they think I'm someone important."

"You *are* someone important."

She laughed that aside. "Only to my father."

He looked at her a moment or two, a rare, soft light entering his eyes.

Her heart skipped a beat. "What's the matter?"

"You are."

"Why?"

He gave a slight smile. "Maybe one day I'll tell you."

Just then someone jostled them and the moment was broken. She quickly glanced down and pretended to check a setting on the camera, his comment reminding her there never was going to be a "one day" for them.

When she looked up again, she trained her camera on some children having their faces painted. The thought that she and Jarrod were going their separate ways at the end of the month brought an unwelcome lump to her throat. Yet she didn't want to feel even the slightest bit miserable about that. So why did she?

"Do you like being a model?" Jarrod asked as they continued their stroll in the sunshine.

She stumbled a little and he put his hand out to steady her. "That's an odd question." She could feel his warm, firm touch through her sleeve. "Why do you ask?"

"You seem to have quite a talent behind the camera."

She was surprised by his perception. "Thank you. I enjoy it."

"Perhaps it'll turn into more than a hobby."

"Perhaps," she agreed in a noncommittal voice, and moved to take another photograph, making Jarrod drop his hand from her arm. She felt awkward, being unused to sharing her dream with anyone. Not even Patrick had noticed her talent for taking pictures. He'd been too busy complaining she had been ignoring him.

Just then she spied a vendor selling hot dogs, and her stomach growled, reminding her she hadn't eaten. "Hey, how about we get some hot dogs for lunch?"

"Pizza last night, hot dogs today. Sure you don't want to go to a restaurant?"

"No, this is fine." She glanced around. "Let's grab some food and go sit on that bench down there on the riverbank."

"Good idea."

A few minutes later, Briana placed her camera on the bench between her and Jarrod to keep it safe, and then she began eating her hot dog.

"You look like you're enjoying that," Jarrod remarked.

She nodded. "I am."

His eyebrow rose a fraction. "So you don't watch your weight?"

"Of course I do, but sometimes I like to break out." She prided herself on the fact that she wasn't anorexic thin like some of the other models. "Still, in the last two days I've eaten enough junk food to last me six months."

His gaze swept over her. "You've got the perfect figure."

She wondered why she didn't care about any other man's compliment, but Jarrod's stirred awareness inside her.

"Then maybe I should be the body of Blackstone's," she joked. "Perhaps I'll even get them to include that in my next contract."

A curious look came into his eyes. "So they're

offering you another contract, then?" he asked in a measured tone.

"I expect so." Her forehead creased. "You sound surprised. Why?"

There was a short pause. "I thought with all the controversy lately, the Blackstones might—"

"Drop me like a hot potato?" she cut across him, stiffening.

He inclined his head. "Something like that."

She suppressed a shiver, refusing to think right now about *not* being offered a new contract. So far no one had held Marise's antics against her. "You may not have noticed, but I was at Kim Blackstone's wedding. I'd like to think that was a good sign."

"Oh, I noticed," he drawled, a sexy timbre to his voice. "And yes, definitely a good sign."

Still, she needed to reiterate something. "Jarrod, as much as you don't like the Blackstones, they *are* professionals."

The lines of his face turned instantly rigid. "Howard Blackstone was never professional," he rasped.

That may be so but, "He was always good to me," she felt obliged to point out.

"And Marise?" he sneered. "Was he good to her, too?"

She sucked in a sharp breath. "What are you implying?"

"What everyone else is implying, Briana. That they were lovers."

"You have no proof."

His gaze sliced over her. "No, but a woman usually

doesn't leave her husband and child to spend time with another man just to be friends."

"Don't," she whispered, feeling a stab of fresh pain. She looked toward the river and away from Jarrod.

God, she hated to think about her own sister doing something like that, but she suspected he was right. She had tackled Marise about being seen with Howard, but had received a smug comment that she didn't know what she was talking about.

Perhaps if they'd been closer as sisters, Marise would have come to her when she and Matt were having problems. Only, they weren't close, and Briana had always felt guilty about that, yet realistically she knew she couldn't do anything about it. Marise had been her own worst enemy. She'd held people at a distance, then pulled them close when she wanted something from them. She knew her sister's faults as much as anyone.

Of course, it still didn't stop her from thinking that if she had been there for her sister, perhaps Marise might not have been with Howard on that plane…might not have died. It was a sobering thought.

"Was she having an affair with him, Briana?"

She looked back at Jarrod, held his gaze, definitely not appreciating the demand in his tone. "How do I know?"

A hint of anger entered his eyes. "You were her sister."

"Her sister. Not her keeper." A knot lodged firmly in her throat. "Look, Marise was my sister and I loved her dearly. And whatever she did, she did for a reason. I have no doubt about that."

Seconds ticked by. "She doesn't deserve your loyalty. She certainly wasn't loyal to my brother. Or to her son."

Briana bit her lip. She knew he was right but she couldn't say it out loud. She just couldn't betray her sister's memory in this way. She owed Marise a sister's loyalty and understanding. Somehow.

"How *is* Matt?" she asked quietly, trying to remain composed. "And Blake? Is he okay?" She hadn't seen Matt since Howard's funeral so she had no idea how her little nephew was doing. The poor little guy must be missing his mother terribly.

"As well as can be expected." Jarrod sent her a hard look, as if everything that had happened was *her* fault. "Rachel Kincaid is looking after him."

She tried to push his silent accusation aside. "Rachel Kincaid?"

"She's a nanny. Her mother is my parents' house-keeper."

She nodded. "Oh, yes. I remember her name now." She'd never met Rachel, but if Matt thought she was good enough to look after little Blake, then that was good enough for her.

A shutter came down over Jarrod's face. "The only decent thing to come out of all this was Blake."

Everything inside her squeezed tight with anguish. It was all such a mess. If only she could go back and somehow help change things. "I agree."

"Your sister left a legacy of heartache, Briana," he said in disgust, then tossed his half-eaten hot dog into the garbage bin a few feet away.

She winced inwardly, knowing it wasn't the food that disgusted him. "I know she did." Her own appetite totally lost now, she stood up and threw her own partially eaten hot dog in the bin before picking up her camera. She didn't bother to take the lens cap off, having lost her hunger for taking any more pictures today, as well.

After that, they walked around for another hour or so, watching the water-skiers and the bands playing music, but the day was flat now. She was quite relieved when Jarrod suggested he take her home, then oddly disappointed when he walked her to her door but only took a few steps inside her apartment.

"You're not staying?" she said before she could stop herself.

"No."

So that was that.

Weekend over.

She squared her shoulders and met his gaze. "This isn't going to work, Jarrod."

He shot her a level glance. "Yes, it is."

"But—"

"We had a deal, Briana. You'll be my mistress until the end of the month. But you'll be happy to know you're getting a small reprieve. I'm off to Singapore tomorrow for a conference."

"Singapore?" Relief warred with disappointment once more, and she told herself not to be silly. Just because he would be away shouldn't mean a thing. And because the following week she had to go to Brisbane, she should be happier about their having less time together.

So why wasn't she?

"What are your plans for next weekend?" he said, as if she had a choice in the matter.

She frowned. "I'm going to the Grand Prix on Sunday. I'm invited to lunch at the Blackstone corporate box."

He nodded to himself. "Okay, that'll work out well then. My plane lands just after lunch and I'm meeting some business acquaintances at one of the corporate boxes. I want you to join me as soon as you've finished with the Blackstones."

Surprise kicked in. "You don't mind being seen with me at a public function?"

He shrugged. "We'll be in a corporate box together, that's all."

"It could cause speculation in the papers," she warned.

"We'll worry about that when and if it happens."

She tilted her head, not exactly sure why they should bring attention to themselves.

"I'll call you on your mobile phone when I arrive at Albert Park," he said, cutting through her thoughts. "Make sure you take a taxi there because I intend taking you home."

All at once his arrogance got to her. "Is that another way of saying we'll be having sex afterward?" she snapped, deliberately sounding crude and as offensive as him.

His dark look said he didn't appreciate her comment. "I don't need to take you home for sex."

"No, you only need a checkbook."

"Shut up about the bloody money, will you?" he growled.

Her mouth dropped open in surprise, yet she'd seen a glint in his eyes that made her wonder who was more shocked by his reaction.

Then he appeared to bounce right back to his usual arrogant self. He gestured toward the telephone on the side table. "Answer your messages."

With difficulty, she drew her gaze away from his face, seeing the red light flashing on her answering machine. "They can wait."

He arched a brow. "Hiding something?"

She thought of her father and could feel herself blush a little. "No, of course not."

He looked at her sharply. "This deal of ours works both ways, Briana. Don't play me for a fool."

"I don't 'play' people, Jarrod," she told him, chin in the air.

"Is that so?" he said, not looking convinced, reminding her that once again memories of Marise rose between them. And it showed Briana that sex and mutual attraction were really all she and Jarrod had going for them.

She stepped aside but he pulled her into his arms. "No kiss goodbye?" he murmured silkily.

Not giving her a chance to reply, his mouth claimed hers in a hard, brief kiss that seemed to punish rather than enjoy. She pushed at his chest, and the pressure of his mouth eased…and then eased some more…and suddenly they were in the middle of a long, languorous kiss that did delicious things inside her blood, pulsing it through every pore of her skin, leaving his mark.

Eventually he put her away from him. "I look forward to having you in my bed again."

Then he headed for her door and closed it behind him, leaving her standing there for a moment, still tasting him in her mouth. Oh heavens. She looked forward to being back in his bed, too.

Thankfully the winking light on her answering machine drew her attention, and she pulled herself together and hurried to listen to the message. Nothing from her father, but Jake Vance had been in town for a couple of hours today and thought they might have lunch if she called him back before he left for Sydney again.

She discovered that Jake had also left the same message on her mobile phone, and she sighed with a hint of regret. She'd accidentally left her mobile on the sofa when she'd come rushing in earlier to get her camera. It would have been so much easier spending time with any man other than Jarrod. But she was committed to Jarrod now. Totally and irrevocably.

Until the end of the month anyway.

Six

Briana had attended the Grand Prix last year, so had previously witnessed the sensation of the world's fastest men racing at incredibly high speeds around the track. It was a four-day action-packed extravaganza of on-and-off-track activities, culminating in the main race on Sunday.

She knew the layout of the corporate boxes above the pit. Thankfully fumes weren't a problem but ear plugs were supplied for use during the races. Invitations were at a premium, so there was always a good turnout of high-profile guests.

Kim and Ric were in the box to greet her.

"Briana, hello," Kim greeted with a quick hug. "I was so looking forward to seeing you."

Briana was moved that Kim thought her worthy of a

friendly hug. "You, too." She offered Ric her hand. "Hello, Ric."

He took it. "She's talked of nothing else all week," he said with obvious affection for his new wife.

"I'm sure," Briana said with a wry smile. "How was the honeymoon? You went up to Leura, didn't you?"

Kim gave a happy sigh. "The mountains are just beautiful at this time of year. It was such a perfect time for us."

"But far too short," Ric added.

Kim smiled in appreciation. "Yes, far too short." Then her smile slipped a little, and her eyes held a hint of worry. "Unfortunately we couldn't take any longer."

Briana knew Kim must be thinking about the fallout from her father's death, and the many rumors in the business community, including the mysterious buy-up of the company shares.

Ric looped his arm around Kim's waist and pulled her in tight next to him. A look of support passed between husband and wife, confirming they would be okay no matter what happened to Blackstone's. They deserved their happiness.

Just then, Ryan Blackstone and Jessica Cotter came through the door. Pregnant with his twins, Jessica looked happy and healthy, with a still small baby bump.

Briana felt a lump in her throat. She was so pleased it had worked out for both couples. She just wished....

No, if she wished for the same thing for herself, then she'd have to find a man who was her soul mate. It had happened for her parents but she didn't really believe that would happen for her.

When most of the guests had arrived, Jessica patted the chair next to hers. "Come and sit down, Briana." She waited as Briana sat on the chair next to her. "Now," she said, lowering her voice. "Ryan and I are getting married next month, so you'd better be able to make it to the wedding, my friend." She named the date.

Delighted, Briana gave Jessica a quick hug, pleased that she would be back from her overseas assignment by then. "I wouldn't miss it for the world, Jess."

Jessica beamed. "Great. It's all going to be hush-hush, but I'll let you know the details later." She waited while the waiter passed behind her chair, then, "So what's happening with the diamonds? Have you heard back from Quinn yet? You dropped them off at his office after the wedding like you said, didn't you?"

Briana nodded. "Yes, I left them with his office manager. But I haven't heard anything so Quinn must still be away. He said it would be a few weeks." She'd had so much going on that she hadn't given the diamonds any thought. Being Jarrod's lover had kept her fully occupied.

And then some.

Even this past week she'd found herself thinking what he was doing at the conference in Singapore. He hadn't called, but she hadn't really expected him to.

Or had she?

Okay, so she had. She understood being busy, but just a quick phone call to say hello would have been thoughtful. After all, didn't being a temporary mistress afford her some consideration?

Obviously not.

"Is everything okay?" Jessica suddenly cut across her thoughts. "You look a little bit—oh, I don't know—tense."

Tense? That was an understatement. Trust Jessica to see through her.

"You're seeing someone, aren't you?" Jessica said, excitement in her voice.

"Kind of."

Jessica stared at her, then just as quickly pulled a face. "You're not back with Patrick, are you?"

Briana snorted. "Wash your mouth out with soap, Jessica Cotter."

"Thank heavens! That guy was such a sleaze."

Briana felt more than a flicker of surprise. "Why didn't you say something when I was going out with him?"

"Sweetie, you had stars in your eyes. Nothing I said would've mattered."

Briana cringed inwardly. That was probably true.

"So who's making you so tense?"

Briana thought about whether to tell Jessica or not. It was probably going to be in the papers soon enough anyway, once she met with...

"Jarrod," she admitted.

"Hammond?" Jessica squeaked.

"Yes. I'm meeting him this afternoon."

"Here?" At Briana's nod, she sent her a shrewd grin. "That's so great. He's such a hottie. If anyone deserves happiness you do."

"Happiness? Who's talking happiness? I'm meeting the guy for a drink," she fibbed, stretching the truth a little. "It's no big deal."

Jessica wagged a finger at her. "That's what I said when I first went out with Ryan."

Briana opened her mouth to speak, but one of the Blackstone clients interrupted them and she was glad to get off the subject.

She thought it was all forgotten, until Jessica came up to her after lunch and whispered, "He hasn't called yet?"

Briana's mind whirled in surprise. "How did you know he was going to call me?"

"Easy. You keep checking your mobile phone."

"Oh." She hadn't realized she was so obvious.

As if their conversation had conjured him up, Briana's phone rang. Her heart jerked inside her chest as she took the call.

"You answered," Jarrod said in a husky murmur that almost made her forget to take her next breath.

"You expected I wouldn't?" she murmured, keeping her voice low.

"Yes."

"Good." A ripple of anticipation shot through her. "I'm glad I keep you on your toes."

"Actually, I prefer to be lying down. With you."

She caught Jessica looking at her knowingly, and that brought her down to earth in a hurry. "Where are you?" she said, making her tone a shade cooler. If he knew she'd missed him, there'd be no end to his demands.

There was a slight pause. "Just getting out of my car," he said, his own tone cooler now. "Come down the stairs and meet me."

Cooler *and* arrogant, she decided. "Why don't you come up here and get me?"

"Is that wise?"

She realized why. He didn't want to meet up with Kim and Ryan again so soon. They may be cousins but there was still a huge gap between them and him.

"I'm only thinking of you," he added quietly.

He had a point. Why put herself under Blackstone scrutiny and put her contract renewal into jeopardy?

"Maybe this isn't such a good idea," Jarrod said out of the blue, surprising her. He wasn't a man who second-guessed himself, and having him do that now on her behalf made her heartstrings catch.

"Yes, it is," she murmured. "Come and get me, Jarrod."

And suddenly she knew she was doing the right thing. For Jarrod, not herself. For his family's sake he needed to touch base with the Blackstones whenever he could. He'd already attended the jewelry launch and the wedding, so he must at least want to try and breach the huge gulf between the Hammonds and the Blackstones.

She knew that Kim would not hold her involvement with Jarrod against her, short-lived as it would be. She just prayed that Ric and Ryan wouldn't either.

"I'll be there in five minutes," he said, an odd tone to his voice, and ended the call.

Briana turned off her phone and put it inside the pocket of her jacket.

"He's coming here?" Jessica said from behind Briana, startling her again.

Briana spun around. "Yes. I hope no one minds."

Jessica eased into an encouraging smile. "Of course they won't mind. He's family."

Briana ruefully shook her head. "Jess, you know as well as I do that there's family, and then there's *family*."

Jessica acknowledged the comment with a nod. "Yes, but I think it's time everyone stopped thinking about what Howard wanted and got on with their lives and with what *they* want."

"I think you're right," Briana agreed, as one of the clients came up to talk to her. For the next five minutes Briana chatted with her and Jessica, even as she kept her eye on the door.

And then the waiting was over, and Jarrod walked in the door like he'd never had a moment of doubt. He headed straight for her, making her heart skip a beat. He looked so handsome. So much a lover. And he was hers.

For now.

But before he could reach her, Kim called out his name in a surprised tone. "Jarrod?" She hurried over and kissed him on the cheek. "How lovely to see you here."

"Kim," Jarrod said, acknowledging her, and Briana swore she saw a trace of affection in his eyes for his cousin. She reminded herself that Kim had worked for Matt back in New Zealand, and Jarrod would have gotten to know her over the years. And just because Kim and Matt were now no longer talking...

"What are you doing here? Not that I mind. I just wasn't expecting you," Kim said as Ric and Ryan moved toward the pair, both men frowning.

Jessica went to move, but Briana beat her to it. "He's

come to collect *me*," she said, stepping forward, just stopping herself from slipping her arm through his. But her chin did angle with a touch of defiance. "Jarrod asked me to accompany him to one of the other corporate boxes and I said yes."

There was a shocked silence.

Kim recovered first with a warm smile. "How nice. But please don't run off just yet. Stay for a drink with us."

Briana watched Jarrod look from Ryan to Ric and back, his shoulders tensing. The two men were standing either side of Kim like a pair of guards. For a moment she thought Jarrod was going to refuse.

"I'd be happy to," he said, his gaze telling the other men he wasn't backing away. That he intended to stay as long as he wanted.

A moment crept by, and it flashed through Briana's mind that perhaps they should leave after all. Jarrod had proven his point.

But before she could say anything, Ric said, "I'll get you a whiskey." He strode away to the bar area and everyone watched him go like he had taken their tongues with him.

Kim asked Jarrod how his parents were doing, and Jessica asked another question, and before too long Ric was back with a whiskey, and talk turned to general things, if a little awkwardly.

Briana stood there and joined in when she could, but she was aware of the speculation in everyone's eyes as they glanced back and forth from her to Jarrod. Did they know she and Jarrod were lovers? Jessica and Kim probably suspected it, but she was certain Ric and Ryan knew. She could see it in their eyes. It was that all-male, all-knowing look that held a new and growing respect for Jarrod for bedding her.

And Jarrod noticed, she was sure. She could tell by the pleased expression on his face. Soon he'd be strutting around like a rooster in a barnyard.

Thankfully Jarrod finished his drink and they took their leave. While Briana was glad to see a slight improvement in the relationship between the men, she didn't like it being at her expense.

As they were heading along the corridor toward the other corporate box, Jarrod drew her into another passageway off on the side where it was quiet.

"What are you—" she began.

He covered her mouth with his for the longest moment, and her legs weakened. She had to grip his forearms to hold herself up.

Eventually he pulled back. "I missed kissing you," he murmured, turning her heart over in response.

She noted he didn't say he missed *her.* He missed *kissing* her. But that's all a man like Jarrod would allow.

"That must be a new feeling for you."

He chuckled in a low throaty sound. "It is actually." Then his gaze lowered over her very feminine, grape-colored suit. "By the way, I love your outfit."

All at once the pleasure on his face reminded her of that rooster look back there. "They know we're lovers, Jarrod."

He frowned. "Who?"

"Ric and Ryan."

His face cleared. "So?"

"You let them think it to boost your ego," she accused.

"No, I didn't."

"You did. You—" He kissed her again, and this time his kiss was even longer and deeper, as if he was trying to stop all thought.

He succeeded.

She sighed deeply with delight.

But when he finally ended the kiss, he didn't wait for her to respond. He took her by the elbow. "Come on. Let's get this afternoon out of the way. I want to take you home and make love to you."

Before she could say anything else, let alone protest, he led her along the corridor until they reached one of the corporate boxes. A Grand Prix staff member immediately opened the door, but not before Briana saw Jarrod's company name on the nameplate. Her head cleared from his kiss.

"You didn't tell me this was *your* box," she said in a low voice as they stepped inside.

He spared her a glance. "Didn't I mention that?"

"No." But then, why should he? If temporary mistresses didn't warrant phone calls from Singapore, then she probably didn't warrant knowing this.

He led her over to a group of men and women about to watch the race. As he began to introduce her, one of the men stood up. "No need to introduce this lovely lady, Jarrod. We all know who Briana is." He smiled at her. "You're certainly a sight for sore eyes, young lady."

Briana put on her model's smile. She didn't always enjoy meeting new people but she never let it show. Most people were genuinely nice.

And then she *did* begin to enjoy herself. And as she saw how the others held Jarrod in high regard, something inside her warmed to him, and before long the incident back at the Blackstone corporate box was mentally filed away. He was a good escort and included her in the conversation, never leaving her side. For a while she let down her guard and forgot all about the family issues between them.

She even caught him watching her with a lazy smile that made her toes curl, and she suddenly felt even more amiable toward him. "I have something to confess. Remember when I said I wasn't taking any of the clothes you bought me at the casino?"

An alert look entered his eyes. "Yes."

"I lied. I took one of the outfits and wore it when I was leaving. I didn't want anyone seeing me wearing the same dress from the night before."

"Obviously you feel safe telling me this while we're in a crowd," he drawled.

"Of course," she said with a shrug and a smile. "But I plan on giving it back to you."

"Keep it."

"No."

"Will you stop being so damn stubborn?" he said in mild exasperation. "The boutique won't take it back, and I certainly have no use for it."

He was right. "Well, when you put it like that…" she

said with a wink, then turned to reply to a question from the gentleman seated on the other side of her.

Jarrod felt the blood rush to his groin at that wink. She'd never been playful before and it had caught him by surprise. He was more than a little charmed, in fact.

Of course he'd always been charmed by her whether she smiled at him or not, he decided as he watched Briana work her magic on his guests during the afternoon. She laughed at exactly the right moments, listened when she needed to, told some modeling anecdotes, and genuinely seemed to be enjoying herself. Not only was she beautiful and intelligent, but he could see that her work ethic was beyond question. She appeared to be a woman with high morals. She wasn't flirting with the other men, or making the women feel less in her presence. Yet he couldn't deny she had slept with him for money.

So why did she appear to have a conscience about that, considering the type of person she supposedly was, according to her sister? That made him wonder now if Marise had been playing games. The other woman had been excellent at stirring up trouble over the years. Certainly she'd played games with Matt, so why not with *him?* More importantly, why had he believed her?

Looking back, all those suggestions about Briana liking money had made sense at the time, but he'd seen no hint of Briana overspending, or of her having a good time now. The Briana he'd been with these past few weeks just wasn't the same person he'd expected from Marise's comments.

Hell, Marise wouldn't have put her Blackstone contract in jeopardy for him as Briana had today. And he sure as hell wouldn't have discussed his adoption with someone like Marise, nor would he have missed Marise like he'd missed Briana in Singapore this past week. It was the reason he hadn't called. He hadn't liked the effect Briana was having on him and he had been determined to ignore it—and her. Now he wished he hadn't. He'd been the poorer for not hearing her sexy voice.

Late afternoon, Jarrod decided to hand over the event to his second-in-charge. They said their goodbyes and were just reaching his BMW when he heard another man call Briana's name. Thinking it was one of her fans he was surprised when a tall, well-dressed man walked up to them and kissed Briana on the cheek.

"Patrick!" she said, and Jarrod saw her face reflect dismay before she quickly schooled her features.

"You're looking gorgeous as ever," this Patrick said, his gaze sliding over her in a way that ate her up.

She glanced at Jarrod as if she knew he wouldn't be pleased, then back at the other man. "What are you doing here?"

"Drinking lots of champagne and enjoying the sights," Patrick said. "And you're one of them." He pulled her toward him and kissed her again. "It's good to see you."

Jarrod watched her step back as fast as she could, and decided it was time to stake his claim. He moved in closer and put his arm around her waist. "Aren't you going to introduce us, Briana?"

Her mouth tightened, though whether because of him or this Patrick he wasn't sure. "Jarrod, this is Patrick. He *used* to be my business manager," she said pointedly.

Definitely meant for Patrick, Jarrod mused. But he could feel her tenseness against him, so it must not have been a friendly parting, on Briana's part at least.

Patrick's slyly amused gaze noted his hand on her hip. "Oh, but we were much more than that, weren't we, Bree?"

Something fierce slammed into Jarrod's gut when he heard this guy call her the nickname. It confirmed what he'd already suspected.

"Were we?" she said coolly.

Patrick quietly chuckled as he looked at Jarrod. "Women! They never forget a thing."

Jarrod's hand must have tightened on her hip because she winced. He relaxed his hold but that didn't stop the feeling that this other guy was a jerk. For the first time in years he wanted to hit another man.

Patrick didn't seem to notice anything out of the ordinary. "I'm really sorry to hear about your mother. And Marise, too."

She inclined her head but her eyes remained cold. "Thank you."

"Look, I don't suppose you want to meet up later for a drink," he said to Briana, and Jarrod had no doubt *he* wasn't included in the invitation.

"No thanks, Patrick. I'm busy."

Patrick looked disappointed but there was a cold gleam in his eyes. "Well, if you change your mind, you know how to find me."

Jarrod's jaw clenched. These two had a past and he didn't like it. Not one bit. Nor did he like the implication that Briana could easily call this idiot and slip into bed with him.

"Goodbye, Patrick," Briana said, then walked to the car a few feet away.

Jarrod shot the other man a hard look then followed her. He didn't say anything as he unlocked the car door, then held it open for Briana. By the time he came around the other side, Patrick was no longer in sight.

He wanted to say something to her about it but noted she had a withdrawn look that said she didn't want to talk. He allowed her that. He could wait.

Once inside his apartment, he could wait no longer. "How long were you and Patrick together? As lovers, that is."

Wariness clouded her blue eyes, but her chin lifted. "A year."

"He's the one, isn't he?" he said, sounding calmer than he felt. "He's the one who stole your trust."

"He stole more than my trust," she said with a touch of bitterness, then seemed to freeze.

"Go on."

She hesitated only briefly. "He invested all my hard-earned savings and lost the lot."

Jarrod swore. "How?" Then he listened as she explained what the other man had done. He swore again.

"The guy looks like a con-artist to me. I could check it out for you. I *am* a property lawyer, after all."

"No!" she blurted, then seemed to pull herself together. "Look, I thoroughly checked the paperwork before I handed over anything to him and it was all aboveboard. I realize now he just gets involved in schemes that sometimes work out, sometimes don't. My one didn't."

He suddenly didn't like the way she was defending the other man so readily. "You still have feelings for him?"

A derisive sound emerged from her throat. "To tell you the truth, I don't know what I ever saw in Patrick."

Relief washed through him, but, "Then why defend him?"

"I wasn't. I—" She stopped, and started again. "Look, what Patrick and I had is dead and gone." Her mouth tightened. "And that's all I'm going to say on the matter."

Something wasn't quite right, but he felt that "something" was to do more with Briana than Patrick. He was sure of it. And it occurred to him that perhaps this was the reason she had slept with him.

"So you recouped your losses by taking my million dollars?"

Her eyelids flickered. "Yes. It was the only way I could get some money."

He saw she had hesitated. And that meant she wasn't telling him the truth. At least, not the *whole* truth.

"Why did you take the million dollars, Briana?" he asked silkily.

Her gaze darted past his shoulder, then back again. "You already have your answer, Jarrod."

"Do I?" He recognized evasion when he saw it. He was a lawyer for God's sake. He knew how to respond to a question without actually giving an answer. And she was doing it well.

Too well.

He started to demand she tell him everything, only he looked at the stubborn angle of her chin and knew she had gone as far as she would go right now. He would bide his time.

Yet suddenly time was the one thing that was running out for them. He pulled her close and started to make love to her, a tenseness in him that for the moment had less to do with knowing Patrick had been her lover, and more to do with letting Briana go.

Briana spent the weekend with Jarrod then had a couple of days at her apartment to prepare for her Brisbane trip on the Wednesday. After all, staying in top shape and looking good kept a model busy.

Still, she couldn't shake the unsettled feeling she'd had since seeing Patrick at the Grand Prix. She had hated running into him. He brought back too many unpleasant memories.

But it had been Jarrod's reaction to Patrick that worried her more than the meeting itself. Could he have been jealous? The thought made her feel light-headed, as if the oxygen had just been sucked from the room.

On the other hand, perhaps he just didn't like another

man wanting what he had, especially if it was an ex-lover. Yes, that sounded more like it, she mused, as she stepped out of the shower and heard the phone ringing.

"I'm taking you to the airport," Jarrod said before she could speak.

She frowned. She didn't have to leave for two hours. "But you'll be at work."

"I'm taking you."

"Why? Don't you think I can find it myself?" she quipped, but she felt uneasy. This wasn't just about him being his usual, arrogant self. This was about him having what Patrick wanted.

"Did it occur to you that I just might like to spend a bit more time with you?"

"Actually, no."

There was a small pause. "Your loss," he said and hung up the phone.

Briana winced. Had she misread him after all? She wasn't sure, but she knew he was right about it being her loss. Any woman would think her mad for missing the opportunity to spend more time with Jarrod Hammond.

But she didn't call him back.

And she didn't call him while she was away either. Nor did he attempt to call her.

The three days went quickly, and Briana was more than a little anxious to see how things were between them once she was back in Melbourne.

Her mind was fully on Jarrod when early evening on Good Friday she stepped off the plane at Tullamarine Airport in Melbourne and got the shock of her life.

Patrick was waiting for her as she wheeled her small suitcase through the lounge gate.

Her mouth dropped open. "Patrick! What are *you* doing here?"

He kissed her cheek, a cold smile lifting the corners of his mouth. "Striking while the iron's hot."

Apprehension rushed through her. "What do you mean?"

"We need to talk."

Her misgivings increased. "Now?"

"It would be in your best interests if you did."

A feeling of uneasiness went through her. "Patrick, whatever my interests are they don't concern you any longer." She went to step past him. "Now, if you'll excuse me."

He put his hand on her arm. "Your father may not agree," he warned, his "Mr. Charming" persona wearing thin.

"Wh—what?" He couldn't possibly know. He couldn't. Just couldn't.

"That got your attention, didn't it?" he said, looking pleased with himself. "Come on. Let's talk over a drink."

"But—" She was still reeling. Still trying to take all this in.

"This way," he said, guiding her forward, his hand on her elbow.

Briana was stunned, her mind going over all the possibilities. If he had said anything else, she would have told him to get lost. But mentioning her father was disturbing.

He took her to a bar along the walkway, then sat her

down near one of the large windows where she could watch the planes take off. She wished she was on one of them right now. She had a feeling she wasn't going to like what he had to say.

"How was your flight?" he asked, once he'd bought their drinks.

She glowered at him. "Cut to the chase, Patrick. What do you want?"

A moment passed, his stare drilling into her. "You're going to Asia soon."

Her forehead creased in a frown. "Yes. So?"

"I want to be reinstated as your business manager. I'm coming with you."

She made a derisive noise. "No chance."

"Is that so?" he said, a lethal calmness in his eyes that worried her.

She shook her head, trying to make him see reason. "I don't understand, Patrick. *Why* do you want to be my business manager again? It didn't work out the first time."

He paused, as if deciding how much to say. "Things haven't been the same since we parted. I need to renew some high prestige connections, and two weeks with you in Hong Kong, Taiwan and China should do it."

"Maybe you should have thought of that before you lost all my money in a bad investment," she choked, not in the least sorry for him. Yet she blamed herself, too. She shouldn't have taken his advice and gotten a second opinion.

"It was a good investment, Briana. It just went wrong." Just as quickly, he pasted on a sly smile. "But then, it's easy to get tangled up in something bigger than ourselves at times, don't you think?"

What was he implying? "Look, I don't know what you're hinting at, but just say what you have to say so I can go home."

"Okay then." He waited for effect. "I *know* what your father's been doing."

She tried not to flinch. "And that is?"

"Stealing money from Howard Blackstone."

Her heart dropped to her feet, but she forced herself not to react. Whatever he knew, he may not be certain. "I don't know what you're talking about."

"Don't play games," he said cynically. "Remember last year when your parents went on that world cruise? Remember how you suggested I stay at their house for a week when my apartment flooded?"

"Yes." Surprising how even then she hadn't wanted Patrick moving in with her, not even for a week. She had the feeling she wouldn't get rid of him, and her parents' house had been a blessing. Or so she'd thought at the time.

"I was using your father's laptop one night because mine was having problems—I think some water had got into it," Patrick said in an aside that made her want to snap at him to get on with it. "And I found something interesting. There was some bank information on it that at the time I didn't realize meant much. It's only now that I've put two and two together."

"Really? That's amazing. But I don't know how you can come to the conclusion my father stole from Howard Blackstone."

"Give me a moment to explain," he said as if he was talking to a two-year-old. Then he deliberately took time to sip his drink before answering. "Okay. It was only after I saw you the other day at the Grand Prix I was thinking about that world cruise and how your parents could pay for it. Your father had retired from his job and your mother was dying at the time, only none of us knew it."

There wasn't even a hint of sympathy in his voice, Briana noticed.

"You had no money to spare, either," he continued. "It was all tied up in your investment. And Marise was over in New Zealand, your parents rarely saw her, and I'm sure if she had loaned them the money I would have heard about it."

His touch of cynicism for Marise was justified, Briana admitted. "So?"

"Well, then I got to wondering how your father paid for everything—the cruise, the medical treatments. And it all fell into place. Your father used to be Howard Blackstone's accountant. All those figures and dates and an account called 'Black Rock' got me doing some investigating. And what I discovered was *very* interesting."

Her hand tightened around her wineglass. "You're making this up."

"Fine. Then let's go the police and I'll get them to check things out. I'm sure they'd be more than interested in anything to do with Howard Blackstone and his death in that plane crash."

Her heart slammed against her ribs. "My father had nothing to do with the plane crash!"

"No, but I'm sure they'd have to investigate everything I tell them anyway."

He was right. Even the suggestion of her father being involved in the crash would be enough to have the police checking out everything to do with their lives.

Defeated, she slumped back against the chair. "So you want two weeks as my business manager?"

His eyes flared with triumph. "In writing." He took a piece of paper out of his jacket pocket and slid it across the table like a snake. "Sign this."

She opened the paper and began reading with a numbness that was comforting. "You've certainly thought of everything."

"Everything except you becoming my lover again," he said in a deceptively relaxed voice. "I don't think we need write that down, do we?"

She shoved the paper at him. "No way. That's not part of the deal. I won't sleep with you, Patrick." Why, just the thought of it turned her stomach. After Jarrod....

He fixed her with a stare. Then, "Okay, we won't become lovers," he relented, and pushed the paper back for her to sign. "But I don't want anyone else knowing that. To the world, we're lovers again. It's the only way I'm going to renew my contacts."

Relief washed through her. There was no way she could have given in to that demand. She had slept with

Jarrod because she'd wanted to. That wouldn't be the case with Patrick.

"What happens after the two weeks and they realize we're no longer an item?" she asked.

"By then I'll have signed up Lily Raimond. She's going to be the next big superstar." His lips twisted. "Move over, Briana."

"Gladly."

He considered her. "You never did realize what power you had at your fingertips."

She ignored that as she picked up the pen and signed. "You stick to your end of the bargain and so will I. Otherwise, my father or not, I'll tell the police about your blackmail—and the rape." She watched his face blanch and felt a measure of power. "Because that's what it will be if you touch me, Patrick."

He folded the paper and put it in his jacket pocket. "I don't remember you being so reluctant to be in my arms before," he scoffed but she could see fear in his eyes.

She stood up. "Think again."

Seven

Briana wasn't sure how long she sat in her car at the airport car park. One minute the sun was setting, the next it was dark and the overhead lights were on. She needed some time to think and sort things out. There was no getting around Patrick over this, of that she was certain.

How on earth had he figured it all out? It wasn't like the account had been one of Howard's regular ones. It was a "secret" account, for heaven's sake. An obscure account in the bowels of some banking institution somewhere in the world, which no one had known about except her father, Howard's previous accountant and Howard himself. And the last two men were now dead.

But Patrick was experienced at walking that fine line between legal and illegal, and like a dog who'd sniffed out a buried bone, he had unearthed the one crime committed from her father's lapse in judgment.

Now she had to phone her agent, who would declare her absolutely crazy to even *think* about reinstating Patrick as business manager, let alone doing it.

And then there was Jarrod.

Oh God.

Yet what business was it of Jarrod's anyway, she asked herself a touch defiantly. He only wanted her for the rest of the month, and after that she was free to do what she liked. Even if she wasn't going to be Patrick's lover, it shouldn't matter to Jarrod what she did with the rest of her life.

So why was she worried? She'd end her relationship with Jarrod, go away on assignment with Patrick, and after that it would be rare that she ran into Jarrod again.

And if at some time he heard she was back with her ex-business manager, well, Jarrod hadn't wanted her anyway.

She felt sick at heart at the thought of it all, but despite everything she suddenly wanted to see Jarrod. Wanted to be in his arms, feel his reassuring presence, even if that reassurance was all in her mind.

But as soon as she pressed his buzzer, she knew she'd made a mistake in coming here. The last time they'd spoken, he'd hung up on her for not letting him take her to the airport. And heavens, what if he had decided to come and get her today? If he'd seen her with Patrick and somehow found out about her going away with Patrick, then that meant the end for them now instead of ten days time. Suddenly those ten days were so extra precious…

She turned back toward the elevator just as he opened his door. "Hey, you're not going anywhere," he said, pulling her into his apartment and into his arms. He kicked the door shut behind them and kissed her, and once again she melted into him.

Then he slowly broke off the kiss. "I think I missed you."

Her heart thudded at his words. He wasn't saying he missed *kissing* her, like he'd said last time. This time he missed *her.* Oh Lord. What did that mean? Did he actually have feelings for her?

She prayed not. Jarrod was not for her. Especially now, not with Patrick blackmailing her. Things would be just too complicated.

She swallowed her anxiety and managed to tease him with, "You only think?"

"If I said I missed you for sure, you'd do that female thing and assume you have a hold over me."

He had it wrong. It would be the other way around. "Actually, I wouldn't."

His intense blue eyes riveted on her face. "You really wouldn't, would you?"

"No."

He didn't give her a chance to reply. He began kissing her again and she kissed him back, and suddenly she felt desperate for him. She so badly needed his touch right now. When all this ended she wanted to remember being in his arms.

Afterward, Jarrod came back from the bathroom and sat on the edge of the bed. "You okay?"

She looked away, then back. She couldn't let him find out about Patrick. "I'm fine. Just a bit tired, I guess."

His eyes seemed to probe her own. "Your job's pretty time-consuming, isn't it? Not to mention sheer hard work."

She almost felt dizzy at his words. It wasn't just his acknowledgement of the many hours she put into her job. It was the growing respect in his eyes. She hadn't felt that from him before.

"Yes, Jarrod, it is," she said, knowing that if she had achieved one thing in their time together, it was this.

His gaze held hers for a moment, then, as if he had better things to do, his face went blank and he pushed himself off the bed. "I'll make us something to eat," he muttered.

Briana watched him leave the room and sighed. He may have new respect for her now, but that respect obviously didn't extend to asking if she actually *wanted* to eat.

And right now she wasn't sure she could.

Briana felt refreshed when she woke the next morning, lying spoon-fashion in front of Jarrod, his hand resting on her thigh. She glanced at the clock and saw it was almost ten and suddenly felt guilty for lying in so late. She had things to do today, including visiting her father and preparing for a fashion show next week and—

It all came rushing back with a vengeance then.

She was being blackmailed.

God, how was she going to find the strength of will to get through this? She wasn't sure she even could. No matter how much she tried, her modeling career, her future monies, would always be tied to Patrick now. He would make sure of that.

Next to her, Jarrod rolled onto his back and for a moment she froze. Last night when she'd arrived, he'd kissed her and they'd ended up making love, but she didn't want that to happen this morning. She needed to get moving.

Thankfully, he continued sleeping, and she slid out of bed and pulled on the oyster-silk robe. He'd brought up her suitcase from her car late last night, so she'd shower in the other bathroom so as not to wake him, then dress and leave him to sleep in peace.

Right before she left, she peeked in on Jarrod again. He was still sleeping, the sheet low on his taut hips, his naked chest muscular and arrowed with hair, a dark shadow of hair on his jaw making him look manly, short rumpled hair on his head very sexy. God, he was incredibly handsome.

Then she saw the dark circles under his eyes, and she felt bad for sneaking out like this. As much as she wanted to run, the least she could do was make him breakfast before she left.

Five minutes later, she'd just finished dishing a fluffy omelet onto a plate when she heard a noise behind her. She spun around.

"So…" Jarrod snarled, behind her in the doorway, making her jump, "it's over between you and Patrick, is it?"

One look at his face and at the newspaper in his hand which he must have collected from outside his door and her heart began to thud. Had they found out about her father? Had Patrick told anyway?

He strode toward her and held the newspaper up in her face. "You call *this* being over?"

She placed the frying pan back on the stove and snatched the paper from Jarrod. Then she glanced at the page and groaned inwardly even as relief surged through her. The papers hadn't found out about her father's embezzlement. This was a picture of her and Patrick at the airport bar yesterday. The caption read "Is Briana Doing *Business* With Her Ex Again?"

"Jarrod, this isn't what you think. I—"

"Am playing me for a fool," he said through gritted teeth.

"No!"

"You can't deny it, Briana. You were even wearing the same outfit." He stabbed her picture with his finger to prove his point.

"Jarrod, look, I'm not trying to deny it," she said, struggling to maintain an even tone. "Patrick *was* there at the airport, but he only came to meet me because—"

"He met you!"

"Yes, he was there when I came off the plane. He wanted to discuss something."

"I can imagine," he said, his voice dripping sarcasm.

She ignored that. She had to stay cool, but she had to think quickly. "It's about an assignment at the end of the month. We're both connected to it and needed to discuss it, and I had to sign some paperwork." It was her turn to stab at the picture. "See, I've even got his pen in my hand. And see, that's the paperwork on the table in front of me."

His mouth clamped in a thin line. "Why didn't you mention this last night?"

She handed the paper back to him and squared her shoulders. "I've done nothing wrong. And despite what you think, I don't have to report to you."

"And that's all it was?"

She met his gaze. "Yes," she lied.

"And there's nothing you want to tell me?"

There was plenty, but her hands were tied. "No," she said, concealing her inner turmoil. "Look, do you think if I was having an affair, I would be sitting in a bar in public with my ex-business manager?"

"Perhaps it's what you did after that—" he suggested, evidently not totally convinced of her innocence.

"I came straight here after that. You can check the time my flight landed." She paused. "So you see, Jarrod, *you're* my alibi."

He scowled at her but didn't say anything.

She arched a brow. "So what's the verdict?"

"I'm reserving judgment for the time being."

All at once this was about more than convincing him nothing was going on between her and Patrick. This was about Jarrod believing she wasn't like Marise. About him trusting her, even as a transient in his life. It may not matter to him, but it mattered to her.

"That's not good enough, Jarrod," she said, standing her ground. "You either think I'm guilty or not guilty."

He held her gaze for the longest moment, then expelled a slow breath. "Okay, not guilty."

Something inside her leaped with joy. If he hadn't believed her they could have gone no further in their relationship. She would be out that door without a backward glance, million dollars still owing or not.

He tilted his head. "I just don't understand how you can have dealings with someone who did the wrong thing by you."

"And like you don't deal with people in your world that you dislike?" she gently scoffed.

He stood there for a moment, then nodded. "You're right. My world is full of people I dislike. It comes with being a lawyer." A glint of wry humor entered his eyes. "I'm usually only involved when someone is getting screwed around."

"There you are then. Having dealings with Patrick is just business, Jarrod. He may have lost my money, but he didn't steal it."

He held her gaze a moment more, then, "Fine."

It was time for a diversion. She looked down at the omelet on the plate. "Your breakfast is cold now."

"So I see. Where's yours?"

She shrugged. "I'm not hungry. I was just cooking this for you before going to see my dad."

His eyes went over her tight jeans, thin knit top hugging her breasts, up to her ponytail but he didn't say anything, though she saw an appreciative light come in them. "You go then. I'll heat this up. Thanks."

"You're welcome." She noted he wasn't stopping her,

and that was just as well. Despite them sorting it out she could still feel things were a bit uneasy between them.

"Are you doing anything tomorrow?" he suddenly said.

"No." That meant she must not be seeing him tonight. It was crazy to feel disappointed but it was probably for the best. It was Saturday night anyway, and she'd had a vague plan to invite her father over for dinner.

"Let's go for a drive down the coast and spend the day at the beach. We can enjoy the last of the warm weather."

She blinked in surprise. "As long as you don't expect me to go swimming," she teased, trying not to show how upset she really felt about everything. "The water's far too cold now."

"No, we'll have a picnic." He gave a bit of a smile that seemed forced to Briana. "I'll be disappointed not to see you in a swimming costume."

She could feel her cheeks grow hot and said the first stupid thing that came to mind. "But you've seen me without my clothes."

Oh heavens!

Desire flared in his eyes and nothing seemed forced now. "That I have." He lifted her chin and placed a soft kiss on her lips. "You are so damn beautiful," he murmured, like he'd never get enough of staring at her. "You really don't know how beautiful, do you?"

She gave a self-conscious shrug. "I look in the mirror every day."

He shook his head. "It's hard to believe a woman so beautiful is so totally unaware of herself."

"Well, you know what they say about beauty."

"Skin deep? No, I'm talking about *you,* Briana. Not the model."

Happiness bubbled up inside her, but she kept it hidden. Everything was going to be okay between them. "Well, right now Briana 'the daughter' had better go and see Ray 'the father' so that I can invite him to dinner tonight."

A humorous gleam came into his eyes. "I'll pick you up at noon tomorrow."

Happy, she stepped around him and hurried out of the apartment. That bubbly feeling stayed with her until she walked into the kitchen of her old home and her father told her he was having trouble putting the money back in Howard's account.

Then the bubble burst.

Her heart sank.

"What do you mean, Dad? How can you take the money out but not put it back?"

He tried to look unconcerned, but she knew he was worried. "Some of the accounts are under scrutiny since Howard's death. And I'm just being extra careful." He hugged her. "Now don't you worry, honey. I'll put the money back and then I'm going to get a job to help you pay Jarrod back his loan. It's time I returned to work anyway."

She frowned at him. "Dad, it's okay. I'll be signing my new contract with Blackstone's soon," she said with more confidence than she felt.

"But that's *your* money. You shouldn't have to use it to help me."

"It isn't just for you, Dad. It's for Mum, too."

His eyes softened with tenderness and love. "You're a good girl, Briana." Then pain crossed his face. "I just don't know where we went wrong with Marise. I know your mother felt she needed more attention than you did, but I didn't always agree. We had many a fight over it, you know."

She gaped in shock. "You did?"

He nodded. "I think your mother's attitude helped make Marise the way she was." He gave a shaky sigh. "God help me, but I shouldn't be speaking of the dead this way."

She put her hand on his shoulder and squeezed comfortingly. "Dad, it's okay. I know Mum loved me."

"Yes, she did, honey. Very much," he said in a choked voice, then shuddered and took a deep breath.

Briana waited for him to regain his composure. "You know," she said gently, "we have to put all this behind us now. We can't change the past and we can't beat ourselves up about it." Easier said than done, she knew.

He offered her a hint of a smile. "You're right, honey."

"Of course I am." She pasted on a bright smile. "Now, how about you come around my apartment this evening for a nice dinner? Just you and me."

"That would be great." He paused. "But I don't want to be a bother. I know you have lots of friends and—"

Suddenly she saw the question in his eyes. "Dad, I know you must have seen the newspaper photo of Patrick and me. And no, we're not back together. I was only meeting him because he has something to do with an assignment I'm on at the end of the month."

The worry in his eyes cleared. "Good. I was never real fond of him." He hesitated. "I like Jarrod, though."

They'd never spoken of Jarrod, but there'd probably been a picture or two of her with him at the Grand Prix. She'd seen a couple of journalists clicking their cameras in their direction, and that had made her even more thankful she'd let the Blackstones know she was seeing him. At least there were no surprises.

"I've been going out with Jake Vance, too," she pointed out wryly.

"I know," he said, just as wryly, his comment reminding her she was news no matter whom she dated. "But there's just something about you and Jarrod Hammond."

Yes, and it was called sexual attraction.

"I guess we've bonded over Marise and Matt. Now, what time are you coming over tonight?"

His smile said he realized she was changing the subject. "I'll be there at six."

Jarrod had stood on the balcony and watched Briana's car drive away. Hell, the last few days while she'd been in Brisbane, he'd checked out this Patrick and found the investment made with Briana's money had all been legal, unfortunately. In the end, Jarrod had put it all to the back of his mind.

And then he'd opened the newspaper to the picture of her and Patrick together. He'd felt like someone had punched him in the gut. She'd made a deal with *him* and he expected her to honor that, not go off and jump in the sack with an ex-lover. Even now the thought of it made him see red. She was *his* for the moment.

So he'd had a few bad moments about believing her when she said nothing physical was going on between her and Patrick. But dammit, he was still confused as to why she would do business with her ex-business manager. Did she want to or didn't she have a choice?

His jaw clenched. No, he wasn't going to doubt her. He'd said he believed her and he did. And to be fair, she was right about one thing. There were plenty of people in his world he disliked, but he still did business with them regardless. Why would the modeling world be any different, he asked himself as he went to take a shower, passing by the rumpled sheets on the bed that suddenly made him want her back here.

So why had he let her leave?

Why not spend the rest of the day with her?

And the night as well?

He grimaced. Because the shock of that picture in the paper had made him feel exposed in more ways than one. It had made him admit to himself that for most of the week while she'd been in Brisbane, he'd been unable to concentrate fully on his job. And he hadn't liked it. He'd needed to clear his head, away from the influence of Briana Davenport. She'd had far too much influence over his feelings lately. More than any other woman he'd ever known. And that was detrimental to a fleeting relationship.

Just after lunch the telephone rang. It was Danielle Hammond, bringing thoughts of family to the forefront of his mind, which was just as well. He'd been trying to concentrate on a client's case, but Briana kept coming to mind.

"I thought I'd give you a call, Jarrod," Danielle said warmly but quickly, as if she half-expected him to hang up on her. "Mum and I are here in Melbourne for some Easter shopping and I thought it might be a good opportunity to have dinner together at the casino tomorrow night."

Jarrod's brows drew into a frown. He'd planned on spending the evening with Briana after taking her to the beach, and he didn't really want to share her with anyone. Still, Danielle was his cousin, and he liked her and Sonya more every time he met them.

"Mum said she'd been disappointed that she hadn't really spoken to you much at Kim's wedding, or at the jewelry launch," Danielle continued. "She really wants to get to know you."

"Does she?"

"We're family, Jarrod," she pointed out, and Jarrod realized she had taken his comment the wrong way.

Dammit, Howard Blackstone had a lot of things to answer for in breaking up the families like this all those years ago. None of it should ever have gotten to the stage where family had been set against family. Hammond against Hammond.

"Dinner will be fine."

"Great!" Danielle said. "And hey, can we keep it a secret from my mum? I'd like to surprise her. She'll be so happy."

Jarrod had to smile at her enthusiasm. "If that's what you want."

"It is. Oh, and Jarrod—" She hesitated, then, "If you'd like to bring Briana, we don't mind."

His smile disappeared. Obviously they'd been reading the newspapers and knew Briana had accompanied him to the Grand Prix. No doubt Kim or Jessica Cotter would have mentioned it, too.

"Of course," Danielle continued, "if she's with someone else—"

"She isn't," he said firmly, knowing she meant Patrick. "Briana will be with me."

"Wonderful. We'll see you tomorrow night."

Jarrod said goodbye, but as he ended the call he realized Danielle may not have meant Patrick at all. She could have meant Jake Vance.

Either way, both men were going to miss out.

Briana enjoyed having dinner with her father that night, but by the time Sunday morning rolled around she couldn't help but wonder how things stood between her and Jarrod now. After their confrontation yesterday, would Jarrod have second thoughts about believing her over Patrick?

But when she opened the door to him at noon, her fears were laid to rest. He presented her with a huge Easter egg.

"Ooh, I love chocolate," she gushed, feeling a giddy sense of pleasure, not just for the gift, but because it seemed like a peace offering. That meant things could get back to normal for them for their remaining time together.

"Some women prefer diamonds," he said, watching her.

Her excitement faded. Yes, they were back to normal all right. She angled her chin. "Not me."

His gaze became guarded. "I'm beginning to realize that," he muttered, then just as fast said, "Are you ready to go?"

For a split second she thought she'd misheard his first comment, but then realized she hadn't. He really was beginning to believe that she wasn't a money-hungry female on the prowl for a good time.

Silly tears of relief pricked at her eyes. "I'll just get my things," she said, spinning away and pretending to check through her beach bag. Did this mean he didn't think she was like Marise any longer? Was it bad of her to be grateful if that were the case? "I wasn't sure what to bring," she nattered on.

"Just yourself."

She blinked to get control of herself, picked up her sun hat and bag, then looked up with a smile. "Ready."

His gaze slid over her body in Bermuda shorts and a tank top. "*More* than ready," he said huskily, making her shiver with awareness.

She went to take a step toward him then stopped, her eyes drawn to what *he* was wearing. Her stomach did a flip.

"What are you looking at?" he asked, something lazily seductive in his voice.

"You. I can't believe you're wearing jeans." She'd never seen him dressed quite so relaxed before.

He broke into a smile. "I'm just a man."

She returned his smile. "Yeah sure."

After that, an inane sense of joy wrapped around her heart. She knew it couldn't last—happiness never did—but today she was determined to hold onto the feeling as long as she could.

The drive down the Surf Coast was pleasant in the autumn sunshine. They talked in a desultory fashion about the breathtaking view and the warm weather and things in general, until Jarrod asked how her father was doing.

Briana felt herself get defensive, even while she tried not to show it. "He's doing okay."

"Did he enjoy dinner last night? You said you were going to invite him."

"Yes. It was nice."

"Speaking of dinner, Danielle and Sonya Hammond are in town. They've invited us to dinner with them tonight."

She was caught unawares. "Us?"

He shot her a quick look. "Do you have a problem with that?"

"Um—no. I just didn't know you were that close." Danielle and Sonya had lived with Howard Blackstone all these years, so she tended to think of them as Blackstones despite their Hammond surname.

"We're not. That's what Danielle wants to rectify."

Her brow rose. "And you're happy with that?"

He gave a careless shrug and kept his eyes on the road ahead. "They've done nothing to me."

She liked his attitude. "Well then, I'd love to have dinner with you all."

"Good. It's at the casino."

"Oh." She could feel herself grow hot. Perhaps she'd been too hasty in accepting the invitation? The last time she and Jarrod had been at the casino they'd ended up in bed together.

He slanted her a knowing glance, but thankfully they arrived at the crescent-shaped sandy beach with a small pier at one end. The whole coastline was covered in glorious beaches like this, and they decided to go for a walk to the most deserted point before coming back to eat the lunch Jarrod had brought with him.

Being at the beach was such an integral part of the Australian way of life, Briana mused as they walked along the path cutting through the tufts of grass to the sand. She loved Aussie beaches... The smell of the ocean and sand... The sun evaporating the stresses of daily life...

Until Jarrod went to hold her hand, and she snatched it back. "No."

His brow rose. "No?"

"I don't hold hands."

He gave a short laugh. "What do you mean you don't hold hands?"

She moved her shoulders in a shrug. "It's so..."

"Romantic?" he mocked.

"If you like." She hesitated. "My first boyfriend always wanted to hold my hand."

His glance sharpened. "Nothing wrong with that."

"There is when it's *all* the time." She'd been young and wildly in love, but after six months they'd outgrown each other. Or perhaps *she'd* outgrown Derek, she admitted, remembering how his constant handholding had begun to make her feel somehow tied to him. A whole new world was opening up for her as a model, but he'd wanted her to stay the same. At nineteen that was the last thing she wanted.

"How many lovers have you had, Briana?"

She stopped dead. She knew she didn't have to answer but she did. "Three."

He had stopped, too. "Including me?"

She nodded. "Yes, including you."

He studied her face with an enigmatic gaze. "You're not very sexually experienced, are you?"

She stared at him, her heart seeming to open like a flower under the sun. This was another indication that he was beginning to see her as the person she was. "No, I'm not, Jarrod."

His eyes held her captive. "Was your other lover serious?"

He already knew about Patrick, so she knew he meant Derek. "At the time, yes."

"What happened?"

"I was young and so was he. It didn't work out."

Looking back, she realized how very young she'd been, and how ill-prepared for emotional commitment. It had been many years before she'd let herself fall in love again—and with Patrick this time. She winced inwardly. Both affairs had merely proven that love wasn't for her.

Jarrod nodded his head, and in silent agreement they started walking again. "You may not believe this," he said after they'd taken a few steps along the soft sand. "But I'm not a virgin, either."

She had to smile. "I'm totally shocked."

"Yeah, you look it," he teased, then they continued walking in silence for a few more yards, a rare sense of harmony between them. A light breeze from the ocean and the lapping of the gentle waves added to the mood.

A little further on, Jarrod said, "I should have said this long before now, but I'm sorry you lost your mother and sister."

For a moment her throat locked up. "Thank you," she managed. It meant a lot to her for him to say that. Then she cleared her throat. "I just wish things hadn't gone so wrong between her and Matt."

Seconds of silence ticked by and she felt a twinge of disappointment. Had she tested his goodwill to the limit? Was he going to bring up that wall of reserve again?

"I had no idea she had left him," he suddenly admitted. "Not until the plane crash."

Her mind reeled in confusion. "But she and Howard were in the papers for weeks before their deaths."

"And I was in New York working day and night on a case. I barely stopped to eat, let alone read the newspapers."

"But didn't anyone tell you?" she said, walking alongside him.

He slanted a brow at her. "Who?"

"Matt?"

He shook his head with regret. "No. He keeps things to himself."

He wasn't the only one, she mused, glancing at Jarrod's profile as they strolled along the sand. To the outside world they must look like a couple merely enjoying their surroundings. Instead they were opening up to each other in a way they hadn't done before—without recriminations. It was a major breakthrough in their relationship. Perhaps after their affair ended, they could be friends?

Perhaps not.

"Marise wasn't an easy person to love," she admitted. "But I loved her all the same."

He pinned her with another sideways glance. "Of course you did."

She gave a shaky sigh. "She didn't deserve to die."

"No, she didn't."

Briana stopped in her tracks as a sudden overwhelming sense of loss swept over her. How Marise had died would always haunt her. That was the worst part. Knowing that her sister had been floating in a life vest by herself with severe injuries. How dreadfully scared Marise must have felt, realizing she was going to die. She would have given a good fight, but not even when a passing ship had picked her up, had she been able to survive. Briana's only comfort was at least Marise had not died alone. Someone from the ship had been with her. She knew that for a fact.

Jarrod stepped in front of her and with compassion in his eyes, brushed some strands of hair off her cheek. "This is why we should live life to the fullest."

"Yes." For once she wanted to lean into him, against

him, take strength from him. She reached out and placed her hands on his hips, stepping closer, seeing his spurt of surprise and knew this wasn't about sex. This was about comfort, about giving and receiving. And that was something neither of them had tried before.

All at once someone screamed, making them both jump. It only took a split second to take in the situation. A small boy with yellow floaties on his arms had been dragged out into deeper water, his mother was on the shore screaming for help, a small baby in her arms.

"Oh God," Briana muttered, forgetting Jarrod as she immediately started to run toward the water. Others were running, too. She could hear the thud of footsteps in the sand. She wasn't sure what she was going to do. She was a good swimmer but not strong enough to swim that far out. But she couldn't let the little boy drown.

Without warning a man brushed past her as he ran into the shallows, splashing through the water. He was bare-chested but had jeans on. He had dark hair.

Jarrod!

Briana reached the mother just as Jarrod dove into deeper water and began swimming through the small waves. A couple of others were milling around the woman, someone taking the baby out of her arms, someone else offering reassurance.

Briana could only stand and watch as Jarrod sliced through the water, her heart in her mouth. She prayed he reached the child before he was dragged out even further. He was getting closer.

And then sheer fright tore through her. Would Jarrod

have the strength to swim back, let alone with a small child in tow? She didn't think so. It was too far.

She began to shake as time stood still. Yet she was aware of the sounds around her. Of the cold water lapping over her wet sneakers. Of the breeze getting stronger. Of the sun going behind a cloud, making the deeper water look even more menacing.

And she began to pray. If anything happened to Jarrod... If he drowned out there doing this heroic thing... If the ocean took him like it had Marise... She wouldn't be able to bear it.

Please God, don't take the man I love.

Her heart seemed to rise in her chest then tumble headfirst into an emotion she'd been fighting ever since she'd met Jarrod Hammond. She *loved* him. He was what love was all about.

Just at that moment Jarrod reached the boy, and a cheer went up, startling her. And then her prayers were answered when a small boat left the pier at the other end of the bay and headed for them. Another cheer went up, and this time Briana's heart cheered, too.

She still held her breath until Jarrod and the boy were in the boat and then safely ashore. There ensued a ton of commotion as the mother cried and hugged her son, then profusely thanked Jarrod with a kiss and a hug. Someone placed a towel around Jarrod's shoulders, and someone else shook his hand.

Through it all, Briana just stood there, not moving, her eyes going over him like she'd been given the greatest gift on earth.

And she had.

All at once he noticed her standing a few feet away. He walked toward her in his sodden jeans. "Are you okay?" he asked.

No, she would never be the same again.

Her gaze went over his dear, dear features. "Are *you* okay?"

He nodded. "Just a bit wet."

She remembered how she'd felt watching him out there in the ocean. "You could have drowned," she whispered.

"Yeah, well, don't make a fuss," he dismissed in a gruff voice, and turned away to collect his polo shirt and sneakers where he'd dropped them in such a hurry.

It was as if someone had snapped their fingers in front of her and awoken her from a trance. A powerful, over-whelming and crushing sensation went through her. Yes, she loved him, but the last thing she could do was tell him. Nothing had changed on his part. He'd warned her at the beginning not to expect anything more than a tem-porary relationship. She wouldn't go back on her word.

Besides, she had to be realistic. There were too many other things between them. Marise...Matt...her father... Oh Lord, if she told him about her father's em-bezzlement what would he do? As a lawyer, would he be obligated to tell the police if he knew a wrongdoing had been committed? She couldn't even tell him that Patrick was blackmailing her for fear of it all coming out in the open.

After the commotion died down, Briana suggested they leave. Though the journey back was quiet, she was inwardly screaming to get some time to herself. Jarrod needed to get out of his wet things and take a shower, only she didn't want to join him. Not when her love for him was pumping through her body...through her heart. Not when she somehow had to keep up all pretences until she could leave next week. Oh God, it was going to be a long, long week. Yet in some ways not long enough.

She was rather distant when they arrived back at her apartment building. "Please don't come up. You need to go home and change."

He stared hard, his forehead creased in a frown. "What's the matter? You've been quiet ever since I helped save the boy."

She couldn't let him dismiss his actions so easily. "You didn't just *help,* Jarrod. You saved his life."

"I couldn't let him drown."

Love swelled inside her. "I know you couldn't." She leaned over and kissed him softly on the lips. "You're a fine man, Jarrod Hammond," she murmured, pulling back. Her heart wobbled with love and a warning quickly filled her. "I just need to be alone for a little while."

His gaze softened with surprising tenderness. "It's because of Marise, isn't it? Seeing me out there in the water reminded you of how she died."

She nodded, gratefully grabbing at the suggestion, though it was true anyway.

"I understand," he said, and skimmed his lips over hers. "Do you still want to come to dinner tonight?"

The casino! She'd forgotten about that for a moment. It was going to be hard returning to the scene of their first time together, knowing she loved him. But she'd still go to support Jarrod, whether he wanted that support or not. She could do it. After all, if he had drowned today....

"Yes," she whispered, then got out of the car, hearing his comment about picking her up at seven. She nodded and said she'd be ready. She just hoped that emotionally, she would be.

Eight

"Hello, Sonya," Jarrod said as they reached the table in the middle of the luxurious casino restaurant, and Briana watched as Sonya lifted her elegant head from the menu, her eyes widening.

In her late forties, Sonya always reminded Briana of a stunning and graceful queen. Queen Sonya. Yes, she certainly seemed to be the queen of the Blackstone family, and deservedly so. The woman had lived at Howard's mansion since her sister's suicide nearly thirty years ago, raising Kim and Ryan along with her own daughter, Danielle. Remembering that, Briana immediately felt a bond with her. Sonya had lost a sister, just like she had.

"Jarrod! Oh my God! What are you doing here? What a coincidence," Sonya said with delighted surprise.

Jarrod kissed her cheek. "No coincidence," he said

as a small smile tugged the corners of his firm mouth. Then he kissed Danielle's cheek. "Danielle planned it."

Sonya swung toward her daughter. "Danielle!"

"I thought it would be a nice surprise, Mum," Danielle said with a wide smile, her golden eyes shining with pleasure, her charm a part of her beauty.

"Oh, it is. It is. It's a lovely surprise," Sonya agreed, her gaze on Jarrod, who looked handsome and debonair in a dark suit. Then Sonya's gaze fell on Briana. "And, Briana, how nice to see you again," she said warmly, and Briana wondered how she'd ever thought this woman was coolly reserved.

"It's nice to see you, too, Sonya." Briana then smiled at Danielle, whose copper-colored curls seemed to want to burst out from their bun. "You, too, Danielle."

"Please. Call me Dani."

Sonya rolled her eyes. "I give my daughter such a beautiful name and she chops it in half." She waved a hand at the two empty chairs on the other side of the table. "Please. Sit down."

Briana thanked Jarrod as he held out her chair for her.

"Well, this *is* nice," Sonya said, glowing with enjoyment. "It's just so good to have you here, Jarrod. We didn't get to talk much at the jewelry launch a few weeks ago, nor at Kim's wedding. I was hoping to catch you afterward but what with all the media swarming around afterward, I decided to go straight home."

"I left a bit early anyway," Jarrod said, confirming Briana's suspicions.

"Wise man." Sonya took a moment to smile at

Briana. "And you looked so gorgeous at the jewelry launch, Briana. I was wishing that was me up there."

"Easily," Briana said, not fawning, merely stating the truth. "But thank you. It all went very well."

The evening went well, too…until Briana's gaze caught Jarrod's by accident and everything came tumbling back. Until now she hadn't let herself think about being here, but returning to "the scene of the crime", the sounds of the casino, the scents of perfume and aftershave, of food, the gleam in Jarrod's eyes, reminded her what they had done together here in one of the casino suites—all for the sake of a million dollars.

And now she loved him.

And he could have died today.

Quickly she lowered her lashes, breaking the invisible thread between them. He may be getting a kick out of revisiting all this, but she wasn't. She would never be able to come into this place again without thinking of the man she loved. She doubted she'd ever be able to go to the beach now without thinking of him either. He would always be a part of her now. And a part of her memories.

Sonya's question broke into her thoughts. "How is your father, Jarrod?" she said casually, but they all knew her interest was more than casual about her brother— the brother she hadn't spoken to for almost thirty years.

For the first time tonight, Jarrod's face became shuttered. "As well as can be expected," he said smoothly, without any hint of the anguish that had passed between their families.

"I was praying Oliver would be up and about by now."

"So were we. But the stroke has taken its toll, I'm afraid."

"Yes, I know. I spoke to Katherine a few months ago," Sonya said, obviously surprising the others. "She's not as hopeful of a full recovery as she was before." She blinked rapidly, as if to stop sudden tears. "It *has* been five years after all."

"These things can take longer than we expect, Sonya," he said, making Briana wonder if in addition to his father's health he meant family issues, as well.

Briana could only think how much stood between these two families. Sonya and Dani were Hammonds yet they'd been shunned by Sonya's brother, Oliver, who was Jarrod's father. Families needed to work things out. How she wished she had her mother back to talk to. And Marise. She'd make it work with her sister if she had another chance, she told herself, despair cutting the air from her lungs.

"Yes, they do take time," the older woman agreed softly, a hopeful looking crossing her face.

An awkward silence ensued but fortunately their first course arrived.

"I must say," Dani began as she picked up her fork, "you have some great shopping here in Melbourne. We were going to come down last weekend, only Mum didn't want to fight the crowds from the Grand Prix."

Sonya shuddered. "I love Melbourne, but car racing is not my thing. Mind you, Kim and Ric were here. Ryan and Jessica, too. They were hosting a corporate box." She paused as she glanced casually at Jarrod. "They said they saw you, Jarrod."

"Briefly."

A moment crept by.

"I was there, too," Briana said to ease the silence. "It was great catching up with them all. Jessica is blooming in her pregnancy."

Sonya sighed. "I'm so grateful they're happy." She glanced across at her daughter with a loving smile. "Children are such a blessing."

Dani pointed a fork at her. "That's not what you said when I told you I was going back to Port Douglas."

Sonya smiled at Jarrod and Briana. "On the other hand—"

"Mother!" Dani laughingly joked.

"As I said, a blessing—" She paused. "In disguise."

Everyone laughed, and then continued eating.

"So, Dani," Jarrod said when there was a lull in conversation. "You like Port Douglas, do you?"

Her eyes lit up. "I love it."

Briana was impressed by Dani's considerable talent. "How is your shop going up there? I loved those pieces you designed for the jewelry launch."

Dani looked thoroughly delighted. "Thank you. I've got so many clients out of that. I've almost paid back Howard's estate the money he loaned me to start the business."

"You design jewelry?" Jarrod said, obviously not knowing. "You must be very good if Howard lent you money."

Dani's chin lifted in the air. "No, Howard Blackstone is *not* my father," she said, a feistiness entering her tone.

"Danielle!" Sonya said, scolding her daughter.

Dani immediately grimaced. "I'm sorry. I'm just so used to everyone thinking Howard is my father that I wanted to set the record straight." She looked across the table at Jarrod. "It's important to me that you know the truth, Jarrod. I mean, I'm grateful to Howard and I was fond of him—but I'm a Hammond, as well."

Jarrod looked directly at his cousin. "Dani, I never did believe any of that crap in the newspaper."

Sonya cleared her throat. "Thank you, Jarrod. This means a lot to me." She reached out and squeezed Dani's hand. "To us."

"Yes," Dani added, her eyes a little watery. "Thank you."

Briana could have kissed Jarrod. She knew how much his family hated Howard Blackstone, how much he disliked the man himself, yet he was able to stand back from that now and realize these two people weren't to blame. Her love for him deepened.

"I once did a magazine shoot in Port Douglas, Dani," Briana said, giving them a moment to recover. "It's beautiful, and you certainly get some pretty famous people up there. I saw a couple of movie stars from the States."

Dani waved her hand in a dismissive gesture. "That's nothing compared to all the hoopla with the Governor-General coming up there on ANZAC Day for a commemoration. You should see those preparations."

Suddenly there was a clang of cutlery and everyone

looked at Sonya, who had dropped her fork on her plate. She'd turned as white as a sheet and had a faint sheen of perspiration on her upper lip.

"Mum?" Dani said, quickly leaning toward her mother. "What's the matter?"

Sonya went to say something, swallowed, then began again. "Um—I'm fine, darling. I just came over cold and clammy all of a sudden." She dabbed at her top lip with a napkin but she still looked white.

"But I wasn't feeling the best before we came," she added, surprising Briana because she'd thought Sonya was a picture of health. Then she looked at Jarrod. "I hope you don't mind, but I think I may need to go and lie down."

"Of course I don't mind." Jarrod got to his feet. "I'll take you to your room."

Sonya waved him back in his seat. "No. Dani and I will manage."

"Come on, Mum. Let's get you up to our suite. I want to get the doctor to look you over." As Dani started to lead her away she promised Jarrod she'd call.

After they left, Briana looked at Jarrod worriedly. "I hope it's nothing too serious."

He'd been frowning, but his forehead cleared. "It's probably just a stomach bug."

"But it did come out of the blue, didn't it?" Briana said, still concerned. "It was like she had a shock, though I guess a stomach bug has the same symptoms." She dismissed her own thought. "Oh well. No matter. As long as she recovers."

"Hmm. I wonder if Sonya planned this," Jarrod said

later. "It's a novel way of getting out of paying the bill, don't you think?"

"Oh, she wouldn't—" Briana began, then saw the twinkle in his eye. "I'm sure you can afford it."

"I guess it's better than the million dollars I spent here last time," he said, more teasing than not.

But she didn't find it funny. She felt hurt. "That's not very gentlemanly of you to bring that up."

His amusement disappeared. "Hey, it's not like you didn't take the money."

Oh, how she wished she could tell him the truth. Things might be different for them. But she had her father to think about first. Herself second. She could never enjoy any happiness with Jarrod at her father's expense. If indeed there was any happiness to be had.

He tilted his head and considered her. "Would you have slept with me without the money, Briana?"

"No."

"Sure?" he asked silkily.

Her heart trembled. "I don't deny I was attracted to you, but no, I wouldn't have taken it further without the money." She would never have let herself be put in the position to sleep with him.

His mouth tightened. "Some things can't be ignored, Briana. And our attraction was one of them. I think you would have."

"Then we'll have to agree to disagree," she said sweetly, but her heart was sinking in her chest. If he knew she loved him... If he knew he held her heart in his hands...

"How about I give you another million dollars to come up to a suite with me?"

The thought staggered her. "Don't be silly."

His eyebrow rose. "So you don't want the money? That doesn't add up. You took a million dollars the first time but you won't take another million now."

"Perhaps I'm not as greedy as you think," she said, encouraging him to think that way about her. After everything, if he thought good about her, then she'd be happy.

For a moment he studied her intently. "Perhaps not."

She ignored a flash of relief. "Jarrod, it's been a long day. Would you mind taking me home? I'm starting to get a headache." She saw his instant concern. "No, nothing like Sonya just had." Her own headache was tension, she was sure. From loving a man who didn't love her, nor would he ever *want* to love her.

Once back at her building she turned to him in the car. "Do you mind if you don't come up tonight?" This was the second time today she'd said the same thing.

The streetlight showed his glance sharpen. "I mind, but if that's the way you feel I won't push myself on you."

"Thank you."

"But I insist on walking you to your door." And he did. Once there, he kissed her goodnight, but it was a brief kiss. "I'll call you later in the week."

"Okay." She breathed easier. She'd asked for time to herself and he was giving her more than enough.

"Miss me," he said, and headed back to the elevator.

It wasn't a suggestion.

She would take it to heart.

* * *

The next morning when her doorbell rang, Briana's pulse started racing. Jarrod! He wasn't waiting to phone her. He wanted to see her now. Today. It made her heart flutter even as she told herself not to care.

But when she opened the door, it was to find a stranger there. A very handsome and impeccably dressed stranger.

"Briana, hello. I'm Quinn Everard."

Her forehead cleared. She easily recognized the smooth, strong voice that would put more than a little spring in a woman's step. Not her step, of course. Jarrod was the only man to make her heart leap.

"Can I come in?"

"What? I'm sorry. Yes, please do come in." She stepped back to let him pass.

"I apologize for dropping by like this," he said as he stepped into her apartment.

She suddenly realized something. "Sorry if I sound confused, but I'm not sure how you got past the doorman."

"There was no one at the front desk, so I just followed another lady into the building."

"Oh—well, I'm glad I'm not being stalked." She smiled to take the sting out of her words, but this time she did intend to speak to the building manager about this. As a high-profile person, she was a prime target for anyone with a grudge or a fixation. The various letters sent to her agent over the years assured her of that.

He gave a slow smile that reminded her of Jarrod. "I hope I don't look the type to cause trouble."

"Not at all. Have a seat. Would you like a cup of coffee?"

"No, thanks." He sat down on the edge of the sofa, resting his elbows on his thighs. "I'm here to tell you about the diamonds you wanted valued."

"You didn't need to come all this way. You could have—"

"Have you ever heard of the Blackstone Rose necklace?" he cut across her.

She lowered herself down on the sofa opposite him. "The Blackstone Rose necklace?" she asked, thinking. Then her face cleared. "Oh yes. There was a vague reference to it in the papers recently."

"That's right. It was a necklace that went missing nearly thirty years ago. It belonged to Ursula Blackstone, Howard's wife, who died just after the necklace went missing."

"She committed suicide, didn't she?" Her brow crinkled. "But what has this to do with the diamonds Marise put in my safe?"

Seconds crept by. An excited light came into his eyes, an aura about him that held her full attention now. "Marise's diamonds belonged to the Blackstone Rose necklace."

Briana's head reeled. "What? But I don't understand. How could Marise have diamonds belonging to a necklace missing almost thirty years?"

"That's what I'd like to know."

What he was suggesting took a moment to sink in.

Then she inhaled sharply. "You don't think I had anything to do with this, do you?"

"Relax, Briana. I don't think you're involved," he assured her. "But I *am* hoping you might inadvertently know something. That's why I wanted to talk to you face-to-face."

She expelled a breath. "I'm happy to tell you what I can, but I just don't know that much."

He slowly nodded, then gave her an encouraging smile. "How about I start at the beginning and we'll see if anything rings a bell?"

She cleared her throat. "Fine."

"Okay. The story goes that in 1970 Ursula's father, Jeb Hammond, was fossicking in the Outback when he found a massive pink diamond that was a rare and extremely valuable find. Jeb called it the Heart of the Outback." He paused to let this sink in. "A few years later he gifted it to Ursula on the birth of his first grandson, then Howard had it turned into the Blackstone Rose necklace."

Her forehead creased as fragments of past information flashed through her mind. "That was the grandson who was kidnapped, wasn't it?"

Quinn's mouth flattened in a grim line. "Yes. James was two years old when he was abducted. But Howard always believed his son was alive, and now it looks like he may have been right."

"Yes, so I'd heard." She remembered thinking how Jarrod may have been the missing heir, and his derision when she'd mentioned it to him.

"Ursula never recovered from losing her son. As you

know, she had two more children, Kimberley and Ryan, but she suffered badly from post-natal depression after Ryan's birth. Eventually she walked into the ocean and committed suicide."

Briana sighed. "Such a tragedy," she murmured.

"But I digress," Quinn said. "The necklace. It was at Ursula's thirtieth birthday that it disappeared from around her neck. Apparently she was quite drunk and fell into the swimming pool. Some of the guests helped her to her room, but by this time the necklace was missing and Howard accused her brother, Oliver, of stealing it." Quinn's eyes hardened. "Of course, Howard also accused Oliver of arranging the kidnapping of James, a claim Oliver vehemently denied, and the brothers-in-law never spoke to each other again. Not that I blame Oliver," he said, a bitter twist to his lips that made her ask a question before she could stop herself.

"You didn't like Howard?"

His jaw clenched. "Howard Blackstone was vindictive and manipulative and very good at using people and destroying them." His face closed up even more. "It's personal."

She took the hint. "So, the necklace was never found?"

"No. And the insurance company refused to pay out because of a loophole in the policy wording."

"And there were never any leads?" she asked.

He shook his head. "Despite exhaustive investigations, no one was ever charged with the theft. Howard continued to blame Oliver."

Briana felt so sorry for Jarrod's father. Oliver had

more than enough justification to cut ties with Howard, though she didn't believe Oliver should have cut Sonya out of his life. A sister was for life.

And speaking of sisters… "Where does Marise come into all this?"

"I don't know," he said. "Perhaps you could start by telling me what she said about the diamonds when she put them in your safe."

"She didn't say much at all, I'm afraid."

"Tell me anyway."

Briana thought back. It hurt to picture the scene but it had to be done. "We were in Sydney for my mother's funeral and—" She stopped, then cleared her throat. "Marise, my father and I were staying at my Sydney apartment, which is paid for by Blackstone's as I do a lot of engagements in Sydney. I remember Marise asking if she could have the combination to my wall safe so she could keep some jewelry in there. Naturally I gave it to her." She took a shuddering breath. "Then after our mother's funeral, I came back here to Melbourne with my father. I was grieving, and trying to keep an eye on him, but I was also trying to fulfill my pre-Christmas engagements. It's all just a blur now."

"I understand," he said, his voice sympathetic.

"Then I started hearing about Marise and Howard and—" She swallowed hard. "I honestly don't know what to believe about them. All I know is that just before I went to Howard's funeral I remembered the jewelry in the safe. I checked and there were the diamonds, so I phoned Matt to tell him I had some jewelry belonging to Marise, but he didn't want to know." She winced, then, "So I mentioned it to Jessica and she gave me your name." She lifted her shoulders in a faint shrug. "Sorry, I'm not much help."

"That's okay. You're doing fine." His eyes took on an alert look. "Did you tell Matt they were pink diamonds?"

She thought back. "No. I just said jewelry. Why?"

He shrugged. "No reason. Was there anything else in the safe?"

"Only a few bits and pieces of my own jewelry." Something occurred to her and her eyes widened. "Oh God, could Howard have given them to her, do you think?"

Quinn scowled. "I don't know, Briana. It would mean Howard either had the necklace all along, or came into it again without telling anyone. And why give it to Marise? Unless—" His eyes flickered away then back to her.

"Unless she was his mistress," Briana said what he'd been too polite to say. "I'm afraid I can't answer that question. I just don't know why Marise was with Howard. I'm not sure we'll ever find out."

"You're probably right."

Her brow furrowed. "What happens with the diamonds now?"

"They should go to the Blackstone lawyers."

She nodded. "Of course. Would you be able to give them to the lawyers on my behalf?"

"Absolutely." He stood up. "I'm returning to Sydney this afternoon and I'll hand deliver them myself as soon as I can."

"Thank you," she said with relief. "Just do whatever

you have to do to make sure they are returned to their rightful owner."

"I will."

She didn't want the responsibility of such valuable items in her care now. God, when she thought about what she'd unwittingly had in her possession... And Matt, he'd be kicking himself for not taking them back. Not that he would have kept them once he found out they belonged to the Blackstones.

Quinn left not long after that, and Briana sat on the sofa again, thinking. How on earth had Marise come by the diamonds? And what had she been planning on doing with them? Not to mention, who had stolen the necklace in the first place?

At the thought, she felt a sudden chill. Would everyone think *she* was involved somehow? After all, it had been her sister with the diamonds, and they'd been in her safe.

What sort of person would Jarrod think she was? She'd taken a million dollars off him, and now she had the stones in her possession. She knew his opinion of her had risen lately, but now, would this set it back? More than likely, she thought with despair.

Oh Marise, she whispered to herself, what have you done?

The only good thing in all this was that the diamonds would now be returned to their rightful owner. More than likely Kim, as the eldest. And Kim would believe her, she was sure. She just hoped this didn't put her contract into question with the other powers-that-be at Blackstone's.

Nine

Time was running out, and Briana was sick at heart for the rest of the day. She felt guilty for keeping the news of the diamonds from Jarrod, yet next week her relationship with him would be over and she'd be on her way to Hong Kong anyway. With Patrick. So why bother telling Jarrod about the diamonds? Why spoil their last week together? Every moment together was precious. She couldn't think beyond that.

The only good news was when her father called and said he'd managed to put the money back in Howard's account. The relief she felt was tremendous. Her father was still guilty of embezzlement but at least now no one could accuse him of keeping the money for himself.

So for her, it was all worthwhile. Sleeping with

Jarrod, spending time in his company. Oh yes, very worthwhile. If heartbreaking now.

Over the next few days, Briana tried to forget about the diamonds while she concentrated on preparing for her overseas assignment. Jarrod had called once or twice, but he was busy with a heavy case. She understood but she missed him. And it made time tick even more loudly in her ears.

And then two days later he took her out to dinner. It was a warm March evening and daylight saving time didn't finish until the end of the month, so it should have been pleasant eating and watching the sun set over the city. Briana spent most of her time trying to act normal, but the pink diamonds from the necklace were at the back of her mind. At the front was the thought of heading to Hong Kong next week and leaving Jarrod.

They ended up back at her apartment where she went into his arms and let him make love to her. Yet no matter that she badly wanted to show him how much she loved him, she still had to restrain herself, knowing that if she gave him her all, she might well fall apart right there and then.

Afterward, she lay in the crook of his arm, a slither of moonlight falling over them. If she could just commit this moment to memory… His masculine scent… The smoothness of his skin… The springy feel of chest hair beneath her palm…

"Is everything okay?" he said, his deep voice rumbling in her ear, cutting across her thoughts.

She mentally pulled herself together. "Why wouldn't it be?"

"You tell me."

She hardly dared breathe. "I don't know what you mean."

"You were distracted tonight."

She lifted one bare shoulder in a shrug. "I've got a lot on my mind."

"Like?"

She hesitated. "I'm leaving for Hong Kong next week," she pointed out, wanting to remind him that this would all end soon. She didn't fool herself that the end of their relationship would impact him like it did her, but it would've been nice to know he'd feel a little sad about them going their separate ways.

He tensed. "So that's next week then?" he said casually, as if he hadn't realized, though she knew he must. Jarrod never forgot a thing.

"Yes. The month will be up then."

A lengthy silence followed, then all at once he gently moved her off him and pushed himself out of bed. "I'd better go home. I have an early appointment."

So much for her thinking he might care, she thought with despair as he dressed in the dark. His movements weren't hurried, yet she had the feeling he couldn't wait to get away from her. He probably couldn't wait to get rid of her for good now.

Then he kissed her and left.

It was a long time before she fell asleep after that.

The last person she wanted to see the next day at a

fashion parade was Patrick. The Chadstone Shopping Center might be one of the biggest in the southern hemisphere but it wasn't big enough to get away from this man.

"So, sweetheart," he said, standing in the doorway with a smirk as he watched her change into another outfit. "You're all ready for our trip next week I hope?"

"Yes," she all but growled at him.

He lifted an eyebrow. "Going to give lover boy the flick this weekend, are you?"

"That's none of your business."

"Yes, it is. I don't want him coming after you and spoiling things on the shoot for me." His eyes narrowed "You make it clear to him that it's over, right?"

She considered him with distaste. "I don't know what I ever saw in you, Patrick."

His lips twisted in a cynical smile. "Do you think I care?"

"No. You care about no one but yourself."

"I'm glad you realize that."

She watched him turn and walk away like he didn't have a care in the world. It was all an act. He cared what people thought of him, but only for his own advantage.

And she knew one thing. If Patrick had known about the pink diamonds, he would have sold them on the black market, and he wouldn't have cared less. Of that she was certain.

Jarrod didn't see Briana again until Saturday. Until then he'd stayed away through choice. He was trying to wean himself off her. She'd begun to play a significant part in his life, and he wasn't happy about it. This was only supposed to be a fling with a beautiful model. He should have worked her out of his system by now. So why hadn't he?

Dammit, he couldn't deny the way his gut had knotted the other night in bed when she'd mentioned leaving. The thought of her going away for two weeks made him ache to hold her in his arms, but it was more than that. It was knowing once she left it would be the end for them.

Hell, he had to have some integrity. He'd offered her money, she'd taken it, they'd made an agreement. And now that agreement was coming to an end. He'd go his way and she'd go hers. Intimate strangers.

And then on Saturday morning his brother called him, and everything Jarrod had previously believed about Briana rose up and punched him the gut, making that knot unravel pretty damn quickly.

"I hope you're sitting down for this, Jarrod," Matt said, an excited note in his voice that immediately caught Jarrod's attention. "Quinn Everard has found four of the five pink diamonds from the Blackstone Rose necklace."

"You're kidding," Jarrod said, leaning back against the kitchen counter. He'd grown up hearing all about the missing necklace and all the heartache it had caused. "Dad must be thrilled."

"He is. It's given him a real boost." There was a slight hesitation. "There's something else. Briana had them."

Jarrod straightened. "What!"

"Quinn said Briana asked him to value them."

Jarrod swore. "Go on."

"Apparently Marise asked if she could keep some jewelry in Briana's wall safe in her Sydney apartment, so Briana gave her the combination. It wasn't until just before Howard's funeral that Briana remembered, and that's when she found the diamonds." Matt paused. "She told me, you know. She said she had some jewelry of Marise's and I told her to keep the damn lot." He cursed at himself. "How the hell was I supposed to know they were diamonds belonging to the necklace?"

Jarrod tried to take it all in. "But what was Marise doing with them? And why the hell didn't Briana at least mention them to me?"

"Who knew why Marise did anything," Matt said bitterly, reminding Jarrod that good news or not about the diamonds, this was going to stir up Matt's ill-feelings again for his late wife. Then, "I hear you've been seeing Briana."

"Yes," Jarrod said tightly.

"Quinn said she had no idea what the diamonds were," Matt pointed out, obviously still having a soft spot for Briana, despite her being Marise's sister.

Jarrod's jaw clenched and his hand tightened around the telephone. "She still should have mentioned them."

Matt didn't speak for a few seconds. "Here's something else that's strange. I heard a recent rumor on the underground grapevine. It was about the Davenports. Apparently, long ago the Davenport name was mentioned in connection to the missing necklace." He paused significantly. "*Before* Marise and Briana were born."

A second shock wave rocked through Jarrod. He tried to take it all in. "How substantial is the rumor?"

"The diamonds pretty much confirm it."

Jarrod expelled a breath. "This is too damn incredible."

Matt waited a moment before asking, "What are you going to do?"

He stiffened. "Speak to Briana," he said, his voice holding an ominous quality.

"Let me know what develops. I've asked Quinn to look for the fifth diamond, but if she knows anything at all, I want to hear about it." His unspoken words said "for Oliver Hammond's sake."

Jarrod hung up the phone and stood there letting it all sink in. He felt gutted. Briana had kept all this from him. It made him wonder what the hell else she was hiding.

Briana started frowning as soon as she heard the buzzer sound on Saturday morning. When she answered, it was to find Jarrod standing there. "You're early for our lunch date."

"I know," he snarled at her as he stepped past her into the living room.

He looked...odd. "What's going on?"

His gaze seared her. "Perhaps I should be asking *you* that."

Her misgivings increased by the moment as she slowly closed the door and turned to face him. The distance was more than the length of the room between them. "What do you mean?"

"The diamonds, Briana."

Her frown deepened. "Diamonds?"

"Pink ones," he drawled with deceptive mildness. "From the Blackstone Rose necklace."

Her forehead cleared, and just as quickly her heart sank. "But how do you—"

"Matt told me."

"Matt?" She shook her head, trying to make sense of what Jarrod was saying.

"The diamonds belong to him now."

Shock ran through her. "But how? Why?" Dear God, she didn't understand what this was all about. And Jarrod obviously blamed her already without a fair hearing.

"Marise was left the Blackstone jewelry collection, remember? On her death, it all went to her husband." He paused. "Matt."

"But I thought the Blackstone Rose diamonds would belong to the Blackstones."

"Howard obviously thought differently. He bequeathed *all* the jewelry to Marise."

"But surely not the Blackstone Rose?" She'd known about the jewelry going to Marise of course, but this was different. This was the Blackstone Rose necklace, for heaven's sake. Howard couldn't have known it was going to resurface, and even if he had, why leave it to Marise in his will?

She let out a shaky breath. "I still don't understand."

"Join the club," he said scathingly.

She ignored that, not sure if it was meant for her or himself. Probably both. "Is Matt going to give it back to the Blackstones?"

Jarrod snorted with derision. "I doubt it. My father will be very pleased to have the diamonds back where they belong—with the Hammond family. It should never have gone to Howard in the first place. The only reason Howard married Ursula was to get his hands on the Heart of the Outback diamond."

"You can't know that."

"I know Howard."

She tilted her head at him. "I didn't realize you were quite so...involved with the family feud between the Blackstones and the Hammonds."

"I'm a Hammond. I'm involved," he snapped.

She realized she'd touched a nerve about his adoption.

He pinned her with his eyes. "Why didn't you tell me about the diamonds, Briana?"

Suddenly she felt a chill. This was it. "I didn't think they were important."

"Oh come on! You must have known Marise had put them in the safe and what they were."

"At the time I knew she put some jewelry in the safe. That's all." Her eyes searched his, and hurt ripped at her insides. "You don't believe me, do you?"

"No," he freely admitted. "Not when there's a Davenport connection to the stolen necklace all those years ago."

Her stomach lurched. "What?"

"Matt learned on the underground grapevine today that the Davenport name was linked to the missing necklace almost thirty years ago."

She shook her head. "No way. Besides, neither Marise nor I were even born then."

"No, but your parents were."

His words hung in the air. She swallowed a lump in her throat. "You can't believe—"

"That your parents stole the necklace, left Howard's employ, moved to Melbourne where they sold one of the diamonds, and in later years told you and Marise all about it? Does it sound so far-fetched, considering the circumstances?"

She stared aghast. "I don't believe I'm hearing this."

"Your parents were pretty cushy with Howard at one time."

Panic flared. She didn't want Jarrod linking her father and Howard. "So?"

One dark eyebrow rose upward. "So you do know about their past association with Howard?"

"If you mean, do I know that Howard fired my mother when she got pregnant with Marise, then yes, I know." Briana still couldn't understand it but she remembered her mother saying those had been the times back then. Howard wouldn't get away with it these days.

"How did Marise come by the diamonds then?" he shot at her. "And why didn't you tell me about them?"

She didn't appreciate his interrogation. "I don't know why Marise had them. And I've already told you I didn't know what the diamonds were. If I did, why would I get them appraised and risk being discovered? Why would I have told Quinn to give them back to their rightful owner?"

"To protect your family."

She stiffened. "What do you mean?"

"You know your parents stole the necklace. You know Marise, as the eldest daughter, had been given the remaining diamonds. And you thought pretending ignorance was the best way of clearing their names."

His words distressed her. How could he think all that? "You've got it all wrong, Jarrod. Very wrong."

"I want to speak to your father."

She sucked in a sharp breath. "Wh-what?"

"I said I want to speak to Ray. I want to hear what he has to say about all this."

Anxiety twisted inside her. "But you can't—I won't—"

"Feeling guilty?" he growled.

"No." Yes, because of the money.

He stared hard. "Then you won't have a problem if I speak to him."

Somehow she had to get through to him. "Look, he's been through so much. His lost his wife and one of his daughters and now you're accusing him of God knows what. Leave him alone. Please, Jarrod."

His face remained rigid. "I'm going to speak to him no matter what you say."

Begging hadn't worked, so she forced herself to look at him with steely-eyed determination. "I'll never forgive you if you do."

He didn't even flinch. "I'll never forgive myself if I don't."

She realized he was deadly serious. He wasn't going

to be swayed. He would talk to her father with or without her. And if her father wasn't prepared…

With a supreme effort, she squared her shoulders and gave in. "I'll come with you."

Ten

"Ray, we need to talk," Jarrod said as soon as her father opened his front door.

"It's okay, Dad," Briana blurted so he would know it wasn't about the money. Despite it, she saw the flicker of apprehension in her father's eyes and prayed that Jarrod would think it was merely confusion.

Her father stepped back. "You'd better come in," he said with a calmness he must not be feeling. Then once they were all in the living room and Jarrod refused the invitation to sit down with a shake of his head, Ray stood, too. "So, what is it we need to talk about, Jarrod?"

"It's about those diamonds, Dad," Briana said, and received a dark look from Jarrod, but she didn't want her father getting mixed up and inadvertently saying anything he shouldn't.

"Diamonds?"

"You know the ones, Dad," she continued. "I told you about them. Remember those four pink diamonds I found in my safe?"

Ray frowned. "Yes, but—"

"They belong to the Blackstone Rose necklace," Jarrod said, obviously deciding it was time to take control.

Ray blinked. "What?"

"Dad, those four pink diamonds Marise put in my safe belonged to the missing necklace," Briana said gently. She understood his confusion only too well. "Do you know why she would have had them in the first place?"

Ray shook his graying head. "No." Then he seemed to realize they were waiting for more information. "Honey, your sister was a law unto herself. She was my daughter but she did what she wanted, no matter who she hurt, may she rest in peace," he said, his voice choking a little on the last sentence.

Briana blinked back sudden tears as a moment crept by. Yes, that had been Marise.

"Ray," Jarrod began, his voice quiet but unwavering. "You and your wife used to work for Howard Blackstone, didn't you?"

"Yes. And I remember when the necklace went missing."

"It was never recovered."

"Not as far as I know." All at once her father's shoulders tensed. "What are you implying?"

"Ray, did you steal the necklace?"

"What the hell!"

"Jarrod," Briana warned at the same time. She didn't like Jarrod playing the lawyer with her father.

"Did you steal the Blackstone Rose necklace?" Jarrod demanded, ignoring her.

"No!"

"Then how did Marise come by it?"

Ray shot him a hostile glare. "Perhaps Howard gave it to her."

"If it had been recovered earlier, Howard wouldn't have been able to keep that to himself." He gave a cynical twist to his lips. "No, I don't think Howard gave it to Marise at all."

Ray shrugged his shoulders. "Then I'm afraid I can't help you."

"Barbara—"

"I can assure you my wife didn't steal it either." If her father's glare was hostile before, it was doubly hostile now.

Jarrod stood his ground. "Ray, look. Try and step back from this for a minute. It's a possibility, isn't it?"

"Anything's a possibility," her father snapped.

Briana had had enough. "Dad, what Jarrod is getting at is that you and Mum stole the necklace, then we moved here to get away with it, that you gave it to Marise as the elder daughter, and that I got the diamonds valued to put everyone off the scent."

"But—but—that's preposterous!" Ray exclaimed.

"Really?" Jarrod said. "Then the rumor Matt heard is obviously wrong."

Her father's forehead creased. "Rumor?"

"From the underground grapevine. They're saying there's a Davenport connection to the missing necklace."

"Good Lord!" Her father looked totally confused. "I don't understand. How can they say that?" He shook his head. "Why would someone jump to such a conclusion?"

"Just like *you're* doing now," Briana said pointedly to Jarrod.

Jarrod ignored her. "I could accept that was the case *if* it had been an open rumor, but for it to be an underground one it must be pretty well substantiated." He watched the older man carefully. "The interesting thing is that only four diamonds were recovered and there were five. One is still missing. Matt believes it's something to do with your family, and seeing that Briana and Marise weren't even born when the necklace was stolen, we can only assume you or your wife must have appropriated it."

"Jarrod, will you stop this!" Briana exclaimed. "Dad knows nothing about it."

Amazingly, Jarrod stood his ground. "I think he does."

"What gives you the right to come in here and—"

"I took it," Ray cut across her.

Briana gasped. "What?"

"I said I took the necklace."

"Dad, no!"

Jarrod's expression became thoughtful. "Then where is the other pink diamond?"

"I—um—sold it."

"To whom?"

"I—um—can't say. It's confidential."

"It was stolen. It can't be confidential." Jarrod stared

hard. "I don't think you're telling the truth, Ray. I think your wife stole the necklace." He paused. "Am I right?"

Ray held his gaze. Tension filled the air. Then he took two steps to the sofa and sank down on it. "Yes," he whispered.

Briana's mind spun. This wasn't true. It couldn't be. Her mother wouldn't do such a thing. "No, you're wrong. You're—"

Ray looked up. "Sweetheart, I'm sorry, but she *must* have stolen it."

Briana frowned. "How do you know that?"

"Because *I* didn't."

Tears pricked at her blue eyes. "Oh, Dad, don't be silly. Just because you didn't take it doesn't mean Mum *did*." She spun toward Jarrod. "This is all your fault. You're browbeating him into a confession so that he can keep my mother's good name."

"Briana, shhh," her father said. "Jarrod's just trying to get to the truth."

"For what?" she choked. "To prove some stupid rumor? There's no evidence, Dad. None at all. Jarrod is just—" All at once she noticed her father's dismayed expression. "Dad, are you all right? Dad, what is it?"

"Oh God. I've just remembered something. Your mother wanted you and your sister to go to a private school. We didn't have the money but then a spinster aunt left her a legacy—quite a substantial amount—and your mother put it into an account for your schooling."

Briana's heart jolted. "What are you saying? That there was no spinster aunt?"

"That's exactly what I'm saying."

"But Mum would never—"

"Honey, I loved your mother dearly, but she was never quite the same after Howard fired her. She rarely mentioned him but I always had the impression she had never forgiven him, and rightly so." His mouth turned grim. "I know she was upset at first when Marise went to work for him, but then she seemed to accept it. And the same thing happened when you were given the Blackstone contract, though I know she didn't let on to any of us."

Briana was trying to take all this in. Her mother…her beloved mother…

Jarrod's voice cut across her thoughts. "You realize that the police may well come around and investigate now that the diamonds have been discovered."

Briana pushed aside thoughts of her mother. "But we gave them back," she said somewhat stupidly.

"The police will still investigate."

Ray swallowed hard. "Then they're going to find out about the million dollars," he said, sending a jolt through Briana.

Jarrod seemed to go on full alert. "What million dollars?"

"The one I stole from Howard's secret account."

"What the hell!"

"Just ignore him," Briana said quickly. "He doesn't know what he's saying."

Ray shook his head. "Honey, the guilt's been getting to me, and this has just made me decide to turn myself in to the police." He turned to Jarrod. "Remember that million dollars you loaned Briana to buy more property?" he said, making her inwardly groan.

Jarrod darted a look at her, and her eyes pleaded with him to nod. "Er—yes."

Ray then went on to explain how he'd taken the money for his wife's medical expenses. "I'll hand myself in to the police tomorrow." He glanced around the room. "I just want to spend one more night in the home I shared with Barbara."

Briana's heart tilted with pain. "Oh Dad," she whispered. "I'll come with you tomorrow. You won't be alone."

"Thank you, honey."

Jarrod cleared his throat. "Ray, embezzlement is embezzlement but there *were* extenuating circumstances. I know a good criminal lawyer who'll take on your case and hopefully will get you a lesser jail term."

At the mention of jail, Briana gave a small sob, but Ray squeezed her hand. "Honey, I committed a crime. I have to go to jail." He gave a forced smile. "You know I love you, but without your mother it doesn't really matter where I am."

"Oh, Dad, that's grief speaking."

"Maybe, but by the time I'm out of jail I might be over the worst of it." He smiled. "Look, you two get out of here. I've got a few things to do now."

A thought occurred to Briana. "Dad, you're not going to do anything silly, are you?"

His face softened. "I promise you I'm not. I just want some time alone."

"Okay." She hugged him then kissed his cheek. "I'll be back first thing in the morning."

"Fine."

"I'll be here for you, too, Ray," Jarrod said, and her father thanked him.

Briana hated that Jarrod had forced the issue, but she had to admit it was a relief to get it all out in the open. If only she could do the same with her feelings for Jarrod. If she could just tell him she loved him.

But that was never going to happen. It couldn't. She had to stay cool and calm in front of him. Jarrod had only ever wanted to bed her, not marry her. He'd told her from the beginning not to ask for more, so there was no way she would go back on her word. Not even after she told him about Patrick and the blackmail.

Once they were in the car, Jarrod looked at Briana in concern. "Are you okay?" he asked, realizing only now how hard this had been for her. The money must have weighed so heavily on her mind all this time.

She looked straight ahead, as if she knew she'd fall apart if she didn't. "Please take me home, Jarrod."

He waited a moment, a distinct feeling of unease rolling through him. Then he started up the engine and drove off, his thoughts turning to what had just taken place back there at Ray Davenport's house. He felt bad about Briana, not for pushing her about the diamonds—no, that had to be done. But for thinking the worst about her all this time.

Dammit, she didn't deserve all the rotten things he'd

thought about her from the beginning. He knew now she was a woman who could be trusted, and a woman who put her family before herself.

Unlike Marise.

Unlike his biological mother.

He owed Briana one hell of an apology. And he would give her one, too, just as soon as they were inside her apartment. He intended to make up for it all somehow—if she let him.

Only, when they arrived at her apartment building, she tried her old trick of telling him to just drop her off out front, but he wasn't having it this time. They needed to talk. And he needed to apologize.

She didn't say another word until they were inside her apartment. Then she stood in the middle of the living room and faced him, a cool look in her eyes. "You were wrong to force my father into a confession, Jarrod."

He couldn't back down. "If I hadn't, the police would have. And they'd have been much less considerate." He paused, then said in his defense, "Hell, I had no idea he was going to confess to embezzlement."

She flinched, then, "Perhaps you should have listened to me when I said to leave things alone. But you never listen to me, do you, Jarrod? It's always about what *you* want."

He inclined his head. "That's a fair comment," he admitted, and caught the look of surprise in her eyes before honing in to further the discussion. "So, the million dollars was actually for your father."

"Yes." Then out of the blue, her mouth began to

tremble. "And now I'm…going to lose…him." Tears bubbled up and overflowed down her cheeks.

Jarrod was at her side in an instant, pulling her into his arms, hugging her tight as she cried it all out. "Shhh. I'll do what I can to help him," he murmured, slipping her his clean handkerchief. He wondered if she'd cried much these last few months, or if she'd stayed strong for her father. More likely the latter, and he admired her for it. But today had to have been an emotional day for her, and things always caught up eventually.

He continued to hug her. "Shhh, Briana. You won't be alone. There are people who…care about you." And he realized he did. He just couldn't bring himself to be personal about it right now. He had to stand back and keep some semblance of detachment.

After a few more moments, she sniffed and pulled back, dabbing at her tears with the hanky, still looking so very beautiful. "There's something else."

His gut clenched tight as he let her leave his arms. "I'm beginning to not like surprises."

She sniffed again. "This one's about Patrick," she said, slamming his heart against his ribs. "He's blackmailing me."

Jarrod's head went back. "Blackmailing you? For what?"

"About the money my father stole from Howard. He figured it out, you see." She took a shuddering breath before continuing. "That's why he came to see me at the airport and why I was forced into signing that agreement. He was insisting I take him back as my business manager so that he could come to Hong Kong with me."

"The bastard!"

"And he wants everyone to think we're lovers again, just until he signs up one of the other models as a client." She hesitated then met his gaze full-on. "I agreed to him coming with me, but I refused to become his lover again." She shook her head emphatically, her eyelashes still damp from her tears. "Never."

Just the thought of Patrick forcing Briana into bed made him want to do violent things to the other man. Physically forcing a woman was one thing he would never do. And it wasn't like Patrick really wanted Briana anyway. Not like *he* did.

He swallowed hard. "Were you going to tell me the truth?"

Wariness clouded her eyes. "No," she said, and he swore. "Not even when I returned in two weeks. I couldn't." She gave a shaky sigh. "Anyway, the end of the month is almost here. It wouldn't have made any difference to you what I do after that."

"It would have mattered, Briana," he growled, admitting the truth. And that was the whole truth. He didn't want to let her go.

He never wanted to let her go. He wanted to keep her in his arms, safe by his side. Always.

Suddenly that thought grabbed him by the throat and had him heading for the door.

"Jarrod, stop! Where are you going?"

Anywhere. Nowhere. Just as long he was somewhere other than here. He needed time to think this all through.

He made himself focus, and he turned to briefly face her. "To see your ex-business manager," he said, letting the anger come. "He's not forcing you into anything, Briana."

She sighed. "It's no use, Jarrod. I signed a contract. Please don't make a scene."

"You can't be serious. You signed that contract under duress," he pointed out. "It wouldn't stand up in court and you know it."

She raised her chin. "Whether it does or it doesn't, I won't renege on the deal, Jarrod, no matter what you say. I gave my word. And if it's good enough for you—"

"Then you're a fool," he snapped, finding it hard to believe that she could even consider going away with Patrick when she didn't have to. He stilled. Perhaps that was the problem. Perhaps she *did* want to go away with Patrick, despite her protestations.

Something shifted in her expression. "Yes, I'm a fool, Jarrod," she said, a sudden catch in her voice. "A fool in love."

Jarrod felt like he'd just been poleaxed. She was in love with Patrick. The thought staggered him, squeezed his heart. And suddenly he knew why.

He loved her.

But he had lost her. She wanted another man. She *loved* another man. God, did he really have the strength to walk away from her? He shuddered inwardly. He had to. He loved her, but when it came right down to it, her happiness was what counted. Not his own.

"Then I hope you two will be very happy," he said, turning away before she could see the anguish that must be in his eyes. In seconds he'd loved and lost the most beautiful woman in the world. Beautiful in more ways than one.

"Oh Jarrod, now *you're* the fool. It's *you* I love. Not Patrick."

He felt his world rock as he spun back toward her. "What did you say?"

She stood her ground like someone expecting to be reprimanded, but defiant all the same. "I said I love you."

He was back at her side in an instant. "Darling, I love you, too. I'm so sorry for what I've put you through."

Her heart stopped. "What?"

He put his hand under her chin and looked into her eyes. "I've only just realized I love you, Briana. Right now when I thought I'd lost you to Patrick."

Oh my. Was she dreaming?

"Then I have to be grateful to Patrick for giving you to me," she murmured, slipping her hands around his neck, enjoying the freedom of touching him with love.

Jarrod's hands slid down to her waist and pulled her lower half close against him. "No," he growled. "We don't owe him a thing. Patrick can go to hell for all I care."

"Jarrod!" Briana said, pretending to be shocked at his words, but more surprised by his arousal against her stomach. But she felt the same way about Patrick. He didn't deserve any consideration. He would have used her if he could and not given a damn.

"Forget Patrick," Jarrod said. "We'll deal with him tomorrow. Together. I'm sure the police will be very interested in his attempts at blackmail."

"Yes." She would report him, if only to stop him doing the same thing to someone else. Another woman may not have someone like Jarrod.

All at once the air softened with love. "And you're not going on assignment to Asia by yourself either," Jarrod said gruffly. "I'm rearranging my schedule so I can go with you."

For once she loved his high-handedness. "No argument from me," she agreed, just before he slid his mouth over hers and kissed her hard.

Eventually they came up for air. "But for now—" He swept her up in his arms and headed to the bedroom. "I think we need some practice."

"Practice?"

"For our honeymoon."

She gave a small gasp. "Are you asking me to marry you, Jarrod Hammond?"

He stopped to look down at her and she caught her breath at the sheer love in his eyes. "Darling, only special people get to come inside my heart and stay forever. And you're the most special person of all."

"Oh, Jarrod," she whispered, his words making her heart turn over and over until she thought it would never stop.

And then she realized she didn't want it to stop. Every beat of her heart would always be for him. Always and forever.

* * * * *

Sometimes Cupid comes with a catch

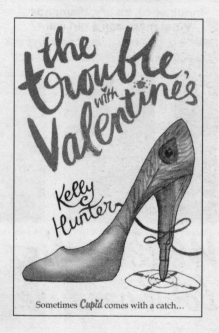

Sometimes *Cupid* comes with a catch...

Hallie Bennett loves flirting with danger. So when a man
with trouble written all over him walks into her shoe shop
she finds him impossible to refuse. Nick needs a 'wife' for
a week to seal a Hong Kong business deal, Hallie needs
£5,000. It might not be the most traditional Valentine's
Day proposal, but she's hardly a traditional girl.

0113/MB40